THE SEVEN MARKETS

THE SEVEN MARKETS

DAVID HOFFMAN

ohbalto

Ohbalto Media LLC
PO Box 2551
Briarcliff Manor, NY 10510
ohbalto.com

Manufactured in the United States of America

Book design by Ben Mautner
The text is set in Minion Pro
The display text is set in SchindlerRR and Priori Sans

PB 10 9 8 7 6 5 4 3 2 1
First Edition

For Jessy

FIRST MARKET

SUMMER, 1726

Ellie spotted the first flier on the road into town.

She was stepping around a particularly large rock that had embedded itself in the dirt when a whisper of movement caught her eye from the side of the road. She stopped and turned, hoping for a finch or perhaps a bluebird. It would chirp, tilt its head at her, and then continue on about its birdly business. Later she could sit down and attempt to sketch it from memory.

Instead, she saw the flier.

Mama had cautioned her against dallying, and while she could feel eyes on the back of her neck, Ellie decided a quick look couldn't hurt.

From the condition of it, the flier had been nailed to the tree a good while. At least a week, possibly two or even three. Funny she hadn't seen it any of the dozen times she'd been back and forth to town.

It was yellowed and cracking, and all around its border were tatters and tears where the wind and the rain had been at it. One corner was folded back, not straight as if by a human hand but rough and uneven. As she stared, a gust of wind picked up from the direction Ellie had come and took the paper in its hands, folding the edge back once more. This was what had caught her eye, almost as if the flier was waving for her to come and take a look.

Ellie pulled her shopping bag up onto her shoulder and, rising up onto her tiptoes, began to read.

THE MARKET, the flier read, each word made of blocky letters, the writing plain but somehow odd, as if written by a person unfamiliar with the language.

MIDSUMMER'S DAY, OBERTON VILLAGE, it continued, and as Ellie read, she was aware of her heart beginning to race. It was a cool morning, with a sharp, chill edge to the air, but she'd begun to sweat.

MYSTERIES, WONDERS, AND DREAMS.

She stood back, searching for anyone out on the road with her. Mama had cautioned her to get an early start, and Ellie, always an early riser, had set out before the sun. She had the morning all to herself.

A sudden, greedy urge came over her and Ellie reached up to snatch the flier down from the tree. A single nail held it in place. It would be but the effort of a moment, the merest twist of her hand, to tear it down, fold it up, and secrete it in one of the hidden pockets in her skirts.

Her hand paused, fingers outstretched. What was she doing?

She caught her breath and stood back a step. She wasn't foolish enough to believe tearing down a single flier would prevent her neighbors from noticing the Market when it arrived in three days. Did she hope to waylay the entire village, concoct some distraction to remove them so she could have it all to herself?

Did she believe this was the only flier that had gone up in the night?

No. She remembered Papa's stories from when she was a girl. There was no hiding it.

Ellie paused, keenly feeling the time she'd spent in the shadow of this tree. She read the flier's words a second time, then, with a terrible effort, turned her back to it and continued into town.

The Market was coming.

She completed her errands in her usual efficient way, a keen ear open for any mention of the Market or the fliers that she now saw were hung all around town.

Early as the hour was, Ellie didn't see many people at Tanner's Goods. She bought several kinds of thread and a few bolts of cloth, as well as a length of lace to tie in her hair. She was tempted to broach the topic of the Market with Mister Tanner, but something held her tongue. The grocer, usually a jovial, boisterous man, was oddly taciturn. Several times Ellie nearly asked him if all was well, but again, the words did not come.

She returned to the street, regretting her silence. She felt foolish and very young. The Tanners had been her neighbors her entire life. She would return at once and ask after him, and that was all there was to it.

Only Ellie did not return to speak with Mister Tanner. Instead she walked a little farther into the village and bought two loaves of bread from Alain McCullough, a boy her own age.

"Morning to you, Ellie," Alain said, his smile open and welcoming.

"And to you, Alain."

Did you see the fliers this morning? she wanted to say. Only to, again, find herself struck with silence. And again, though he looked every bit the boy she knew, Alain McCullough had a drawn look about him. Ellie's first thought was that his mother, who frequently suffered from pains in her hands and elbows, had taken a bad turn, but the shadow hanging over his face was different. Ellie saw that it came from within.

She paid for her bread, thanked Alain and his father, and went on her way.

At the apothecary, Ellie waited while Mister Garrett measured and mixed her reagents. Mama's list was extensive; Ellie suspected she was getting a jump on stocking up for the winter. It had been a lean year in some ways, and such would be in keeping with Mama's character. Ordinarily this would give Ellie a good bit of time to mill about in the shop, talking with and listening to the other customers.

She counted six other people in the shop. All were folk she recognized. Every one of them had lived in or near Oberton as long as she could remember. Neighbors and friends, just the sort you'd expect to find in town running errands early in the morning.

Seven of them, counting Ellie, in Mister Garrett's small shop.

The place was silent as a tomb.

Ellie watched from the sides of her eyes as Mister Anderson, the solicitor, browsed a shelf of powdered digestive aids next to Mister Gabriel, one of two partners at Oberton's only bank.

Ellie had seen the men in town before, laughing and talking together, thick as thieves. Now they might have been the most distant of strangers.

She saw Greta Jacobs, a year younger than her but certainly no stranger. Ellie met the other girl's eyes. They exchanged a curt nod, and though they had plenty to say to each other, Greta quickly turned away, back to browsing the shelves.

Ellie collected her shopping, tucked it away in her bag, and exited the shop. As she left, it seemed the silliest thing in all the world that she didn't turn around and strike up a conversation with any person at random. Another flier flapped in the morning breeze not two steps distant, daring her to shout it over the rooftops.

The Market! Coming to Oberton!

She kept Mister Garrett's shop at her back, finished her shopping, and left the village to begin walking home.

The farther she traveled, the more foolish she felt. When she came again to the yellowed flier she had seen on her way into town, she approached it with caution, feeling the same way she'd have felt standing before a hissing, foam-mouthed animal.

Taking small steps, Ellie drew ever closer, never taking her eyes off the gently flapping paper. A single double-headed nail, hardly more than a staple, held it in place. Each time the wind touched it she was sure the flier would tear free and be whisked away. If she couldn't read it again, how could she be sure, positively sure, she'd read what she thought she'd read?

Finally, in a burst of brave action, Ellie shot forward and pressed a hand against the flier, flattening it up against the tree. She devoured the words on its face in a single quick breath, reading aloud. They had not changed. Gratified, she read it again. Proof to Ellie that she had neither imagined them nor that was she mistaken in their meaning.

The Market was coming to Oberton. Coming in three days' time.

"What a foolish people we are," she said, understanding her silence and the silence of her neighbors had stemmed from uncertainty. None of them had wanted to be the first to say the words. None of them had wanted to find out they were imagining it.

Ellie licked the tip of her pinkie and touched it to the tip of her thumb. She drew a quick, simple sign in the air before the flier. She spoke two short, twirling words under her breath. *Protection*. A second passed in which nothing happened.

Ellie took the flier between her fingers and pulled it off the tree.

Still, nothing happened.

Nothing continued happening for several more seconds before Ellie decided yes, it was safe.

Relieved, she folded the flier in half once, twice, three times. She tucked it into a hidden pocket in her skirts. She could show the flier to Mama and Papa and they would believe her when they saw it.

Ellie hurried home.

Papa's reaction was not what Ellie expected.

"You take it back," he said. There was a faint tremor of fear in his voice she found utterly unfamiliar. "Right back where you found it. That you'd be so foolish! An' I thought we raised you smarter than that."

Ellie pouted and looked to Mama for help. But Mama was busy cataloging her groceries. If she had anything to say, she wasn't offering it up yet.

"It's safe, Papa," Ellie said. "I promise it is. I did it just like Mama taught me. Said all the words just perfect. It's safe, I'm sure it is."

"Sure, are you?" He wagged the flier in her face.

"Yes, Papa." She was on the verge of tears. Seventeen summers and ready to bawl. It took everything she had to keep from fleeing to her bedroom.

"After everything I told you about the Market, you'd go and pluck a flier right off the face of a tree? Ellie, I thought we taught you better."

"You did!" she said. "But Papa, you didn't see, you weren't in town. The fliers, they were everywhere. Everywhere! Just like in the stories. But no one was talking about them. No one was talking at all. Just *morning to you, ma'am* and *here're your goods*, sir. If I hadn't brought it back, I wouldn't have had the words to say, I know it."

She was standing by the table and fairly collapsed into a high-backed wooden chair, burying her face in her hands.

Footsteps sounded from the kitchen as Mama approached. She laid a hand on Ellie's shoulder and Ellie could feel her breath on the fine hairs covering the back of her neck.

Mama whispered several words, almost too low to be heard. Ellie recognized them as the words she'd spoken when taking down the Market flier. *Protection*. She looked up, and careful not to let the tips of her pinkie and thumb touch, traced the same lines in the air.

"It's all right, Rennie. Let the poor thing be. No harm done."

Papa blustered, but gradually the redness left his cheeks. After a short time he became again the genial man Ellie knew. He sat opposite her at the table, laying the flier out between them.

"I still say—"

"Done is done," Mama said, cutting him off. "And anyway, she's done right. Which you would know if you weren't letting your excitement get the better of you. *The Market*, you silly man. The Market."

Ellie looked up and saw the broad, familiar smile of her Papa beaming across at her.

"I suppose we were due, weren't we? If the stories are to be believed. Still, it is quite a thing." He reached across and squeezed his daughter's hand. "Apologies, dear heart, I surely meant no harm. It's just, well, it was a bit of a shock. But your Ma's right: I know you'd do it right."

"Thank you, Papa."

He turned the flier around so the words were facing him.

"Three days," he said. "Just like the stories. Still, a bit more warning would've been nice. And you say no one in town would talk about it?"

"About *anything*," Ellie said. "It was terrible. I was so excited I wanted to jump up and shout, but I couldn't get the words together."

"Well, I don't expect that quiet will go on too much longer, eh, Tara?"

"No," Mama said. "Before noontime enough folks'll have seen that someone will muster the words. Once the cat's out of the bag it's going to spread like wildfire."

Papa considered a moment, scratching the stiff hairs on his chin. "Well, someone's already let the cat out, I figure. Don't you agree, Ellie?"

"Papa?"

He examined the flier, fingering the torn bits, separating them and holding the split edges right up to his nose.

The flier was printed on heavy linen stock that might have been a bright, festive yellow at one time. The sun and elements had faded it, and what Papa held in his hand now was the creamy color of drying oatmeal. The center of the flier was lighter than its outside border, creating the illusion of a dull glow spreading out from the middle.

The words printed across the page showed none of the wear of the page itself. They might have been set there only the night before.

"Bet you anything," he said. "Only thing anyone's talking about in town right now is the Market. Tara?"

Ellie knew Mama had good instincts for the invisible world. Her charms always held, and when she wanted a bread to rise or a pie crust to hold its shape, it did.

"Your da' may have a point, hon."

A shiver tickled its slow way up Ellie's spine, catching the breath in her throat. She felt her cheeks flush red and was grateful again to be sitting.

Papa comforted her, holding her hand tight in his.

"I didn't mean to," she said, full of the need to apologize, to make it right. "What can I do?"

"Do?" Papa said, smiling broadly. "Nothing to do, and no reason to do it. Ellie girl, the Market is a good thing, one of the best.

And there's no shame being the one who tells folk about it, least no shame I've ever heard."

"It's true, baby," Mama said, approaching from behind and rubbing Ellie's shoulders. Mama had magical hands. It was impossible to feel worried or afraid when she was there.

Ellie read the flier again, still expecting to find she'd gotten the words wrong. She was a good reader and had been for some years. Still, a person can see things they want to see if they're not careful. She read aloud, "Mysteries, wonders, and dreams."

"That's what it says," Papa said.

"Just like you told me, Papa."

"Yup, just like I told you."

Sure enough, when Ellie took herself to town the next day, the Market was all anyone could talk about. She fielded questions from everyone she saw—who had told her? When had she heard? Did she believe it? Could she believe it?—but if anyone guessed it was Ellie who'd broken the village's spell of silence, they didn't raise the point within range of her hearing.

The largest question, in point of fact, was *where* the Market would be held. The flier specified only "Oberton Village," and there was some dispute over just what that might imply.

Mister Tanner, when she stopped in with a fresh shopping list from Mama, insisted the Market would be held right in the center of town. "Where else would it be?" he said. "Nice, big open space out there, and plenty of shops for visitors to wander." He'd hired Mitch Danvers' son, Robbie, as temporary stockboy for the three days specified on the flier. This was, he told anyone who'd listen, not just to cover the till when the crowds began piling up but also so he could sneak out and have a look at the Market with his own two eyes.

Reverend Childs told Ellie, in terms that left no room for interpretation or negotiation, that the Market would occupy the fields before and on either side of his own church. "There's no other place for it, really," he said, acting out for Ellie, with his hands, how the land could be best used for both Market and visitors.

Everyone had an opinion. And what Ellie noted for herself was, as insistent as a person might get, as utterly convinced as they might be that their theory was the correct one, the conversation never seemed to devolve beyond one person explaining, calmly but still with great enthusiasm, not why the other person was wrong but simply why they were correct.

It was the most congenial discussion she'd ever seen. Remembering the furious debate that had erupted over the location and construction of the new schoolhouse the previous summer, Ellie couldn't help but find it rather remarkable.

She lingered in town, enjoying the energy the Market's impending arrival had injected into her neighbors. She did a small amount of shopping, buying little things Mama had asked for and which Ellie suspected she did not need. As she started home her shopping bag felt emptier than when she'd arrived. She secured it over her shoulder and began the long walk home.

"Heading out without saying good-bye," came a voice from behind.

"Joshua!" Ellie spun to find Joshua Bullock, a year older and nearly a head taller than her, stepping out of Tanner's carrying a good-size burlap sack of flour.

"I didn't see you there," she said.

"I wasn't," he said, gray eyes alight with pleasure.

They stopped short of embracing, propriety demanding she maintain a ladylike distance with the eyes of half the town on them.

"I've missed you," Ellie said, swelling at the sight of him.

"I can tell from the way you raced past, eager to escape town without seeing me."

"Shush, beast. Have you heard?"

"Aye. The Market. I always figured it for a tale."

Ellie appeared stricken and he fell back in mock regret, nearly dropping his sack as he floundered.

"Well it's a delight to be proven wrong," Joshua said. "My sister hurried home to tell us when she heard. She was buying bread from the McCulloughs. My poor ma fainted at the news."

"Is she all right?"

"Of course. You know how she gets." He shifted the sack to his hip before thinking better of it and setting it on the ground. "Not looking forward to carrying that home, I'll tell you."

"It does appear quite heavy," Ellie said, hoping he'd take it as a compliment.

"It's light, actually, but unwieldy. Still, Mister Tanner wouldn't send anyone out with a delivery until after the weekend and Ma insists she needs to 'bake, bake, bake' like there's company coming. I suspect she believes the entire Market will be dropping by for a bite."

Ellie giggled, imagining Joshua's mother darting around her small kitchen baking cakes and desserts for the weekend's visitors.

"If you didn't have your flour there," she said. "I'd have you walk a bit of the way home with me." The Bullock farm was on the opposite end of the village from the MacReady farm; walking Ellie home would only lengthen the distance he'd need to lug the heavy sack.

"I can go a short way, I think, if you'd like."

"I would," Ellie said. "Very much so."

She waited until they were a good distance outside town before letting him hold her hand. His palm was damp with the day's humidity, but she didn't care. His hand could have been on fire and she wouldn't have complained. When they walked together like this, she frequently felt the need to verify that her feet were touching solid ground, for she felt she could have been flying.

Joshua asked how she'd come to learn of the Market and Ellie related her tale, offering her stolen flier as evidence. She held it out and was overcome with the sudden, perverse certainty he would snatch it from her and run away. Instead Joshua turned it over in his hand, examining it back and front. When he returned it, Ellie folded it up and hid it away in her pocket like the most precious of treasures. If Joshua noticed her urgency, he did not let it show.

She asked his plans for visiting the Market and he told her, plain as day, "I was planning to attend with you. If I might be so bold, Miss MacReady."

Ellie composed herself and squeaked out a response in a voice that hardly seemed her own. "You may, sir," she said. It was all she could do not to jump for joy.

By that point, Joshua Bullock had been courting Ellie MacReady for a hair more than a year. They'd become familiar with one another—walking together as they did now and kissing on more than one occasion—and Joshua's father had begun negotiations with Ellie's papa on his son's behalf. They were young to be considering marriage, but both families were successful and all parties agreed the match was a good one. "Within the year, Ellie," Mama had said. "You're still so young and there's no need to be rushing."

In moments like these, however, Ellie could not agree with her mother. The heat rising up from her belly told her there was every reason in the world to rush.

"Would you like to stop a minute, rest your arms?"

"Please," he said.

They were passing the site of the old Finnegan place, which had lain fallow for two summers since the family had picked up stakes and moved away to the coast. The house had not borne the harsh winters well with no one to care for it and was little more than a skeleton. Ellie made out its face, the bare windows and doorless entryway, and its limbs, the half-flattened barn and bare ribs of what had been their grain storage.

"Here," she said, arranging her skirts so she could sit.

He thudded the unwieldy sack onto the ground, rounded his shoulder twice to loosen it, and took his place beside her. Joshua still held her hand in his, only now as they sat together it had come to rest in her lap.

"Ellie…"

"Hush," she said, turning to place her lips on his. His height was less of an obstacle sitting than standing. It would be no obstacle at all if they were lying down.

She pressed his palm to her breast, sighing at the heat coming off his hand. She brought her hands up to his face and rubbed the rough stubble of his chin as she continued kissing him. He tasted of salt and sweat and dust. Of hard work and most of all, it seemed, of desire for her. She opened her mouth and nibbled his lower lip, pulling at it playfully and letting it go.

"Ellie…"

He was twisting in place, letting her lean on him, letting her press up hard against him, when the sudden awareness of eyes on the back of her neck came over Ellie. She sat abruptly up, then stood, flattening her clothes, making herself proper once more.

Turning in place, she saw they were alone. Still, she wondered if she would receive a talking-to when she returned home. Mama and her charms.

"I'm sorry," she said. "I was—I don't know what came over me."

He smiled, his rough features vulnerable, his dark complexion ruddy. He looked more like a boy than she'd ever imagined he could. Unable to resist, she reached out and ruffled his hair.

"Quit it!"

She leaned over to kiss his forehead and, promising herself she would behave, again took the spot next to him in the fractured shade of the old farmhouse.

"This is a nice place, isn't it?"

"It is," he said. She felt his fingertips on the back of her neck and decided that was a degree of chastity she could oblige.

"They were talking in town. Perhaps you found yourself caught up in the conversation—I know I did. About the Market and where it would be held. Everyone had a theory and if I had to offer mine, I'd say this spot right here."

"The Finnegans'?" he said, surprised.

"As good as any other place. Owned by no one, nearby to town but not right on its doorstep. Farther from home for you but not so far to walk—if one isn't lugging a fat sack of flour, that is."

He considered this, an easy smile on his face. The fingers dancing along the back of her neck stepped up to her braid of nut-brown hair and insinuated themselves like field mice in a thicket. She shuddered with delight, his fingers tiny feet scrambling along the back of her neck.

"It's a fine place. Finer now, I should think."

"Hush," she said.

He slid an arm around her shoulder and Ellie lay her head in the crook of his arm, against his chest. They sat that way a while, speaking idly but mainly enjoying each other's silence.

When they returned to the road, Ellie and Joshua spent several minutes competing to see which of them would walk away from the other first.

She kissed him on the cheek—but only after searching in all directions lest they be seen. Then she shooed him on his way.

"You first," he said, grinning like the oversized fool he was.

"Very well," she said, turning and walking—but only a handful of steps.

She stopped and spun, hoping to catch him with his back to her, the sack of flour slung over his shoulder.

He stood in the road, beaming.

"You," she said.

He crossed the distance between them and this time it was he who kissed her. He leaned down and pecked her cheek.

"Go," she said, knowing he would not.

But he did. She counted four steps before he turned, and, seeing her still anchored in place, head cocked, hands on her hips, he dropped the sack of flour and darted back to her waiting arms.

When they separated this time, it was Joshua who had the bright idea. "On the count of three," he said. "We'll both turn and both walk away and that way neither of us is leaving first."

Ellie nodded. It was a very sensible idea.

"One," he said.

"Two," she said.

"Three," they said, speaking together.

Neither of them turned. Ellie broke out laughing and Joshua joined her, slapping the flat of his hand on his thigh and falling back, planting his bottom on the dirt road. Tears streamed down his cheeks.

Ellie helped him up. As she pulled his hand, he pulled hers and she toppled over, landing across his lap. She should have been scandalized but somehow it only made her laugh harder. It was unseemly; if *anyone* came along at that moment it could very well prove their end. But she couldn't help herself and neither could he.

It was some time later when they were able to disentangle their limbs and stand. Ellie brushed herself off and turned so Joshua could whack the dust from the back of her blouse. It was cream-colored and attracted filth the way a magnet drew iron nails across a wood floor. A losing battle. Still, he did what he could.

"For real this time," she said, planting her hands again on her hips and staring him down.

"Yes, for real." He hoisted his sack up again and met her eyes. The edge of his lip twitched and Ellie knew in that moment she could, if she chose, send him back down to the ground again, howling like a loon.

"On three," she said. He agreed. They counted, and when they came to three, miracle of miracles, both of them turned.

And turned back.

"You're impossible," she said.

"Me?"

"I was only looking to ensure you *weren't* looking."

"As was I."

She harrumphed. Her papa had a truly grand harrumph, which was what Ellie aimed for. In her estimation, she came quite close.

"Joshua Phineas Bullock, if you do not leave this instant, then ... then I am going to. I will turn and march away and I promise you, you foolish, foolish boy, I will not look back, not even if you follow me flicking my ear as if we were in our first year of school together."

"Such a cute thing," he said. "Whatever happened to your golden hair?"

"I grew out of it," Ellie said, tossing her braid of nut-brown hair back over one shoulder. "Are you going?"

"Fine, fine," he said. Joshua walked three steps before turning, only partially, and speaking over his unburdened shoulder. "You're going to watch me the whole way?"

"Until you are the tiniest speck on the horizon, sir. Now go."

He raised his foot to walk and held it in midair. Then, in a flurry of movement, he dropped the sack and raced back to peck once more at Ellie's cheek.

"For good luck," he said. Joshua scooped up the flour and commenced running from Ellie as if fleeing for his life. He paused only once, a tiny figure she could only make out by shielding her eyes from the sun and squinting. He turned, her faraway man, lifted a hand, and waved.

And then he was gone.

Ellie stood in place a while longer, convinced he was going to reappear in the distance, running with his head down, sprinting to catch up to her before she could spot him, starting the whole ridiculous game all over again. Part of her wished he would but the day was beginning to stride away on long legs and she was well past due home. She adjusted the strap of her shopping bag and started walking, only checking occasionally to make sure he wasn't sneaking up on her from behind.

She walked, and as she was approaching the borders of her family's land, Ellie became aware of something approaching.

Her first thought was that Joshua had somehow gotten past her by cutting across the open land and was now coming upon her from the wrong direction. This made her smile and feel quite warm inside. As the object grew closer she was able to make out details, and hear noises, and she observed that it was not Joshua coming to surprise her.

It was a wagon.

Iron wheels rattled and groaned as they turned over the uneven road. Ellie could hear the tinkling of bottles brushing against one another and the clatter of what she guessed to be pots and pans whenever a wheel found a divot to fall into or a large rock to crash over. Whoever loaded the wagon, she thought, had done a poor job.

It moved faster than it looked, closing the distance between them with haste. When it was near enough she could hail the driver, Ellie stopped. She raised her hand and called out.

"Hello!"

"Hail," the driver said, easing to a stop before her. "Is this the village of Oberton?"

"It is, sir," Ellie said. "Where are you bound from?"

"Oh far, quite far, my lady. May I ask you, is it Midsummer yet?"

Ellie told the man, who was short and stout with a great, red beard, that Midsummer was yet two days distant.

"Bugger," he said. "One day, I tell you, one day."

"Sir?"

He shook his head, and Ellie could see the shape of a smile forming beneath his nest of facial hair.

"I'm early, of course. Always early, or late, but never on time. I swear, I don't know what it is with me. You, you live here, don't you?"

"Yessir," Ellie said.

"Has word come yet of the Market?"

"Yesterday," she said. "Three days' warning, just like in the stories."

He snorted. It was almost a laugh.

"In the stories. Of course 'just like in the stories.' Why wouldn't it be? Where d'you think the stories is from, after all? That's jolly, it is."

"Sir?"

He shook his head again, as if trying to force all the contents into their proper locations. "Apologies, my lady, it's been a long journey. Your village is lovely, I'm sure, but hardly convenient for traveling. Probably for best my flubbing the dates, now that I reflect upon it. Better late than never, they say. I say early beats them all."

She couldn't think of anything to say better than "yessir," so she nodded, hoping that would be sufficient.

"Can I ask you," he said, tying off the mules' reins and stretching, first his arms and then, standing, his legs. He twisted his back and cracked his neck and leapt down to join her on the ground.

Standing fully upright, the bearded man barely came to Ellie's waist.

"Always a bit pesky, sorting out what's appropriate, what I can show and what needs be held back. Don't suppose I could enlist your aid for the briefest of moments, could I? Make it worth your while, I will."

"It would be my pleasure," Ellie said, glad for something different to say, unsure of what she'd just agreed to.

He rounded the wagon, opened several latches, and threw up a panel on the side so they could peer inside. As Ellie watched, he dove in and rummaged around. He came up with a long-handled shovel with a dark iron face.

"Y'got these, do you?" he said.

"Pardon?"

"These, er, shovels, eh? Y'got 'em?"

"Do we have...shovels?" Ellie said, considering. "Yes, we have shovels."

"About this size? All done up like?"

She reached for the shovel and turned it over in her hand. Papa and Tom Johnson, the hired man, did most of the manual labor around the farm. Ellie had handled a shovel before. For all she could tell, this was a match to their own. She told him so.

"Fine, fine," he said, tossing it back into his mess. "You've shovels, how marvelous. Stands to reason then...and here... very well. How about, d'you have these?"

He produced what was recognizably a lantern and held it aloft for Ellie to see. She began to tell him that, yes, they had lanterns in Oberton, when he touched a spot on the top of the lantern and it suddenly lit up brighter than any lantern she'd ever seen.

"Ah, I see," he said. "Lanterns but not 'lectricity, is that it? Is it candles? No. Oil, surely. You've oil, don't you? Pour a bit in and lower the taper and there we are, good and bright, eh?"

He made as if to return the lantern back into the wagon when Ellie told him to stop. "May I see it?" she said.

"Oooh no, can't do that," he said, ducking it down away from her. "Truth be told, I could get into frightful trouble just for the glance I gave you there."

"Just a moment," she said. "I won't tell."

"It's not the telling," he said. "It's more, well, there's rules, y'see?"

"Whose rules?" She stood up on her toes to peer inside the wagon. There were a great many unfamiliar items amid the general clutter, but she had no way to make sense of them all.

"Just rules," he said, tucking the lantern away. He rummaged a bit more, muttering under his breath about photons and tera-bytes and several other words Ellie was unfamiliar with. From what she could tell, he was separating his goods into two piles: those he could sell and those he would need to keep hidden.

"How about this?" he'd say, holding a thing up for Ellie to look at. "Y'got these?"

"Earrings?" she'd say. Or, "Pocket watches?"

Whenever he held up something she didn't recognize, no matter how she tried to conceal her curiosity, he was too quick.

"What does that do?" she asked, after he held up a round, silver box scarcely wide enough to fill her palm, only to hide it again just as quickly.

"Plays music. How about this?"

"Yes, we have eyeglasses."

"These?"

"We have books as well, though none so fine as that. May I see?"

"These?"

Ellie recognized a pair of dice when she saw them. She began telling him so when she saw the way they sparkled in the day's light.

"Are those glass?" she said.

"Up—right. No 'lectricity, no CD players, *definitely* no plastic. Sloppy that. Apologies."

It was becoming late and the light was failing. After her time in town and then her time with Joshua, she'd already been on track to arrive home quite late. With this latest distraction, Ellie would likely come in after Mama had dinner on the table.

"Pardon me, sir?"

He looked up, his hands empty.

"Ah, growing dark, is it? Here you go."

He reached over to a flat, silver panel Ellie could see inside the wagon. A heartbeat later it became as bright as midday. She cried out in surprise, protecting her eyes with her hands. The little man, realizing his mistake, swore loudly and extinguished the wagon's lights.

"Rules, rules, rules," he said, shaking his head. "So easy to forget. Just like dates, there and gone in the blink of an eye.

Ellie rubbed her eyes, blinking away the fading embers of light imprinted on the undersides of her eyelids. "Was that the same as your lantern?"

"Yes."

"Do it again."

"No."

"Do it," Ellie said. "I'm ready now. I won't be blinded. Do it."

He made to protest, and then saw he was beaten. Shoulders slumped with resignation, the little man tapped the same silver plate again and the light returned.

Ellie had shielded her eyes from the sudden brightness. After giving herself time to acclimate, she was able to see into the wagon.

"How does it work?" she said, unable to help herself.

"All right, that's about enough of that," he said, switching the light back off.

"But it's wonderful. And you seem so nonchalant. Do it one more time, won't you?"

His face spoke his feelings plainly enough: *I've created a monster.* "No no," he said. "Hadn't you best be off for home?" He sniffed the air, nostrils flaring, the great bushy mustache inflating as he did so. "Dinner's almost ready. You'd best be off."

Ellie started to argue—she wanted to remain out here on the road with him all night and all day tomorrow—but she saw an easier path than arguing.

"Do you still need help?"

He mused and told her he had it pretty well sorted out. "Once you factor out 'lectricity it's a relatively easy line to draw."

"I could come in the morning," she said, undeterred. "I could help you sort out what stays and what goes. You don't even have to pay me. I'd be happy to help out, honestly."

She saw him perk up at the idea of enlisting her services at no cost to himself and knew he would agree.

"Very well. But—stop bouncing like that—I like to sleep in after a long journey and I like my morning tea. So I don't want to see hide nor hair of you until I'm good and settled in."

"Perfect," Ellie said.

"Now away home with you."

"Yessir," Ellie said. "But I'll see you tomorrow."

"Not until after tea."

"Not until after tea, yessir."

He grumbled some, clanking away inside his wagon. Ellie understood that was his way of ending the conversation. She thanked him, bid him good night, and hurried away home, hoping to arrive before dinner became cold.

She arrived home in time to help with dinner—it was earlier than it felt. Ellie expected her parents to have a score of questions relating to the late hour and how she had occupied her afternoon, but they surprised her by almost doggedly avoiding the subject. Papa bragged about how much work he'd gotten done that day, talking like he'd been alone out in the fields and not with Tom Johnson and three other men he'd hired for the season.

"Will you have much work tomorrow, Papa?"

"Enough," he said. "But we're ahead, and will get further ahead, and when the Market arrives, we'll be ready." He scooped a forkful of food into his mouth and looked down to find his plate very nearly empty. Ellie watched as he filled it with heaping portions of meat and vegetables and broke off a thick hunk of the bread she'd brought from town the day before.

He continued describing his busy day, lingering on an especially harrowing adventure he'd had clearing a rock from a stubborn patch of soil. Ellie was ashamed to find her attention wandering. She was mindful of her Papa and did not find his story uninteresting, but whenever she let her focus waver the slightest bit, she returned to that spot of road and the short man's wagon and all the wonders he carried within.

"I met a man today bound for the Market," she said, unable to contain herself any longer.

"A traveler?" Mama said, looking up from her plate.

"A merchant."

"Was he...?"

"I don't know, Mama," Ellie said. "He barely rose above my waist, but his manner was strange."

"Did you give him your name?"

"No, Mama. You know I know better."

Mama nodded, satisfied, and returned to her meal.

Papa spoke between mouthfuls. "What'd you speak about, this odd little man and you?"

"He had questions," Ellie said. "He seemed unsure of his location—he had the day wrong and was fussing greatly—and had questions about several items up for sale."

"Some of his own items?"

"Yes, Papa."

"How odd. Wouldn't you think a merchant should know his own inventory?"

"What sorts of items?" Mama said.

Ellie shook her head. "I don't know exactly. One was a lantern that required neither oil nor taper. Another was a rounded, silver box about this large"—she indicated the size with her hands—"which he claimed made music. He called it an *eye pod*."

Papa raised a single eyebrow in disbelief. "Indeed?"

"Yes," she said. And suddenly Ellie wished she had said nothing at all. *What did you do this afternoon, dear heart? Why, nothing, Papa. Though I did cross paths with Joshua Bullock and he was gentlemanly enough to walk me home, all while c arrying a very heavy sack of flour.* Why had she told them about the short man?

"What else, Ellie?" Mama said.

Ellie considered trying to describe the blinding lights the man had inside his wagon, but she could not do it.

"Very little else, actually. A shovel, some eyeglasses, and a book as an example. Much of what he will have for sale is mundane indeed."

Mama seemed to be considering Ellie's tale, weighing it to see what she thought. For her part, Ellie forced down several small bites, chewing slowly and swallowing with some difficulty. Her throat seemed to have shrunken down to nothing.

"Very well," Mama said at last. "Perhaps if we see your new friend at the Market, you will be able to introduce us."

"Oh, of course!"

"Don't see what kind of a merchant he can be if he can't tell a shovel from a pair of eyeglasses," Papa said.

"Stories change over time," Mama said. "Stories about the Market as much as any. But I'm glad you met this fellow, Ellie. He sounds a good sort, if a bit confused. And now we have something of an idea what to expect day after next."

"A shovel," Papa said, stuffing his mouth and chuckling. "Well, we will see, won't we?"

Neither Ellie nor her mother argued. As the meal continued, they spoke of several other things. Papa said he'd had a visit from

Aaron Bullock, Joshua's father, that afternoon. The two men had discussed at some length more details of a union between the two families.

"The chief headache is land," Papa said. "Old Aaron would prefer his son wed and expand their own holdings. 'If you were only our neighbors,' he told me, 'this would all be so much easier.' Wants to take that farm of his and grow it until it gobbles up the whole village, I think."

Papa stabbed a large chunk of meat with his fork and looked up at both women to see if either had a contradictory word to add.

"We dickered for some good time, I can tell you. But I think we may have reached the start of an agreement. It's technical and I won't bore you, but assuming the old sod doesn't get a better offer, your old da' might well have you sorted out before first snow."

"Oh, Papa!"

If she'd been standing, Ellie would have flung her arms around him and squeezed until he popped. Good luck for him, they were all sitting.

"A fair good, too," he said. "You know the Finnegan place up the road, eh? If'n we can sort out who it would be to collect the money, old Aaron and I will club together to buy the place for you two. 'How's that for a dowry?' I asked him, and even old Aaron couldn't argue with me there."

Pushing back her chair, Ellie did hug him now, unable to control herself. He remained in his seat—possibly from a sense of self-preservation—and patted his daughter to help settle her down.

"Engaged isn't married, Ellie," Mama said. "You'll remember yourself around that Joshua, girl."

"Yes, Mama." Ellie planted a kiss on her papa's head and returned to her seat. She wondered if Joshua had known about this when they'd been together that afternoon. Then she realized of course he had. The idea for buying the Finnegan farm had actually been hers.

They finished eating and cleared the table. By the time they were drying their hands and the dishes were soaking, it was dark outside. Ellie asked Mama if she needed any more help and Mama told her *no, go on along* with a kiss and a quick hug.

What Ellie wanted to do was take to her heels and run all the way through town and right to Joshua's front step. That wouldn't do, of course; there was more than poor behavior waiting for her out in the growing dark. There'd been wolves in Oberton that summer, and several great bears seen milling about in the woods. No one had actually been hurt yet, but it would be foolish indeed for an unescorted girl to venture out so late. She wondered if more visitors had arrived for the Market.

Ellie found Papa outside sitting in his chair, enjoying a pipe. He blew wide, white smoke rings and pointed through them, showing his girl the stars.

"Papa," she said at length. "Is Mister Bullock really going to let Joshua marry me?"

"Seems as like," he said, not looking at her. "Can't imagine why he'd trouble to come all the way out here if he wasn't serious. But don't you worry, dear heart, I've got old Aaron wrapped right around this." He held up his pointer finger and jabbed it straight up into the sky, as if he were hooking Joshua's father on it and making a trophy of the man.

"What d'you think made up his mind?"

Papa shrugged, tapping his pipe out onto the ground and refilling it without looking.

"The boy, I expect. If he had any trouble with you at all, which I doubt. Aaron Bullock fancies himself a businessman, Ellie, pure and simple. Safest bet is he wanted to make sure he couldn't get a better deal for his son. Now me, I wouldn't be surprised if he didn't try and buy the Roderick place out before too long."

The Rodericks, Ellie knew, owned the land between the old Finnegan farm and her own parents' land. They were silver-haired and had no children.

"He'd do that?" she said.

"Oh, I figure. Add up the Finnegan place and the Roderick place and our place right here and you've got a tidy piece of land for yourself. Couldn't do it for himself, but he'll do it for his son, I'd wager."

"It's so much," she said.

"That it is, Ellie girl. Is that all right with you?"

She smiled. "I suppose." The three properties combined would make up the single largest farm in Oberton. Ellie shivered in spite of the warm weather.

"All right?" Papa said.

"It's scary thinking of that much land. Papa, with all that, would Joshua and I be rich?"

He nodded as if the conversation had finally come to the point he'd been anticipating.

"Rich enough, if you take care. And I think you both would. Is that all right?" he said, a third time.

"I don't know." Ellie was unsure of how to express herself. "Thinking about living in a big house and filling it with children, I like that. I know Joshua would be a good father, Papa, but too much money, Mama always says people with too much go mad."

"Smart woman, your ma."

Ellie agreed.

Papa lit up his pipe again and blew more smoke rings into the night air, pointing up at the stars and the moon, naming them as he was wont to do. Ellie leaned back onto her elbows so she could look up where he directed. For as long as it took him to empty his pipe again, she felt as if she were a girl again. Skinned knees, dirt under her fingernails, looking at the sky through the eyes of her papa, the biggest man in the whole, wide world. She would have been that girl again, if she could.

"Tell you what," he said, standing and then helping her up. "It's getting late and your papa's got plenty of work yet to do tomorrow. I imagine you've got a busy day ahead of you as well. And the day after—well, the Market's exciting and that's for sure, but *I'd be surprised if your Joshua didn't have a question for you.* Good luck getting engaged at the Market, or so I've heard tell."

He opened the door and ushered her inside. The house was quiet. Mama had gone to sleep while they'd been stargazing. Papa kissed Ellie on the cheek and told her to mind the hour and not stay up too much longer.

She went to her room and tucked herself in. She would have slept if she could. There were too many thoughts in her head as she lay in the dark, trying not to think about Joshua, trying not to think about being rich, trying not to think about the Market or the short man's wagon or the others who might be coming to Oberton right at that moment. She decided she'd never be able to fall asleep. She'd lie awake all night, tossing and turning, and be exhausted come morning.

"Joshua," she said, greeting him in the darkness. She imagined his hands on her, his lips on hers, the weight of him upon her in her childhood bed. The thought of him made her heart pound with a most unladylike urgency. But when it slowed again at last, she slept.

The short, stout man with the bushy red beard grumbled and complained when Ellie arrived. It was too early. He hadn't had his tea. She'd just be underfoot. Best if she came back later, perhaps after lunch or—better!—a little before suppertime. It didn't take long before Ellie realized he was just trying to get rid of her.

"I brought cakes," she said, showing him the basket she'd filled before leaving home.

That perked his interest up some. She sat him down and fixed his tea while he picked at the goodies she'd brought. He ate with shy fingers, the way a bird will peck at its food. Ellie wondered how a man could be so stout eating so little but she kept the thought to herself.

"Very well," he said, once the tea was gone and Ellie's cakes transformed, as if by magic, into nothing but crumbs. "Y're obviously not leaving, so we might as well get on with it."

She made her best whatever-do-you-mean face, more out of playful habit than any hope he might fall for it. The short man chuckled and stood, brushing stray bits of cake from his lap. But when Ellie moved to follow him around to the wagon's entrance, he stopped her with a single wagging finger.

"Up, up. Your place is out here, my lady."

"Ellie," she said. "My name is Ellie."

For the longest time the only answer she received was a raised eyebrow and a studious look. He was waiting for her to say more. She held her lips shut and waited him out.

"Your true name?" he said at last.

"Of course not."

"Fine, fine. Safe, that. You may call me Beesix, then, if you like."

"Beeswax?"

"Beesix," he said, enunciating the syllables better, emphasizing the last. "It means 'bouncing bird' in my language."

"I'm not sure if my name means anything at all," Ellie said. "By which I mean, it means me and nothing more."

"Good thing to own your own name, girl. Hold on to that if y'can."

He climbed the few steps into his wagon, threw open the side, and began producing items for Ellie to identify. His attention was as keen as the previous day; the instant he brought out something she didn't know, poof, it disappeared, down into the space behind the counter where he hid each item away.

Over the course of the day she identified the following: a spinning wheel, a violin, a baby's bonnet, a left slipper that might be worn by a lady at court, a knit sweater, a purple scarf with yellow stripes running through it, a ship's sexton (which she only recognized because she'd seen a picture of one in a book), a pocket watch, a hairbrush, and a silver-framed mirror that went together in a set.

There were many more things she could not identify, which went down into the short man's collection of goods to conceal before the Market proper. Some of them glowed with their own unearthly light. Some of them made noises, a loud buzzing or music, as if an entire orchestra had been shrunken down and tucked away inside for safekeeping.

And there was the rare item of interest that Ellie recognized, but which, like his lantern, defied her understanding just the same. A writing implement he produced from a bell jar was clearly intended for putting ink to paper. But when he clicked its far end, a point stuck out from the tip and it was this she could write with, if she only had a few scraps of paper.

"Pens?" he said.

"Yes, but—"

"But what? Pen's a pen, no? Y'got pens?"

Ellie nodded her head, thinking for the first time about the rules he'd alluded to the day before and what happened when one broke them, even if it was only by accident. It was odd how in all the stories Papa had told her about the Market, he'd never mentioned that some things just couldn't be sold there.

"It's this part here," she said. "See how it clicks? I've never seen the like."

He snatched the pen from her hand and clicked the end several times with his thumb. Then he dove back into his wagon and produced several more pens of varying colors and sizes.

"Try these," he said, spilling them out onto the counter.

Ellie sifted through them, selecting out the ones with curious appearances or unfamiliar attachments. She asked if he had any paper to test them on, and he allowed that yes, he had paper, but it was all in the form of books and those were for reading or for selling but not for writing in.

"Oh, I have this," she said, remembering the folded Market flier in her pocket. She smoothed it out, face down, and began testing the pens. As she did this, the short man, who Ellie kept thinking of as Mister Beeswax, recommenced digging through the mess in his wagon.

She hated to scribble on the flier, so instead she wrote her name on it over and over again. First just "Ellie," then "Ellie MacReady," and finally, the same way she might try on a new blouse, "Ellie Bullock." When he looked up to check her progress, she had separated the pens into two roughly equal piles. She folded up the flier and tucked it away in her pocket.

"Chimeglass," he said. "Been carrying these since I don't know when. Good quality, too. Give a listen."

He handed her a small glass, about the right size for a single gulp of water. Sure she was doing it wrong, sure he would snatch the glass away and hide it from her sight, Ellie pressed the glass to her ear. She held her breath, listening, waiting for him to scold her for a fool and say, "Ah, no chimeglass then, eh? Right, right."

He said nothing. And when her panic had subsided, Ellie realized she could hear music in the glass.

It flowed like water sliding over flat stones, reminding Ellie of her mother's mother, who'd lived with them when she was young and who loved singing in the morning, lullabies and hymns and nonsense melodies she made up as she sang. More, it was her Nana's voice Ellie heard within the glass. She felt tears welling up in her eyes as she realized how long it'd been since she'd even thought of her Nana, and how much she missed her.

"Most days I can't even," the short man said, holding out a hand for the glass. "Hurts too much, don't it? Good hurt, sure, but it's still a hurt, innit?"

Ellie nodded. It was with some effort and no small amount of relief that she removed the chimeglass from her ear and passed it back to him. He took it and added it to a line of six more similar glasses.

"I heard my Nana."

"Liked to sing, did she?"

Ellie nodded.

"Tha's how chimeglass works—oh, don't be putting on hurt eyes. Best part though, is it's real, it is. Dunno how they works but put that back up to your ear and I could lean in and listen just as well. Your Nana?"

Ellie nodded again. She wiped at fresh tears on her cheeks.

"Gone long, is she?"

"Several years, yes," Ellie said. "I'd forgotten how much I missed her."

He reached out a hand in an awkward gesture of comfort. Suddenly Ellie couldn't care less about his trinkets and geegaws. She wished she could sit down with him and find out where he came from, what his people were like. What he was really like, once you got past the merchant worried about breaking rules she knew nothing about.

"Have you been traveling long?" she asked.

"Seems," he said. "Still, home goes with you, I reckon. And you get to meet interesting people and make a buck or two, so it evens out."

"I think you're very nice, Mister Beeswax."

He laughed and did not correct her. "Here now, d'you have these?" he said, producing another item—it might have been a stubby black candle minus the wick or a sizable chunk of rich chocolate—from within the wagon. By the cautious way he held it, though, she decided it was neither of those things.

"Hup, nope nope. Okay, d'you have these?"

* * *

It became dark while Ellie's back was turned. It wasn't a long walk home for her, but Mister Beesix insisted on escorting her as far as her front door.

"Night before the Market and sniffings of wolves about. A great bear to boot. Wouldn't sit right with my conscience if'n I let you get gobbled up alive walking home, now would it?"

She thanked him for his company and invited him to join them for supper. The short, stout man declined with a regretful shimmer in his eye.

"Wolves, I said." He paused as if choosing his words with care. "Tell me, Ellie, when y'go to the Market tomorrow, will you go alone?"

"Alone? No, not alone."

He nodded. "Husband?"

Ellie lifted her hand so he could see her ringless finger.

"Ah."

"But I will be with my Joshua. May I—may I bring him to meet you?"

"Joshua," Beesix said, tasting the name. "Is he your man?"

"He will be. He is. His father is buying us the land where your wagon sits. The old Finnegan place." She remembered their time there the day before. Remembered the feel of his lips, the rough strength in his hands. "He will make a fine husband."

"But not married yet?"

"Soon," Ellie said. "Perhaps tomorrow. Papa says it's good luck exchanging vows at the Market."

"I've heard that. Yes, promises made are promises kept, when made at the Market."

His words pleased Ellie to no end. She imagined Joshua dropping to one knee, asking for her hand in marriage. That the

Market should come, that the timing should be so fortuitous, it was almost as if it were meant to happen.

"Tell me about him, your Joshua," Beesix said.

Ellie opened her mouth to tell her new friend how handsome Joshua was, how broad his shoulders, how strong his back. Then she realized none of those things were who Joshua was. None of those things were the reason her heart quickened whenever he was near. Oh, they were good things—didn't her knees wobble just the tiniest bit, thinking about him now?—but they weren't the important things. If Joshua's face was scarred working the farm, if the corded firmness fled from his muscles, would she love him any the less?

"He's terribly kind," she said, speaking without realizing which words were going to come out. "Most people don't see it, because he's so—well, they don't see it. He smiles and makes every man his brother. He'd pull your wagon out of a pool of mud, single-handedly if necessary. He'd give you the clothes off his back and the last coin from his purse."

Beesix smiled; Ellie thought it looked false, like a child's paper mask.

"You don't believe me?"

"I believe you love him. And love paints the world many colors."

"Joshua Bullock," she said, feeling her cheeks flush in anger. "Is a fine man."

She thought he might apologize. Instead the little man shook his head, almost as if scolding himself. "Course he is," Beesix said. "Tell me, how'd you two meet?"

"Meet?" It was the oddest question he could have asked. "I don't know. We've—we've both lived in the village all our lives,

His family on one side, my family on the other. I have no idea when the first time was we met."

"Love, then," Beesix said, a warm smile peeking out from behind his fiery whiskers. "Tell me how y'fell in love."

If Mama had asked her this, Ellie would have blushed and changed the subject. Papa, of course, would never ask such a personal question; if he had, Ellie might have fled the room in embarrassment.

"Love," she said, surprised to hear herself speaking. "I don't know if that's how it works. How did we fall in love? Slowly. We got to know each other, and now I can't imagine *not* loving Joshua Bullock."

Ellie waited to see what he'd say to that. He crossed his arms and nodded his head, as if telling her to continue.

"I told you we grew up together," she said at last. "And that's true. Our families were not close—if we played together as children, it was in town, or along with other children. For much of my life Joshua was as much a part of Oberton as Tanner's Goods or the stone bridge leading east out of town."

"Not childhood sweethearts then?"

Ellie laughed. "Hardly. He was a boy from outside town, nothing more. Not to say there was anything...wrong with Joshua. He was, well, inoffensive. Almost part of the landscape. He was Aaron Bullock's son. Tell me, have you ever lived in a town like ours?"

"I've visited more than my share."

"It's not the same," she said. "Visiting as opposed to living there, is what I mean. When winter falls, if a family wasn't able to stock its larders for the long cold, the rest of us will help out.

There's a community here you might not see in big cities. Still, that kind of closeness creates a sort of distance, too. You know everyone, but in knowing them, you might also keep them at arm's length."

Beesix appeared to consider this point a moment. He patted his pockets as if searching for something, perhaps she'd reminded him of home, or of his family, but gave up after a short time.

"Joshua was part of my life, but not a part I ever gave much thought to. If his family picked up stakes and moved away one day, I doubt I'd have given his absence—their absence—much thought at all."

"Something changed," Beesix said.

"It…I suppose something did change. I noticed Joshua. Does that sound terrible? Do you find me awful? I noticed him. Or he noticed me. I think it might be the latter, now that I say it out loud. After all, it was him that came up to talk to me."

She closed her eyes, remembering the day. It had been warm. She remembered that because the night had been so frigid. The calendar said it was spring, inching into summer, but Ellie's bed was still piled high with blankets.

"Papa was traveling," she said. "And Mama had her own business on the other side of town. She does some healing, helps people with small charms, that sort of thing. So I had an afternoon to myself. I offered to accompany my mama, but she told me to enjoy the pretty day. That was what did it, I think, when she reminded me how pretty the day was."

Ellie's hand drifted to her bag, but did not delve inside.

"I fixed a small lunch and took my drawing pad. I draw a little. Sketches mostly." In a hurried breath, she added: "Nothing special, I'm not very good, of course.

"Joshua came upon me out by the old Miller place, trying to sketch a piece of their fence that had come down that winter, and which they hadn't gotten around to repairing yet. Grass and flowers had sprung up between the fence posts, poking up like rabbits searching the landscape for hungry foxes.

"I was on the opposite side of the street, my lunch gone, my bag open on the ground. I was sitting on a flat stone, engrossed in my drawing."

"'Hullo, Ellie,' he said, crossing the road to me."

"I looked up. Do you know it took me a second to recognize him? How silly that must sound now, but it's the truth. I saw him, and knew I knew him, but I had no idea what his name was. 'Good afternoon, Joshua,' I said, plucking his name out of my mind like a berry."

"'How are you?' he said. Just like that. Very formal. Then I watched his eyes move from my face down to my lap. Down the drawing pad resting in my lap, I should say. 'Are you drawing?' he said."

"I told him I was, and indicated the broken section of fence."

"'I didn't know you drew,' he said.

Ellie shrugged her shoulders. "He sat down and asked to see my drawing. It wasn't very good—it wasn't good at all, I think—but he just seemed so fascinated to learn something new about me. Before I knew it, the afternoon had slipped away from us. Joshua was late getting back home—he'd been to the Millers' delivering goods for his father, saving him a trip in the cart—and Mama was likely wondering if I'd wandered off and forgotten the way home.

"A few days later, I ran into him in town. Instead of exchanging the usual pleasantries, we stopped and talked. He asked me if I'd been drawing. We spoke for a quarter of an hour before remembering ourselves."

"And then it continued," Beesix said.

"Yes. It wasn't long before we were coordinating our visits to town. 'When will your mother send you for errands?' he'd ask. 'Tuesday next,' I'd answer."

"And now you're to be married."

"Engaged," she said, correcting him.

"Engaged, yes. Tomorrow?"

"Papa thinks so. I hope so."

Beesix nodded his head as if agreeing with Ellie. "I ought to be getting back," he said. "Market day tomorrow. Big day. Lots to do. Stop by and say hello. Bring your fella and we'll dazzle him with a little shiny off the bottom shelf."

"I will. Definitely."

She thought he'd leave then, but he remained where he was.

"Sir?"

"We initially spoke of payment," he said. "I know you said it was unnecessary, but fair is fair and at the Market a deal is a deal, even when y'show up a couple days early."

Ellie wanted to tell him *oh no, that's fine*, but curiosity kept her lips sealed tight. She nodded in acknowledgment; it was all she could manage.

"I can't be selling them anyway—wrong time, wrong place— but there's no rules against giving gifts, least not so's far as I've ever heard." She watched him dig into a deep coat pocket. "Just the same, let's not make a fuss, shall we? Rules is rules and sometimes they just change one and don't bother telling anyone. Still, gifts and such."

He stepped toward here and Ellie realized she was holding her breath. He opened her hands and placed something small and cold in them.

"Thanks, an' such," he said.

Ellie looked down and recognized the chimeglass at once.

"And do stop by tomorrow. Might be tricky finding your way, but I'll be right where you left me and that's a promise."

He sniffed the air, giving Ellie the impression he was searching for the scent of wolves or bears. Satisfied the night was safe, Mister Beesix turned and headed back to the road, to the Finnegan farm and to his wagon. It was dark enough that after he'd taken a dozen steps Ellie could find no trace of him at all. She sat on the stoop, where she'd talked with her father the previous night, and listened to the chimeglass a while before remembering herself. She wiped away her tears and went inside for dinner.

Ellie fell asleep remembering old stories.

She dreamed of trapped princesses and valiant princes; of ferocious, fire-belching dragons and splendid golden unicorns; of magical beanstalks which led to bellowing giants; of fabulous treasures, wish-granting genies, pixies and fairies and satyrs and sailing ships and desert caravans and gleaming steel towers that split the sky and cast impossible shadows the entire length of the land.

And, of course, of the Market.

A familiar voice recited the old catechism: *once in a century, for three days only, the Market will come.*

Another voice, the one she saved only for herself, asked: *do the three days always come together, Papa?*

A hearty laugh, a warm feeling of security. *Perhaps. With the Market, anything is possible, or so I've heard it said.*

Her voice, high and young but still unmistakably hers, said: *it wouldn't make much sense to split it up. Better all at once, I think.* She heard a tinge of doubt and remembered thinking, *if it was split up, though, it'd seem to last longer, wouldn't it?*

The younger Ellie shifted her feet. Through the veil of night the older Ellie was aware of kicking her bedsheets away. It was warm and her room was stifling. A distant part of her considered rising and letting in some air, but the dream held her and she did not want to risk slipping from its grasp.

Three days only, and ten days would not be enough to see it all. Dream a thing and it will be at the Market. Imagine a taste and you can sample it at the Market. Wish for your heart's desire and find it made real at the Market.

Young Ellie thought then of her favorite cookies and cakes. She thought of her favorite doll, who shared her pillow every night. What if she brought Janey to the Market and she came to life? Why, it would be just like having a baby sister!

The dream began fading, Papa's words turning first into echoes and then into the shadows of echoes. Her eyelids grew heavy and she understood she was falling asleep. Falling asleep within the dream, as she had fallen asleep listening to her father's stories as a girl.

Ellie slept and did not dream. And when she woke, it was morning and the Market had come to the village of Oberton.

Ellie counted three suns blazing in the sky. They were too high for the early hour and monstrous compared to her expectations of what a sun should be. The rightmost sun, whose face was the jelly red of fresh blood, seemed close enough to touch.

"Joshua," she said, feeling for his hand. "Do you see?"

"I do. But I don't know what I'm looking at."

She stepped away from him, reaching out to the sky. She could imagine plucking one of those suns down and dropping it into her purse. A souvenir of their visit to the Market. The idea was so reasonable, so obvious, she was surprised when it didn't work. Ashamed and feeling deeply silly, Ellie turned back and found Joshua had stepped up to join her. His arms were outstretched, his fingers grasping at the center sun, the smallest, which burned a fierce white beside its siblings.

He caught her watching him and blushed, actually blushed. Joshua Bullock blushing! For a moment Ellie could forget her surroundings, forget her excitement, and simply marvel at the flush in his cheeks.

"Don't," he said, his voice halting. "I was—I wanted to bring the little one down for you. As . . . a present. I was going to have it set into a necklace so you could wear a tiny sun with you as a—"

"Souvenir?"

He nodded but did not say any more.

Ellie flung her arms around him and, with no thought of her parents or anyone else, kissed him full on the mouth.

"Sweet, wonderful, ridiculous man! What did you think I was doing?"

"The same?"

"The very same," Ellie said. And then, feeling the need to add a small white lie, added, "Though I hadn't gotten so far as picking out a setting."

He leaned down and kissed her forehead. Then he realized where they were, jerked back, and looked at the ground, shuffling his feet. As if pretending he didn't know her would fool anyone witnessing their horrendous behavior into forgetting what they'd seen.

Glancing around, Ellie saw Papa and Joshua's father dickering with a young man whose face seemed oddly off—too long in the chin and something disconcerting about his nose—over a pair of sausages. A ways from them, Mama and Joshua's mother were engrossed in browsing the collection of what she took for a bookseller's stall. Tables were lined up in the shadow of a high brick building, and the two women, who'd never gotten on so far as Ellie knew, were gabbing and passing books back and forth, acting like the oldest of friends.

"Shall we go?" Joshua said.

"Go?"

"Go. Explore. Just the two of us, I mean."

"We can't!"

He slouched his shoulders and opened his eyes wide. This had the effect of turning Joshua into a contrite eight-year-old. "I'm sorry," he said, making his voice climb several octaves higher than normal. "I thought you were right behind us. We certainly never would have wandered off on our own on purpose."

"You are a rotten man, Joshua Bullock."

He shrugged. "An honest mistake. It could happen to anyone."

As they fled, Ellie marveled at her surroundings. All the times she'd imagined the Market growing up, she'd imagined it as a sort of open-air bazaar. Meeting Mister Beesix and seeing his wagon had only reinforced this notion. She'd traveled with Papa to sell their goods at harvest time and had seen firsthand what a proper market looked like: tables covered in trinkets, racks filled with clothing, steel drums serving as cooking fires for meat and ears of corn.

The Market was a city.

No sign of the Finnegans' old farm was anywhere in evidence. The shell of their home was gone as surely as if it'd grown legs in the night and wandered off in search of a family to care for it. The familiar dirt path, which they'd strolled together only the day before, was now a paved road wide enough for two carts to pass side by side. It branched off time and again, creating avenues and side streets, alleys and cul-de-sacs.

Close to the entrance, closer to the road into town, the Market had been wagons and tents, vendors perched behind tables peddling their wares. Farther in, these gave way to buildings: first of stone and wood, then of materials neither could name. Joshua made Ellie stop more than once, not to browse a shopkeeper's wares or consider a pretty trifle, but so he could lay his hand upon the side of a building and feel its skin for himself.

"It could be glass," he said, pausing before a shop filled with gleaming crystal flowers and flitting, twittering birds crafted seemingly of light. Ellie joined him, laying her own hand upon the outer wall.

"It's warm," she said.

"Is it?" He moved his hand to the spot she was touching and held it there a second, considering.

"Here."

"Oh—ow, that is hot!" He jerked his hand back.

"Oven's on t'other side," said the shopkeeper, a young woman with long, plaited golden hair. "Careful not to hurt y'self."

They walked farther along. Joshua bartered with a stringy green-eyed fellow for a pair of pastry rolls. They were cool to the touch but emitted copious billows of steam when bitten into. Ellie said hers was the sweetest thing she'd ever tasted. Joshua kept his opinion to himself, afraid his mother, who was known for her baking, might be lurking nearby.

As they sampled the Market's wares, Ellie noticed the buildings, two and three stories where they'd stopped for their breakfast, were now growing taller. More than once Joshua made her wait while he stood staring straight up, searching for a building's peak.

"Look here," she said, ducking into a high, slender tower. It climbed into the sky, but inside there was barely enough space for the both of them, and no sign of steps or a trapdoor to the higher floors.

"There are no steps. I can touch the ceiling but there are no steps."

"Employees only," the shopkeeper said, glancing up from behind his counter. "No customers allowed."

Ellie thought of waiting for Mister Tanner to fetch her orders from the stockroom and tried to imagine a shop with so much stock it had to soar up into the sky to hold it all. She pulled Joshua away, leaving without looking back. When he asked her some time later what the "tall, twisting shop" was selling, she had to admit she had no idea. To her memory, the walls had been bare and the shop empty.

Every turn revealed a new surprise. Every breath carried a provocative new aroma and the promise of flavors more tantalizing than the last. Ellie and Joshua alternated between rushing from shop to shop and lingering to savor whatever the moment held. It didn't matter; fast or slow, the Market was overwhelming. Ellie's head began spinning, and just as she was about to ask if they could sit a spell, he told her to stay put a moment and dashed off without another word.

Where was he going? She watched him disappear into a shop they had not visited. The exterior was purple, the walls round. It reminded her of nothing in all the world so much as an eggplant. What had drawn him there? People flowed past her, neighbors and strangers and vendors alike, their voices melting together until she couldn't make out a single individual word. She was caught in a cacophony of noise, a symphony of musicians playing their instruments with no conductor to guide them.

Noticing tables nearby, Ellie navigated the throng and found a place to sit. A serving girl, younger than her and wearing clothes so indecent Ellie couldn't help blushing, approached and offered her something to drink. A cup of tea, a beer or perhaps a pint of ale?

"Ale?"

"Aye, and good too. Tempt you?" The serving girl shifted from foot to foot, constantly in motion. Watching her made Ellie's eyes hurt.

"Yes, two please," she said, sure Joshua would not demur at the prospect of a drink when he returned.

She sat observing the crowd, waiting for her man. It began to dawn on her where he'd vanished to. Papa's words came to her then, I'd be surprised if your Joshua didn't have a question for *you*, and Ellie knew she had the right of it. There was no money for an engagement ring or a fancy necklace, but he obviously had something in mind. Joshua was not a complicated man. The way he'd rushed off, Ellie knew he'd found whatever he was after.

"Joshua," she said, feeling the need to speak his name aloud. A personal sort of charm. Not for protection or for raising bread, as Mama tended to do. Not for discouraging pests or keeping the horses healthy, as was Papa's wont. Just the one word, just his name. A wish, almost. The happiest of wishes.

Ellie didn't notice when the stranger sat down. She didn't notice when the inappropriate serving girl returned with their drinks. Nor did she notice when the stranger thanked the serving girl, tossing a coin Ellie would have found unfamiliar onto the circular serving tray.

"It was good of you to order," the stranger said, sipping the ale she'd ordered for her fiancé-to-be. "Thank you ever so much."

His voice snapped her out of her daydream, out of the house she shared with Joshua, away from the children they would have, the animals they would keep. She turned and saw him raising Joshua's glass to his lips.

"How dare you!" she said. Or started to say. She got out the first two words, "how dare," but not the third.

"I beg your pardon," he said, cutting her off. "Sometimes I do forget my manners. But you are waiting for me, aren't you? You were holding this seat for me, weren't you?"

She tried to say no but...couldn't. And Ellie was surprised to discover she *was* waiting for him. She *had* been holding the seat for him.

"Ah, there we go then. Perfect, perfect." He lifted the glass a third time. "Excellent choice, by the way. Always come here, always drop in, every time. Best ale in seven realms. Almost as good as Trafalgia, but don't tell anyone I said so, will you?"

Ellie nodded. she'd never breathe a word of it. The mere thought!

The stranger leaned back in his chair—*his* chair—opening his hands as if to say the entire world was his but he was only too happy to share. He smiled, and Ellie felt herself sinking into him.

"You shouldn't leave it sit too long, really you shouldn't. Here."

He gestured for her to find her own glass and Ellie did. Her throat was dry as dust. She drained it in three giant, thirsty gulps.

"My goodness," he said. "Don't overdo it now. People will think I'm taking advantage of you." His eyes were the red-gold of summer sunsets when she was a girl.

He finished his own and held a hand up for the serving girl. *If you please*, he mouthed, once he had her attention. From the way she hurried off, a casual observer might have thought him royalty.

But the thing was, there were no casual observers in that part of the Market. Not right then. Everyone was watching their table from the sides of their eyes or from beneath the wide brims of their hats. A woman wearing yellow from head to toe, resembling an enormous canary, right down to the tail feathers, hid behind a yellow fan, hanging on the stranger's every word.

"Remind me, remind me," he said, gesticulating richly. "Your name. I'm afraid I've lost it. Terribly sorry."

"Ellie," she said, the word escaping more than being spoken.

He smiled again. Her heart slowed to a crawl at the sight of him.

"No no no. Your *true* name. It's right on the tip of my tongue. How could I have forgotten?"

She knew better, but Ellie could no more have held back than she could have spread her arms and taken flight. "Eliwys

Aithnea Lily MacReady. Aithnea is for my father's mother. Lily is for my mother's. Eliwys is for me and me alone."

"Lovely, lovely," he said. And then, as if pulling on a shirt or fastening a band around his wrist, he tried her name on for size. "Eliwys Aithnea Lily MacReady. Lovely, just lovely."

The serving girl arrived with a fresh round of drinks. Her hands shook as she set them down, and she left without collecting another of the stranger's coins. "On the house, sir," she said, and scurried away, her shoulders hunched, her head down.

He savored his ale, sniffing the mouth of the glass in between languid sips, which he sloshed around before swallowing. His hair gleamed like spun gold and his skin bore the deep, handsome color of one who spends all his time lounging in the sun.

"You haven't touched yours," he said, indicating Ellie's drink. "Aren't you thirsty?"

She was! She was parched! But she also sensed she *wasn't* thirsty. In fact, the mere notion of even another drop of ale made her stomach shudder.

"I fear I may be sated," she said. "Would you like it?"

"Don't mind if I do," he said, chuckling as if at a private joke. He leaned across the table and fetched her glass. Some part of Ellie judged the table too wide for such a move but he managed it just the same. Managed it with elegance and a certain amount of finesse. His every movement was refined and calculated. Even his laughter had an air of nobility about it, as if only someone who'd done the things he'd done and seen the things he'd seen could ever laugh in such a fashion.

There was movement in the crowd, and in short order, the spectators parted to allow someone through. It was a young man, tall with stormy eyes and a dark complexion. He carried a bouquet of wildflowers in one hand and a box the size and shape of a small eggplant in his other.

The stranger looked up and Ellie, sensing there would be nothing amiss in such an action, mirrored him. She recognized the young man the same way she might have recognized a place she'd only seen in a book or in a painting, but never in real life. When he knelt and set his hand on her shoulder, Ellie recoiled.

"Good sir!" said the stranger, flying out of his chair. "Such cheek!"

The young man looked up at the stranger, his eyes full of desperate confusion. He stood, taking his time, weighing options. "May I help you?" he said, at long last.

The stranger laughed again and then he thanked the young man for fetching the bouquet of wildflowers. He popped the lid off the purple box, peered inside, and returned it. "A fine gesture, sir, and I thank you, but I believe I can do better."

The stranger glanced up at the triple suns, downed the last mouthful from her glass, and offered the wildflowers to Ellie. "My dear," he said.

She accepted the flowers and stood. She liked flowers, enjoyed having them by her bedside or on the table during breakfast. These were lovely and had obviously been picked with care. He was so thoughtful.

"Eliwys," the stranger said. "We really must be going. Darling?"

He offered his arm and she took it without a moment's hesitation. She shifted the flowers to her free hand and was about to leave when the other man, the tall man with the gray eyes and dark complexion, grabbed at her.

"Ellie!"

"Do something with the boy, would you?" the stranger said. And as they left together, the assembled crowd pulled the young man back, away from the happy couple. They held him and kept him from following even as he, himself, was unsure of who he was trying to pursue, or why.

Ellie and the stranger walked together to the center of the Market, pausing here and there so he could point out an interesting sight or converse briefly with an acquaintance.

It was thrilling.

He knew everyone and everyone knew him. Vendors hailed as he approached, offering their goods with never a word said about payment or barter. Musicians played for him, and for her, singing ballads of eternal love and endless beauty. Children—for there were children this deep into the Market—dashed up to touch his cloak or pull at her dress. They giggled and fled with their heads down.

A woman dressed all in green, with eyes as dark as the sea during a storm, stopped them and offered them a gift. "For you and your love, my grace," she said, searching through her cart before presenting Ellie with a chain woven of fine gold. From the chain hung a red gem of surpassing brilliance.

"Blessing on your union," the woman said, bowing and shuffling backward.

By the by, after having her hand kissed umpteen times and after being told how lovely she was, and how fortunate a thing their pairing was, they came to an inn.

The front door opened at their approach, and as they entered, they were met by a lanky man with blood-red hair and a jagged scar across his cheekbone. His eyes were the green of the deep forest, and though Ellie could tell he was clearly quite upset, his voice was melodious and lacked the barest hint of urgency.

"Off for a walk, your highness?" he said.

"Obviously," the stranger answered. Ellie felt herself wanting to rise to his defense—who did the lanky man think he was?

Before she could utter a word, though, he turned his brilliant green eyes in her direction. Ellie felt herself being appraised. The stranger tightened his hand around hers and she knew not to worry. He might have the feel of danger about him but he was no threat to her.

"I suppose congratulations are in order then, sire?"

"Indeed. And a joyous day this is. Love really brings out my eyes, don't you think?"

The lanky man nodded and stepped aside, making way for Ellie and the stranger.

The interior of the inn was cavernous. For all that, it was only the three of them, a bartender, and a serving girl within. The stranger seemed to waver, considering the air, the roaring fire, the softness of the cushions upon the chairs. He sniffed to see what was cooking, and that tiniest of motions, the flaring of his nostrils, sent Ellie's heart racing.

"I think we will have a table, Cutter."

"Of course, sire."

"By the fire, I think."

"Very good."

The lanky man, Cutter, followed behind them. Ellie saw the innkeeper wave at the serving girl, who rushed over to pull out first her chair, then her companion's.

"Ale?" the stranger said.

"That would be lovely," Ellie said.

"Two of your finest," he said. The serving girl zipped off to where the innkeeper was already pouring their drinks.

"Cutter, have you eaten?"

"No, your highness. I thought it best to wait until I'd ascertained your location."

"From here at the inn? I might question the dedication of your efforts."

"Market Peace, sire," Cutter said. Something about how he said it sent a flash of disgust through Ellie's heart. *You didn't need to be with my love to watch him, did you?*

"Of course, of course. These things are so easy to lose track of. Well, we are celebrating and you simply must join us." He raised his hand for a third glass of ale, catching the serving girl mere steps away. She stopped in place, thought a second, then returned for the lanky man's drink.

"You are too gracious, sire, but I'm afraid I must decline." He spared a glance in Ellie's direction. "I suspect I have work to do out in the Market proper. Tell me, will you be venturing out for the festivities tonight?"

"Will we...no, I believe we shall stay in tonight, Cutter. First evening and all, two more to go. Best to stagger these things, don't you think?"

"Of course, sire."

"Besides, I believe I have other matters to attend to tonight. Isn't that right, dear?"

"Oh yes, my love," Ellie said.

Cutter rolled his eyes as the stranger grinned a wolfish grin.

The serving girl delivered their drinks and described the night's offerings.

"It all sounds delightful," the stranger said. "Cutter, are you certain I cannot tempt you?"

"Regrettably, sire."

"Two of everything, then," the stranger said. He raised his glass. Ellie did the same. "Cutter, I know you're not going to leave without raising a glass with us."

"Of course not, my Prince."

Ellie flushed crimson, nearly spilling her glass onto the table. *My Prince! My Prince!*

They toasted and drank and the Prince summoned the serving girl for more. "Nothing for my loyal bodyguard," he said. "Nothing but work work work for him, the poor thing. We two shall have to forge ahead in his absence, won't we, my dear?"

"We shall persevere," Ellie said, grateful that the bodyguard would not be remaining with them for dinner. She longed to have the Prince all to herself.

"You see, Cutter? 'We shall persevere.' I daresay I'm in safer hands than yours tonight, eh?"

"Truly, your highness." He stood and excused himself, thanking the innkeeper and the serving girl for their hospitality. "Shall I check in on you when I return, your highness?"

"If you must. If you must."

Cutter bowed to Ellie, removing his hat.

"Cutter," she said.

"My lady."

He left through the same door they'd arrived by, his cloak billowing out behind him. Ellie was surprised to see he wore neither sword nor pistol. If it hadn't been for the glinting hilt of a dagger hanging off his hip, she would have thought him unarmed.

"Good man, good man," the Prince said. "But a royal pest, just the same. Loyal, my dear. Eternally loyal, as you shall see. Now then—"

He bade her lean into him, and as Ellie did, he fingered the red gem the black-eyed woman had given her. His brow furrowed in concentration as he caressed the stone with his thumb, balancing it on the tips of his fingers.

"There it is," he said.

He spoke her name aloud, but so low only the two of them could hear. He closed his eyes and drew his lips so tight they might have been a scar at the center of his face. Ellie saw a single bead of sweat materialize from his brow and travel down between his eyes, across the bridge of his nose, finally coming to rest on his upper lip.

"Eliwys," he said. And another word she did not know, could not even be sure she heard.

"There. Too right."

He sat back in his chair and in short order their dinner arrived. Ellie found she was famished, absolutely starving. She ate with relish and sensual delight, savoring the juices as they ran down her chin, the steaming berries as they burst within her mouth. She tore hunks out of a loaf of bread and buried herself in them. She ate until she could not eat anymore, then continued eating until she felt she might burst, or if not burst, collapse from sheer exhaustion.

Against her bare skin, the blood-red gem pulsed, a second heart beating in time with her own.

SECOND MARKET

FALL, 1831

Waves crashed against the hull of the *Esquatorious*, spraying her decks, soaking any of her crew not already drenched to the bone. The ship rose over the crest of another surge, boards creaking in protest, prow climbing high into the bleak, moonless dark. At its zenith, the ship looked ready to leave the sea, fleeing the maelstrom below by launching itself into the sky. She reached and reached, only to thunder down once more into the raging whitewash.

Ellie stood on deck beside the Prince, holding on with both hands. She was not the slightest bit wet. Not a single hair was out of place. The Prince was immaculate, as always. He stood with his hands behind his back, feet planted almost as if daring the storm to come and take him.

"Cutter," he said.

The bodyguard dragged himself over, fighting the sea and the wind and the sickening rise and fall of the ship. He had to shout to be heard over the gale.

"Sire?"

"This is taking entirely too long, Cutter," the Prince said without raising his voice. It was not necessary. Her love's voice could not be engulfed by a mere storm.

"Ah, apologies, your highness." Over Cutter's shoulder, one of the sailors was flung overboard by a sudden flush from the sea. As Ellie watched, the other men hauled him back onto the ship by the heavy line fastened around his waist and shoulders. "The sea, it would seem, has other plans for us."

"Nonsense," said the Prince.

Cutter's eyes were tired. Ellie could have stabbed them out for their impertinence.

"Cutter, we're going to be late."

"Yes, sire."

"Cutter," said the Prince, drawing an infuriated breath. "You know how I feel about being late."

The bodyguard opened his mouth to speak—Ellie knew he was going to say *Of course, sire*—when the sea again rained down on them. He choked on his words, nearly losing his handhold.

"This is tedious," the Prince said.

The storm stopped.

The sails, sopping wet, shook like a dog drying itself off and puffed out to fill with wind. The sailors scrambled to gain control of the *Esquatorious* as she shot forward with the sudden gust, laying an uneasy line with no steady hand to guide her.

Cutter slumped forward onto the deck, the wind he'd been fighting no longer blowing. He shook his head, swearing under his breath.

"No more distractions," the Prince said.

"Of course, highness."

Ellie suspected Cutter had more he wanted to say. The lanky man, his red hair turned natty and dark with seawater, turned from them to direct his men.

"Storms always make me ravenous," the Prince said, taking Ellie's hand. "Would you join me belowdecks for a bite?"

Ellie's stomach grumbled. The Prince beamed and led her down to his stateroom to await supper.

The messenger had found them three days prior, bearing news of the Market's imminent arrival at Lancaster. He hunted Cutter down, perhaps seeing the wisdom in allowing someone else to bear the Prince's wrath.

"How far by sail?" was the Prince's only response when Cutter came to him.

"Four days at the least, sire."

"I see. And then how far by land?"

"Not more than half a day."

The Prince frowned and consulted a yellowed map spread out over the surface of a table. "Show me the nearest intersect."

Cutter searched the map and pointed out several spots.

"Each farther than the last and all farther from us than the Market itself. This is very poor planning, Cutter."

"Yes, your highness. Inexcusable."

They'd departed almost at once. The Prince, Ellie, Cutter, and several servants rode out while the hired men remained to break camp. Cutter sent the messenger ahead with no rest and a warning not to fail the Prince again, the obvious threat implicit in his manner and bearing. The messenger would ensure the Prince's ship was ready to depart when they arrived. They would have a fresh crew and a change of horses for their journey to the Market.

Four days later, just before sunrise, they made landfall. The Prince was in a foul mood, his frustration burning off of him in waves.

"When will we be ready to ride, Cutter?"

"Shortly, highness."

"Is that all you can say? 'Shortly, highness.' The Market is already one day gone, if your fool messenger even had his days right. How much of today will we sacrifice to incompetence and sloth?"

Ellie waited to see if the bodyguard would respond. He served the Prince well enough but contradicted far more than suited her. Would he now plead the winds or the storm or the distance they'd traveled and would travel yet? Would he accuse the Prince of lingering too long in far-off lands when he knew, so many years later, the Market's return must be approaching?

Cutter stood his ground but did not reply. Eventually the Prince put his back to the man and came over to where Ellie waited.

"The man is a fool," she said, unbidden.

The Prince, his eyes aflame, did not answer.

"He does not heed your wishes. He treats you like a venal child."

"Does he now?"

"He should not challenge you so before the men."

"The men are of little consequence."

"He should show you the proper respect."

"True, true. But he will bring us to the Market. And he is true in all things, if a trifle slow in this instance."

The Prince's outward calm began working its magic on her, as it always did. And by the time the horses were saddled and they were ready to ride, she had not a trouble in all the world. She was riding with her love, riding to see the Market for the second time. How many people ever visited the Market twice in their lives? How many had ever walked its avenues and breathed its air and were able to remark how that building there had been different last time? That brewery, the one run by the mine-dwellers, they had that fine apricot ale last time; I wonder if they brew it still?

Her memories of the first Market came to Ellie as she rode, drifting through her mind like faces carried by the wind. She remembered dining with her love that first night, and the suite of rooms he'd taken at the inn. They'd gone to a great ball the second night, and though she'd protested she did not know how, when they stepped out onto the gleaming floors and the band began to play, she had danced—oh, how she had danced—all night long.

They'd met the sun on the third morning, touring every corner of the Market, every hidden alley, every street vendor with a folding table and goods to set upon it. They'd shopped, the Prince choosing an entire wardrobe for his new bride, dresses and shoes and blouses and boots and hats and cloaks and bags. All the clothing she could ever wear and more, some of it cut and sewn from fabrics the likes of which she'd never imagined.

That night, the last night of her first Market, they'd sat under the stars of an unfamiliar sky as the Prince described each of them in turn. He'd pointed up, identified the star by its inhabitants, and mused for a while about the color of the their sky or the taste of their water or the nature of their people.

"Will we go there?" she'd asked.

"Someday, my dear. But not just yet. I've been away from your lands for too long and wish to take in the changes for myself. This pleases you, I hope?"

"So long as we are together," she'd said.

They'd ridden from the Market the following morning, before dawn, as they were bearing down on it even now. How much longer until they arrived? How much farther would they need to ride before Ellie saw three suns burning overhead instead of one? Would she feel the Market as it drew closer? Or would it surprise her, peeking over a ridge or a hill as if to say *hello, daughter, there you are.*

They rode and Ellie thought of stars, hoping her Prince was finally ready to share them.

It was midday before they arrived, driving their horses hard right up to the stone gates. The Prince leapt to the ground, his mount shaking and glistening with a sickly sheen of perspiration. It groaned, staggering off blindly at an odd, uneven angle.

Ellie patted her own mount's neck, whispering into its ear as she waited for Cutter to attend to her. She could dismount on her own—her life on the farm was still with her, in some ways—but she knew the Prince would disapprove. Better to wait. He was so cross from the slow journey; it was certainly better to wait.

With a helping hand from the cook's boy, Cutter assisted Ellie in returning her feet to the ground. She brushed the dust from her skirts and jacket and ran her fingers through her hair, smoothing the errant strands away from her face.

I must look a fright.

They would take rooms at the same inn as last time. There would be a bath and fresh clothes. Ellie wished she could blink her eyes and vanish, only to reappear once she'd had time to compose herself. It would not do for her to enter the Market looking as she did.

"The horses, sire?"

"Leave them," the Prince said. "Let them graze or rot; we do not leave here by horseback."

Cutter nodded and signaled for the horses to be taken away. Ellie noticed that his mount seemed to have fared best out of them all. The bodyguard was, among his many talents, an excellent rider. His mount looked fresh enough to make the same journey twice again.

"Come," the Prince said, holding out a hand for her. She went to him, as was her wont, and when they touched she felt a shimmering pass over her. The Prince's clothes were clean and pressed, his hair as perfectly coiffed as ever. The very picture of masculine beauty, the most startling man she'd ever beheld.

They entered the Market arm in arm, passing through the great stone gate as if trumpets sounded to announce their coming. Ellie caught a glimpse of her reflection in a window and was not surprised, standing with the Prince as she was, to see her jacket and skirts were as clean as the day the seamstress had delivered them. Her hair was as tidy as it had ever been.

Cutter followed behind, his men close at heel, ears tuned for the slightest utterance from the Prince's lips. Ellie was aware of them the same way she might be aware of a small dog chasing after her feet, hopeful for attention and afraid, always afraid, of a scolding or a swat across the nose.

"It has been too long, hasn't it?" The Prince shone at her side, raising his hand in a formal wave. "Too long away. So much has changed."

Ellie agreed. She raised her own hand to match his wave, turning her wrist and keeping her elbow high.

"Second night, just in time for the ball." He called over his shoulder at Cutter. "It is the second night, isn't it? You haven't made us so late we've missed the ball, have you, Cutter?"

"No, sire," the bodyguard said. Ellie didn't find his tone warm in the least.

"Then we shall visit the ball tonight. Would you fancy a dance, my dear?"

Ellie could barely contain her excitement. The memory of their first ball at the Market was still fresh and cherished in her mind.

Deeper and deeper into the Market they went. And she could feel the Prince's agitation and impatience radiating off of him like the heat from a baker's oven. They came to the inn he'd brought her to all those years ago. She and the Prince stood back while Cutter negotiated for their rooms and tended to the matter of their luggage, meals, and other trivialities.

"See her upstairs," the Prince said. "I have business."

He left without another word.

* * *

In the Prince's absence, the glamour that had hidden Ellie's disheveled state faded in short order. She examined herself in a tall, gilded mirror. Still the same, unlined face. The same nut-brown hair and opal eyes. The same slender shoulders, coltish legs, and slim hips. In all their years of travel, no matter where they visited or what they found there, no matter her clothes or adornments, it was always the same Ellie looking back in the mirror.

"My love," she said, fingering the blood-red gem that hung evermore, a second beating heart, around her neck.

She ran a bath, marveling, as she always did, at the simple miracle of running water. She'd beheld wonders with the Prince, seen skies alight with brilliant color, oceans rising up to take the shapes of men. She'd taken every marvel in stride but somehow the act of turning a knob or pulling a chain and summoning water, fresh and clear, never ceased to amaze her.

She added oils and scented powders to her bath. She washed her hair, rinsing it and combing it out. There would not be the slightest hint of road on her when she saw her love again.

A folded towel drawn from a nearby shelf provided Ellie with a headrest. She lay back, covered in lavender and honey-scented bubbles, and closed her eyes. She might have dozed but for the Prince, who she knew would not be long with a ball to prepare for. Still, she soaked much longer than she'd intended, emerging from the still-steaming waters of the tub red as a beet, her fingers wrinkled like a congress of tiny, disagreeable old men.

As she dried, there came a knock on the door. Ellie called to her visitor and Cutter peered in at her.

"My lady," he said. "I apologize for the interruption."

"Of course not. Your timing is impeccable."

He bowed his head.

"My Prince will expect much of me tonight, Cutter."

"I anticipated, my lady. If I may?"

He pushed the door further open and let in two girls, younger in appearance than herself, and a tall man with stringy golden hair and tanned skin. His eyes narrowed to a razor's edge as he examined Ellie in her bathrobe with her hair still wringing wet.

"Splendid, splendid," the tall man said. "Yes, yes."

Cutter bowed again, excusing himself.

The tall man directed Ellie to stand in the middle of the room. His assistants removed her bathrobe and retreated to let their master work.

"Your Prince," he said after a long silence. "How does he feel about blue?"

"It is one of his favored colors," Ellie said.

"Light or dark?"

"Light like the sky or dark like the sea. He says it brings out the sparkles in my eyes."

He leaned close so their noses were almost touching.

"Yes, yes. It will be blue, then."

One of the assistants rushed forward with a bolt of cloth. If she'd hurled it out the window and up into the sky it would have been lost at once in the brilliance of the day. The colors were so close Ellie could see clouds drifting in a breeze that was not there.

"Unless my lady objects?"

The Prince would approve; Ellie said as much.

"Splendid." He produced a measuring tape from a hidden pocket and quickly fitted Ellie for her new gown. He called out measurements to one of the assistants. When he was finished he instructed them to return Ellie's bathrobe. "Don't want you to catch a chill while I'm working," he said.

Ellie sat at her dressing table, sipping a cup of tea she did not remember steeping or asking for. One of the assistants—she had a hard time telling them apart and suspected they might be twins—set to work on her hair. The other attended the tall man, handing over pins and thread when asked, acting as an impromptu mannequin when needed.

It came to Ellie, watching him work, that the tall man's name was Sartha and that his hands had crafted the garments her Prince had worn the first time they'd met. His assistants she could not name, but somehow this did not bother her. She had the sense it would not bother them either. The one who'd styled her hair and was now applying gentle brushstrokes of makeup to her face Ellie named Esme after a nymph they'd encountered long ago. The second assistant she named Resme, after the nymph's younger sister.

"Come," Sartha said, holding out a hand. "Let us see how we did today, shall we?"

Ellie rose, sparing a glance at her now-unfamiliar face in the grand mirror. She was a stranger to herself. Her cheekbones were more pronounced, her eyes at once brightened and oddly deeper, as if one might lose himself staring into them. Her hair rose in an impossible pile of curls and waves. Esme had worked a miracle with her plain hair, transforming it into a living thing, a halo of dark, moving flame.

"Your right arm. Now your left. Deep breath and then exhale, please. Hold."

She froze in place as he adjusted the gown around her. He frowned, dove in with a needle and thread, adjusting the dagged sleeve so it matched its sibling, coming to a point where Ellie's knuckle met the base of her longest finger on each hand.

Ellie allowed him to work almost without interruption. He'd satisfied himself with the length of the gown, the complicated lacing on the back, the shoulders and the sleeves. The hips accentuated her form in a startling fashion, tricking Ellie once again, in the mirror, into thinking the girl looking out at her was a stranger.

When he moved to enhance her bustline, moving the blood-red gem aside, Ellie jerked back and rose a hand to caution him.

"My dear?"

"Have a care, sir."

A curious expression passed over his face.

He is recalling my lack of modesty when he'd first arrived and asking what this sudden shyness might be.

"It is not for me," she said.

"No?"

"I am the Prince's. I beg you to have a care."

He studied her expression, searching for falsehood and finding none.

"Your necklace?" he said. "I'm afraid it does not match the color well. I was hoping we could—"

"The gem will not come off, but that was not my concern. For some, for some men I mean to say, it may not be...safe."

Sartha roared with laughter. "I assure you, my dear, your virtue is at no risk in my presence."

"Even so. You have been kind and labored hard and I would not have you come to any harm it is in my power to prevent."

He thought a moment before asking her to spin the necklace so the gem hung down her back, nestled and slumbering in her cascade of hair. Next he summoned Esme and Resme and directed them in the final adjustments to her gown.

"I'm still not happy with the color," he said, when they were complete.

"My necklace?"

"Yes."

Ellie found the stranger again in the mirror. She concentrated on the shimmering red eye at the center of the girl's chest. She thought of the Prince and how pleased he would be to see her arrive in such finery. It beat in time with her own heart; first a deeper red, then nearly black, then lightening to blue. When she let it rest between her breasts, the gem was the same shade of blue as her gown.

Ellie danced. The orchestra played and the Prince twirled her and dipped her and lifted her. His stamina was, as always, unending. And she matched him step for step and move for move. When the music sped up, they flung their arms and kicked their feet. When it slowed down, the dance floor dropped away and they floated through the night air under the watchful gaze of a dozen moons. It was the perfect night, the perfect homecoming after nearly a century of travel.

Until the shooting started.

It was during an airwaltz. Slow reeds and soft strings as the Prince held her in his arms. The wilds of Ellie's hair swam, weightless, through the star-filled sky of the ballroom. She felt the Prince's satisfaction, his enjoyment, as they turned in space. He'd always been fond of dancing. It was one of the first things she'd learned about him.

The assassin dove down at them, appearing overhead with a bang and a flash of light. He was hooded, dressed all in black, with a long, tattered scarf tied around his neck, streaming behind him as he flew. In one hand, the assassin gripped the bone handle of a curved blade that reached back past his elbow. An oiled pistol stared at them from his other hand, an angry red eye flickering as he fired again and again.

The Prince, nonplussed, twirled Ellie away in a dervish of movement. She gasped and soared through the air over the ballroom, coming to a rest next to a bearded couple by the far wall.

He sidestepped, placing himself outside the arc of the assassin's blade. The way he moved, one might forget his feet were so far from solid ground.

"Revenge!" The assassin's voice was choked with incoherent rage. He struck the ground, rolling to absorb the impact, and was back on his feet instantly. He slashed up at the air, missing the Prince's feet as he danced once more out of range.

"Revenge!" The assassin raised his pistol, leading the Prince as he danced across the ballroom, waiting for the inevitable moment when he would need to pause and rebound off a wall.

With a wail of inchoate fury the assassin fired his weapon again and again. Bursts of golden energy erupted across the ballroom, zeroing in on the Prince for the split second he hung, exposed and vulnerable, in midair.

The first shot struck him in the thigh, twisting him back into the wall. The second took him in the arm below the elbow. His hand curled into a withered, darkened claw. It twitched, withdrawing into the Prince's body, seeking shelter in the shadow of his torso.

"Nooooo!" She reached out across the ballroom to him. If she was only closer she could have shielded him with her own body.

The third and fourth shots hit together, the former striking his chest and the latter catching him high up on his temple. The Prince flashed in agony, blazing for a moment like a summer star, before collapsing onto the floor.

There was not a single drop of blood anywhere on either the wall or the floor where he came to lie.

Ellie raced to his side, cradling her beloved's head in her lap. She expected, for all the world, to be comforting him as he spoke his dying words. If it wasn't too late already. She wept. Her hands shook. The world was a bottomless pit from which she could never escape.

"Where is he?" the Prince said, using her shoulder to push himself up off the ballroom floor.

He had been shot four times, in the leg, the arm, the chest and the head. Yet there was not a single mark on him. His fine clothes were unmarked. Ellie glanced at the hand squeezing her shoulder—it had been a gnarled claw only moments ago—and saw only the familiar hand of the man she loved.

"Here, sire!"

Cutter knelt over the assassin, his knee pressed into the man's throat, the strange pistol and the curved blade cast aside where they could do no more harm.

The Prince helped Ellie up from the floor. Together they went to Cutter and the assassin.

"Who sent you?" the Prince said, bending down.

"Revenge!"

"Ah, that." He turned to Ellie. "Revenge is so tedious, don't you think, my dear? Look at this poor fellow. He's gone mad with it."

"Revenge!"

"Yes, so you said. Your revenge, or are you working for someone? Please do tell, it's so important to be specific with these things."

"Sire," Cutter said, an anxious tremor to his voice.

"Yes?"

"There may be more, sire. We should continue someplace safer."

The Prince rolled his eyes. "If there are more, let's hope they're as incompetent as this fool. Still, we must credit him for showing up at a formal ball all in black. Masked even. Why, Cutter, I can't remember the last time a masked man attempted to dispatch me."

"No, sire," Cutter said. He flexed his hands, opening and closing his fists. All his attention was focused on the man beneath his knee.

"Revenge!" It came out less as a warning and more as a sob.

Ellie was standing back several paces. Not as near as the Prince and Cutter but still closer than the others in the room. She studied the man sprawled out helpless on the ballroom floor. His clothes were curious. More than mere cloth, but like no armor she'd ever seen. It bent and flexed when he shifted his position. Cutter's knee was not held back by its strength, but accommodated. Still, there was a hardness to it that was plain to see.

"I've never been a fan of masks," the Prince said. He reached down and tugged at the man's hood, pulling it back. His eyes were covered in thick, dark goggles, and beneath that, a mask of the same material as the rest of his dark uniform. The Prince removed mask and goggles in a single motion. As he stared up at them from the floor, the assassin's eyes met Ellie's. For an instant, she saw a flash of recognition cross his face. And something else: fury.

"You," he said, his voice scarcely more than a croak.

And then, with a scream that was equal parts rage and agony, he turned to dust before their eyes, crumbling as if aging whole centuries in the span of a single heartbeat. Cutter thumped heavily to the floor, his knee suddenly unsupported by the man or his odd armor.

The Prince stared at the mask and goggles in his hands. It might have been the assassin's head he'd removed and not his garments.

"Sire?"

"Strange evening, Cutter," the Prince said. He dropped the mask and goggles onto the empty pile of clothes and reached to examine the man's weapons. He picked up the blade by its bone handle, turning it over in his hand, appraising the workmanship. "Exquisite," he said, a smile growing on the edges of his mouth.

He picked up the pistol and shrieked in pain. The Prince fell back. The pistol clattered to the floor, its single hollow eye still searching the ballroom for a fresh target.

"Sire!"

The Prince panted, tucking his injured hand into the folds of his jacket. Ellie could see beads of sweat forming on his forehead. He licked his lips before speaking.

"Iron," he said, gasping in pain. "A child's mistake, really. To survive the attack unscathed and then suffer so foolish an injury…"

Cutter stared across the floor at the discarded weapon. It seemed to have its own gravity, its own unspoken strength. A faint steam rose from its dark skin, and the wood floor beneath it sizzled.

"The girl. Cutter, she must—"

"Yes, sire. I understand." Cutter waved to two of his men, who'd been lingering nearby. "Return the Prince to the inn at once. Search his rooms thoroughly before allowing him to enter. Make sure the windows are secured, then stand guard until I arrive to relieve you. Do you understand?"

"Yes, sir," they said, speaking as one.

Cutter extended a hand to help the Prince up. "Go with them, sire."

"Thank you, old friend."

Ellie thought she'd never heard her Prince sound so haggard, so frail. She watched him depart with the two guards, leaning on one for support, holding his injured hand close, taking short, unsteady steps as he went.

Cutter turned to her. His face was grim but resolved.

"Ellie, I need you to do something."

"Anything for my Prince," she said. It occurred to her this might be the first time he'd addressed her as anything but "my lady."

"Yes, of course." He indicated the pistol, the assassin's clothing, and his blade. "You are human. The iron will not burn you. I need you to collect these items and aid me in disposing of them."

"It would be my honor." Her face was alight with joy at being able to help. At being, according to the bodyguard, the only one who could.

Working with care, afraid of triggering the weapon again, Ellie gathered the pistol and blade into the assassin's dark uniform. There was no separation between the pants and his shirt. She was able to bind it all together with a pair of simple knots.

"Good, good," Cutter said. He motioned for her to follow him.

They walked through the Market, and as they had years ago, the assembled guests and vendors parted at their approach. This time it was not from a sense of reverence or honor; it was fear. She heard whispering from the crowd as they passed. Ellie paid them no mind. She was protecting her Prince. What more could she ever do?

"Wait here," Cutter said, leaving her outside the entrance to their inn. He disappeared inside and was gone for several minutes. Ellie waited with a glad, patient heart. Her arms did not tire, nor did she consider for even an instant lightening her load or setting the bundle of armor and weapons down on the ground.

When Cutter returned, he was not alone.

"This is Rossi," he said.

"I know. The cook's son. You've traveled with us for some time, haven't you?"

"Yes, mum," the boy said, his voice shaking. She knew him to be a shy, wide-eyed boy who constantly snuck her extra rolls or a second glass of wine. She guessed he was a year or two younger than she'd been when the Prince first swept her away for a life of adventure and romance.

"He's going to accompany you in your errand. He will...look after you."

"Thank you," Ellie said. Burdened as she was, she still managed a rough bow in the boy's direction.

"Mum," he said, cheeks flushed, eyes turned down.

"You understand?" Cutter said.

"Yessir."

"And the danger?"

"Yessir. Absolutely, sir."

"Good." Cutter spared a glance at the fat moon overhead. His eyes, perhaps of their own accord, moved up to the high window of the Prince's suites and then down to Ellie and the cook's boy. "Rossi," he said, as if to remind himself.

"Captain?"

"Nothing, nothing," Cutter said.

"Very good, sir. We should go then, shouldn't we? Mum?"

It seemed the lanky man had something he could not articulate.

"You are always so serious," Ellie said. "Don't give us another thought. We'll be back before you know it. This brave boy will be a capable escort. Go and look after my Prince."

"My lady," Cutter said. He opened the door to the inn, hesitated as if he had still more to say, and then vanished within.

Together, Ellie and the cook's boy, Rossi, began walking. They passed through the different layers of the Market, following streets she was pleased to discover she could navigate without the slightest thought.

The Market, of which I dreamed as a girl, is now my home. How many worlds will we see together? I know it as well as I know my own heart.

The first of the three suns was peeking over the distant tree-tops as they came to the wide stone gate. Ellie paused to shift the wrapped weapons into a more comfortable position. Rossi adjusted the leather pack on his back.

"You her?"

Beyond the gate stood the largest man Ellie had ever seen. His shoulders were broad enough to ride on; if they'd arrived before sunrise, the gleam on his bald head could have been the moon hanging in the sky. As Ellie watched, he began growing larger and larger, towering over her as if he'd been launched up over the wall.

And then she realized, *oh my, he's not growing. He's standing up.*

Ellie and Rossi bowed.

"I's Dhaleb," the huge man said. He himself bowed—the swoosh of air nearly knocked them off their feet—then extended a hand to Rossi in greeting.

"Sir," Rossi said. He looked in danger of being swallowed whole within the giant's hand.

"Good man. I heard what you done. Good man, you."

"Thank you. I—d'you have horses for us?"

"Course," Dhaleb said. "Tha's the job, innit?"

He moved to lead them away to, Ellie supposed, where their mounts were waiting. He stopped in mid-stride and looked down at himself. It gave Ellie vertigo just watching.

"Lords!" he said. "How'd I—lords, you won't tell, will you?"

"Sir?"

"M'glamour. Lords, I can't let the townfolk see me this way. Did any, d'you think? You didn't see anyone, did you?"

Rossi turned his head back and forth and assured the giant they were alone out on the road. "It is still very early, sir. I do not believe anyone saw you."

As if on cue, Ellie heard voices approaching. A couple by the sound of it, a local couple. She moved to warn the giant but he was gone before she could even move. A second later a man and a woman, walking together but not touching, lost in private conversation, appeared from around the bend. They walked past her and Rossi without a second glance.

"Lords, that was a close one," Dhaleb said. "Y'won't tell, will you? I's usually so good, y'know, but then your captain had me fetching horses for you—'strongest you can spare, Dhaleb' he told me—an' I dozed off waiting. But no one saw, did they? You said no one did, din't you?"

"I did," Rossi said.

"You are quite safe, sir. And your indiscretion will remain between just the three of us." Ellie was hoping to reassure him, and by the way his shoulders rounded and the tension went from his face, she felt she had succeeded.

Dhaleb led them a short way down the road to where a pair of fine roan horses were tied off.

"Figured the white one for the lass and the gray for you, sir. Saddles should be right, I think."

Rossi examined the horses and nodded his satisfaction.

"D'you need help, lass?"

"I believe I can manage," Ellie said. She looked to Rossi for confirmation—the Prince and Cutter had assigned him the role of accompanying her, and in her mind that made him into a surrogate for both her husband and the bodyguard.

"Do you have a good saddlebag we can use?" the cook's son asked.

"Yessir. Just give me half a moment." He raced off, moving with such speed Ellie decided she must have imagined his large size before remembering one of the first things she'd learned about glamours; they did more than slip past your eyes and your ears, they slipped past your memories.

Dhaleb returned with a weathered saddlebag in no time at all. Ellie let him fix it into place on the rear of the white horse and then, working under Rossi's watchful eye, unwrapped the assassin's uniform, freeing the strange pistol and the bone-handled blade from within.

"Gods," the giant said, his voice hushed for so large a man.

She tucked the pistol and the blade into one side of the bag and folded the armor, face mask, and goggles up into the other. Under Rossi's direction she did not allow Dhaleb to help or even to touch anything until both pouches of the saddlebag were closed and secured. Then and only then would she step aside so he could satisfy himself they were done up properly.

"What do we owe you?" Ellie said.

"I couldn't," he said. "Not after y'done right by me. S'a gift. A gift for your journey. An' good luck to you, as well."

"And to you," Rossi said, mounting his horse. He waited until Ellie was steady in her saddle and then, with a final thanks to the stable master, the pair of them began following the road away from the Market.

Ellie traveled with a song in her heart. She decided, wherever they stopped to dispose of the weapons, she would buy a small gift for Dhaleb. He'd seemed so worried about them, and so concerned with wishing them good luck.

It was almost as if he thought we were leaving the Market for good. What an odd thing! The Market is my home now—both of our homes. We will run our brief errand and be back by nightfall, if not sooner. My love is going to show me the stars.

She rode, wondering what sort of thing a man like Dhaleb would enjoy as a gift. Perhaps a hat to protect his great head from the beating sun. She spent some time lost in thought, being led by Rossi, imagining different hats and how they might look on the giant's head. Many people passed them as they rode, all heading in the opposite direction, toward the Market instead of away from it. Ellie spoke to many of them, smiling and confirming that yes, they were going the right way, and no, it wasn't far, not far at all.

When, after a time, they stopped meeting people riding to the Market, and walking to the Market, and stopped being asked if they were going in the right direction, Ellie was grateful for the chance to concentrate more fully on the question of the stable master and what sort of hat might suit him best. It seemed an important question, one with weight. She knew a poor gift would embarrass not only herself and the stable master but her Prince as well.

They stopped for the night. Rossi produced a tent and several warm blankets from his pack. He prepared dinner over an open fire and suggested they rest after their eventful day.

"We've a long way to travel tomorrow, mum, if we want to make it back before the Market closes."

They rode out at first light the next morning, continuing in the same direction. As Ellie had decided on a proper gift for Dhaleb the night before—she envisioned him in a dark, wide-brimmed hat with a thin leather band rounding the brim—she instead took to asking Rossi about himself, about his father, the cook. She was familiar with his father, of course, and had spoken to him on many occasions. This was different, however. In all those other instances, she was either complimenting him on an excellent meal or requesting some special dish for the night, something the Prince had tasted once or dreamed about as a boy.

"No matter what, your father always made it."

"That's Da," Rossi said, smiling. "And before you ask, I can save you the time. No, he never told me."

"Never?"

"Nope. Never. 'Trade secret, boy,' he always said."

"But weren't you apprenticing for him?"

The boy nodded. "I was and I wasn't."

"Well, which?"

"I wasn't, I suppose. My Da always said there was a difference between a job and, well, a job. One you do because you have to do something. The other you do because you are compelled."

"And you were never compelled to cook?"

"I thought I was, but well, he always said he saw more in me. That's what parents do, though, isn't it? Look for more in their children?"

They rode until the moon rose, which Ellie confided reminded her of Dhaleb, the stable master, her voice hushed as if he might step out from behind—or over!—a tree at the mere mention of his name.

"I want to get him a fine hat," she said. "As thanks for his assistance."

"Yes, that would be a grand idea. What sort?"

The moon continued its journey through the inky blackness as Ellie went over her perceived options and the reality that, wherever they ultimately stopped, there was a marginal chance the hat selection would be quite limited. She found a folded piece of paper in her pocket, yellowed with age and tattered around the edges, and sketched on its blank back. Rossi nodded his approval of her choices and offered to act as a head model, if it would help.

"Oh, it would! Thank you so much!" She was nearly squealing with delight.

When the moon reached its apex, Rossi closed his eyes and said his father's name once, only once. It sounded to Ellie like a prayer. Like he was saying good-bye.

"You will see your father soon enough," she said, hoping to reassure him.

He gave her a weak smile and judged it was high past time they made their beds.

"We've a long way to travel tomorrow, mum," he said, the good humor drained from his face. "If we want to make it back before the Market closes."

THIRD MARKET

WINTER, 1920

Ellie saw three of them, three massive, burly men with filthy hands and untended beards. Rossi marked them at once, alerting Ellie to their lurking presence on the far side of the street. "We should go," he said.

She nodded and quickened her pace. The sound of her boot heels on the cobblestone avenue brought Ellie to mind of a tinker's invention they'd seen some years back, traveling overseas. *It's my doomsday clock*, he'd explained, a raspy laugh present in every syllable. *Counts off the days until your doom. The days you have left.* She had found the idea enchanting, the clock almost too tempting to leave behind.

"I'm a fool," Rossi said, panting with exertion. "I don't know what I was thinking."

"He'll watch out for us. I know he will."

Rossi's answer was to reaffirm his grip on her hand and urge Ellie along. The ticking clock sped up, doom approaching, footsteps instead of turning gears. She stifled a dry laugh and strained to keep up, cursing her boots, which were fine for show but useless for more than teetering along at her companion's side. An affectation she hoped she would not regret.

The men pursued, adding their footsteps to hers and Rossi's. Slap of heavy leather on stone. Slow at first, patient, then speeding up, echoing off the low canyon formed by the high brick buildings on either side. Their murmured voices filled the street, obscuring their whereabouts, turning the sounds into high, mocking laughter.

Rossi swore under his breath, hurrying her along even faster. If they'd dare stop, she would have kicked off the hateful boots and fled barefoot.

"Not much farther, I think."

"Good," Ellie said. Shadows danced madly about them. Was it just the three men, or had they somehow become surrounded? The Prince's wedding gift slipped out from within her jacket and flung itself this way and that as she ran.

She saw light ahead. Not the feeble streetlights that had been, she was convinced, designed not to chase away the gloom but to amplify what darkness there was, but light, real light. Was it their hotel? She dared allow herself to hope. They would make it back in safety. No one would be hurt this night.

Her doomsday clock stopped. All clocks stopped; hers, Rossi's, the men stalking them. There was a weightless moment when her feet left the ground and Ellie was brought back to that night so long ago when she and her Prince had danced on the air. She became aware of a crushing pain in her throat, a rush of movement, and the sudden pressure of being flattened against the rough brick face of a wall.

"Hello, missy."

His accent was thick, his hair and beard dark as pitch; his breath was somehow dark as well. Dark and dank and so foul it made her choke. His eyes were tiny black holes punctuating his features, his nose a burning ember of coal. She smelled rotgut and sweat and sawdust and ash.

"It's early yet, missy. Where were you going in such a hurry?"

He had a laborer's hands, thick and callused. Ellie could breathe but not speak. She pleaded with her eyes, dug into his fingers with her own, but did not fight back. She didn't want to make him angry. There was still a part of Ellie MacReady hoping this could be resolved peaceably.

"Please," she said, gagging.

"This way, boys." He lifted her up with one hand and, keeping her well collared, carried Ellie off the street, into the alley.

Rossi was nearby. She felt for him with her mind and the telepathy of long acquaintance. There, deep in the alley. One man was bracing him while the other was occupied with delivering blows to his midsection. Ellie shuddered with every punch; she might have been feeling them in her own belly.

"Well, let's see now. What've we caught here, boys?"

He released her throat, and in a single, smooth movement she feared was well practiced, swung her around so she was once again pinned against the wall, this time not by his hand but by his entire weight. He planted his left hand on her shoulder, the palm more than sufficient to hold her fast. His other hand was occupied searching through her mass of skirts for what he and his friends had come for. With stinking breath, he licked Ellie from her neck to her temple.

"Don't," she said. "I beg you, sir, don't."

He howled with malicious delight. His friends jeered and stamped their feet. The man holding Rossi up decided the girl's companion had no more fight in him. Husband? Brother? What difference did it make? The pounding they'd delivered, he'd be lucky if he ever walked again.

"'Don't,' she says, boys. Have you ever heard the like? Missy, when we're through with you, 'don't' won't be a word you'll be likely to use again." He laughed once more and resumed unraveling her undergarments.

"Don't," Ellie said, one more time.

And exploded.

It wasn't light, not exactly, pouring out of her. It flowed from her eyes and her mouth and her hands and the blood-red gem hanging from her neck. It radiated outward, a tide of brilliance consuming everything it touched. Her assailant moved to cover his eyes, blocking the light with hands that turned to cinder before Ellie's flowing luminescence. Now he howled in pain, falling back, feet scrambling for purchase and finding none. His chest split open like an over-ripened cantaloupe; his guts and viscera could not spill out fast enough to keep from burning up before they hit the ground.

One of the other two men reacted quickly, turning and fleeing deeper into the alley. His wit abandoned him, however, when he saw it ended in a steep brick wall. The light caught up a heartbeat later, and where there had been a man casting a shadow now only the shadow remained, its arms raised as it attempted to scramble up the sheer face of the wall.

The one who'd held Rossi up found his feet rooted to the ground. He watched his friend burn and did not act. Something had frozen in his mind, and it would later occur to Ellie that by that point it was most likely a kindness to let the Prince's light take him. It snaked up around his ankles, rushed up his legs, hips, and chest, and pulled him down into the ground itself. He came back to himself at the end, clawing and fighting to keep from being subsumed entirely in the wet, dark surface of the alley. His fingernails scarred deep furrows in the ground that claimed him.

Rossi coughed and pushed himself up, using the wall for support. He brushed the dust and ash from his pants, spitting blood into a pile of trash.

"I tried to warn them," Ellie said, speaking between violent sobs.

"I know," Rossi said, helping her to stand. "I know you did. I heard you. It wasn't your fault."

He wrapped an arm around her and helped her out of the alley. The hotel's light was closer than ever. They walked to it without making a sound.

Ellie felt every eye in the hotel lobby on her as they stepped inside. She leaned on Rossi for strength, wishing she could shrink to the size of a pea and hide away in one of his pockets. She willed the tears to remain in her eyes until they were safely behind the door of their suite. She told herself none of these people wished her harm; they were nothing but travelers like Rossi and herself. Travelers and nothing more.

She made the mistake of glancing into the hotel's lounge as they passed.

"No!"

If Rossi hadn't been supporting her she might have crumbled into a boneless heap on the plush, carpeted floor. The strength went out of her legs and he had to haul her up, a puppet master winding up the puppet's strings.

"Keep it together, Ellie. Just a little longer."

She tried to point at the thing in the bar. Her arm wasn't working. It wouldn't lift. And her hand, her fingers—they weren't working either.

"Do you see?"

He turned to look and frowned. "Should I get you a glass of water?"

"No!"

He smiled and made an excuse for her behavior. He repeated it several times to a passing couple, a bellhop, and a rail-thin woman with a smoldering cigarette hanging off her lower lip.

"What is it?" he said, returning his attention to Ellie. There was a tremble in the air before and after he spoke. An audible glamour, masking their words from those around them.

"In the lounge," she said, tucking into Rossi's glamour. "The blue man with all the arms."

He looked again. Rossi shook his head. "I don't see any blue people. Do you mean the man in the blue suit?"

"No, *the blue man*." She jerked her head at the mahogany bar. Four patrons sat on high-stooled perches, nursing their drinks. The second from the right looked like he'd be ten or fifteen feet tall if he pushed away and stood on his own two feet. His glass was tall and thin and had a pink umbrella and a sword-skewered piece of fruit hanging over the lip. As she watched he used his many arms to take a sip of the drink, straighten his dark suit, scratch his behind, adjust his hair, turn the page of a newspaper, and tap on the bar to summon the bartender for another round.

"I don't see any blue people," Rossi said. She hated him then, could have snatched up an ashtray from one of the guests and bashed that knowing smile off his face.

"It's not funny," Ellie said. She moved to point again, and a thing with too many legs to count skittered past. It was close enough to touch, close enough that she could make out the sickly-sweet smell of sugar, mountains of sugar, trailing in its wake.

She stumbled again, nearly slipping from Rossi's arms. If that had happened, she might have fled. Away from the hotel and out into the night. Better to take her chances with the drunks and the ruffians than risk embarrassing her Prince before his subjects.

A dozen more came into view. A green beast more animal than man, its long, angular snout opening into several rounds of enormous teeth. *He's made for ripping and tearing, chewing and biting.* She didn't suppose there was much to come between a creature of this sort and its next chosen meal.

A swirl of colorful smoke passed Ellie. It had no mouth but it spoke just the same: "The sea of Liir, truly?"

Truly. She saw no one walking with the swirl of smoke, heard no voice. But there was someone there just the same. Someone who was no one. And it spoke, only without using words. She felt its answer the way she would have felt warm or cold or tired or hungry.

"Well, I've never heard the like," the smoke said. It paused within arm's reach of Ellie and Rossi. She could imagine a gentleman holding his position a moment to adjust his shoe or straighten his tie.

Certainly it's unprecedented, I'll grant you, but that doesn't mean it's impossible.

"Irresponsible is what it is. Thoughtless and irresponsible. What are the rest of us to do?"

No one laughed, burbling like fast-moving water. *No argument here.*

"I tell you," the smoke said, drifting away. "There'll be hell to pay. Mark my words: hell to pay."

If no one answered, the pair was too far away for Ellie to hear. She felt Rossi's hand on her arm, urging her forward. She glanced over at him, and was momentarily shocked at how old he looked. *All these years. Older and older, and I just stay the same.*

"No," she said. "I believe I would like a glass of water. Perhaps something stronger."

He might have protested, but with her resolve came a renewed sense of strength. Ellie shrugged his hand off and strode through the lobby to the hotel's lounge. She located a small table in a far, dark corner and sat down, pulling out her own chair before Rossi could catch up and do it for her.

She sat with her back straight, her ankles crossed, and her hands in her lap. The outward calm she projected was in stark contrast to the storm raging within her mind. Her eyes stared sightlessly forward, focused on a single overhead light.

"What is it?" Rossi said, sliding into the chair beside her.

"You don't see them. Why don't you see them?"

"Tell me."

Ellie raised a hand from her lap and pointed the monsters out to him one by one. The towering man with the blue skin and extra arms was on the far side of the lounge now but the nearest table was populated by a rangy, twitching thing with too many eyes, a red-skinned woman who seemed to communicate by sniffing the air and exhaling at her companions and a short, stout man with a tuft of fire where his beard should have been.

Rossi shook his head as Ellie described them. "I see a short man with a gray beard," he said. "A quiet woman, and a boy who looks even younger than you."

Ellie shook her head. She seized Rossi's hand, pleading with him to believe her. When his eyes met hers they grew wide in recognition.

"Ellie," he said. "Your eyes."

"What?"

Her handbag was by her left foot. Rossi picked it up and removed a small palm-size mirror. He held it to her face so she could see what he saw.

Her eyes. Even in the dimness of the hotel's lounge they sparkled. But there was something more. A thin tendril of light, curling up like a wisp of smoke, seeped out of Ellie's reflected eye.

"No!"

She clapped her hands over her eyes, held them closed so tight it hurt. She was keenly aware of the fevered beating of the Prince's gem against her chest, matching her own racing heart beat for beat.

The air in the lounge had suddenly become very thin.

She saw in her mind's eye the gnashing teeth of the green creature with the long snout. Imagined the blue giant rising to his full height and, club in hand, flattening her to a bloody pulp of crushed bones and exploded organs. Felt the eerie calm as the red woman at the next table glided over, leaned in close, and pulled the life from her in a single, sharp inhalation.

Ellie felt her eyes blazing beneath her hands. Felt the tips of her fingers beginning to tingle and burn as the light overwhelmed her flesh. Soon. Soon she would be burning, and the horrors in the hotel lounge would burn with her.

"Ellie, it's all right. Open your eyes. No one's trying to hurt you."

"No."

"Ellie, it's me. I promise."

She held her breath, trying to decide, the light building and building. What finally decided her was Rossi. How could Rossi lie to her, or hurt her, if her Prince had tasked him with her protection?

"See?" he said as she lowered her hands.

She watched the creatures at the next table raise their glasses in a toast. The blue giant at the bar bellowed with laughter, clapping one of his companions on the back. The predatory half-lizard stepped away from the bar to let an ancient crone in tattered rags step up close.

"Do you see them?" Ellie said.

"No. But I believe you. And I don't think they mean you any harm."

She continued watching and realized that, apart from an occasional worried look, not one of them appeared the least bit interested in her or Rossi. They drank and talked and told stories. They laughed and embraced as old friends who hadn't seen one another in many years. They were creatures, true, but that was all they were.

As she calmed down, as the Prince's gem slowed its beating to a soft, steady, unhurried pace, their features melted and blurred and became as normal as hers and Rossi's. The blue giant shrank and became a fit man in a sharp blue suit. The half-lizard became a woman with thin features, a pointed nose, and a long drape of unruly hair that fell to the center of her back.

"Glamours," she said, marveling.

"Ellie?"

"I was seeing through their glamours. They must be here for the Market, same as us. Did you know there were so many walking the world? Why haven't we seen them before?"

"Maybe we have, but without realizing it. Ellie, do you know how much power it takes to see through a glamour?"

She shook her head.

"I'm not even sure if your Prince could do it. His father, perhaps."

"He gave me this," she said, holding up the Prince's gem, remembering the three men in the alley. "It protects me. What if that extends to…I don't know…letting me see through things that aren't there?"

"To protect yourself?"

"It wouldn't be the strangest thing we've seen."

"True, true. Even so."

Ellie nodded at the table beside them. "Maybe I can prove it to you."

"You don't have to," Rossi said. "I told you, I believe you."

"Even so."

Before he could stop her, Ellie leaned over to their neighbors, the man with his bushy gray beard, the thin, quiet woman whose dress was cut a hair tighter than modesty would allow, and the wild-haired boy who couldn't seem to sit still.

"Pardon me," Ellie said. "May I ask where you all are from?"

"Cleveland," the bearded man said, answering without turning.

"No, not where you've come from for the Market. Where you're really from."

The thin woman remained silent as she glared at the bearded man. The boy drummed on his legs and made a soft, mewling sound.

"Market?" the man said.

"Of course. You're travelers, as my companion and myself are."

"Fraid I don't catch your meaning, girly. We're from Cleveland." He shared a look with the thin woman and poured the rest of his drink down his throat. As a group, they rose to leave.

Ellie had no more luck with any of the other lounge patrons, earning herself several threatening looks and a few harsh words before Rossi insisted that she stop before someone tried to hurt her.

"You don't want that again, do you? Twice in one night?"

No, she didn't. She'd rather he think she was losing her mind.

They left the lounge together, Ellie shooting defiant looks at the patrons who'd remained after she spoke to them.

"What did you expect?" he said once the door to their suite was closed and locked.

"I don't understand."

"Just what I said. If they're hiding behind glamours, they've probably been doing it a long, long time. I've only met a handful of things that can create a proper glamour. I'd be willing to bet not a one of the people downstairs can swing it. How many do you think even remember the sight of their true faces?"

Ellie fell onto the couch. Removing her boots, she was brought back to their attack in the alley.

"Who do you think they were?"

"Who?" Rossi said, loosening his tie and struggling to get his jacket off.

"The men from outside. From—"

"The street? The alley? No one. Monsters who don't need a glamour to appear human. Monsters worse than anything downstairs."

Rossi finally managed to extricate himself from his jacket. He tossed it over the back of a chair, kicked off his shoes, and sat down as if he was afraid the impact with the cushion might shatter his bones.

"Are you all right?" Ellie said, spotting his distress.

"Fine, just fine. Little banged up is all."

She puzzled for a second before fitting the pieces together. "The alley? I'm such a fool!"

"Now, now, not a fool, just a girl with a lot on her mind." Rossi began unbuttoning his shirt. For the first time, Ellie noticed a line of dried blood on his face. It trailed from his chin, up his cheek, over his lip and to his right nostril.

"You're bleeding."

"I was. It's fine, honestly. Nothing to it."

"Let me see."

She forced him back and made him sit still while she unbuttoned and removed his shirt. When she pulled up his undershirt, she discovered a blossoming field of purple, green, and yellow bruises all across his chest and midsection.

"Looks worse than it is," Rossi said. When Ellie didn't respond, he spoke again, "You're supposed to tell me, 'It looks horrible,' and then I'll tell you, 'Oh, then it looks about right.'"

"Don't joke." Her voice was so small it might have come from a thousand miles away. She touched a star-shaped bruise on his shoulder with the tips of her fingers, feeling like a child reaching out to feel the soft skull of a new baby brother, curious what the tender flesh would feel like.

"See, that doesn't hurt at all," Rossi said through gritted teeth. "Do it some more, if you like. Please do."

She pulled away, then fled to the far side of the room, by the tall windows that opened out over the city.

"I'm sorry," she said at last.

Rossi stood. He forced a smile and went over to her.

"It's not your fault, dear. Nothing is your fault. I'm here to watch over you, and on occasion, it gets a little rough and tumble. But just you watch: I'll be right as rain before morning."

He kissed the tips of two fingers and pressed them against her forehead.

"Can I count on you not to go out again? We can try talking to some of the other guests in the morning, if you like, but right now I just need to sleep."

She shook her head. "I'm not going anywhere without you."

"Nor I." He managed a wobbly sort of smile before giving her another kiss-by-proxy and retreating to his own room for bed. Ellie closed the lights and dragged a chair over to the tall windows so she could watch the city. The next morning she would wake in her bed with no memory of rising from the chair and tucking herself in for sleep.

Ellie insisted on inspecting Rossi's injuries. She refused to set one foot outside their suite until he removed his shirt and let her see his chest once more.

"I can order food up to the room, you know? They will deliver."

She punched his arm—a reflex—and regretted it a second later. Rossi flinched back, but seeing her distress, waved her away with his palms to show he was joking.

"It's not funny," she said. The pleading tone of her voice cut through his resistance, and he removed his shirt so she could examine his bare torso. His skin was unmarked; the injuries he'd suffered on the street had vanished.

"How?"

"I told you, a good night's sleep would do me right."

"But—"

He shook his head and put on his undershirt. "We all have our little tricks, dear. If it makes you feel any better, it was hell getting to sleep last night banged up as I was."

That didn't make her feel better in the least. "Is it a spell? A charm?"

"A parting gift from a mutual friend. You remember Captain Cutter, don't you?"

"Of course."

"Smart man, that. Even keeping a low profile as we have, waiting out the Market, he knew I'd need a little boost to keep up with you." He finished buttoning his shirt, tucked it in, and squared his tie away in short order. After selecting a hat and a jacket, he opened the door to their suite and gestured for Ellie to follow him.

"Where are we going?" she said.

"Breakfast. I'm famished. And I think you wanted to try talking to some of the other guests when they haven't spent the past few hours soaking whatever they have to pass for brain cells in the local flavor."

She snatched her bag from the table and followed him out the door.

Ellie didn't recognize any of the guests downstairs from the night before. She tried talking to a group of likely-looking people, eventually asking where they were from, where they were *really* from, only to find her questions met with blank, concerned stares.

"My niece," Rossi explained. "Means well but she tends to get excited and, well, turned around from time to time."

"Pity," said one of the men. Rossi excused himself to rescue an older woman in a dark, high-collared dress who Ellie was badgering for her place of birth. The woman's hair was pulled back tightly enough that the strain showed on her cheeks and forehead. Even if she hadn't been put out by Ellie's questions, she would have looked ready to begin screaming.

"You can tell me. It's all right. We're here for the Market, too." Ellie was cooing right into the woman's ear, oblivious to her clear discomfort.

The woman addressed Rossi as he approached, sliding away from the mad young girl's fevered assault.

"Sir, is this... girl with you?"

"I'm afraid so," he said. Ellie shook him off and pulled out the Prince's gem. She held it up in the old woman's face.

"See? Look—it's all right. Just tell me where you're from and"—Ellie leaned close to whisper right in the woman's ear—"what you are. I promise I won't tell."

"I'm so sorry," Rossi said, pulling Ellie away.

"I should say so. Are you responsible for this girl?"

"My niece. She gets confused from time to time. Again, I apologize."

Ellie dangled the Prince's gem directly before the old woman's nose. "You know what this is, what it means. I *order* you to tell me what you are!"

Before the woman could express her utter outrage at Ellie's terrible behavior, Rossi had pulled his "niece" away and was leading her through the hotel's lobby.

"What was that?" he said.

"Don't be dumb. I think she was the green thing. With all the eyes last night. She changed glamours to hide from me, but come on, look at her: you can see the green peeking out from the edges, can't you?"

"Ellie, she's old and possibly unwell. But she's not an insect."

"You didn't see her last night!"

"I didn't. But even if she was, what then?"

"Then I'd know," Ellie said. "I'd know what I saw was real. And I'd know my dreams are real."

Rossi stopped. They were standing just before the hotel's entrance. He drew her away to an alcove.

"Dreams?"

"Yes. I see my Prince. We are dancing across the deck of a fine, great ship. He spins me and brings me back into his arms. I see his face, his eyes, and I know it's real. It's real and if I can prove what I saw last night was real then I'll know this is real as well." She realized she was nearly shouting and stopped to get herself under control. "He's calling me, don't you see? All of it, it's him calling me back."

* * *

They walked from the hotel toward the river, Ellie stopping people from time to time to ask after their origins. Sometimes she pulled out the Prince's gem, other times she didn't. There was no rhyme or reason to her behavior. She'd stop one person and comment on the weather, the light dusting of snow that had fallen in the night. Another person she'd take by the shoulders and order them to reveal themselves to her.

Rossi did a good amount of apologizing.

It wasn't their first time in the city—they had traveled so much in the years waiting for her Prince to return—but much had changed since her last visit. New buildings had sprung, seemingly fully formed, right out of the ground. Parks had been replaced by odd, featureless structures looking weathered to have stood a century or longer. It was somehow an old city and a new one, a longtime friend who'd lost his hair, bought new clothes, shaved his beard, and started wearing spectacles.

"We should have brought the dogs," Ellie said.

"They'd be miserable. You know they hate going to the city."

"I didn't mean like that. I'm going to miss them. I hadn't thought of it before, but the Prince isn't going to come home with us, is he?"

"I'd doubt it."

"Then we should have brought them. Will they be all right, do you think?"

"I left instructions for their care."

She was genuinely pleased by this—at least for a few seconds. Then Ellie frowned. "Do you think they'll miss me? It's not the same if Cindy lets them out for a run, is it? Not the same as having me there to throw sticks and shout for them?"

"I suppose not."

They followed the streets until they came to the river. Rossi brushed off the surface of a bench with a handkerchief and they sat. A cargo ship steamed past and Ellie waved at the sailors. Rossi removed his hat and joined her.

"The Prince's ship is much larger, in my dream," she said. "I can only see a small part of it but even that much is enormous. Two hundred people could fit on the deck, but it's just the two of us dancing in the moonlight. Isn't that nice?"

"It sounds lovely," he said.

"It will be. Three days' warning and then the Market. Today is the third day. Do you think it will have changed much?"

"I doubt it. Nor your Prince neither. Some things in this world are content to remain as they are."

"Like me," Ellie said. "And you. Oh, taller than the boy who rode with me and beginning to show some gray. And perhaps not so sprightly in your step, but you wear your years well, don't you?"

Rossi nodded and did not reply. He might have been caught in a sea of memories. He might have been simply keeping his thoughts to himself.

"I suppose it's good, though. No telling where we'll be going. No telling how the Market may have grown. Like this city. Look at the size of it! The new buildings barely fit on the island, and how many sites did we pass where more are being built?"

"I didn't think to count."

"I tallied a dozen before stopping. Think of that. The next time we visit, it'll be fit to burst."

Ellie turned from the water's edge. Rossi followed her gaze.

"Look, do you see that?"

She pointed at an advertisement painted on the side of a building. THE MARKET, it read. NEW YORK CITY, MIDWINTER'S DAY. ALL YOU SEEK SHALL BE WITHIN.

"You'd think it was just for me, wouldn't you? 'All you seek shall be within.' All I seek, all I've ever sought, is the Prince. And he'll come and bring the Market with him. It's been so long since I danced, Rossi, but I'll dance again when I'm with my Prince."

Ellie heard a grumble of thunder rolling down the street. Booming thunder, crash of metal and glass, groan of a transmission that wanted nothing in all the world so much as to be taken out behind the woodshed and put out of its misery.

The driver downshifted as he rounded the corner, tailpipe belching out tarry black smoke. Toss in a lick of flame and you'd have something any dragon would be proud of. The smoke hung in the air, thick enough to slice and serve on a plate with a scoop of ice cream. Rossi pulled her away, covering his mouth, indicating for her to do the same. Ellie gagged and fanned the air with her hand, to no avail. She'd have had more luck moving that smoke with a shovel.

As the faded yellow truck ground to a halt, the passenger-side window stuttered down. A pointed hat the color of deep water peered out at them. It swore, ducked down, and seemed to grow the topmost part of a head. A tangle of bushy red hair, lined, squinting eyes, and a rosy, pointed nose looked down from the truck's cab.

"A horse," it said. "Ah, what I'd give for a horse."

They heard sounds of a struggle and then the door opened. Ellie expected to see the owner of the hat fighting for his life against two, three, or even four opponents. What she saw instead was a short man with a rough, but pleasant face, his fingers clutching the door handle as he swung himself down to the street.

"Never heard a horse make noise like that, did you? No, I say. Just one horse, that's all I ask for. A mule, even. I had *great* mules once upon a time, I did."

He was short enough that he needed to scuttle around and slide feetfirst from the truck. It wasn't graceful, but after some struggle he managed to lower himself to the sidewalk, landing in a great cloud of dust. As he straightened himself, Ellie saw that he barely came to her waist. Rossi, who was several inches taller than her, towered over the little man.

"What day is it?" he said, straightening his disheveled clothes.

"Thursday," Rossi said.

"Not that kind of day; t'other kind. What day is it? Am I late again? Always late. Or early. Sometimes I'm early. Never on time, though. More pity, that."

Rossi repeated himself, telling the man again that it was Thursday. Before the stranger could counter, however, Ellie broke in. "You're a day early," she said. "It's not until tomorrow."

"Early? Better than late, innit? Now, let's see who we got here."

He circled them where they stood, looking the two of them up and down. Ellie tightened her grip on Rossi's hand. The little man walked in a wobbling, kneeless fashion, like a penguin with a bushy red beard and a tall garden gnome's cap.

"Y've got something about you, y'do," he said. "Where are y'from?"

Rossi clapped his mouth shut, but the laugh escaped anyway. It was a rough bark and the short man jumped reflexively back.

"Lord, boy, what's wrong with you?"

"Please pardon my…cousin," Ellie said. "He gets confused from time to time."

"Does he now? Family can be a pain, can't it?"

"I am not confused," Rossi said.

"See what I mean?"

"Aye. Poor lad."

"I am not confused," Rossi said again.

"Then he starts repeating himself." Ellie shook her head in mock regret. "It happens every time."

"You're good to look after him the way you do." The little man pressed his hands together, palm to palm, as if saying a silent prayer on Rossi's behalf.

"Family," she said, giggling.

Rossi rolled his eyes, unsure of how exactly he'd become the odd man out. It was the truck driver who cracked, bending over and wheezing out peals of laughter that sounded like rocky teeth grinding up shards of broken glass. When Ellie joined him, it wasn't the sweet, proper lady's laugh he'd grown accustomed to during their years together; she howled and slapped her leg, gasping for breath.

"You're a good sport, lad," the truck driver said, offering Rossi his hand.

"Thanks, I suppose."

"It's a good man who can be the butt of a joke and a great man who can laugh at himself." He sized Rossi up again. "I figure you're decent at best."

"Oh, he's a delight," Ellie said, standing on the tips of her toes to kiss Rossi's cheek. "Aren't you, 'cousin'?"

It was a weary smile Rossi showed them, and very nearly enough to set the pair bawling again if he hadn't added his own short, low chuckle as punctuation. The truck driver clapped him on the back and offered another sideways compliment.

"There you go, lad."

The little man's truck, perhaps jealous of all the attention its master was getting, cut a terrific fart that blotted out much of the early afternoon sunlight. Ellie noticed that the snow by their feet was no longer white, but a sooty, filthy gray like dirty wash water.

"Is this your first Market?" she said, thinking to regale the stranger with tales of her two previous visits. Rossi could describe traveling with his father, perhaps gain a little prestige in the short man's razor-thin eyes.

"My first?" he said. "Not my first. Nor my second neither. I kept count for a time, yes I did, but some kinds of counting turn around on you if you don't mind them. Get out of hand, they does. Take a life of their own. Dangerous, that."

He slapped the side of the truck with his palm; the sound was flat but not hollow and there came a rattling from within as if he'd toppled some precarious tower of small items. Ellie guessed the old, grumbly thing was packed from floor to ceiling.

"Oh, curiosity?" he said, noting her hungry look. "Well, we can see, can't we? Market a day away, but a customer's a customer and a deal's a deal. What are you coming to the Market seeking, dearie?"

"My husband," Ellie said, answering without thinking.

His eyes shifted over to Rossi then back to Ellie. "Any husband at all or one in particular?"

"My husband," she said, stressing the *my*. "We became separated some time ago. Rossi—my cousin—has been accompanying me ever since."

"Your cousin?"

"Yes," Rossi said. "Or good as, at any rate. You are a nosy one, aren't you?"

The short man tutted and tapped his chin with the knuckles of his left hand. "Travel long enough and y'get nosy. A good story's worth its weight in golden eggs. Worth its weight in just about any currency you care to trade. But hold on, you…"

He reached to take the shoulders of Ellie's coat in his hands and pull her down toward him, almost as if he meant to plant a kiss on her nose. But he didn't touch her, except to lower her down to his height. He only looked, staring into the heart of her, studying her face and hair and lips and eyes.

"We've met before, haven't we?"

"I don't believe so," Ellie said. "I would remember."

He pulled her down farther so that Ellie's head was touching his chin. He sniffed her hair three times, *sniff sniff sniff*, and let her go. Ellie stood back up again, unsure of what had just happened.

"Different but the same. You're her, aren't you? The girl from the road. Lords, your people don't live this long. Which Market is this? *When* is this? I've really hit it wrong this time, haven't I?"

"What road?" Ellie said.

He boggled, watching her for some sign that the tide had turned. Now it was Ellie and Rossi who'd have a touch of fun at his expense. But neither of them laughed.

"You remember, surely. Ran into you walking by the road, the cat who swallowed one canary, then went back for all his friends and family. You helped me out a spell. Helped me prepare. Lords, girl, how old are you? You don't show a day!"

"My husband's doing, I'm afraid. I'm sorry, but I don't recall meeting you. What road are you speaking of?"

He scratched his head and licked his upper lip with the tip of his tongue. If he'd had a pencil close at hand, he could have chewed on the tip. Instead he smacked his forehead and let out a low whoop of realization.

"Y'helped me," he said. "Long time ago. Didn't expect you'd forget—you being so excited and all. Also wouldn't have expected to find you here today. How'd that come to pass, I wonder?"

"Her husband," Rossi said.

"Yes yes, of course. Husband. Lots of those around, feral cats out for a prowl. Doesn't tell me what she's doing here though, does it? You neither, come to that."

"Where are *you* from?" Ellie said.

He shook his head. "Nowhere. Not anymore."

She poked him, prodded his shoulder with her fingers. "Is this what you really look like?"

He gaped at her. "What else should I look like?"

"A bug? A blue giant?"

The short man raised a finger on either side of his head, forming makeshift antennae. He wiggled his fingers and buzzed with his lips. "Like this?"

The wind changed direction and the air coming off the river was bitter cold compared to the air from inland. The fine powder of snow that had drifted companionably about the trio as they became acquainted suddenly and without warning began accumulating in a wet, frigid mass around their feet. Ellie's ears became numb and her lips, when she examined them in the grime-coated glass of the truck's window, were turning blue.

"I met a giant once. Big as a tree. Dumb as one, too. Sold him his own right shoe and y'wouldn't believe how stunned he was to discover I had a left one to match."

Ellie's giggle turned into a shiver. Rossi removed his coat and laid it across her shoulders. "We should get back to the hotel," he said.

"I could give you a ride, if you like," the short man, who still had not introduced himself, said.

Ellie nodded, eager with discomfort. "Yes, please."

Rossi helped the little man up into the cab of the truck, ignoring protests that he could do it himself if they'd only let him be.

"Lemme see, some heat would do right, no?"

He punched a button behind the steering wheel and waves of impossible heat issued forth from vents in the truck's dash. Soon the layer of snow and ice was falling away from the windshield.

"My seat is getting hot," Ellie said.

"Latest thing," the short man said, winking at her. "Don't tell anyone. Rules and such. Right place, wrong time, all that."

"Yes, rules."

He turned the key in the ignition and the truck began its slow, trudging way up the street. Ellie expected they would have to give directions—she couldn't imagine that this odd little man actually knew where he was going—but they cut a sure and direct path to the heart of downtown. When they arrived at a building only a couple blocks from their hotel, the driver cautioned them to find something to hold on to.

"This next bit may be a touch...dicey. Truth be told, never done this with passengers. Still, the principles is sound."

He shifted the truck into reverse and backed away, cutting the wheel so they were traveling perpendicular to the building where they'd paused before. The engine groaned, and the halo of dark smoky exhaust surrounded them. Ellie heard a shrill *beep beep beep* as they reversed. It ceased when he shifted the truck back into drive.

"Here we go," he said.

Bearing down on the steering wheel as if afraid he might be thrown clear, the short man floored the accelerator. The truck shot forward, the engine purring for the first time since they'd heard it approaching out of the drifting snow. The building grew larger and larger until it filled the windshield.

Rossi let go of his handhold on the door and threw himself in front of Ellie, shielding her body with his own.

"There we are, then. Right as rain. Care to walk around?"

Ellie pushed Rossi off of her and followed the short man out the driver's side door. The truck, no longer spewing noxious black fumes, had been reduced to a silent observer.

They were in the building's basement. A few steps from the truck's grill was a rusted, silent boiler. A puddle of brackish water covered the floor in one corner, and beyond the range of the truck's headlights Ellie could hear small things with too many legs skittering about in a mild frenzy.

"I was on time for something once. Didn't suit me."

"The Market is coming here?" Ellie said. Behind her, Rossi had recovered from their non-collision with the building and was climbing down to join them.

"More like here is going to the Market, but that's close enough. Safe here, though. Y'said you had a hotel?"

"Yes," Rossi said. The lone syllable was all he could get out.

"Well, come on, then. Three days of busy trade builds a powerful thirst. Best to get ahead of it is what I say."

There was an additional room in Ellie and Rossi's suite when they arrived back at the hotel. Neither was especially surprised to find the short stranger's luggage waiting for him there.

"You know, I can't remember your name for the life of me," he said.

"Ellie. And this is Rossi."

"Your cousin?"

"Not by half," Rossi said.

"Call me Beesix," the short man said. "S'close enough to right and I'll mostly answer when I hear it."

"Beesix," Ellie said without a hint of recognition.

"No? I'd swear it was you, girl."

The hotel room seemed to have warmed itself for their arrival. Ellie excused herself to tidy up and change out of her damp clothes before they went downstairs for dinner. "Will you please entertain our guest, Mister Rossi?" she called over her shoulder, closing the door curtly behind her. It was a light door and it shooshed closed as if floating on a curtain of air. If she was quiet, Ellie would be able to hear what Rossi and the strange man said in her absence.

"Nice girl," Beesix said. "Hasn't changed at all in two centuries."

"No," Rossi said. She could imagine the look on his face. It was not a happy one.

"How'd you end up tied to her? 'Cousin' my foot."

"As she said, it's a service for her husband, the Prince."

That same rough stone-on-glass laughter. It sent waves of cold shooting up Ellie's spine. "Husband. Got you trained, no? What's your game?"

"I'm looking out for her."

"Are you?"

"Someone had to. Can you imagine?"

"Don't have to. Seen it. That's all there is to it?"

"What more would there be?"

"Oh ho. 'What more,' indeed. Never seen the like, have I. Almost the whole distance, isn't it?"

"It is," Rossi said. "You won't tell her?"

"Me? I'm here for the trade, and that's all. Job t'do. Might be better for you if I took the load, though, don't you think? That storm's going to bear right down on you. Think you can survive it?"

"For her," Rossi said.

Ellie's curiosity was piqued. They seemed to be having a rather serious discussion but whenever she attempted to focus on the substance of it, she found herself distracted by memories of her Prince. Anticipation of seeing him again. Thoughts of his touch, his vigor, his masculine beauty. Was Rossi upset or merely tired from a long day out in the elements? Was this new friend, who seemed to be staying overnight with them, agitated over some matter or was it just the long day of travel he'd passed?

She asked herself what her Prince would think and decided he would carry on his affairs without concern for those beneath him. Rossi was her friend, certainly, but he was also a servant. And this peddler, this tinkerer, while a cheery enough fellow, seemed inclined to rambling when he spoke. He couldn't find the end of a sentence from its beginning with a length of rope, a head-mounted light, a map, and a compass.

She abandoned her vigil at the door and removed her clothing. She could imagine the Prince's hands appearing from the air to touch and caress her, his lips to kiss her. He took her hands and led her, dancing, across the deck of the ship from her dreams.

The lobby was deserted, the lounge closed. Behind the front desk a lone concierge snored with his feet up on the counter and a cap down over his eyes. Ellie carried her boots; she wore only the thick wool socks she'd tucked away beneath the bed before telling the men she was turning in early.

"Big day tomorrow, Ellie," Rossi had said. He and Beesix had become fast friends. The table between them was covered in empty glasses, playing cards, and scattered toothpicks, which they were using in place of money.

"Don't stay up too late, you two. We're getting an early start, remember?"

But they had stayed up late. Ellie had lain awake for hours waiting to hear the two of them stagger off to their respective beds. From the sound of it, Beesix had cleaned out Rossi's supply of toothpicks and her companion was none too happy about his losses.

She gave them another hour to settle in before pushing aside her covers. Dressing in darkness, Ellie almost changed her mind a hundred times. Rossi would be waiting for her in the living room. He'd have his *I'm very disappointed, Ellie* face on, and this time when he saw her to bed, he'd make sure the door was locked from the outside. Might even prop up a chair to hold it shut. Or bring a blanket out to doze on the couch, one ear cocked for the telltale sounds of wayward youth. All for her own protection, of course.

Her bedroom door stuck. Ellie turned the knob and leaned against the stubborn thing with all the strength she dared. She expected it to give up the fight without warning and spill her out onto the common room floor.

Help me, my love.

She shouldered the door, bracing her feet and hoping she wouldn't spill through when it opened, hoping the door wouldn't fly open and bang against the outside wall.

It opened, the click of the lock impossibly loud. Ellie held her breath and counted to a one hundred, poised to fly back to bed at the slightest sign of wakefulness.

The night was a looming tombstone, impassive, silent. She pushed the door open and stepped out into the common room. Her boots waited by the door, along with her coat, gloves, hat, and scarf. As bitter as the chill had been earlier, she expected it would be well below freezing when she left the hotel's warmth. She slung her cold-weather gear over one arm, cradled her noisy boots in the crook of the other, and exited into the hall. The wall sconces were miniature suns compared to the darkness within her suite. Ellie shielded her eyes and eased the door shut, terrified of making a noise loud enough to wake Rossi and his new friend. She didn't like thinking about the little man with his flaming, bushy beard. He was genial enough, that was true. But when she looked at him, when he looked at her, Ellie felt a rotting emptiness at the pit of her being. They'd only just met, but the sense she got from him was disappointment. How she could disappoint a complete stranger was beyond Ellie's ken, but there was no mistaking the man's contempt.

She took the stairs down to the lobby, afraid of risking the elevator. It pinged when it opened on their floor, and that was bad. The muscular grinding it made as it parked on a floor and settled into place was worse. There was no way Rossi would sleep through a racket like that.

She should have put her boots on, but every whisper was a scream, every creak of old construction a tortured wail. She couldn't conceive of how noisy the tick tock of her boots would be if she attempted to hoof it all the way down to the lobby in them.

She passed through without incident, stopping at the hotel's un-manned front entrance—it appeared doormen didn't work through the wee hours of the night—and sitting to pull her boots on. Ellie wiggled her toes, remembering how difficult it was to move with any speed in these ridiculous things. The only other footwear she had were fancy shoes, a pair of open-toed sandals and another pair of high heels. Her feet would have turned to icicles the instant she stepped outside in those, so: uncomfortable boots.

The night was *much* colder than the day had been. Tightening her scarf and pulling down the ears of her hat, Ellie still felt the knife of winter sliding between her ribs, between the joints in her fingers. She was grateful the walk ahead of her was not long.

"Here for the Market?" came a raspy voice from overhead.

Ellie turned to look, certain Rossi had followed her down-stairs. For an instant she allowed herself to hope he would understand. He might even come with her.

Not Rossi. "It's very late for a walk," the dragon said. It was blue in the moonlight and curled up on the balcony above the hotel's broad double doors. A close-cropped beard like a dusting of snow covered its chin and its right ear was pierced in nearly a dozen places. There was nothing in all the world it could be but a dragon.

"You shouldn't try to eat me," Ellie said, screwing up her courage.

"Eat you? Why would I possibly do a thing like that?"

She racked her brain. Why *would* a dragon want to eat her?

"Because you're big and I'm small," she said after some consideration.

"You think I eat everything that fits into my mouth?" The drag-on uncoiled its body, which was long and slender, like a prowling jungle cat, and much bigger than she'd initially thought. It dropped down to the ground without making a sound. "You think they'd let me visit the Market if I started eating everyone?"

"I suppose not," Ellie said.

"Of course not. Anyway, have you ever eaten a human? Horrible, wriggling things. You don't cook up right, and the screaming, heavens above, the noise is just unbearable. Hardly matters if you pop the head off first or save it for last; all you do is scream and scream and scream."

"I wouldn't scream," Ellie said.

The dragon moved with a sinewy ease that belied its obvious size and weight. It reminded Ellie of the feral cats that stalked the woods behind her and Rossi's home.

"You wouldn't scream? Listen: are you *trying* to convince me to eat you? It's been a long day and I had a nice supper, but I've never been above performing favors for pretty girls. Or for midnight snacks."

Ellie stepped back, feeling for the hotel's doors. She'd only taken a step or two, but they seemed as distant as the morning sun.

"I swear," the dragon said. "I never met a people so excited about being eaten. It's all we ever hear, 'Please don't eat me' and 'I'll do anything if you don't eat me.'" It leaned down and in a conspiratorial voice said, "Between you and me, that last bit is worth its weight in gold. The 'I'll do anything' sort tend to be well off and used to buying their way out of trouble. Scorch the hedges a bit, take a bite out of one of the horses, and you can write your own ticket."

"What—"

It shook its massive anvil of a head. It tried to smile. "Let's start over," it said. "Preferably without the screaming and the running away. Which, to be fair, you didn't do. Come to think of it, your whole 'you shouldn't try to eat me' bit has the vague air of a threat, doesn't it? What's your game, little girl?"

Ellie felt the Prince's gem against her chest, beating in time with her own heart. "Just what I said. You shouldn't *try* to eat me. My husband protects me."

The dragon's eyes grew drawn and distant as the horizon. It looked both ways up the street, left and right. "We seem to be alone, miss."

"Even so."

"He must be fearsome indeed, your husband."

"Oh yes." Ellie found she rather enjoyed her sudden boldness. It felt somehow appropriate that she should be bold. Like shrugging on an old coat you've found in the attic and remembering how perfectly it fits.

"Then I appreciate the warning. Is he up in the hotel?"

"No." Ellie shook her head.

"I see. Are you going to meet him, then?"

"I am. At the Market."

The dragon chuckled, snorting out puffs of steaming warmth. "The Market isn't here yet, is it?"

"No, but it will be soon. I know where it will come to and intend to wait for its arrival that I might greet him properly."

"You have not seen him in some time, have you? The Market comes to these lands but once in every century." It looked her up and down, its head snaking around Ellie as she stood prone. The heat it gave off felt wonderful in the frigid wintry stillness. "One as young as you—I've never been good at estimating human ages, but you're, what, sixteen, seventeen? This is your first Market, dear thing."

"My third, actually."

"Certainly not." It sniffed her from head to toe, the snow-white whiskers beneath its nose tickling Ellie's face as it lingered there. "I don't sense any power in you, not the smallest bit."

"Nevertheless, what I've told you is true."

The dragon stretched, drawing back and extending its forelegs straight out onto the street. Its haunches rose high into the air and its tail whipped back and forth with a lazy grace. When it extended its wings Ellie couldn't help but gasp aloud. They were the same shade of blue as the rest of its body, and while they were strong enough to fill the street with a gusting breeze, they were so thin she could see the moon and stars through them.

"First dragon?" it said.

"Actually, no. But you're the first I've seen up close. If it's not inappropriate to say, may I just tell you that you're magnificent?"

It puffed up its chest and unfurled its wings again. "You may. These other dragons, where did you see them?"

"Far away, traveling with my husband before we became separated." She saw its quizzical expression and continued, "At the last Market. I was late in returning and it had gone."

"And you've waited for him ever since? I misspoke before. There is power in you, miss, only of a different sort."

The dragon rose up on its hind legs, bracing itself against the face of a building, digging its claws into the brickwork. It raised its head high and sniffed the air, this way and that, up the street and down the street. When it returned to her, Ellie saw stony resolve in its eyes.

"If you would go to the Market now, to see it arrive, I would accompany you. If I may be so bold, of course."

"That would be fine," she said.

"You know the way?"

"I do." Ellie pointed up the way they'd come from parking Mister Beesix's truck. She waited to see if the dragon would scoop her up onto its back, spread its great wings, and soar up into the encroaching darkness. Instead it bowed before her, brushing the snow away with its whiskers. It offered its foreleg in a mock display of gentlemanly behavior.

"Milady, if you would do me the honor of accompanying me."

She suppressed a giggle and accepted the dragon's "arm." It could not walk in this fashion, requiring all four limbs to maintain its balance, but it hobbled a few steps, juggling its weight so as to keep from losing its footing, toppling over, and crushing her flat.

"You are very graceful," she said as it slipped on a slick patch of wet street. It fanned the air to regain its balance, and then, gingerly, as if afraid it might tear her hand clean off, the dragon freed its foreleg from her grip.

"Perhaps it would be best if I kept all four feet on the ground."

"Or," she said, indicating its wings, "we could always fly."

With its oceanic hue, Ellie didn't think it possible for the dragon to blush. Its features became hot, though, and she feared she had embarrassed it somehow.

"I...I cannot fly," it said.

"No?"

It shook its head. "These old wings can't command the air like they used to. Not good for much apart from gliding or swooshing snow around." It stomped its feet several times as if to illustrate. "It's my own four feet doing the work these days. Still, a dragon's grace and speed are measured in more than the span of its wings."

It grew quiet, and Ellie feared she'd offended it or caused it un-due distress. She saw they'd arrived at the site of the Market, the building her new friend, Mister Beesix, had parked his truck in.

"We are here," she said.

"Are we? That was much closer than I'd expected."

"Not all journeys must be long."

"Indeed." It sniffed the air, fanning its great wings. For the first time, Ellie was able to perceive how thin the membranes were and how pocked with holes and tears its wings were. She felt supremely foolish for her suggestion of flight.

"It's cold," the dragon said. "Aren't you cold?"

She realized she was, and shivered.

"Come, over here." The dragon darted across the street, to the steps of the building opposite the one that would play host to the Market. It curled up on the stoop, its tail wrapped back around its legs, resting flat behind its head.

"Sit, sit," it said. Ellie stood, shaking from the cold. Did the dragon mean for her to join it on the stoop? Did it intend for her to nestle up against it where it lay?

"For warmth," the dragon said. "You're freezing and we've al-ready established that I have no interest in eating you. Come, come."

With some reluctance, Ellie joined the dragon on its stoop. She sat, ankles crossed, at the foot of the steps, the dragon's warmth radiating off of it in waves. It wasn't long before she succumbed to temptation and curled up against the furnace of its belly. Soon Ellie had her hat and gloves off and was unbuttoning her coat.

"Isn't that better?" the dragon said, its voice somnolent. It un-furled one of its wings and laid it across Ellie. And now she was surrounded by its warmth, by the heat baking off every inch of it.

She told herself she was here to see the Market's arrival, here to greet her Prince on his return. How pleased he would be to see her. How surprised he would be that she was here, waiting for him, the first thing he would see upon his arrival.

The dragon's heat ebbed and flowed as it drew in breaths, its chest rising and falling with the steady, even rhythm of a ship astride a calm sea. She felt her eyelids grow heavy as the day's exertions and the gentle, rocking motion of the dragon's respiration drew her away from this cold street to the Prince's ship once again, where she would dance with her beloved.

She heard the sea, the patient lapping of waves against the ship's hull. And she heard the music, lilting and faint as a lover's whisper. And the shuffle-step of feet as they danced alone beneath an alien sky.

How often had the Prince described the strange lands he would take her to, if only she could wait for the Market to return? "More worlds than stars in the sky," he'd said. And here was the proof. They were reunited at long last. And surely this was but the first leg of their longer journey together. A pleasure cruise to celebrate finding each other once again. The sails were furled, the current carrying them in the gentlest of hands. She could have knelt to the deck and balanced a coin on its edge, the water was so still.

Twin moons shone overhead and she was brought back to the Market. *The Market—it comes soon. I must not linger.* For she knew, even as she trod across the sanded deck, her feet bare, the constant braid of her hair undone, that she was dreaming. For wasn't it always so? Didn't the Prince come to her every night as she lay sleeping? *But soon, he will not have to. Soon we will be together.*

Soft music drifted through the air like spun gold. Ellie felt a whoosh of air take her in its arms and she spun around and around, twirling in her lover's embrace. He guided her with effortless grace; she closed her eyes and gave herself over to him. Her Prince. He would be there when she woke. And this ship, this languid sail, it was their second honeymoon. His gift to her and she was relieved, though she had not realized before that moment how anxious she was that he might blame her somehow for abandoning him. *I rushed to you, my love*, she pleaded. *Rossi and I, we did all that we could. But we were too late. The Market had gone, bearing you away with it.*

But he was not angry. He smiled and took her hand and turned her around and around. On the very tips of her toes she danced, the music and her lover's touch one and the same. He led her and she followed, as was right. He led her and she trusted him because, in this above all other things, she knew he would never hurt her.

"My darling," the Prince said, laying a hand upon her hip, pushing her back as he drew her in with his other hand.

I am coming, my husband, Ellie said, her words gossamer in the cool night air. She danced with her eyes closed, her feet scarcely touching the deck as she turned and spun, her lips open and waiting for her lover's kiss.

"Isn't this better, my darling? So much better without the crowds and the noise and all that bother."

It is better when it is just you and me, my husband.

"Truly," he said. "And here we are."

She was watching from a distance, in his arms and far away at the same time. His warmth radiated through her, filling an emptiness she had not known was there. A century gone and now in his arms again, knowing the dream would soon become real, Ellie was finally whole again.

"Sire?"

She turned. The Prince sighed, boredom and impatience plain on his features.

"What is it, Cutter?"

"I have it, sire."

Her love's face brightened. "Ah, excellent. Excuse me, my darling. I won't be but a moment."

The Prince left her looking out over the glassy sea. She watched as a spindly, multi-legged creature dashed past, running across the surface of the water, what she took for its head skimming the shallows for small things to eat.

"She was quick, Cutter."

"She understands your urgency, highness. Here."

Cutter passed a flat, square case over to the Prince. When her love held it in his hands he hefted it as if testing its weight. "Heavy," he said.

"Sire, if I could implore you, one last time."

"Cutter."

"Sire, there is still time. There is an intercept in Batharia. It is old and rarely traveled but—"

"Cutter, enough! I have made up my mind. I will not dance on his strings. Now, away with you. This is," he said, glancing back over his shoulder, "a very special night. Magical almost, wouldn't you say?"

Frowning, the bodyguard turned away.

"Cutter, you didn't answer."

"Yes, sire. Most magical."

The Prince returned to her. He carried Cutter's box with delicate care, almost as if afraid it might rear back and snap at him, a slobbering mouthful of fangs exploding from within. He was behind her, whispering into her ear. One hand was on her neck, caressing gently. With his free hand he popped the box open. No monsters erupted from within, no hoary beasts lusting for warm, wet flesh.

It was only, she saw, a necklace.

It looked *so* familiar.

The chain was gold, the links thick and solid. From the center of the chain dangled a gleaming gem dark as the surrounding night. The Prince whispered more words, opening the clasp on the chain and fastening it around her neck.

"My lady Gaira Norena Al'ti Hohnas," he said, his tongue dancing in his mouth, his eyes alight with golden fire.

Ellie stared in horror and disbelief as her Prince, her beloved Prince, slipped a necklace identical to the one she wore over another woman's neck. He spoke her name, her true name, and she understood this bound her to him.

He weds another. This is their honeymoon.

The placid sea raged around her, kicking the small craft—how had she ever thought it grand?—like a child's toy. The wind gusted, fattening the ship's sails, breaking them loose. They flew away as if disgusted by what they'd witnessed. Forks of lightning streaked across the sky. Ellie wished she could look away, wished she could see nothing at all, if only to forget what he'd done.

The Prince, his ship steady, his deck level, caressed his new bride's cheek and led her away, belowdecks.

Ellie stood, shattered, alone, her heart racing. She could not believe the evidence of her eyes. But she could not deny them either. She had seen what her Prince had done, and there was no resisting the truth in his actions. He could not lie to her. Rather, she could not see anything but truth in his actions, could not hear anything but truth in his words. A century apart and he did not remember her, did not care that she had come at last to him. She saw into his heart, saw her reflection within and understood there was no more room there for her.

With a scream of impossible fury, Ellie's heart broke. The pain radiated outward from her, a nimbus of blazing, destructive energy consuming all in its path. The ship was gone, the Prince's honeymoon lost to time and tide. She was back on the street, back waiting for a Market that would never come. Her pain expanded, writhing and blindingly white, devouring the very street beneath her boots. She fell to her knees, the jarring impact nothing to the tortured wails of her own heart.

Her gem, the Prince's gem, splintered down its center, exploded with blinding energy, blasting the tops off of buildings, reducing all in its path to wisps of dissipating smoke. Tentacles of light thick around as an oak tree snapped up, grabbing at passersby, burning where they touched, dragging them away into nothingness.

Ellie screamed, her pain too great to be contained. She saw him caressing her neck, sliding the necklace over her head, speaking her name low so that none but they two could hear. She saw him marrying another, the dagger of his betrayal infused with such cold her blood steamed and hissed at its touch. It flowed out of her, inexorable, unending, the overwhelming love she had carried with her now twisted, corrupted into a hatred strong enough to crack the world.

* * *

For a hundred years and a hundred years before that Ellie's every thought had been of the Prince. When she'd been with him, her utmost concern was his pleasure. Being where he wished her to be. Behaving the way he wished her to behave. Dressing how he preferred, wearing her hair a certain way, laughing at the appropriate time and holding her tongue when silence was all he desired. When apart, her mind drifted constantly to him. She could recall a thousand memories from her time in Rossi's care; everything she saw, everyone she met, every bite of food passing her lips accompanied by the same, overriding thought: *what would the Prince make of this? If only he were here to share it with me.*

The first thing she did every morning was roll over in the hope of finding him there, their separation revealed as a trick of the Market, a dismal fantasy, even a malicious plot engineered by his enemies. He was her questing hero, leading his men in tireless pursuit of his lost love. Whatever the scenario, not a morning had passed that she did not search for him on the empty pillow beside her own.

She would bathe and dress, always asking herself, *what would he think of this skirt?* or, *would he prefer these shoes to those?* For Ellie there was no doubt he would find her, only how long their separation would last.

Through those years she would have lost herself if not for Rossi's company. It was nothing the man did so much as knowing that the Prince had tasked him with her well-being. If her love existed as a constant presence in her mind and heart, Rossi was the physical proof of that. Not that she needed any proof; she had all she needed in the gem beating in time with her own heart. Her Prince's love made solid, binding her to him for all time.

Still, without Rossi she might have been lost. She might have forgotten to eat for days and weeks at a time, wasting away to nothing. She might have gone mad, holing up in her room, curled up in the corner with her eyes closed, lost in dreams and imaginings of her Prince come home at last. Rossi kept her grounded, kept her from sliding too far into the black hole of their unending love.

It was this that fueled her hatred now. She saw the Prince's face, handsome as ever, but terrible in its beauty. His eyes flashed brilliant gold, capturing her heart. Only now, instead of surrendering to him, she was brought back to the deck of his ship, to the sight she could not unsee no matter how she might wish to.

No! She did not wish to unsee it. She burned it into her memory. Held the thought of him professing his love for another as an anchor to drag herself back to earth. She collected the disparate strands of herself, calling them back, wrapping them up in her impenetrable hatred of her vile betrayer. Love? How dare he speak of love? She would hold his heart in her fist and squeeze until it burst. Let him see the effects of a love strong enough to stop a heart. Let him bear witness to the thing he had created with his false promises of love.

She held the thought of him in her head—and it became easier by far to pull herself back together. She scraped against the shells of ruined, smashed buildings, her body became the burning wave of destruction. She saw the swath she'd cut through the city. It was as if an arrow had fallen from the heavens, scorching the streets and their inhabitants. The air was filled with twisting wisps of dust, the fading remains of those unlucky enough to have fallen in her path.

Ellie pictured him again, imagined digging her fingers into his neck, imagining what it would be like to squeeze and squeeze until his eyes bulged and she felt his throat crush beneath the strength of her fingers. It focused her, visualizing his pain in this fashion. It drew up a wall between Ellie and the Prince, armoring her against further incursions into her will.

So long as she held her hatred close he could not get to her again.

She felt the last of the blazing energy draw back into the shattered gem. It fizzled like a fork of lightning crossing the sky and was silent.

All about her was evidence of the damage she'd done. Shattered buildings, jagged fissures in the snow-covered streets, helixes of dust and ash where people had been. How many had died during her childish tantrum? How great had grown the price the Prince now owed her?

She followed the path of destruction. It led back the way she and the blue dragon had come, back to her and Rossi's hotel. With a start she remembered the kind dragon. She'd been kneeling in the snow, but now she shot to her feet and spun in place, searching for its quizzical face, the spread of its tattered wings.

The dragon was nowhere to be seen.

She returned to the stoop, dreading what she might find there. An azure-tinted mound of ash, all that remained of her new friend? No. Apart from several patchy remnants of snow, the stoop was clear. If the dragon had been here, it had gone, fleeing her fury. Would it return? Did she dare to wait?

No. She refused to offer her neck up for the noose. For when the police arrived—she could hear their sirens already—what else could they think but that she was to blame? They would see her, untouched in the midst of so much destruction, and they would decide the fault was hers. They would lock her up, perhaps unsure of why, exactly, they were doing so, but unable to see such tragedy and not levy blame on someone. And she would rot away in a cell, never knowing the feeling of squeezing the life out of the Prince who had taken so very much from her.

Ellie began walking back to her hotel. Gazing skyward, she saw the top few floors had been raked as if by an enormous claw. Through one of the jagged fissures she saw a glow like flickering flames. This evoked a thought in her mind that she couldn't place, a memory of something that hadn't happened yet. Déjà vu in the worst possible way. All around her were the ruins of brownstones and storefronts, but not a one caused her the same sense of foreboding, of abject dread, as staring up at the broken hotel. She thought of Rossi, told herself that Prince or no, he would be able to help her sort it out. And with an almost audible click, she realized the cause of her distress.

Their room was on the top floor. The top floor she had destroyed.

Ellie broke into a run, uncomfortable boots be damned. A crowd of hotel guests, some of them Market travelers with their glamours thrown off, milled about on the cracked street. All eyes were directed to the smoking ruins high above. Murmured voices spoke of lightning strikes, freak fires, and—yes—of the Prince and of his family, and how wrathful they could be when they did not get their way.

She dashed past them, pushing through the double doors into the hotel. It was dark inside, a low haze hanging over the lobby. She could make out shapes, but not much more. Through a combination of memory and trial-and-error she was able to find her way through to the elevators.

"Oh, foolish girl."

Of course the elevators were not running. The left-hand pair of doors was shattered beyond repair, the car having obviously plummeted from a high floor when her wave of destruction hit. The right-hand doors stood open, their car undamaged but plainly not moving.

After stumbling many times and once falling flat on her face, Ellie found a door that led into a stairwell. As she felt her way through the darkness, she cursed the Prince for his selfish ways. At this moment, it was easier to hate than to hope. She was already blaming the Prince for what she knew she would find. Blaming him for what she had done.

The stairs ended abruptly in a wall of iron and debris. Ellie tried pushing on it to no avail. She'd lost count of how many flights of stairs she'd climbed, but surely she couldn't be too far from the top. She backtracked to the closest intact floor and let herself out to investigate. The ceiling was missing, and as she'd climbed, the sun had risen high enough that she could make out her surroundings. She tripped over a prone body that ended up being nothing more than an ordinary hotel guest who'd knocked her head in the commotion. Ellie shook her awake, directed her to the stairwell, and promptly forgot about her.

The floor was a rectangle. Ellie was able to walk all the way around and return to the door opening out to the stairwell.

She found no sign of Rossi or their new friend Mister Beesix.

"Wait," she said. How early was it? Rossi had always been an early riser. Even turning in as late as he had, his fortune in matchsticks depleted, he'd have been up with the sun. Especially for a Market day. And then? Wouldn't he have come to wake her so they could get an early start? Wouldn't he have woken their guest, who'd need to get an early start himself with the first batch of Market-goers?

"You woke up, didn't you? And you're downstairs. I bet I ran right past you." She turned to retrace her steps back to the lobby, back to the street. Before she could exit, though, she heard her name being called from above.

"Hello?"

"Ellie...Ellie?"

"Who are you?" she sad. "Where are you?"

"Up...above..."

She craned her neck, and saw blue sky and plumes of dark gray smoke rushing up to fill it...and the corner of a boot, hanging just over the edge of an outcropping in what was left of the ceiling.

"Help me," he said.

Ellie hunted through the debris for something to stand on. She found a cushioned bench and dragged it over so she could climb up and reach the owner of the boot. With no small amount of difficulty she was able to reach and pull on it until she could haul its owner down. She told herself it might be Rossi, but she knew better.

"Thanks," Mister Beesix said when she had him propped up against the wall. His beard was singed, the festive red turned a sooty black. His eyes were bloodshot, his pajamas burnt all over.

And his left arm was gone from the elbow down. Ellie bent to care for the wound, to tie it off and stanch the bleeding. It was smooth as a skipping stone. He might have lost the arm ten years earlier.

"Tried t'get me. Not tha' easy, m'afraid. Took a nip just th'same."

"Your arm," she said.

"Got another, near as good an' twice as pretty. Ellie, what happened?"

"What happened?"

"Yer...Rossi, he woke me up. Said I had t'leave right away. Said t'just go, just run fast as I could. Kep' lookin out th'window. Kep' tellin me to go. Just go. What was it? What'd he see?"

She shook her head. Of course Rossi would recognize the Prince's power coming for him. How many times had he seen it through his custodianship of her? She imagined him waking, early as always, and finding her bed empty. A look out the window at the advancing wave of pure white would have told him in an instant what had happened. Not the details, no, but the fact that her careful control had finally slipped. He'd have seen that at a glance.

"He gave me this," Mister Beesix said, holding out a small pouch. "Said t'give it to you if I saw you. Said you'd keep it safe for him."

"He didn't flee with you?"

The short man couldn't meet her eyes. "He tole me to go, then slammed the door behind him. Said he had somethin' t'do but that I shouldn't wait. 'Be right along, just you see,' he said, then slammed the door on me. Thought he was a nutter, I did, right off his rocker. Tell me, girly, please, what was it? What happened?"

"Me," she said.

His eyes grew wide and she saw the question on his lips as surely as if he'd spoken it aloud. *How? All this destruction come from a slip of a thing like you?* If she'd had the strength to explain she might have tried. Then his eyes tracked down from hers to the fractured gem hanging around her neck. And impossible as it was for her to believe, she saw recognition flash across his features in an instant. He knew. Maybe not everything, but enough to put the pieces together.

"Poor thing," he said. "Truth, I never wanted this. None of it."

"You never—what?"

"Still?" he said. "C'mon an help me down an I'll tell you what I can. Tell you what y'told me the first time we met."

FOURTH MARKET

WINTER, 2013

"Tony Hart, you've just been dragged halfway across the country on a wiiild goose chase—what're you going to do next?" Hart paused, plastering a movie-star smile across his craggy face. "Why, I'm going to Disneyland, Ed!"

Major Presley swatted the back of Hart's head. "Stow it, Captain."

"Yessir, Major sir, consider it stowed, sir."

"Wiseass."

A rumble of laughter passed through the other men. Presley glowered at them, daring them to add to Hart's insubordination, quieting them down in a hurry. "Captain, if it's not too much trouble?"

Hart straightened up. He zoomed the display and highlighted a few key landmarks from their briefings. "Target's most likely location is here, at the inn, name unknown." He looked up a moment at the silent old woman at the head of the table. "He'll take supper there, sir. Intel says he always does, first night."

"Very well. Proceed."

Hart ran them through all the landmarks, one by one, highlighted in green on their display. He felt like a king idiot, reviewing data on a bakery, a beer garden, a haberdashery, and other similar businesses. Were they going to storm the bakery, commandeering the hot cross buns for use against the target? Was the haberdasher going to provide them with cover-fire as they advanced against the enemy's lines? It was ludicrous. It was idiotic. It was a game they were playing for a wealthy, senile fool, and every one of them knew it.

But hey, the money was good. And crazy cash spent just as green as the regular kind.

"Target's rooms are on the sixth floor, accessible via the main stairwell, which is in turn accessible from the inn's common room. Which is also where target will take supper, if intel is correct. No other points of ingress, but we have visibility from here, here, and here." Hart highlighted the rooftops adjacent to the inn's location. "Any one of which makes an excellent sniper's perch should the need arise."

"Excellent, Captain. Anyone have anything to add?"

McBride raised a timid hand; it was out of character for the man, who had trouble fitting through some doorways.

"Yes, Captain?"

"Can we stop and ride the Matterhorn, sir?"

The men broke out in an explosion of laughter. Hart could have strangled McBride, stealing his joke like that. Uncreative ass.

He looked down and saw the major digging his hands into the edge of the table, knuckles gone white. And Hart reminded himself that, crazy or not, the old bat had only paid half the money up front, something he knew would be on the major's mind as well. Punch a hole in the crazy and see if Grandma Moses here took her money elsewhere. Hart stole a look in her direction. If she was put out in the slightest by their mockery, he couldn't tell it by the utterly serene expression on her face.

Presley must have seen the same, because he relaxed his grip on the table's edge and chuckled. "Funny guy," he said. Hart watched the color drain from McBride's face. "You're a real comedian. Tell me, then, Mister Comedian, what are the target's defensive capabilities?"

"Sir?"

"No?"

"Sir, we weren't briefed—"

Presley roared across the table at McBride. For once, Hart was glad he'd let someone else get off a good one. Let the big man suck it up.

"I know you weren't briefed, Captain! That's because we don't have any intel on their defensive capabilities, do we? Guards in the inn? No. Guards outside? No. Guards in his rooms? No! We have zero actionable data on what we're about to jump into, so I'd like to know why you think it's acceptable to begin telling knock-knock jokes!"

"But sir," McBride stammered. "Tony—"

The major's face, awash with fury, became suddenly placid. "Don't go laying your inadequacies off on Captain Hart. God knows he's got enough of his own. But he knows his job inside and out, and he's not going to find himself hip-deep in whatever's waiting for us inside that inn." Hart followed Major Presley's eyes as they zeroed in on the old bat parked, silent as ever, at the opposite end of the table. "He's babysitting, which means while your face is being chewed on by God-knows-what, he's going to be watching *from a distance*. If I were you I'd worry a whole lot less about telling jokes and a lot more about what's waiting for us inside that inn. Doesn't that sound a just bit more productive?"

There was no sarcasm in McBride's voice when he responded. "Yes sir!"

Presley closed the display and turned away from the briefing table.

"Something you lot need to get through your thick skulls. We're going in, no question about it. According to intel, target has already resisted one assassin's intentions, with devastating results for said assassin. If you thought you were catching an easy gig, if you thought we were going to spend another five years living the high life, think again. The target is live, the clock is ticking, and when we land in Cleveland, we are going in guns hot." He turned to the old bat, who might have been a statue for all the emotion she showed. "A job is a job. And we've got a job to do. You could have stepped out years ago, but today is the day and I expect nothing but the best from each and every one of you."

Major Presley stormed off to the rear of the private jet, leaving Hart, McBride, and the rest to digest his words. Hart suspected the major was fixing himself a drink, or checking his load out. He waited what seemed an appropriate time and then hotfooted it after him.

"Need to keep your jokes to yourself, Captain," Presley said.

Hart grinned. "Yessir. Never happen again, sir."

Presley rolled his eyes skyward, dropping several ice cubes into his rocks glass. "Wiseass."

"So my mama always said."

"And she was right. Never could keep your damn fool mouth shut. Most days, you're more trouble than you're worth. Tell me again why I keep you around?"

"No idea, sir. Bad habit, probably."

"Too true, Captain." Presley offered a glass to Hart. "Disneyland. Jackass. You almost cracked me up. What d'you think old nut-typants would think then?"

Hart shrugged. "Who knew she'd come with? I figured..."

He didn't need to finish his sentence. They'd all had the same thought: take the old lady's money, fly off to points unknown, and return with wondrous tales of the magical fantasyland they'd found there. Her husband? The fairy-tale prince she'd sent them to bag? Oh, he must have skipped the market this year, ma'am. And it's 'Hart' with a 't' on those checks, thank you very much.

"Disneyland," Presley said, downing his drink in a single gulp. "You've got to watch that. The other men see you smarting off and think it's okay. If they see you being serious..."

"I know, I know. They'll act serious. Boss? Tell me, what do we do when we get to Cleveland and there's a parking lot where her market is supposed to be?"

"Dunno, Captain. Park?"

Two identical black SUVs were waiting at the airport when they landed. Major Presley stood aside with the old woman while Hart and the men broke out their gear and ported it into the trucks. Shotguns and assault rifles, flak jackets and body armor, hand grenades, plastique explosives, remote detonators, night-vision goggles, combat knives, and zip-ties.

If everything went according to plan, all they'd need were the zip-ties.

Hart rode in the first SUV with Presley and the old bat. He expected her to be full of nervous energy; she'd chatter on and on about their preparations, her expectations, maybe make a vague, not-so-veiled threat about how unhappy she'd be if things went pear-shaped. Rich folks thought hiring a guy like him was the same thing as ordering an expensive dinner; if their steak didn't come out right, they'd just holler at the waiter and send it back.

But she didn't blather on. She didn't threaten him or take an opportunity to remind him how godawful important this was. As if you spent a quarter of a million on a whim. In fact, she didn't say a word until they were nearly there. And when she did finally open her mouth, it was something of a relief to him.

"Remember what we discussed, Major. Remind your men."

"They've all been fully briefed," Presley said, working hard not to smirk. But when the SUVs stopped and the men were assembled out on the street, he did take a second to remind them. Not like it made a difference—Disneyland and all that—but Hart figured he felt better getting it out.

"Okay, you all know the drill. We're going in by the numbers and we're taking it slow. If our intel is right, we won't see any opposition unless we make it ourselves. For clarity: I'm not going to see any one of you starting trouble. Keep your weapons holstered and your knives sheathed. We're just eight friends taking a trip to the market. The eight little piggies. Browse around if you like. *Don't* eat or drink anything."

Hart saw the old bat nodding her head in agreement. This was, he thought, the oddest part of her story, the idea that eating food from her fantasy market would somehow get under your skin. They weren't going in sightseeing, though, and there was no reason for any of them to stop for a burger along the way.

"When we reach our objective we'll assess the situation. We'll book a couple rooms, stake out the bar. Again, we will not provoke violence and we will not be goaded into it. Use your weapons as a *last resort only*. Is that clear?"

Hart enjoyed the surprise in Presley's face when, instead of the mumbled assent he clearly expected, the men shouted as one, "YES SIR!"

Hamming it up for the old woman. Fantastic. At least she couldn't complain they weren't enthusiastic. But she wasn't even paying attention. She'd moved past Presley's show and was fussing about in the back of her SUV.

"Ma'am?" Presley said, catching her attention. "Anything else to add?"

"Presents, Major. One for each of you."

The men quickly crowded around. They'd discussed bonuses for a successful mission, but Hart thought it was damned strange passing out the cash before going in. Still, he wasn't going to argue.

It wasn't money she was handing out but capes. No, he corrected himself, not capes but cloaks. Freaking *cloaks*. His was forest green and long enough it would drag behind him when he walked. He tried to hitch it up but she stopped him.

"Let it drag. It's supposed to. Here."

She undid the clasp he'd fastened, turned it around and suddenly his shoulders were free. The cloak might have become weightless.

"You've got secret pockets here, here and here. And if you pull it closed you'll be able to hide away. From some folks, at least."

The other men looked miserable. Presley was doing the best, collecting the yards of shimmery fabric up in a ball so it wouldn't tangle in his equipment. To the major's credit, he was willing to hold still while she adjusted his cloak the same way she'd adjusted Hart's. When she spread out his cloak so it surrounded him, Presley let it hang where it fell.

And Hart noticed something as she finished adjusting each of them; the bulk of their weapons vanished beneath the cloaks. Each man had either a shotgun or an assault rifle strapped to his back, but there was no hint of these when she'd done her work. The cloaks sucked up the sound as well. McBride loaded his shotgun and gave his Glock a final check, but neither action made more than the slightest tickle of sound to Hart's ears.

She slung a final cloak over her own birdlike shoulders and fastened a long, bone-handled knife to her belt. With the hood of her cloak drawn, Hart found he had to keep reminding himself where she was standing—next to the SUV, behind Andrews—or he lost track of her.

Good tech, these things. Money buys the best toys, doesn't it?

"Okay," Presley said, a grim smile on his face. "Let's go."

The Market was right where she'd told them it would be.

The twin dark stone pillars stood like towering guardians over the gateway. Extending from each pillar was a wall, at least twelve feet high, running to the end of the street in either direction. They were too high to see over but it was easy to imagine what was on the other side. Lord knows they'd spent enough time studying her maps and drawings.

"Sir?" Hart said.

"I see it."

"What d'you see?" Robb said. His voice had that *you guys are screwing with me* tone Hart associated with the moment just before things went pear-shaped.

The problem was, no matter what he was looking at, her fancy market was impossible. The park across the street was barely two blocks from end to end. The maps they'd memorized showed a city bigger than all of Cleveland. He reminded himself that the very rich will often do very weird things. Why not build up a farce market to keep her delusions alive? Anything to fill the days.

Presley cleared his throat. "Okay, we'll do this by the numbers. Vulgari and Docherty, you're going in first."

"Sir?"

"Is there a problem?"

"No sir."

"Good. Also, remember, once we're inside, no more 'sir' or 'Major.' I'm Presley. Use each other's names as well. This op will work for one reason and one reason only: because no one's going to know we're there until it's done."

They all nodded but did not answer.

Hart watched as Vulgari and Docherty stepped up to the stone gate.

"You good?" Docherty said, socking his partner on the shoulder.

"Just you keep up."

Hart watched them cross the street, inwardly amused at how hard they were working to *not* look like soldiers advancing on an enemy's position. Funny how unarmed ex-Navy SEALs always look like they're carrying. They exchanged a quick look as they passed through the opening in the stone wall, squeezing together to avoid brushing against either stone pillar. If Presley was waiting for something—a flash of light, a boom of thunder—he didn't get it. Docherty turned from about ten feet past the gateway to wave.

No, he wasn't waving. He was calling them to follow.

And Vulgari, who should have remained at his partner's side come hell or high water, seemed to be wandering away.

"Sir? Sir? Where'd they go?"

Hart recognized Robb's voice at once. It took him a few seconds to figure out the keening wail, like a dog that's been run over on the road and can't figure out where its guts have gone. That was Collins.

Robb was grabbing at the collar of Hart's cloak, shaking him, begging him to explain. McBride was down with Collins. Hart slapped Robb twice across the face, *slap slap*, and shouted something about pulling it together. He could have been talking to a statue.

Presley pushed Robb back and got into Hart's grill. "Hart, report."

"Don't know, Maj—crap, sorry, Presley—he seems to have just gone to pieces."

"Where'd they go? Docherty and Vulgari, sir, they're gone!" The panic in Robb's voice gnawed on Hart's spine like a rat working a hunk of spoiled meat.

He twisted his neck to find the pillars and the gateway. Docherty was right there, waving for them to come in. He shouted for them to hurry on up, hurry on in. Vulgari was no-where to be seen.

"They're right inside, Robb. Pull yourself together, man."

"They're not! Just the playground, the slides, a few kids run-ning around. Where'd they go, sir, oh crap, where'd they go, sir?"

The old bat chuckled and shook her head. "Just two of you. That's a relief. I was afraid it would be more."

"What are you talking about?" Presley said. "'Just two?' Just two what?"

"Just two that can't see. *Only those with eyes to see*, that's how it goes, isn't it? I think I must have mentioned that at some point, no?"

Her hood was up so Hart couldn't make out her whole face. She was smiling, though. It was a sickly sweet smile, and he un-derstood she wasn't just crazy; the old bat was mad.

She pulled Robb's hands free from Hart's cloak, as if he were a baby and not two hundred and fifty pounds of ex-Marine who could kill her with a hard stare.

"You're Robb, aren't you?" she said, her voice so soft it was almost a song. She didn't continue until he'd looked at her and nodded, his eyes full of panic, his jaw quaking.

"You're going to need to look after Mister Collins over there. He's having a worse time of it than you are, if you can believe that. Can you help him back to the SUVs?"

Robb nodded again. Some of the tension went out of his shoul-ders. He might have fallen if the old bat—who couldn't weigh more than eighty pounds soaking wet—wasn't holding him up.

"You knew," Robb said. "Didn't you?"

"And told you all. But don't worry, sweetie. Can you help Mister Collins back?"

He nodded and she released him. Robb swayed in place but did not fall. He knelt to where Hart and McBride were working to settle down Collins, pushed them aside, and fought Collins to his feet.

"Wait by the SUVs," he said in a robotic voice, and began shuffling back the way they'd come.

While all this was happening, Major Presley had stood silently by. As two of his men—who were clearly having some serious and uncharacteristic difficulties—started leaving, he snapped out of his fugue and shouted after them.

"Let them go," the old bat said. "They're useless to us now."

"Useless? Those are my men!"

"They'll still be here when we get out. It's just, well, the Market can be hard for some types of people."

Hart watched as Presley threw up his hands. He wanted to lay it all out on the table. He'd give the money back if that's what it took, but he was sick to death of this madwoman and her ridiculous stories.

"Major! Major!" It was Docherty. He'd come back through, past the stone pillars, and was shouting for their attention.

Presley waved to the man and mimed a *cut it out* gesture by slashing his hand sideways across his own throat. Instead of returning to his partner, Docherty ran across the street.

"Major, come on! You've got to see it!"

"See it? Docks, are you losing it too?"

"No way, sir!" Docherty shook his head hard, like a dog coming out of the rain. "Come on! You've got to see!" He seized Presley's sleeve and pulled at it, trying to drag him to the stone pillars and the gateway.

Hart knew Presley well enough to know the major wanted to stop, to wait. There seemed to be no fighting Docherty, however, and it wasn't long before the two of them passed back between the twin stone guardians.

McBride exchanged a look with Hart, shrugged, and in his big, lumbering way, crossed the street to enter the Market. That left Hart alone with the old bat. But she was gone, standing by the left-hand pillar, looking up at it as if lost in memories. A wild thought came to Hart's mind then: *she's thinking about horses, and riding.*

It was impossible, of course. Another of the madwoman's tricks.

But Hart had to give her credit; it was a *good* trick. She was really pulling out all the stops. Was this what rich, crazy folks did with their cash and spare time? Never mind their little game of tag with the old bat's husband; he wanted to know how she'd managed the trick with the wall. Must be mirrors or some kind of illusion, like a magician sawing a woman in half.

And it was hot in here. Not uncomfortably so, but hot enough to make his fingers and toes tingle as the cold left them. Cleveland was rough this time of year, but it might have been the tropics inside the old bat's market. No, that wasn't exactly right. It was hot, sure, but it wasn't uncomfortable. Even in full combat gear and under her silly Ren Faire cloak, he wasn't sweating. *Bottle this and you're set for life.*

Hart gathered himself, watched the others doing the same. *Time to get into character here. She's paying a lot for this show.*

Presley took immediate command. "Okay, let's move like we've got a purpose. Docherty, where's Vulgari?"

"In the pub, Major. Can you believe it?"

"Pub?"

"He just took off. I couldn't stop him."

Hart scanned the rows of storefronts on either side of the dirt road. He saw it on the right, past several racks of colorful, wispy clothing, a wooden cart covered with candles, and what he took to be a kite shop. Vulgari was seated outside, at the head of a long, high table piled with food and drink. He had a beer stein the size of his head in one hand and a monster of a salty pretzel in the other.

"Go fetch him," Presley said. When Docherty didn't seem to understand, Presley jabbed a finger at Hart and gave him the same order.

Hart trotted off to the end of the street. He and Vulgari exchanged a few words and then Hart double-timed it back.

"He says he ordered for us, sir."

"Ordered for—you must be joking?"

"No sir."

Presley scowled down at the old bat, training a killer stare at her. Hart had seen strong men wither under the major's evil eye, but hell if she didn't seem bothered in the least. Ah, money.

"It's not a bad place, Mister Presley," she said. "Though it can be dangerous. Let's try and snap him out of it."

But there was no removing Vulgari from his table, not without calling undue attention to themselves. Whenever they came close enough to grab hold and drag him away, he'd force one of the enormous steins into their hands and burst into song. When Presley signaled for Hart, Docherty and McBride to seize hold of Vulgari and haul him off, he shrieked as if they were tearing him limb from limb, biting and scratching, and would not relent until they allowed him to return to his feast.

"Let that boy alone, why don'cha?" a tall man with a high, sloped forehead and squat cauliflower ears told them. Hart was drawing on the man before Presley could stop him; thank heaven the old woman was there to rein him in.

"No fighting, remember? Ease off, Mister Hart."

He felt the blood pounding in his ears, war drums calling him to battle. She diffused him with a few soft words and a gentle touch of his arm. *How'd she do that?* Hart shook the cobwebs off and felt supremely foolish. If this whole fantasyland was one big playground for the old nutter, it made sense she didn't want her big, scary soldiers perforating the natives. They were just actors, after all. He didn't like to imagine what the insurance would look like if a couple of them got put down.

"Remember what the lady said, boys," Presley said, his lips tight. "No fighting. Harsh language and rude gestures only."

They left Vulgari to chow down while the rest of them earned their paychecks. Presley adjusted their line, slotting McBride into Vulgari's abandoned position beside Docherty. He'd fill in the middle position while Hart filled in the rear with the old bat. Out in the real world, saddled with a civilian, that was a two-man job. Here in the Magic Kingdom, Hart was confident he could one-man it just fine.

He drew her attention. "Any other surprises?"

"Probably," she said, the thin line of her smile all that was visible beneath her cloak.

He swore to himself, then fell in beside her as McBride and Docherty led them up the road. It wasn't long before blacktop replaced the dirt, and the rickety carts and shimmed tables were taken over first by low stone buildings that were little more than huts, and finally, as they approached the center of the market, by multi-story structures and shining crystal towers like buildings out of a dream. Staring up at one, searching the sky for its apex, Hart felt his heart suddenly leap up to his throat.

"Major, you see that?"

"Captain?" Presley said, stopping in place.

"Look."

Ellie MacReady was, by all accounts, a rich woman. A *wealthy* woman. The quarters she provided for Hart and the rest of them were top of the line. Every amenity was provided for. He didn't want to think about how much the private jet they'd flown in that morning must have cost. And this market, all the actors she had working here, plus that weird special effect when they walked in—it just seemed to go on and on forever—all that must have cost a bundle of money.

But no matter how much she had, there was no way she could hang a pair of extra suns in the sky.

"What'm I looking at, boss?"

"Tell me so I don't think I've lost it."

Hart scratched his head. "Think I'm seeing three suns up there. Big one looks too close to be right. The other two are tiny, I think. Can suns have moons? Or sun-moons? How'm I doing, boss?"

"Better than me, I think."

The old bat caught up to them. Old as she was, she still moved at a good clip. Seeing how fast she could run when she felt like it, Hart decided she'd been holding back. Taking her time. Acting the part of a doddering old fool. Now he saw she'd been lying in wait until they realized they really, truly weren't in Kansas anymore.

"It's a shock, isn't it?"

"Where—where are we?" He wanted to say, *You lied to me! You lied to all of us!* But of course she hadn't, unless telling people things you know they won't believe counts as lying.

Everything she'd told them was true.

"Honestly, I don't know. Ask one of the locals and they'll tell you it's the Market. That's the only answer you're likely to get, though you're willing to take it for a spin yourself."

"But...there are three suns?"

She nodded.

"It's impossible. Cleveland doesn't have three suns."

"Today it does. Or today it has the Market and the Market does. Tell me, Major, are you and your men all right?"

Major Presley looked straight at Hart. He didn't utter a word, but he didn't need to. They'd served together so long, in so many different places, it was second nature to communicate in silence.

Thoughts?

Crazy as a bedbug.

Still, opportunity here, no?

Opportunity for what?

McBride and Docherty had sussed that something was going on behind them. They'd doubled back as casually as they could and were now standing off to one side. Any pretense that the five of them were strangers had been abandoned.

"You guys okay?" Presley said, unable to peel his eyes from the sun-filled sky above.

Hart mumbled something about getting the job done. McBride said he needed a drink but was otherwise good.

Docherty, perhaps already shaken by the loss of his partner, simply nodded his head and waited for orders.

"Good," the old bat said. "Because we're almost there. Time to earn your money, gentlemen."

They found an empty table by the dormant fireplace, ordered a pitcher of ale and several plates of food.

"You said not to eat anything," Hart said, after the serving girl had left.

"I said *you* shouldn't eat anything. It's far too late for me."

"And why shouldn't we eat?"

The inn was packed with a noisy lunchtime crowd. Visitors happy to be returning home? If the old bat was to be believed— something he was becoming more and more convinced of— they'd been away from home going on two centuries. Long time to let the mail pile up.

"You saw the suns, right? You're not in the human lands anymore. The food can ... well, it can have an adverse affect on you. It was in your briefings." A playful smile crossed her face. "You're only just asking now?"

Hart scowled. He didn't like being taunted, even if she was right.

"What else did you tell us that was real?"

She turned to Presley, who had asked the question.

"Everything. Don't eat the food. Don't drink the water. Don't tell anyone your real names. Don't, under any circumstances, try to hurt anyone."

"Is the food poisonous?" McBride said. He was drooling over a hank of meat the man at the next table was shredding with teeth that had no business appearing in a human mouth.

"Not poisonous, no."

"Will we—will what happened to Vulgari..."

"That was a new one for me, actually. I've heard tales of visitors falling headfirst into the Market. Guess we know what that looks like now."

"But aren't we good this far in?"

"Told you to eat before we left," Presley said, almost growling. Hart didn't think he'd meant it as a joke, but all of them, including McBride, laughed just the same. When the food came and the old bat dug in, Presley ordered them all to stand down. "You can wait until we get back home. We're already down three men, remember?"

McBride grumbled but didn't press the issue. Docherty stared at the head of the old bat's ale with obvious longing.

Hart didn't care one way or the other. "So we're just going to wait here for your husband to show up?"

She shook her head. "He'll be busy in the Market until nightfall. Business, affairs of state, that sort of thing. I don't actually know much about that, I'm afraid."

"So he might not come here at all?"

"He always stays here. They hold the entire sixth floor for him."

"The sixth floor," Hart said. "That was in your briefing. I thought I was remembering it wrong when we got here. Ma'am, begging your pardon, but this place is only five stories tall."

"Don't be ridiculous."

Presley sat up in his chair. He might have been paying attention for the first time since they saw the three suns. "Five stories?"

Hart nodded. "I counted out on the street. One, two, three, four, five. Didn't take but a second. Always excelled at math,

I did." He watched as the major glared at the nutty old broad. Dinner and a show.

"What do you have to say about that?" Presley asked her.

"I don't doubt Mister Hart's powers of observation, but the Market...it's not like the world you know. Trust me when I tell you there's a sixth floor and that's where my husband's rooms are."

"Your husband," Presley said. Hart recognized the brilliant gleam in his eyes. His engine might have stalled but it was humming now. He almost felt badly for her if the major had his head screwed back on straight.

"Yes. Major, we're not going to have a problem, are we?"

"You know, kidnapping isn't very nice, ma'am."

"Neither is my husband. Trust me, it couldn't happen to a nicer guy."

"And you?"

"I beg your pardon?"

Presley gesticulated wildly with his hands. "I'm sure he's a proper bastard, but what about you, Miz MacReady? Who hires a gang of rough men like us to nab her husband? Not exactly landing yourself on Santa's 'nice' list, are you?"

"I only need him for a little while," she said. Hart shivered at the sudden chill in her voice. "I might not even have to hurt him. Much."

"Catch him with another woman? Hell hath no fury, right?"

"Not exactly." She pushed her plate back and refilled her mug of ale from the pitcher.

"Just pissed off, then? Okay, I can get behind that. So we'll nab your old man and you can have your fun. Still, you should have leveled with us."

"I thought I had."

"No. You spun us a yarn you knew we wouldn't buy and dangled enough cash in front of our noses you knew we couldn't resist. That's not quite lying, but it's not leveling either. Like this 'don't tell anyone your name' garbage. What's that all about?"

"When you give someone your name—your real name, your full name—it gives them power over you. It relinquishes any power you might have and renders you helpless before them. In some cases they can hurt you, or worse, just by having your name."

"Bullshit."

"I only wish, Major Presley."

Docherty raised his hand. The sight of him acting like a kid at school almost made Hart laugh out loud. "What about hurting people? Why can't we, you know, just shoot the place up when he shows, knock him on the head and go on our merry way?"

"Look around you," she said. "Do you think these people care one whit about you or me? Most of them aren't even people, at least not the way you'd reckon. They're just visitors looking to get home to their loved ones. Visitors gone too long, as I believe I've mentioned. I can't have you shooting them up, can I?"

"So the lady does have a conscience," Presley said.

"It lingers."

Hart mimicked McBride and raised his hand. He caught the old bat noting the look of amusement on his face as she pointed at him.

"Okay. We can't eat or drink—fine—and we can't tell people our names—also fine. But politely asking your husband to please step into the SUV isn't going to go too far without the juice to back it up."

"They've seen guns here before, Captain Hart. They know what they do. Wave yours around, shout and make a fuss, maybe shoot up into the air once or twice, and they should be properly mollified."

"If not?"

"If not, then do what you have to do. But I need my husband and I'm not leaving without him."

Presley sent Hart with the old bat to book a room in the inn. They had no intention of staying the night, but it was important to scout the rest of the building, and checking in offered the simplest way to do so without arousing suspicion.

"Ask for something on the top floor," the major said.

McBride added, "Something with a view and not too near the ice machines."

Hart ignored him. He and the old bat wound their way through a crowd that was becoming increasingly less human. "They're shedding their glamours," she said, without explanation.

They had to wait for the innkeeper, but when he arrived he happily assigned them to one of the fifth-floor rooms.

"See?" Hart said.

She didn't respond, but he caught the innkeeper's curiosity.

"See what?"

"Oh, my wife here, she heard there was a sixth floor. Said something about renovations and how you'd added a floor to accommodate more guests during the, you know, the high season."

The innkeeper burbled laughter. If he'd noticed or cared about the gap in their ages, he didn't say a word, discretion being a valuable trait in a host. "No, no sixth floor here, I'm afraid. Where did you hear this rumor?"

"A friend who stayed here some time ago. She said she stayed on the sixth floor." She mustered her strength before speaking again. "On the sixth floor with the Prince."

He bellowed laughter now. "The Prince! I'm never sure *where* his rooms will show up. Once I think he was in the cellar. Something about his lady friend being averse to sunlight, I believe. But the penthouse does seem much more his fashion, doesn't it? Sweeping views of the whole Market, suns out every window." When he realized he'd confused his new guest, he stopped short and backed up. "He brings his own rooms, the Prince does. Likes his comfort, doesn't he? But our rooms here, nice as they are, surely aren't up to his standards. No, he's kind enough to bring his rooms and we count ourselves lucky to have him."

"And where," the old bat said, speaking with such deliberate slowness Hart couldn't believe the innkeeper could fail to notice. "Where are his rooms now?"

Hart pushed in front of her. "I'm so sorry, I must apologize. My wife, it's all she could talk about all day after hearing he was here. You know how it is with royalty, don't you?"

"Of course, of course. But I'm sorry, ma'am, I don't know. Only his staff can reach his suites. For the rest of us, well, we could be standing in his doorway and not know it."

"Even to deliver food? Surely a man as powerful as the Prince doesn't dine down here with the commoners?"

"He does, sir, as a matter of fact. Great man, the Prince, great man." The innkeeper was visibly puffed up with pride. "But there is a door in our kitchen right to his dining room. Likes a private breakfast, the Prince does."

"Who doesn't?" Hart said. He signed a false name to the register as the old bat had instructed and led her, arm in arm, up the stairs to their room on the fifth floor.

Hart waited until they were exploring the second floor before he started talking. "So tell me what's really going on," he said.

"I'm afraid I don't follow."

"Sure you do. You played us for fools and hey, I get it. Five years on stand-by for an op like something out of *Hansel and Gretel*. Who wouldn't take that money?"

"But now it's real and you want out?"

Hart's grin was bigger than his entire face. "Out? Hell no. I just like to know what dog made the mess I'm getting ready to step in."

She nodded as if to say, *fair enough*.

"I've already told you everything I know, and guessed at a fair amount on top of that. I *did* think his rooms were on the sixth floor. The times I've stayed here with him, at least, that's where they were."

"Come on."

"Pardon me?"

"I mean, come on. Don't feed me that line. You think I didn't read your reams of backstory on this place? Pops up every hundred years or so. Different place each time. Come in for a visit and do a spot of shopping. But look at you. Listen, my granny's older than you and she wasn't walking and talking a century ago."

"To be fair, it was more like ninety years ago, but the Market didn't come that time."

"No?" He caught her trying to change the subject and veered back on course. "Even so, if you were here two hundred years back or whatever, you're looking pretty spry. How do you explain that?"

"It's complicated. But if we get our hands on my husband maybe I'll be able to explain. Anyway, that wasn't my first visit."

His eyebrows raised in disbelief.

"This would be, if the Market had come in 1920, my fourth Market."

"Sure it would."

"You don't have to believe me, but given the things you've seen, why wouldn't you?"

"What things?"

She pointed up while knocking on a bare spot of wall. They were finished on the second floor and ready to proceed up to the third. "We should have gone to five and worked our way down."

"We can skip up if you like."

"Perhaps."

"You're changing the subject," Hart said. "If you're the four-hundred-year-old woman, how come all you're sporting is some gray hair and crow's feet?"

"Clean living?"

"Ha ha. If I'd known you had a sense of humor we could have started swapping dirty knock-knock jokes five years back. Really?"

"Really?"

"I'm asking, aren't I?"

They were on the steps. She stopped to catch her breath—the way she hunched over, wheezing, he could almost believe she'd been walking and talking for four centuries.

"Here," she said, pulling at the chain around her neck. It caught on something, and he was forced to watch for more than half a minute as she struggled to extricate it.

"What's that?"

"My wedding gift. It's safe to touch. Now, at least."

"It's cracked."

"Yes. That happened in New York, incidentally. But that wasn't what kept the Market away."

"What did?"

"My husband. He was away on his honeymoon."

"Ouch. I take it you weren't invited?"

"Hardly. I went there hoping to be reunited with him. We'd become…separated after my second Market. He sent me on an errand, and while I was away the Market moved on."

Hart shook his head. "You know how that sounds, right?"

"Of course. But I also know how it sounds when you and your friends carry on about real-time satellite connections and laser-sighted rifles. Imagine what that sounds like to someone who was born in the early eighteenth century."

"Sure. Of course. Naturally."

"It's fine either way, Captain Hart. But you asked and I'm trying to tell you." She fingered the fractured gem, stroking it like she might a cat. "Before this broke, it would pulse with power. It beat in time with my own heart. And it kept me young and vital, saving me up for him."

"Saving you up?"

"Literally. More than keeping me young, it kept me *his*. His in mind, body, and soul. No man could touch me unless he wanted to burn. But that didn't matter because so long as I wore this I didn't want anyone else's touch but his."

"Take it off, then."

She smiled. "Now why didn't I think of that?"

"None of this can be real, you know that? I mean, I've been out in the world, lady. I've seen things. I've done things. It's a rough life, but there are no magic gems that let you live four hundred years without aging."

She dangled her wedding present from its chain so he could get a good long look at it. Her eyes went cloudy and for a second he believed her, believed all of it. More, he saw what she'd lost, why she was after her louse of a prince. *You were in love once. He took that from you, didn't he?*

The gem sparked white along its fissure. A shower of tiny, blazing stars showered forth, singeing the stairs and the walls. Hart pulled his hand back before he was burned. He nearly lost his balance and tumbled down the steps.

"Whoa!"

She caught his hand and kept him from falling.

"Got you," she said, holding on until he steadied himself.

"Lady, how'd you do that? I should have dragged you down with me."

She shook her head and resumed climbing. Hart seriously considered hiking down the steps, out of the inn, and back to the real world as fast as his feet could carry him, but in the end, he followed. She was going at a good clip now, but he caught up to her at the landing between the fifth and sixth floors.

"Son of a—"

"You see them too, then? I wonder if that's because you're with me or if it's something else. Curious, isn't it?"

Where the stairs should have ended at the fifth-floor hallway, they instead wound around and continued up to the floor above.

They were a perfect match. The banister as well. Even the framed pictures on the wall went with those they'd climbed past during their ascent.

"Who is this guy?" Hart said, his voice filled with terrified wonder.

"My husband. Come on."

He followed her up the stairs to the sixth floor, the floor that wasn't there. Instead of an open hallway, however, the stairs ended in a wooden door that rang like steel when he knocked on it.

"Don't do that," she said.

"Why not? Nobody's home, right?"

"It's been a long time. People change, of course, but not him. Not my husband. Oh, he'll put on airs of change as it suits him, but the capacity for true change, even on so small a scale...it just isn't in him."

"Let's see."

The door was undecorated apart from a single doorknob set slightly higher than normal to accommodate her prince's height. No keyhole, no lock, none of the more modern appliances one might find out in the real world.

As he watched, she eased her hand around the doorknob, moving with the kind of caution people use around hungry bears. Hart remembered a bodyguard from one of her briefings—Butter or Hutter. Would her prince's protector have insisted on guarding the suite, or would he have counted on people's ignorance of its existence to safeguard it?

She turned the doorknob and pushed the door open.

"Ladies first," Hart said.

"Chicken."

He grinned and stepped past her, drawing his sidearm. He walked in a half crouch, taking small steps with bent legs, the gun's barrel pointed at the floor.

"Clear in here," he said, calling back. She was still standing in the stairwell. He heard footsteps, soft as a kitten's, and she joined him in the entryway.

"Which way?" Hart said.

"What are we looking for?"

He shrugged. "Didn't think we'd get this far."

She slid past him. Ahead, if her briefings had been accurate, were the living room and the morning room, the bedrooms and the Prince's dining room. There was a kitchen, of course, but it was more for show than actual cooking.

"Follow me. You can holster that, if you like. I'm not sure this is technically still part of the Market."

He followed her down a hallway and through a door into the most opulent bedroom he'd seen in his entire life.

"Right where I left you," she said, frowning, eyes far, far away.

"What's this?"

"My rooms," she said, after a time. "Come in and close the door behind you. We might be safe in here, for the moment."

Hart was long past the point of asking questions. Hart pulled the door shut and stood, still holding his sidearm, while she dug into a chest of drawers. She covered the floor of the room with clothes, blouses, skirts and dresses. Hart felt absurdly embarrassed watching her empty several drawers of outdated undergarments onto the floor. He turned his head and waited for her to finish.

"Here! Help me, would you?"

He turned to find her struggling to remove an enormous chest from a much less enormous drawer. There were handles on the ends and he was able to, with some difficulty, free it from its home and lift it up.

"Onto the bed, please."

He hefted the trunk up onto the bed. If it was as old as she claimed, the mattress should have groaned in protest, but the bed was silent. Aside from a slight indentation in the blankets where the chest dug in, it showed not the least sign of strain.

"Thank you." She pressed on the chest's catch and pushed up the lid. Inside he saw three levels of trays that she was able to slide apart. Each tray was mounted on a clever accordion-style bracket that allowed her to examine the entire contents of the chest at once.

"Where are you...where are you...there!"

She stood away from the chest and the bed. He saw a small shot glass in her hand.

"Thirsty?"

"Actually, I am. Too much salty food downstairs. I'll pay for that later, but for now—well, here." She pressed the glass into his palm. "Welcome to the Market."

"Um, thank you? Didn't you say no food or drink?"

"It's not for drinking. Press it up to your ear. Wait, sit down first, then listen."

Possibilities swam through Hart's head. The most likely was that she'd hoodwinked them all. First she separated him from Presley and the others and now she was going to take him out with...a shot glass? Hart couldn't decide if he felt moronic or curious, but it was a day for taking leaps of faith. He closed his eyes and pressed the mouth of the shot glass to his ear.

At first, nothing. Then a single note in the darkness, high and long, stretching out to the infinity in his mind. Another note joined the first. This one was low, reverberating with power. He could imagine a steel guitar being strummed over and over—*burm burm burm*—as the audience screamed in anticipation.

More notes, faster, an explosion of sound. The song was familiar but he couldn't place it. It wasn't a single song, it was *every* song, played together, layering one on top of the other, fitting together like a four-dimensional puzzle. The beginning was the end and the middle enclosed them all. Song after song played in his head and he wasn't Hart the soldier anymore, Hart the Navy SEAL, who'd obeyed his orders in Iraq heedless of the cost. Hart with his tough-guy exterior, always itching for a fight because the alternative was your CO asking, *hey, what's up, you okay, man?* The one question he couldn't answer, would never be able to answer.

Hart with his kid brother who'd wailed on the guitar and died way, way too young.

Her hand was cold on his as she loosened his fingers and withdrew the shot glass from his ear. Hart the soldier would have knocked her hand away, pushed her over, and taken the glass for his own.

Hart the man sat a while, eyes closed, savoring the resonating silence.

"It's all real, isn't it?"

"Yes."

"But…how does no one know about it? I mean, we're in Cleveland, aren't we? How are people driving past all day without flipping out?"

She didn't answer right away. She turned the shot glass over and over in her palm. She hadn't listened to it, not yet. He could tell she was tempted, but something in the way she handled it told him she was also terribly afraid. Her prince still had his claws in her. What effect would hearing Billy play have on those claws?

"Someone once told me the reason the Market only comes once every hundred years or so was so people would have time to forget. That makes about as much sense as anything else I've ever heard."

"I'll never be able to forget."

"No? Okay, but you'll tell your kids and maybe they'll tell their kids. And right about the time the Market's ready to come back, all the folks who've heard your story will be joking about crazy old great-grampaw and his trip to Disneyland."

"You heard that, huh?"

"I hear a lot."

"How about you, though? How'd this happen to you?"

She shrugged. "I sat at the wrong table, attracted the wrong man's attention. I suppose it happens. Can't seem to shake it even all these years later."

"How old were you when he took you?"

"I was seventeen. I think I was about to get engaged."

Hart balled his hand up into a fist and swore. "Seventeen. You don't look seventeen, not anymore. Are you aging?"

"Not at first. I am now."

"Slowly?"

"It was slow at first. It's been picking up recently. I have another gift from a friend. It helps some of the time. I try not to think about it." He noticed her twisting a ring on her finger as she spoke and wondered if she was aware she was doing it.

"We should go," she said.

"Go? We should stay. Especially if no one can see this room. Hell, we should bring Presley and the others up here and set up a little ambush action. Catch your husband flatfooted when he comes home. Nice and private up here. Don't have to worry about civilians, either."

She shook her head. "I don't know quite what this counts as. These rooms—I don't know how they work."

"So we'll find out. Fortune favors the bold, right?"

He saw she was tempted. But there was something else, something she wasn't telling him. It might even be something she was keeping from herself.

"It cannot be. This place, it's his. I don't know how powerful he'll be here."

Hart nodded his agreement and stood to leave. He opened the door a crack and listened for signs of movement. When he'd assured himself they were alone, he led her out into the suite's main rooms. As her hand lighted in his, weightless as a bird in flight, he imagined her as a girl of seventeen years, flushed with anticipation of marriage. He imagined Billy with his guitar slung over his shoulder and decided, no matter what, her husband was due for a major ass-kicking.

Presley greeted them at the bar with a frosty mug in his hand and a stupid, distant grin on his face. He tried to kiss the old woman's cheek, missing only because she pulled away before he could. He embraced Hart like a long-lost brother, announcing to everyone how glad he was to have his friends back.

"Boss, what's going on here?"

Presley raised a finger to his lips. "Shhhh. Camouflage. You were gone too long."

He pulled Hart with him. There was a large crowd gathered around one of the tables by the fireplace. Docherty was in the thick of it; he wore the same dazed expression as the major. And when he saw Hart and the old woman he threw up his hands and called for a fresh round of drinks to celebrate their return.

McBride was sitting at the table, opposite a wall with vaguely human features. It had a beard and eyes and something resembling hands jutting out from its body. McBride had his shirt off. He was limbering up his right arm, rolling the shoulder, shaking his hands for circulation.

Hart tried telling Presley they'd found the target's suite. The major couldn't have been more uninterested. "Always were a real stick in the mud," Presley said, sloshing his drink onto Hart's boots.

"This is bad," the old woman said, pulling Hart back from the table.

"No, really? You're my resident expert, what can we do about this?"

"Coffee and a cold shower? A fistful of aspirin? They're drunk, Captain, not doped up. It's just that the food here, the drink, it's different from what they're used to."

"It's not, like, magic?"

She swallowed a sad laugh.

"Okay, not magic. So we need to drag them upstairs and let them sleep it off? What about Vulgari?"

"The guy by the gate? I told you, I've never seen anything like that before. But look at them. Remember what he was like? Shoveling food in, gulping pint after pint of ale. This is different."

He sighed loud enough to be heard over the din. "Okay, upstairs to bed. Cold shower. Hot coffee. Do you know what I did before I met you? Bodyguard duty, mostly. Standing in the shadows making sure nobody takes a shot at your client. Fighting to stay awake. Can't believe I miss it."

He picked Presley out of the crowd. The major was in the center of it, shouting right into McBride's face. Hart let himself hope Presley had come to his senses, and was dressing down McBride for losing control.

Then Presley slapped at McBride's forearm. He took the other man's hand and held it up high, hooting and hollering as he did so.

The wall slammed its elbow down on the table. The floor shook and several mugs clattered to the ground. Hart realized what was going on.

They were going to arm-wrestle.

In spite of himself, he almost laughed. He'd been getting worked up, expecting the worst, but it was just McBride losing at arm-wrestling. Let the locals have their fun. Once the wind went out of Presley's and the others' sails, they'd be more than happy to retire upstairs and sleep it off.

The wall growled something that might have been words. McBride slammed his own elbow down on the table. He wrapped his hand around the wall's, shifting his weight so his whole body was behind his right arm. He couldn't win—anyone watching could tell that—but it was plain to Hart and the entire surrounding crowd that he intended on putting up a good fight.

They roared as the wall lowered itself until it was in position. A blue thing with too many arms separated itself from the crowd and asked if both men were ready. The wall made a sound like stone blocks being dragged over gravel. McBride changed his grip and told the blue thing to quite stalling.

It counted down from five, the words strange but their meaning crystal-clear. Hart could almost hear the numbers as it called them out:

"Five…four…three…two…one…go!"

McBride and the wall pushed all their weight, all their strength, into their arms. To give McBride his due, the contest looked to actually be a contest. Hands shot up throughout the crowd, waving coin purses and, in some spots, actual paper money. Legal tender, though it was anyone's guess what that might mean.

The wall fought to keep its arm up, losing more ground than seemed believable but losing it just the same. It was a man arm-wrestling a great stone wall, and that should have made for a one-sided contest. But McBride was hanging in there, even gaining ground. Hart couldn't believe his eyes.

"Something, innit?" Presley forced a mug into his hand. Hart had it halfway to his mouth before he remembered himself.

"I'm driving, boss, remember?"

Presley nodded and did not argue. He drained his own mug, then snatched Hart's away. Docherty was right at McBride's back, rooting him on, screaming in his face not to quit, not to give up, you've got him, Mac, you've got him.

McBride's shoulders shook as he fought harder and harder to bring down the wall. His free hand dug into the edge of the table; there would be deep furrows in the wood once the match was over. He bore down, pushing all his strength into his arm, and with superhuman determination hammered the wall's hand twice into the flat of the table.

The crowd exploded. Even the old woman, who was hiding once again beneath her hood, skulking back into the shadows, was peering through the mass of visitors for a look at

McBride. Hart told himself it was pride he was seeing on her face. She'd brought them here. McBride was her guest, after a fashion.

She spoke, but was too far away for him to hear. A moment later she shrank back against the wall, her face receding into the shadow of her cloak's hood. The abruptness of it and his experience as a bodyguard told him she thought someone had spotted her. Someone had recognized her.

"Dammit."

He pushed through the crowd, away from Presley, McBride, and Docherty. They'd have to manage without him for a minute. His job was to watch over her and he'd let her get too far away for safety's sake. Presley might not care now, but when he sobered up, he'd rip Hart a new one for letting the client get hurt. Especially if it meant they wouldn't get paid.

Also, he was becoming somewhat fond of her.

"You okay?" he said.

"Cutter. It's Cutter. He saw me. He *heard* me."

He started to tell her *no way, it's too noisy in here for that.* Before he could, however, a gunshot rang out, and the inn fell into stunned silence.

Hart took a reflexive step backward, swinging the old woman around so he was between her and whatever Presley and the rest of his squad was facing. His hand dropped to the weapon at his hip, flipping open the holster's safety-snap.

"Wait," the old woman said, laying her hand over his.

Across the bar, Presley had his .45 drawn. Wisps of smoke rose from its barrel. As Hart watched, the major leveled his weapon at the ring of onlookers, centering his sights on the closest, largest of them. It was the wall-shaped thing McBride had been arm-wrestling.

"All I'm hearing are excuses," Presley said. "You made a bet. Your friends made bets. You lost. We won. Pay. Up."

The wall didn't seem capable of speech. A gray, wiry creature next to it stepped forward. It waved its arms at Presley—if you could call the pulpy, wriggling things arms—in what Hart thought was a clear plea for level heads and patience. Hart couldn't understand its gibberish, but the meaning got through somehow. *My brother should not have been making bets*, it said. *I'm sure we can work something out, friend.*

"Sure we can," Presley said, shifting his aim from the wall to the gray creature. He seemed to consider a second before squeezing off a pair of shots, one aimed at the creature's head, the other at what Hart took for its chest.

A splatter of viscous purple gore erupted from the back of the creature's head, painting the wall with its brains. It fell back, chest oozing in a slow but steady flow. As the crowd parted, the onlookers suddenly remembering other places they needed to be, Hart was able to see the gray creature's leg twitch several times before becoming still.

Then it moved. It hitched itself up with a few of its spindly arms. Hart watched the wound on the back of its head shrink and then vanish. The spray of brains and blood and who knows what else remained on the wall.

The gray creature sat up and opened its eyes.

It spoke. Again the words were nonsensical, but again, its meaning was clear: *you gonna be sorry for that, man.*

Presley laughed, leveling the barrel of his gun at the creature's face. "Neat trick," he said. "See if you can't—"

He never got to finish his sentence. Hart felt the floor of the inn rumble beneath his feet, a high, keening sound reverberating through the air. It was in his teeth and the pit of his stomach. In his heart. His eyes itched and his tongue had gone dry as sandpaper. It was as if every cell in his body had developed a terrible itch at the exact same moment.

Across the room, Presley was waving his gun around, beating at his left ear with his free hand. "Quit it!" he said, shouting to be heard over the increasing wail.

The gray creature, the wall, and the other onlookers drew far away from where Presley suddenly dropped to his knees. The major fired off several more rounds, not bothering to aim. He dropped his weapon, cradling his head in his hands, squeezing as if trying to keep his brains from squirting out through his ears.

"Quit it! I told you to quit it so you quit it!"

The wail became a hum, like feedback from a microphone held too close to an amplifier. Hart heard voices beneath that hum and understood they were speaking the major's name. He drew his Glock, ready to charge forward and force the creatures to stop whatever they were doing to Presley.

"Stop," the old woman said. She guided his hand so that he returned the gun to its holster. She pulled him back, away from Presley. He felt the hum of sound receding, the voices fading.

"You should be safe now," she said.

Hart stood silent as McBride, still bare-chested, forced his way through the crowd. Docherty was right behind him. McBride's hands were empty but the other man had armed himself. They bookended the major, who was writhing in apparent agony on his knees. Docherty waved his weapon around as if the travelers were not still backing away, giving them as wide a berth as possible.

"Oh crap, oh crap. What'd you go and do that for?"

Docherty detached the assault rifle from his back and passed it to the unarmed McBride, who switched the safety off and aimed the barrel of the rifle into the crowd.

"Tha's my boss," he said. His eyes had gone blank and a thin line of drool hung from his lower lip. When he began pulling the trigger, there was nothing human left in his eyes; he was as empty as a rain barrel sixty days into a drought.

Docherty backed him up, silent, calm, and in control. He sighted target after target, squeezing the trigger with the steady, focused pressure they'd taught him all those years ago. Squeeze too quickly and you'll throw off your aim. A shooter had to be cold and solid, a veritable rock. Exhale. Squeeze. Exhale. Squeeze.

McBride screamed in agony, cracking his own bones as he contorted himself into unnatural shapes. His arms bent into his chest—and kept bending. A bone jutted out of his shoulder and one of his elbows was spitting blood onto the floor. His head pressed down until his chin was cutting into his chest. His knees folded back until he was kneeling; then they kept bending, until his heels were touching the back of his head. He was being folded up and put away, a toy no one wanted to play with anymore.

Docherty was melting into the floor. No, he wasn't melting; the floor was consuming him, pulling him into itself, taking only the choicest cuts of meat. It trimmed him down, shaving bone and organs and skin, gobbling up the rest with a wet, smacking sound like a big dog licking its chops.

Hart didn't want to watch, but he couldn't turn away. Not until the old woman, perhaps sensing his condition, pulled him back toward the stairs, up, away from his friends' deaths.

She stopped on the first landing, halfway between the first and second floors, clutching at her chest. All the color had drained from her face. She stumbled and nearly fell, catching Hart's arm with a wild grab.

He lowered her to the carpeted floor, remembering out of nowhere how, before Presley had lost it, she'd thought she'd been noticed.

"Up...room..." she said, gasping for air.

Hart's eyes darted between the old woman and the melee below. Instinct and training insisted his team needed him. It might not be too late to help them, maybe save them.

"Please..."

She'd never make it to the fifth floor without help. He dragged himself up, hardened his heart against the sounds of his comrades' suffering, and reached to lift her.

"Easy does it. Hold on, lady."

He slung her over his shoulder in a fireman's carry, stunned at how light she was. He could have carried two of her with ease. More, even. It was as if there was no one there at all.

Their room was at the end of the hall, far from the stairs up to the Prince's suite. Hart carried the old woman the whole way, pausing only when he realized they had no key to the door. He cursed his lack of preparation; why hadn't he thought to bring his lock-picks?

"D-Disney," she said. It was enough. He laid his hand on the knob, waited as a tingling like millions of tiny feet crossed his palm. Amazed at how ridiculous he *didn't* feel, Hart pushed the door open. Keys? Who needed keys here?

The room was spartan compared to the Prince's suite. That suited Hart just fine. He pulled back the blankets and laid her on the single wide bed.

"Looks like the couch for me, eh?"

She smiled and managed a few words. "I'm a married woman. Remember?"

He walked to the window. It wasn't locked, but they were too high up to jump. He had a length of cord in his pack. It might be long enough to lower himself, but that wasn't going to work for her. Could he carry her down the line and try to drop her onto something soft? He leaned out as far as he could, searching the street for a conveniently placed hay cart or a truck hauling pillows. Nada.

"Well, I think jumping is out. Don't suppose you thought to pack a pair of wings, did you?"

She groaned and pulled herself up into a sitting position. Some of the color came back to her cheeks. Her eyes were no longer seeing things a thousand miles away.

"You okay there?"

"I will be," she said. "Thank you."

His instinct was to dismiss her gratitude. To tell her it was no big deal, all part of the job. Trouble was, it *was* a big deal. He'd left his team downstairs. Everything he'd seen told him they'd gone down hard and messy. And he couldn't shake the feeling that he could have left her on the steps and helped them out in some way.

"It wouldn't have made a difference."

"You read minds, too?"

"No. Faces. Listen to me, Captain Hart: there was nothing you could have done for them."

"Yeah, I—wait. Hold on a second. Nothing I could do for them? Did you—did you know that was going to happen? That they would...that's why you told us not to get violent with the natives. You *knew*!"

She pushed up farther in the bed. "No. I just...well, there are stories you hear, all right?"

"What stories?"

"They say the Market protects its visitors."

"And you knew?"

"It was just a story! I warned you all not to get into a fight. I begged Major Presley not to let you bring guns at all."

"Because you knew?"

"Because I'd heard. And I suspected."

"So you knew."

"No! Listen: nobody fights at the Market. Nobody cheats you and nobody ever, *ever* tries to kill someone. Because even if we don't know, we're worried the Peace might be real."

"What's that?"

"The Peace? It's what people call it. The Market protects its visitors, protects the folks who live and work here. And it doesn't have to be real, don't you see? Because if they believe it they'll stay out of trouble."

"But it is real."

"Seemingly."

"And that wasn't your husband or one of his flunkies there putting a whammy on my team?"

"No. No whammies, Mister Hart." She felt the Prince's gem twitch against her skin. "That's not how it works."

"Tell me how it does work, then. And tell me how it happens to be that you forgot to mention this whole 'Peace' thing. Seems a mite important, don't you think?"

"You're angry."

"Damn right I'm angry. Even if those men weren't my friends, I wouldn't want to lose them like that. But they are my friends—*were* my friends. If you knew something that could have saved them, you should have said so."

"What if I did? What then? I told you all a lot of things, didn't I? Funny how it wasn't until you saw for yourselves that you started listening."

"I'd have remembered this."

"All any of you remembered was when to come pick up your checks."

He shook his head, walking back to the windows. They reached from knee level all the way to the ceiling. Hart pressed his face against the glass and made himself count to ten before answering her.

"Never told you, I think, I was married once. Nice woman. It was back when I was with the teams. She couldn't take the life, you know? Navy SEALs don't get a lot of free time. If you're not training you're planning an op. If you've got the day off you never know when that phone's gonna ring and rip you away."

"I'm sorry."

"It was a while ago. My point is, my ex, she had this neat trick she did. Whenever she was losing an argument—or when she knew she was going to lose—she'd change the subject. So instead of explaining why I found another guy's toothbrush in the bathroom, she'd start screaming about how the teams were more important to me than she was. See, then it's not about what *she* did, it's about how *I* screwed up. It's not that she slept with someone else, it's that I drove her to it."

"I don't understand."

"Don't you? Why'd you hire us, lady? It wasn't to kidnap your husband, was it? Because I'm failing to see how that plan can work when you have to worry about the floor eating you, you know?"

He was shouting. And she was so small, so shrunken, propped up on the pillow with her legs and hips covered in blankets, almost as if the bed was gobbling her up as well. It would serve her right. It was better than she deserved, getting his friends killed like that.

"You don't understand. You *can't* understand."

Hart had to join her on the bed to hear. All the strength had gone from her again. If he opened the window, the breeze might have picked her up and carried her away.

"I was seventeen, I told you that. He kept me for a hundred years and that was bad. But then he cut me loose, and for a hundred more all I wanted—all I wanted *all the time*—was him. I couldn't think, I wasn't myself. But at the same time, I was. I was walking and talking, caught in a fog, but I couldn't free myself. I couldn't even *want* to free myself."

"So you're angry? That's your excuse?"

"I have to be angry. If I stop hating him, I'll fall back into the fog. Back into him."

Hart shook his head. "No go, princess. I'm sorry if he did wrong by you, but that doesn't give you the right to get my friends killed. And make no mistake, that's exactly what you did.

Sending soldiers into hostile territory with lousy intel, well, you don't have to pull the trigger to be the one lining up the crosshairs."

"You won't listen," she said. "And I understand, but you have to understand, too. I was in New York in 1920. Something...happened. It knocked me loose, but there was a price. A cost. I was free and I was myself again, but I'm dancing on the edge of a blade. The tiniest nudge, the slightest breeze, and I'll be lost again."

"Boo hoo."

"You don't have to be cruel," she said. He kept his response to himself, so she continued with a question. "Do you know what a glamour is, Mister Hart?"

"Women's magazine?"

"It's magic. Very powerful magic. My friend, Rossi, he wore a glamour. It let him live someplace he shouldn't have been able to live. Let him walk around like everyone else. He took care of me for a century, but I still don't know what was under his glamour."

"And he died in New York?"

"Yes. He left me some things. One of them was this." She held out her right hand. He saw a gold ring with a small, dull emerald set in its face on her middle finger.

"His class ring?"

"It was his glamour. A very powerful glamour, as it turns out. He left it for me. I think he knew I'd need it."

"Listen: I'm glad you got a nice piece of jewelry out of the deal but none of this is screaming *it's not my fault your friends are dead*. Is there a point? Are you going somewhere with this or are you just changing the subject again?"

"Both, actually."

She turned the ring once around her finger. Then she pulled it off in a single quick motion.

The old woman was a corpse. There was no other way to put it: she was a corpse. Her skin was gray and dark, pulled taut over her bones. Her eyes had sunk deep into the recesses of her skull. Her teeth had long since gone yellow. Many were cracked or outright missing. And her hair, somehow that was the worst of all: her full, lively braid of twisted gray had been replaced by a desiccated mockery. It had the texture of a wire brush, sticking out in all directions, but was at the same time wispy and insubstantial.

"He kept me young at first," Ellie MacReady said, her voice like sandpaper against rough stone. "But that spell broke. Rossi knew it would; he was ready for me. His glamour lets me act. And now that I know the Peace is real, next time I can come back and kill him. And maybe then I can finally die."

FIFTH MARKET

WINTER, 2143

"Ready, Doctor Beauregard?"

Bo took a deep breath as Ellie, unseen, watched. "I hate this, you know?"

"You don't have to," the technician said. "Just use a screen."

"She'll ignore me. Especially today."

"Headset?"

"God, no. Those things kill me. No, I should be used to this by now." Bo rubbed the back of her head. Ellie knew there was an uplink port there, disguised as a birthmark. Bo'd often complained about how queasy needling into the headnet made her. "Do it."

Ellie killed the feed and took a millisecond to tidy up, pulling herself together for company. The world flashed red three times, indicating a new user was logging in. When Bo appeared, she was in mid-sentence.

"—remember to close my eyes."

"Did you forget again, Bo?" Ellie soared past, flapping her arms as if they had anything to do with her weightlessness. Most users would close their eyes when needling in. Bo, somehow, always forgot.

"Every time. How're you today?"

"Antsy. Excited. Delirious."

"I'm sorry you can't be with them. You know we tried."

Ellie backstroked past, flipping in midair and pushing off a wall that wasn't there. Doing laps. Bodiless exercise.

"Are they live?"

"Can't you see? Oh, sorry—had them on private. Here."

The landscape erupted with color. Screens appeared all around them, hanging unsupported in the nothing. The images were startlingly three-dimensional, though the screens themselves occupied only two dimensions, height and width. Viewed from the side, they would vanish entirely. Or they would have, if the UI—the User Interface—allowed viewing from that angle.

Bo surveyed screen after screen of nearly identical images. A man dressed in black combat gear riding in a truck. Another one. Another ten. A view of the road from the truck's window. The rear of the lead truck by way of the second truck's driver. Ellie piggybacked as Bo selected a screen. The others faded as it zoomed to fill her entire world. Bo became the soldier riding in the truck, holding a folded map of the Market in one hand and a spare power-pack in the other.

He turned the power-pack over and over with his fingers, flipping it over the back of his hand with practiced ease. He opened

184

the map and studied it before closing it again. Cramming in the final moments before the exam.

"Zoom out," Ellie said, sending the feed away. Normal users couldn't do stuff like that, manipulating another user's UI. But Ellie had her own set of admin preferences. There wasn't much she couldn't do, here in the nothing.

"Who were you peeping?"

"Didn't look." Bo shrugged. Ellie gave up her laps and hung upside-down, her face lined up with Bo's. When the doctor shrugged, it was eerie and unnatural; some body language only works right side up.

"When are they going in?"

"Any minute now. Are you going to stay and watch?"

"I can. I did have some things—"

Ellie cut her off. "Later. Whatever it is, it can wait, no?"

"I suppose. But—"

Bo disappeared. Everything disappeared. Ellie felt a tingling in the back of her head was she was disconnected and reconnected in rapid succession.

"Ah!"

Her world returned; she crumpled to the ground in a boneless ball. "Ground" being a relative term. Bo was standing at a ninety-degree angle from her. As Ellie struggled to stand, Bo rotated her UI by one quarter, orienting herself to Ellie to help her up.

"Still?"

"Always," Ellie said. "At least, 'always' so far. What do you think?"

Bo fell silent. She was activating her doctor subroutine, summoning her examination tools. With Ellie's hardline, examining her avatar would serve the same purpose, essentially, as examining her physical body. In Ellie's case, examining her avatar was actually more effective. Safer too, by far.

"Heart failure. Again. Ellie, do you know you're the only person on the planet to die of heart failure in probably fifty years?"

"You've told me." She thumped her chest twice with her fist. "I'm old-fashioned that way."

"Don't joke. What if they…what if they get him?"

"If we get him then it doesn't matter. I've told you before, we're a package deal. No tears from me."

Ellie waited as Bo called up a screen of her own. The UI was touchless, but Ellie knew her doctor preferred the tactile experience of gestures. Bo's fingers danced across the virtual keyboard.

Ellie's body appeared on the screen. Blackened bones rose up through fissures of ashen skin ready to split at the slightest touch. Veins and arteries stood out as a network of plump, dark lines pulsing with machine-driven superblood. Empty eye sockets, their residents long since dissolved, were sheathed in a clear, rose-tinted gelatin. This last was to protect the shriveled stew that was all that remained of Ellie's brain.

"It's impolite to stare," she said, killing Bo's screen.

"You can't be alive. You know that, don't you?"

"So my body keeps insisting. And yet here we are. I look pretty good for a dead woman, don't I?" Ellie tilted her hips and pushed out her chest as if posing in front of a mirror.

In here, she had the body of an eighteen-year-old. Her hair flowed in a gravity-free, nut-brown starburst around her face. Her arms were bare, her skin soft with hints of muscle beneath its smooth surface. Her face was ageless and unlined, and her eyes, oh, her eyes. They sparkled with all the colors of the shifting waters of a rough sea.

"I'm serious, Ellie."

"You're *always* serious, Bo. Can't you give me just today? Do you have any appreciation for how long I've been waiting for this?"

"Of course I do. But do *you* appreciate how hard we've been working to free you from this...place? And I think we did it, Ellie. I think we cracked it."

Depending on UI and settings, a user could convey as much or as little emotional response, in terms of facial expression, tone of voice, and body language, as they liked. Ellie adjusted her response slider to its lowest setting. Her arms and legs became stiff, her back straight as a board. Her face was as blank as a sheet of paper.

"Are you okay? Ellie? Ellie? Did you...freeze up again?" Bo tried to move closer, but Ellie ordered the system to hold her in place.

"I can't right now, Bo. I'm sorry. I know how hard everyone is working, but this is an important day for me. When it's over—one way or the other—when it's over, then we can talk about this."

"Ellie—"

"Please!"

Ellie summoned a menu no other user had access to and ejected Bo from the system. The nothing flashed three times and she was alone.

Bo didn't understand. How could she? It wasn't the sort of thing you could explain. The Market. The Prince. Four centuries of life. Two of them spent in a haze made unbearable by how impossibly pleasant it had been. Two more spent in a state of constant, rabid hatred.

Ellie spread out to occupy her nothing. She couldn't do this when guests came calling. Alone, she could abandon her pretense of physicality and stretch her legs, so to speak. She scrolled through the feeds, searching for the one she wanted. These systems, this network, they'd been built to her exacting specifications. Who knew the eighteenth-century girl had a knack for computers? When she found the feed she wanted, she brought it up, full sensory data, and let it carry her away.

Ellie stepped off the carrier, straightening her body armor. It was lightweight, felt no thicker or heavier than ordinary fabric, and was nearly skintight. Her goggles dangled from around her neck; her hood was split down the middle and hanging against her back.

Her vantage point was off; she was taller in this body than in her own. She moved differently, too. Her limbs felt heavier, her footfalls plodding. But the strength this body held was intoxicating. Even as an observer, this was better than her bodiless life in the system.

A soldier in matching gear approached from along the carrier's side. "Commander Hart."

"Yes, private?" she heard Hart say, his voice stuffy in her head.

"The men are ready for your inspection, sir."

"Very good, private."

The military honorifics were for show, nothing more. Ellie had found over the years that military men needed their titles and their ranks. It gave them a sense of order. A sense of purpose, in some funny way.

She inspected the men, tightening a strap here, a buckle there. Like the ranks, this inspection was also for show. Their armor was foolproof, conforming to the wearer's body, fitting itself to each one's height and weight. Once activated, the light, pliable fabric became stronger than steel. Only the holsters and scabbards required any adjusting, and that, she knew, Hart left to the men themselves.

Still, one must maintain appearances.

He was her third Hart, his body cloned, his consciousness ported over from one to the next. Raw technology the first time they'd tried it. Now, she mused, there was nothing to it, though renewal technology was getting good enough it might soon put the cloners out of business.

Hart instructed his troops to pull up their hoods and don their goggles. "Examine the man next to you and the man next to him. Even one millimeter of exposed skin can be deadly. No exceptions!"

He watched them prepare. When each man had stepped back into formation, Hart ordered weapons distributed. Pistols were slotted into holsters, blades into scabbards. She knew he was disappointed with their armaments—the man was a fool for big, noisy shotguns—but the Market came when the Market came. There had only been time for the pistols and the blades, so that's what they were going in with.

Hart was the only one with bare skin still exposed. Ellie lost interest in his unending inspections of the men. She minimized his screen and brought up several others at random. Each man— and her soldiers were all men, a condition Ellie would not budge on, no matter how qualified the woman—kept his eyes on Hart as he made his way down the line.

In appearance, at least, he was much the same as when they'd first met. Sadder, perhaps, and driven by more than a desire for money, an urge to prove himself indomitable. More than anyone save Ellie herself, Hart had been waiting for this day, for the Market's return.

She switched back to him when the inspections were over.

"Here it is: the last time I walked through those gates I lost my entire squad. Period. That is because we were unprepared, and frankly, because we thought the whole thing a giant, ridiculous joke.

"Not today.

"I've given you every scrap of information I can. I have spoken to each and every one of you personally, at length, and you are only here because I believe in my heart of hearts that *you* understand what you're getting into.

"You know your jobs. I expect you to do them. Period. These suits"—he patted his chest with both hands—"will protect you inside. More than that, however, they will protect you from yourself. We will let nothing deter us from our objective today. You hear me?"

Their response was a lion's roar. "WE HEAR YOU, SIR!"

Hart pulled on his hood, fixed his goggles over his eyes, collected his pistol and blade, and faced his men once more.

"Don't talk to anyone. Don't touch anything. They won't see us if we don't want them to. We do this by the numbers and we all come home. All of us."

It was a short walk to the Market's gates. Ellie marched with them in Hart's shoes, anticipation mounting with every step he took. There was the great stone wall enclosing the Market. There were the twin stone pillars bordering the gateway. There was the Market, just beyond.

He stepped through the gate without hesitating, setting a proper example for his men.

The feed went dead; Ellie was alone, once again, in her nothing.

If she'd been flesh at that moment, Ellie would have slammed her fist down on the console, kicked over a chair, found herself someone to scream at. She would have demanded they bring the feeds back *immediately*. She would have sent a dozen technicians to crawl over every inch of line to search for breaks, ordered diagnostics up the wazoo. And she would have fumed—literally, thanks to the Prince's wedding present—as she waited for them to come scurrying back and tell her what she already knew.

The problem wasn't on their end.

She briefly considered coalescing back into her Ellie-shape, conjuring a chair out of the nothing and venting her frustrations by kicking it around a bit. That seemed counter-productive, however, so she tabled the idea for later.

What, then?

Through her hardline, she could order those same diagnostics. She did. A little rejiggering of the monitors and she could check the lines by running a burp of power through them. This she did as well. Screaming at someone might have helped her mood, but it wouldn't have brought back the feeds, or told her anything about what was happening at the Market.

Her UI blinked red three times. Someone was trying to come in.

She was tempted by the request. It would be someone to scream at. For the moment she let it go unanswered. Whoever it was, they could wait.

She skimmed the feeds, searching for some residual signal, some remnant image which might be sneaking through. Hart's feed had gone silent the instant he entered the Market. Was it possible his hostile intentions had been noticed and dealt with so swiftly? She forced herself to remember how his men had died a hundred years past and decided, no, his death would not have come so quickly.

The Market liked to play with its food.

With instantaneous death ruled out in the absence of more data, Ellie moved on to the next likely suspect: the sub-net feeds themselves. The sub-net was checked out, according to the literature, "up to five star systems away." She'd seen the math but it had made her head hurt, even with the full processing power of the system at her disposal. The Market was in Great Los Angeles, well within the sub-net's realtime transmission range, which meant the Market must be keeping the signal from getting out.

She breathed a sigh of relief. Hart and his men were transmitting, but no signal could get through. It was obvious, actually. She'd witnessed firsthand how the Market had its own weather—its own suns, for heaven's sake! They'd been so wowed by the fancy new sub-net tech that they'd neglected to apply a little common sense to the problem.

Still, their implants would be recording. She could watch the feeds to her heart's content as soon as Hart and his men returned.

Patience. It always came down to patience. Even four hundred years later, she was still learning patience.

The UI flashed red three more times. Ellie brought up the request and Bo's profile popped up. Hadn't the doctor wanted to talk about something earlier? Not the raid, certainly not. Ellie knew Bo was appalled by her and Hart's hunger for revenge against the Prince. What, then? Had she had some kind of break-through in her own projects?

"Come on in," Ellie said, gathering the extant parts of herself from the system. A Bo-shaped space appeared, then filled up with Bo-colors and Bo-details.

"Ellie, I saw the feeds go down, are you okay?"

"I'm fine. It's just the Market snubbing its nose at us."

Bo looked surprised. Ellie had to remind herself that not everyone knew the extent of her access. "Knowing you, Doctor, that's not why you've come calling. What's going on?"

Again, surprise. She'd probably come expecting Ellie's not-inconsiderable wrath, and here she was practically being offered tea and crumpets. Bo was brilliant, there was no denying it, but sometimes she was a little slow on the uptake.

Ellie gave her time to sort herself out. It wasn't long before Bo got to the point of her visit.

"It's your Mister Rossi, Ellie."

"Rossi?"

"Yes, he's . . . well, it's working."

One of Doctor Beauregard's conditions upon agreeing to take Ellie's case was that her laboratory and operating theater would remain, for the duration of her employment, unmonitored. That meant no cameras, no spy-eyes, and a field that disabled the implants Commander Hart and his men wore should they cross over into her workspace. Before today, Ellie hadn't cared; she could access Bo's data as easily as anything else in the system. Now, however, she wished she'd insisted on tucking away a couple hidden eyes somewhere Bo wouldn't have noticed.

"I hate that thing," she said, unable to ignore the smile on Bo's face.

"Then we're even. Come on, be a big girl and put on your hologram. I'll get you an ice cream cone."

Ellie scowled. She doubted if Bo had ever tasted real ice cream.

"Fine. But this had better be good."

Bo vanished again from the nothing, leaving Ellie no choice but to follow. She brought up the hologram actualization controls and gave a nudge to the one marked SCALE. If she and Bo had ever met in real life, the doctor would have towered over her; the median height had risen by a hefty margin since the early seventeen-hundreds. Ellie would wear the hologram, but she'd be damned if she'd let Bo see how short she was.

The world fizzled. Ellie's mind collapsed down into the cramped space of the holo-control module. She maintained her connection to the system but could no longer access her advanced controls. It was as close as she came, these days, to feeling human.

Bo was waiting when she blinked into existence. She must have needled in right from her lab.

Ellie stretched her arms as if she could feel them. The solid-light projections could interact with the world in real time, but sight and sound were the only senses available. Taste, touch and smell, considered trickier for some reason, were still in beta. The manufacturer had told them those final three senses were not recommended for users running a hardline, as Ellie was. The potential feedback was too dangerous. It couldn't be lethal in her case, but she didn't like to imagine what the Prince's gem would do with, say, the heat from a burning match looped over and over again approaching infinity.

So: eyes and ears and a dumb body she couldn't feel. Not as bad as being back on the slab, but nothing compared to her private universe within the system.

"Where is he?"

"He's right here," Bo said, stepping around a large, expensive-looking piece of equipment Ellie did not recognize. "But listen, I don't want you to get too excited. He's not much to look at."

"You said it was working."

"It is. But working to me and working to you might mean two different things. I just don't want you expecting miracles."

"Miracles are what I pay you for."

"Ellie."

"Fine. No miracles today. Let me see him."

Bo keyed a quick sequence onto the screen and stood back to let the top of the machine open up. Within, Ellie saw a fist-size bean filled with pink liquid. The skin of the bean pulsed as feeder tubes cycled the pink liquid in and out.

"He's a bean?"

Bo chuckled and lowered a screen over the incubator. The view magnified until they could see a pinprick of dark matter floating within the sea of pink.

"Hello there, Mister Rossi," Bo said, beaming with pleasure. "How are you today?"

"Okay, explain. How excited am I supposed to get about a microscopic dot?"

"You should get very excited. And he's not microscopic, just hard to spot if you don't know where to look. Ellie, this is further than we've ever been before."

"A dot. Bo, if you're trying to, I don't know, distract me from the fact that we've lost contact with Hart and his men, you're going to have to do better than this."

Bo closed the cover of the incubator and guided Ellie to a large screen suspended nearby. The screen was filled with incomprehensible data, graphs and charts. Bo cleared it with a single keystroke.

"We tried cloning, but that same shine you've got on your DNA keeps us from growing him a viable host body. Not that he has a consciousness to transfer, but it was a good first step.

"Next up was renewal. That's only good for an organ or three. Brain cells are iffy at best. Heart, lungs, liver, kidneys, etcetera, no problem, but most bodies can't stand doing everything from scratch. Bottom line: that wasn't doing the trick either.

"Still, it gave us something to go on. We had hair and a couple fingernails from your, what was that thing called?"

"A jeroboam," Ellie said. She accessed the memory and a golden locket appeared in her hard-light hand.

"Right. We had enough to clone from, but obviously, not enough to grow from. And our clones looked less like human beings and more like raw hamburger. Even if we could get you out of your body, we don't have anywhere good to put you."

She tapped keys on her virtual keyboard and the screen filled with pink light. At the center was the dark blot Bo insisted was Rossi. "You can't see it, but this pink gloop is actually filled with Mister Rossi's cells. What we're doing, in essence, is running a full-body renewal on a body that's not there. We're growing a new Rossi from within the existing one."

Ellie couldn't manipulate the screen with her stupid hologram hands. She could touch things—she could have knocked Bo's coffee mug onto the floor—but she bore only the appearance of flesh. The screens were capacitive, requiring actual, conductive flesh to move things around.

But she could interface directly with the software. She ordered the screen to zoom to its maximum magnification.

"Why is it pink? You didn't grind up a clone, did you? Ick."

"One of my techs suggested it, actually. Wouldn't work. Running the renewal in a matrix of failed flesh would only give us more failed flesh."

"If you can't clone him—us—how would you get good flesh?"

The smile that spread across Bo's face was priceless. Ellie knew she'd asked the question Bo had been waiting for.

"The pink isn't a clone. Or it is, but it's a clone we didn't bring to term. We created it and we're replicating the cells, but we're not quickening them. It's a clone at the very first stage of development and that's as far as we're letting it go. Second one of creation, before anything can go wrong."

"And it's working?"

"See for yourself." Bo cleared the screen and brought up a new display. A DNA helix spun on the left side of the screen while numbers flowed past on the right. Ellie ordered the stream to stop and studied it. She didn't know enough about DNA or biology to gauge whether what she was looking at was good or bad, but she knew that when Bo's team found faulty cells or damaged DNA strands, they were highlighted in red. Scrolling through the text, all Ellie saw was white.

"It's working."

"So far. We're cooking him slowly, taking our time. Right now he's nothing but a few thousand undifferentiated cells. It'll be another week or two before we have anything resembling a human fetus."

"And then what?"

"Assuming no genetic abnormalities appear, we'll continue bringing him up slowly. Don't get me wrong; this is just a first step. Apart from your DNA, I've never seen anything like your Mister Rossi in my entire life."

"He always was one of a kind. If this works—if—what then? How do we use this for me?"

"This won't work for you."

"Then why—"

Bo cut her off. "Your necklace keeps anyone from harming you. We can't draw your consciousness out because—this is the theory at least—it thinks you're dying, so it stops you leaving. In a strange way, your Mister Rossi's being dead has made things easier on us."

"Be sure and thank him when you see him."

Bo chuckled. "So we can't get you out of there. And anything we do which might threaten to harm you gets thrown back at us. I'm sure you remember how well our attempt at a heart transplant went?"

Ellie nodded. She'd been anesthetized but had watched the recording. The theory had been that a series of transplants might pull her together enough to have a go at renewing her. They knocked her out well enough, but when Doctor Knox—Bo's old boss—made his first incision the Prince's gem flooded the room with its white, killing light. She hadn't allowed further transplant attempts after that.

"So what then?"

"So we don't do anything to hurt you. But that damned ugly thing doesn't seem to mind if you hurt yourself, does it?"

Bo brought up an image of Ellie's ruined body on the screen. On all the laboratory's screens. The empty eye sockets stared in mock surprise from every direction. The mouth gaped in eternal, agonizing pain.

"Bo, that's enough."

"No, wait. Don't you see? If we can grow a new, viable body for Rossi from within a sea of his own cells, we can apply that same procedure to you. If anything, it's easier with you than it is with him. We can't clone you—the clones all fail within days—but we're not trying to clone you. If anything, your necklace will help the process along."

"You've lost me. And get that off the screens."

Bo killed the screens. To Ellie, it seemed a soundless wail had been suddenly silenced.

"One more time, Doctor, if you please."

"We grow a new you from inside the old you. There's no one doing it to you, so there's no one to get upset with. It's literally your own body doing the work. We can immerse you in a vat of your own cells to help the process along, but all we're really doing is turning back the clock."

"And you think this will work?"

Bo clapped her hands together. "It should. We'll see how our Rossi develops over the next few months. But even if he fails, I know we're on the right track. Ellie, I just know we've cracked your problem at last!"

"Turning back the clock, huh? If it doesn't work, well, I'm no worse off than I was before, is that the thinking?"

"Yes," Bo said, her voice hushed. "And to answer your next question, Ellie, it's probably not going to be a...pleasant experience.

And no, you can't hide away in the system. We're afraid it could be dangerous if your port healed over while you weren't home."

It seemed a good opportunity for pacing. Ellie cued the pacing subroutine on the hologram while she thought.

After the Prince's gift had cracked in New York, after Rossi and who knows how many others had died, she'd begun aging. Slowly at first but in less than a decade her hair had turned first gray and then white. She'd used Rossi's ring and the glamour it provided to make her way through the world, hoping she could last to the next Market and force the Prince to release her. When that tree failed to yield fruit, her degeneration had grown even faster. It wasn't long before she'd been unable to stand or move. Just breathing had been an agony. Her organs failed one by one; she'd died a hundred times a week, the flash of light pushing against the approaching darkness.

She hadn't thought much about that time since her hardline had been installed. It was always in the back of her mind, however, a whispered voice that could never be silenced.

"Ellie, I'm sorry. We are working on other things, too. Maybe one of them will be…" She trailed off, then spoke again as if remembering some bit of good news. "There is something else, though."

"What?"

"See, this you're going to like, I think. And best of all, you get to ditch the hologram."

"Thank God."

"Help me needle back in and I'll show you."

Bo climbed into her chair, put her feet up, and waited for Ellie to slide the interface needle into place. Such fine motor skills were beyond her dumb holographic hands, so she let the system take control. The needle slid unerringly into place, and with a loud *click*, Bo was gone from the world of man.

"Awful damned thing," Ellie said, shutting the circuit in her mind. She fizzled again and felt the warm, comforting flow of data envelop her as she returned to her familiar world of nothing.

Bo was waiting, as Ellie'd known she would be. She had someone with her.

"Ellie, I would like to introduce you to a friend of mine."

"Hello," he said, extending his hand. "My name is Rossi."

She fell into his arms without thinking about it. He was Rossi, sure as anything. He was shorter than she remembered. Then Ellie realized it wasn't him; she'd left herself "tall" from her visit to the real world. She dialed back her height and settled into the old, familiar physicality of being held by him.

"Boy," he said, his voice at once familiar and new. "You weren't kidding, were you?"

"I told you, Clay, she's very happy to see you."

"Clay?" Ellie said, looking up but unwilling to let go.

Bo shrugged. "Everyone needs a first name. Clayton was my grandfather's name. I didn't think you'd mind."

Ellie would have said tears were impossible within the system, a "ghosted process" it wouldn't allow. Either they'd updated the specs without her noticing or she'd grown beyond its parameters. She rubbed her damp cheeks on his shirt as she'd done so many times during their time together.

"How?" she said, opening a private channel with Bo which Rossi couldn't hear.

"Perhaps we should all sit down," Bo said. Ellie assumed it was a private message from Bo to her until Rossi extricated himself from her—with some reluctance, she was pleased to note. His hands remained on her shoulders.

Ellie summoned chairs for them all. Couches. Big, comfortable couches they could each stretch out on. To these she added coffee tables and—why not?—steaming mugs of coffee. Once she'd started there was no sense in stopping. By the time they sat down, her nothing was replaced by the drawing room of the house she and Rossi had once shared. The fireplace crackled and snapped and the picture windows opened out onto a snow-covered landscape she still saw in her dreams.

One of her dogs, Brutus, padded over, leapt up onto her couch, and curled up at Ellie's feet. When she scratched behind his ear, his leg twitched with delight. Her other dog, Rufus, sprawled out with his belly exposed to the fire.

"How nice," Bo said. "Where are we?"

"Maine. Near the coast. This was our home." She dug into Brutus's neck. "These were my dogs. I can't imagine why I never thought to do this before. I always loved this place. Even when I was…well, even then. It's beautiful, isn't it?"

"I lived here?" Rossi said.

Ellie examined him. He was young, so young. It was Rossi as she'd known him nearly from the beginning. Not the boy who'd accompanied her at the Prince's order, nor the man he grew into. This was Rossi in the full flush of his youth. Twenty, maybe twenty-five years old, by the looks of him, with his dark hair cut close, not as he'd worn it but as was the current style. His face was tanned, and his eyes, though confused, cut through her just as they always did.

"We lived here," she said. "We were—you looked after me. For a long time you were the closest thing I had to family."

He smiled; it lit up his whole face. Her memories of Rossi—the Rossi she'd known—were of an old man lying back in his favorite chair, an open newspaper spread across his lap as he dozed. One of her great fears was that her recollections of him were colored by the spell the Prince had set upon her. She was pleased to feel genuine affection for the man sitting across from her. Wherever he'd come from, he was unmistakably Rossi.

"Please, Bo, tell me how you did this. Where is he from?"

"He's something of a side effect, actually. What you might call an 'unplanned consequence.'"

"He's not from the bean, is he?"

"He is."

"That's impossible. Clones don't have consciousness."

Bo shook her head. She looked pleased with herself. "I told you, Ellie, it's not a clone. Okay, the gloop is made up of cloned cells, but the Rossi we're growing, that's right out of the hair and tissue samples you supplied to us." She was referring to the captured hair and fingernails within the jeroboam, the enchanted phial he'd left for her with Mister Beesix. Ellie couldn't remember how long ago she'd entrusted it to Bo's care.

"You can't get a consciousness out of a few scraps of ancient hair, no matter how well they're preserved."

"I agree, normally. But I think I told you before that you and Mister Rossi are proving rather different as subjects. The normal rules don't seem to apply to the two of you."

"So it's him? He seems confused. I'm sorry, Rossi. Clay. But it's true."

"It is. Doctor Beauregard, you can explain it better than I can. Please?"

Bo sat forward in her chair. Ellie felt a lecture coming on.

"No," she said. "Bo, give it to me in fifty words or less. It's been a hell of a day."

"There's not much to it, not really. Remember all those tubes we had going in and out of the bean's incubator?"

Ellie nodded, yes she remembered.

"One of those was a hardline, similar to yours. We use them for cloning to upload data to the new body. Think of a building: it's like laying the foundation before putting the frame up. With Mister Rossi here, the opposite happened. The server started filling up with data. Data we couldn't understand. It was even weirder when we tried to analyze the upload. It was raw data. No, it was more than raw data. It was absolute nonsense. An unending sequence of numbers and letters pouring out every nanosecond. We had to double the storage in the first day. By the second day we had to double it twice more. Finally, this morning, the stream slowed to a trickle. And when the trickle dried up, what we had was our friend here."

"Me," Rossi said.

Ellie squeezed his hand. "His memories?"

"Nope. On that front he's a blank slate. Still, there's something of your Rossi in him. I'd never publish this—not even if my contract allowed it—but for lack of a better word, it was the spark of his life."

"Come on."

Bo raised her hand in mock salute. "Scout's honor."

"Do you even know what that means?"

Bo admitted she did not. "But I'm telling you the truth. I can't quantify it better than that. Somehow, some tiny remnant of your Rossi survived in those hair and nail trimmings. We had to stumble on to it, but I credit him as much as my team for the bean doing so well. Ellie, he's helping it grow."

Ellie was able to access Bo's systems without expanding to fill the nothing, and without, she was confident, Bo knowing what she was doing. She pushed through firewalls and security measures, brute-forcing her way through the passwords as if they were made of air. Rossi's file was right on top of the data stacks. It took her less than a second to pore through it all.

"You're serious," she said. "Bo, when did you get religion?"

"I could be excused for it, don't you think? The things I see here with you. But no, Ellie, I'm not talking about some man-in-the-sky madness. We can transfer consciousness from one body to the next—not yours, regrettably, but it works for the rest of the population. And is it really so crazy, when you get down to it? I told you his DNA has that same shine on it yours does. Almost like it's too good, too perfect. Maybe the lingering spark of life is a side effect; too small to detect but waiting to turn on with a nudge of encouragement."

Ellie thought of Rossi's ring, which she'd worn for a time to mask her true nature. If he'd been wearing it the day he'd cut his hair and nails for the jeroboam, might some of the glamour have clung to those discarded bits of him? She'd always thought of glamours as parlor tricks, little more than camouflage. Walking around with four arms and blue skin? Put on a glamour and you're ready for a night out on the town with no one the wiser. What if there was more to it than that?

"It's his glamour," Ellie said.

"I'm sorry?"

"It's like—oh hell, it's magic, Bo, pure and simple. Rossi had a ring he used to wear. It made him look younger than he really was. I wore it, for a time, and it was more than just a costume. When I wore it, I *felt* younger, too."

"And he was wearing it when he died?"

"Yes. No. I don't know. I found it after he—it's not important, though. He was wearing it when he filled the jeroboam, so whatever was on him went into it."

"But you don't have a glamour, do you?"

Ellie looked around. She was sitting on her favorite couch with a dog that had been dead more than two hundred years, sitting next to a friend who'd been dead even longer. With a thought, she could turn this place into the bottom of the sea, outer space, or anything else she liked. Earlier she'd wished herself taller without batting a virtual eyelash. She had a glamour, that was certain, but that wasn't what Bo was asking.

"No. I did, a while back, but I stopped using it. But Bo, just because I'm not fooling people into thinking I'm thirty again, that doesn't mean there isn't magic crawling all over me."

Bo came to it almost at once. For Ellie's part, she was surprised they hadn't stumbled onto it a few decades back.

"Your necklace."

"Bingo. It's from *him*, and we know it's packing heat, even split down the middle. You can't imagine how powerful it was when it was whole. If Rossi's glamour is mucking things up, you can bet that shattered supernova hanging around my neck is in on the game too."

She expected Bo to be dejected; surely this meant her experiment with the Rossi-bean was doomed to failure. The doctor surprised her, though, by laughing aloud. There was a maniacal edge to it Ellie didn't like. She could imagine towering Tesla coils crackling with energy and a hunchbacked henchman hauling jars with brains sloshing around in them.

"Bo, what is it?"

"It's been staring us in the face the whole time—we were just too stupid to see it. Ellie, the shine in your DNA, the shine in his, *that's* the glamour doing its work. We've been trying to work around it for so long, it never occurred to us to just let it do its thing."

Ellie felt excitement rising up within her. Bo was going to tell her they could fix her, fix her body. Use the pink gloop and this new understanding to grow her a body from the inside out. It would hurt, sure, but the pain wouldn't last forever. And when Hart and his men returned, they'd have the Prince hog-tied and willing to do anything for his freedom. She wasn't going to ask for much; just her liberty. If she had to ask more than once...well, after four hundred years, who could blame her if her darling husband came away with a bruise or two? She'd been willing to settle for the freedom of the grave but now, if Bo could do even half of what she said...

A screen blinked on, blocking the fireplace. Rufus sprung up, nothing but a sub-routine pretending to be a dog, but it still tugged on Ellie's heartstrings. The face which filled the screen belonged to one Louis Bloch. He was her head of engineering, and in command while Hart was out in the field.

"Ms. MacReady, ma'am, we've got a signal coming in. It's them."

Ellie wiped away the drawing room with a sweep of her hand. Screens appeared all around, filling the nothing. She was disappointed to find the vast majority of them blank. No signal over the sub-net. A bad sign if ever she'd seen one.

But a handful of the screens were live. She separated them from the blanks, clustering them together in one place. Five in total. She recognized the names appearing on each one's UI, but only in a purely academic, informational way. She knew of them, but she did not *know* them. An oversight, to be sure, but not one she cared to examine right now.

Each live feed showed roughly the same thing: a bouncing view which she recognized as a man running. The five soldiers had emerged from the Market, but they hadn't missed a step. She feared they might run all the way through the city and straight to the ocean if she couldn't get them to stop.

"Doctor Beauregard, what's going on?"

"Hush a moment, Clayton," Bo said, taking the man's hand. Ellie would have swatted her away if she hadn't been so busy. Business for another time, she decided, skimming from feed to feed, piecing together what had happened.

"Here," she said. "Rossi, I'm sorry but bear with me here. Bo, can he take it if I focus in on a single feed?"

"I think so. Why?"

"Because," Ellie said, selecting one of the soldiers and casting herself, Bo, and Rossi, together, into the soldier's mind.

Private Anslo Ramirez entered the market on hesitant feet. His palms were sweaty and he couldn't seem to keep his eyes focused on one thing for more than a second. Telemetry told Ellie, watching the feed, that Ramirez was terrified, his vitals spiking across the board. The fact that he continued advancing was a testimony to the private's fortitude.

The Market was as beautiful as she remembered it. The sights and sounds were the same but somehow minimized. Blame it on long absence, or on software inadequately interpreting the soldier's signal. She wanted to explain to Bo and Rossi that this wasn't the Market, the real Market, they were seeing. The muted colors, the dulled sounds, they were all distant shadows of the true Market.

"Ellie, it's…" Sharing the soldier's feed was different from being alone inside his head. She was aware of Bo and Rossi, like waking up in a strange place and knowing you're not alone.

"Where is this?" Rossi said, his voice filled with wonder.

"It's the Market. This is where we met. In another life."

"It's beautiful. The air, it smells like…I don't have the words. Bo, what am I looking for?"

"Baking," she said. "Pies and muffins and steaming hot rolls. And flowers and running water and cinnamon and honeysuckle and sweet beer and a thousand other things. You've been to the Market, Ellie, yes?"

"A few times now."

"How did you ever bring yourself to leave?"

Ramirez stopped. Their view shifted as he backed away from a storefront where a man with sandy hair and a huge soup-strainer mustache was pulling a tray of morning buns from the oven. As the soldier continued distancing himself, the man squirted dollops of icing over the top of each bun, whistling while he worked.

Hart's voice filled the world. "Everyone back. Barnes, just like we discussed."

A lone soldier broke from the pack. He approached the baker, pausing to sniff the man's wares. Ellie, Bo, and Rossi couldn't hear what he said, but after a brief conversation, the baker removed three pastries from a rack behind the counter, dropped them into a small sack, and passed them over to Barnes.

Barnes nodded.

"Everyone be ready," Hart said, the voice of God in their ears.

Barnes drew his sidearm, an oily pistol with a long, straight barrel. The baker regarded it with curiosity, almost as if he didn't believe it was real. He smiled and said something Ellie guessed was, "Anything more for you today, sir?"

Barnes shot the man three times in rapid succession, twice in the chest and once in the head. It took several seconds for the baker to realize he was mortally wounded. Confusion passed over his face in a wave as he slumped down, the strength gone from his legs forever.

Bo shouted something, but Ellie muted her. What happened next would decide everything for her. Everything.

Barnes stood with his weapon lowered but still unholstered. He looked left, then right, then left again. He pivoted in place to check his rear. He stepped back, away from the baker's stall. He left his sack of pastries behind and walked, taking his time, back to where Hart and the rest of his squad waited.

"We are go," Hart said, booming in their heads. "I repeat, we are go. Proceed to rally point one and fall into positions."

Ellie had to minimize Private Ramirez down to a single screen to deal with Bo. She was inconsolable, livid with rage.

"You knew, didn't you? You knew they were going to do that!"

Ellie conjured up the drawing room again. The soldier's screen hung over the fireplace. She saw the men proceeding through the Market at a quick march. She had time to talk to Bo before they arrived at the inn.

"Ellie!"

"Yes, of course I knew. Who do you think wrote the original brief on this mission?"

"You?"

"Sure. Bo, we needed to know if it was safe before our men went too far in to back out."

"Shooting an innocent in cold blood is safe?"

Ellie nodded. "Better one of them than all of us. What did you think we were going in for? I know you've seen them running drills, testing the armor and the weapons. Did you think it was so they could go in and do a little light shopping?"

"No, but—"

"We had to know if the Market would resist us. We *had* to. Believe me, if there'd been any other way...but there wasn't."

"She's right," Rossi said. "Doctor Beauregard, don't you see? They had to find out if it was safe before they went in too deep. But Ellie, you're also wrong."

"What?"

"They didn't need to kill the man, did they? If the Market was going to fight back, just pushing him around, maybe knocking him unconscious—wouldn't that have worked just as well?" He rubbed his head, squinching his eyes shut. "The Peace, that's what it's called, isn't it? It's not just for killing. It protects them all. But you figured out a way to beat it. How?"

"We didn't need to kill him?"

"How did you beat it, Ellie?"

"Hold on a second."

"Ellie, please, how did you beat it?"

She pulled up a scan of the original Market flier she'd stolen all those years ago. It was a digital copy, but indistinguishable in the system from the real thing. Even the words had changed, CLEVELAND, OHIO replaced with GREAT LOS ANGELES, CALIFORNIA.

"I...know this," he said.

She explained what the flier was and how she'd come to possess it. "You—the other Rossi—once told me it was a piece of the Market. You're not supposed to be able to take something like that, but I did. I don't know the science, but they found something in the paper they can use. It's in their armor, the goggles, and their hoods. The knives and the guns, too. So long as they stay covered up, they're safe. The Market can't see them, can't hurt them. They can get to the Prince and no one will get hurt."

"No one *else* will get hurt," Bo said.

Ellie didn't correct her. On the screen over the fireplace, Hart and his men had arrived at the Prince's inn.

For the soldiers, the waiting must have been the hardest part. For Ellie it was a matter of zipping through the replay to just before the Prince arrived at the inn.

"There should be twenty of them waiting inside," Ellie said. "No one will notice them unless they do something stupid. If he goes upstairs they'll follow and take him before he gets to his suite. If he sits down to eat they'll just surround his table and—"

An explosion rocked the soldiers' feed. Fire vomited from every one of the inn's windows, raining flaming debris over the surrounding area.

Hart barked orders into the soldiers' ears. "Fall in to surround the inn. Fall in! We've taken the target but are meeting with heavy resistance!"

Private Ramirez leapt to his feet and sprinted after the rest of his squad. Other black-clad soldiers closed in all around him, all with their weapons drawn.

Another explosion from the inn, this time not of fire but of searing white light. The top floors flashed with the Prince's energy and were gone in a heartbeat, leaving only steaming ruins. A wave of energy radiated from the shaking inn, knocking Ramirez off his feet.

The light flowed over them, consuming all it touched as if made of nothing but biting, ripping, tearing teeth. Where skin was exposed to the air, the Market also took its due, reaching up with grasping claws to pull flesh from bone, sucking whole men into the ground with orgiastic fury.

The few soldiers who remained began retreating. In the ruins of the inn stood the Prince and Cutter, the former guiding his tide of white light out to hunt for more enemies, the latter with his long sword drawn, fighting the few who remained.

Ellie zoomed in the view and found Hart in the thick of things. He wore the same dark suit of armor as the rest of his soldiers, but she recognized the shreds of his old cloak fluttering from his shoulders like a tattered scarf. He stood toe to toe with Cutter, blade drawn, exchanging blows with the bodyguard, giving as good as he got.

The Prince raised his hands and stared at Hart and the few men still fighting. They dove for cover or fled into the street, Cutter hot on their heels, then disappeared from Ellie's view. The Prince guided the torrent of rushing whiteness as it searched for more prey. His face was twisted with rage, no longer the least bit beautiful. His hands were brown and gnarled, as if made of old, sick wood. He screamed and the light rushed back into him, filling him up, healing his many wounds. With a disgusted snarl, he leapt from the rubble after Cutter and Hart.

Private Ramirez stayed in place for more than a minute. They waited to see if he would flee to the Market's exit or if curiosity would get the better of him and go after Hart and his pursuers. Ellie said a silent prayer—to whom she wasn't sure—that the man would knuckle up so they could see Hart's fate.

"There he goes," Bo said.

Ramirez picked himself up and, slow with caution, trotted after his commander. He didn't have far to go; just around the next corner, by a round-faced building with a wide, open doorway, Cutter and Hart were ripping each other to shreds as the Prince stood glowering nearby. The bodyguard had suffered a number of small cuts and one long, jagged wound down his left arm, which hung limp at his side. The loss did not seem to make him any less dangerous as he slashed at Hart again and again with his long, curved blade.

Hart backed up toward the open doorway, blocking Cutter's blows with short, measured strokes. When he found an opening, he darted out with unbelievable speed, nicking the bodyguard here, cutting him there. His sidearm remained in its holster. The time necessary to draw and aim it would have given Cutter all the opening he needed to finish the fight with a single blow.

"No!"

Hart caught his foot and stumbled, lowering his guard for a heartbeat. Cutter swept his blade in low, aiming to disable his foe, realizing too late the clumsy move had been a ruse. Hart trapped the blade between his arm and his ribs, twisting it out of Cutter's grip, sending it clattering to the ground. He heel-kicked Cutter's leg out from under him, and now, finally, reached to his holster.

"Finally, revenge for my friends." His voice boomed through the soldier's head as he took aim at the Prince.

"No!" Ellie screamed at the feed. "No, don't kill him! I need him!"

Before Hart could fire, the Prince unleashed a focused blast of energy directly at him. Hart dove clear as an explosion of debris erupted from the spot where he'd been standing only a moment earlier. The force of the blast flung him, head over heels, into the round-faced building. There was a flash of green light, a scream of terrible pain, and then nothing more. Hart was gone.

Private Ramirez remained in his hiding spot for a few minutes longer, waiting to be discovered. They watched as the Prince and Cutter entered the building Hart had been thrown into. The two men looked around, conversing briefly. Ellie's blood froze in her veins as she watched the Prince throw his head back and laugh. They exited the building together, Cutter's sword sheathed, the Prince unbearably beautiful again. Ramirez waited for them to leave before breaking cover and double-timing it back to the Market gate and home.

They sat in silence, the light of the roiling fire a stark contrast to the otherworldly glow of the blank screen hanging in the air between them. Bo dismissed the screen when she saw Ellie had no intention of doing so. Now it was only the firelight illuminating the trio. The night beyond the drawing room's windows was moonless and shrouded in darkness.

Ellie sat with her head down, all her attention seemingly focused on Brutus, who'd made a nest of her legs and was now involved in having his head scratched. She smiled, and her face was filled with terrible sadness.

"Ellie, I'm so sorry," Bo said. "I know how very close you were."

The UI flashed red three times. Ellie ignored Bo's sympathy and authorized the visitor.

Commander Hart appeared before them. A fourth chair—a beat-up leather recliner with an afghan folded over one arm—blinked into existence for him.

"Ma'am."

"You've watched it?"

"All five, actually. About what we expected, no?"

"Just about," Ellie said. Brutus rumbled contentedly in her lap.

"Wait, hold on," Bo said. "How is he here?"

Ellie held up her hand and ticked off fingers. "Commander Anthony Hart the fourth, meet Doctor Emily Beauregard the first."

"Ma'am. Though technically we've already met. Topside, you understand."

"Topside?"

He glanced up at the ceiling. "Topside. Out in the world. You sat across from me at lunch last Tuesday. Borrowed a napkin when you spilled your tea."

Bo's look as she put two and two together was priceless. "That was you?"

"Hart the third was on maneuvers. SOP—that's Standard Operating Procedure—is to let any man who wants to take his clone's place. My brother and I, we've got a bit of a bone to pick with her ex."

"Moreso now, I'd imagine," Ellie said.

Bo sat forward, startling Rufus out of his snooze by the fire. The dog shot to his feet and dashed out of the room. "Those were all clones we saw dying?"

"Mostly clones." Ellie grimaced. "Like the commander said, you get the option of going in if you want it. I think forty-seven of the men were clones, not counting Hart. He was third-generation."

"But that's—why?"

"Because we expected to fail, doctor," Hart said.

"But now we know our suits work. We know our weapons can wound him, even if only temporarily. Also, Cutter's not the ultimate badass we thought he was. Did you see your brother there? He'd have had him if the Prince hadn't stuck his nose in."

"Cheap tactics. Won't work a second time."

"Also, did you see?"

"I sure did. Just like you said. Next time we're gonna steamroll them."

Bo stamped her foot on the ground. Brutus looked up but remained in place, poured across Ellie's legs. "Sorry to interrupt your little love-in, but perhaps you'd like to share with the rest of the class?"

Ellie and Hart exchanged a look. He nodded for her to explain to Bo what they were talking about.

"Their weapons, Bo. Their tech, all of it. Whether by design or by necessity, the Market is stuck in the dark ages. Okay, there's running water and roads, but Cutter was still fighting with a sword. Take away the Market's teeth and the Prince's magic, and you've got a bunch of pointy-eared wannabes playing with sticks in their backyard."

"So?"

"So that's the way it was in Cleveland. They haven't learned a thing in a hundred years. And what do you want to bet, in another hundred, wherever the Market pops up, it's going to be same show, different day, all over again? The commander's right. Next time we're going in to get the job done for real."

SIXTH MARKET

SPRING, 2260

Word of the Market arrived early in the evening. The Duke's envoy found Cutter leaning against the trunk of a tree, just within the firelight of the Prince's camp. The night's wind bore a bitter chill, but Cutter was in shirtsleeves.

"Good evening, Captain," the envoy said, leaping down from his horse and bowing low.

"Evening. I know you, don't I, son?"

The envoy radiated pride at being recognized. "Aye. You passed several weeks at my father's estate some years back."

The bodyguard nodded, pressing the mouth of his pipe against his lips, inhaling and then blowing sweet smoke out in rings. If the cold bothered him, if he noticed it at all, he gave no sign. "What news, then?"

"The Market, sir." The envoy produced a folded paper from his coats. "It returns to the human lands again. His majesty's presence is requested."

"Required, you mean?"

"Aye. Though it is not for such as I to say."

Cutter drew in another lungful from his pipe, holding the smoke deep, deep down before exhaling once again. "We're a long way from the human lands. My lord will not be pleased at this news."

"I don't imagine so, Captain. I set out as soon as word came. It was only this morning the news reached us."

"Three days?"

"Aye, three days. And one almost gone."

"Very well. How far did you ride to come to us? Will you join us for the night before setting out?"

"Thank you, Captain, but I must refuse your generous hospitality. With your permission, sir, I will ride ahead to prepare the way."

A brief flickering from the camp's fire illuminated Cutter's features. As their eyes met, Cutter perceived a shiver running through the boy's body. Was he afraid? "You presume much, son."

"Begging your pardon, sir. I meant only to say—well—if the Prince must ride for the Market, he will travel by intersect, no?"

"Possibly. Are you offering, then, to travel ahead and warn them of our coming?"

"Only with your permission, sir."

Cutter studied the young man. His hair was fair and long past his shoulders. He wore it pulled back, exposing his ears. A brave thing in most lands, given the state of the world. He asked himself if the boy was reckless, foolish, or merely showing off, hoping to impress the Prince and his bodyguard.

"You may ride ahead of us if you wish, but do not name the Prince when you arrive. State only that travelers are coming with urgent business at the Market. That may be enough to identify us but there is no percentage in advertising our movements, especially to that hateful place. You are aware, I hope, what the Prince went through the last time he sailed to those climes?"

"The attack?"

Cutter nodded, but would not dignify the cowards' actions by naming them.

"I will forget for whom I ride the moment I set off."

"And a good lad, at that. Tell me, do you fancy presenting yourself into his service?"

The young man nodded, but could not seem to muster his power of speech.

"It is a good thing, to seek service. Perhaps allow yourself a handful more years, time to grow and love a bit. There will always be time to serve your Prince."

"Thank you, sir."

Cutter tapped out the bowl of his pipe into the snow. "Let us replenish your supplies and water your mount before you set out. Come with me. If you meet the Prince, do not speak of your task. It will be my duty breaking that news to him."

The envoy bowed, indicating he would not enter the camp if the Captain did not precede him. With a sigh, Cutter pushed away from the tree he'd been leaning on and trod fresh tracks in the snow. His feet were bare, his breath trailing behind him as they approached the blazing fire.

* * *

The Prince, predictably, was furious. Cutter took his fury in stride, choosing his moments with care.

"I've half a mind not to go at all," he said. Cutter kept silent, knowing there was no point in reminding the brat of the uproar over the debacle two centuries past. He would rant and rave and fuss and in the morning they would ride for the intersect. If the young envoy succeeded in preparing their way, it would stand ready when they arrived.

"I suppose we'll just pick up and go at a moment's notice then, eh, Cutter? Have you ever heard of such a thing?"

"No, it's preposterous, sire. Still…"

"Still still still. You are a cautious minder, aren't you, old friend? And what if I rode east in the morning instead of west? What if I refuse?"

"You know I cannot force you, sire. But it is your duty." The words on the tip of Cutter's tongue—"it is your *only* duty"—remained mercifully unspoken.

The Prince rolled his eyes. "Duty? Of course, that old saw. Tell me, Cutter, what do you think the King knows of duty?"

Cutter stiffened. "I could not say, sire." The mere mention of his King sent paroxysms of pride pulsing through the bodyguard's heart. His King—the mere mention of him was enough to bring Cutter to his knees. That he should serve such a man…

"I thought not." The Prince sighed, gazing back into his tent. Cutter had interrupted him with three women who'd joined their party at the last village. "Interrupted"—it was a kind word, at that. He wondered if the women would join them on the way to the Market, or if the Prince would simply leave them in this wild place to fend for themselves.

"Very well. Make preparations to depart at first light. Select an envoy to ride ahead and warn them of our coming. It's an intersect we'll ride for, isn't it?"

"Yes, your highness."

"Dreadful things. This is poor planning, finding ourselves this far from civilized lands and with a need to travel. I'm disappointed in you, Cutter. Honestly, I thought you knew better after all this time."

The Prince returned to his tent without another word. Cutter stood, silent as the night itself, tamping down his rage like a musketeer packing the barrel of his weapon. Only when the red had left the edges of his vision and he could once again see the hallowed visage of his King clearly in his mind's eye did he uproot his bare feet from the snow and rouse the Prince's servants to begin their preparations.

They would work through the night so all that would need to be done in the morning was break and pack the Prince's tent. The whelp would still complain of the delay but Cutter comforted himself with thoughts of his King and the goodly service he did the man each and every day.

The intersect was ready when they arrived. Cutter felt it calling him all through their second day of travel.

He was gratified to see the young envoy had not spread news of their coming. Spiriting the Prince into town unnoticed was a simple matter. They'd made excellent time, riding hard, swapping horses whenever possible, leaving a trail of exhausted servants the entire way. Those who could would catch up. Those who could not would be forced to make their own way in the world. So it had always been, so far as his charge was concerned.

The Prince announced he would take lunch in his rooms. "Go examine the intersect and see about hiring more servants."

"Yes, sire."

When he was outside and well shod of the brat, Cutter allowed himself a fresh pipe and a moment's peace. The day was balmy; what snow remained on the ground was melting and would be gone before nightfall. He checked their horses in the stable, ordering their saddles removed and stored, and walked an easy, winding path to the intersect's location just beyond town. Cutter found it by following the familiar tug in the back of his head. This close, it would have been harder missing the intersect than finding it.

"Sir! Sir!" Cutter spotted the young envoy a good distance away. He'd exchanged his fine clothes for a more appropriate traveling cloak. His face was streaked with dirt, and for all Cutter could see, he had not slept since they'd first met. As he closed the distance, Cutter noticed the boy was standing barefoot in the snow. His toes burned bright red and were going gray in spots.

"Boy, where are your boots?"

"Away, sir."

"And why is that?"

The young man glanced down at Cutter's feet. He looked surprised to see the fur-lined, heavy boots the bodyguard wore.

"Ah, I see. Let me tell you, if I'd had my boots, I'd have been wearing them. Come, let's get you warmed up."

They found a tree that had been downed in one of the recent winter storms. Cutter laid out his cloak for the young envoy and assisted him in drying his feet. His boots were fine and warm. Examining his feet, Cutter decided any damage he'd suffered from his foolish attempt at heroism would not be permanent.

It was an unlikely circumstance that his posting as the Prince's bodyguard had earned him a certain infamy in many of the lands they traveled. Youths like this one, hardly more than a boy himself, found him standing barefoot out in the snow and sought to emulate the feared Captain Cutter.

"Use your head, boy. You think I chose to go bootless in ankle-deep snow?"

"Of course, sir. Our lands are distant, but we have heard your tales."

"My tales," Cutter said, suppressing his dismay. "If half of them are true I'll eat my own hat. Boy, if you hope to make yourself useful, the first task you must complete is gaining an ounce of common sense."

"Yes sir."

But Cutter could see his entreaties fell on deaf ears. He drew his sword.

"Do you know this blade, boy?"

"Of course, sir, that is—"

Cutter pressed a finger to the young man's lips, silencing him. "Well if you know its name, surely you can tell me how many men it's killed. A blade such as this must drink deeply of the blood of its foes, no?"

"Sir?"

"Now you're thinking. But a drawn blade is no different from a man standing barefoot in the snow. It tells a tale, yes, but perhaps not the tale you expect." Cutter sheathed his sword and threw an arm over the young man's shoulders. "Tell me, do you have a name, boy?"

The young envoy impressed him then; he nodded and said, "Yes, sir" instead of blurting out his name. There might be hope for him yet.

"You're a quick study. I've seen more than a few fall for giving of their names too freely. Now, what may I call you?"

"My mother called me Felwyn, sir. Will that do?"

"Is it your true name?"

"No, sir."

"Then it will do. Hold a minute, that I might do my duty. Then we will return to town and you can tell me of your heroic deeds."

"Sir? I have performed no such deeds."

"Did you not just this day arrive to guard this intersect for your Prince? Did you not, foolishly or otherwise, execute this duty with your bare toes upon the frozen ground?"

Felwyn nodded, lowering his eyes.

"There's heroism enough in that. I imagine if we continue talking we'll discover even more bravery in your heart. The trick is filtering out the foolishness. Really, it's just as brave standing guard with your boots on, and more comfortable, too."

Cutter left the boy sitting on the downed tree and left to inspect the intersect. It was a simple enough thing, a doorway formed from the trunks and branches of two trees growing close together. He laid his hand on the wood, careful not to pass into the space between the sister trees. It was warm to the touch, warm as an oven filled with baking bread. The air shimmered with radiant heat, distorting the rolling field beyond so that it might have been a mirage out on the wide desert. Smiling to himself, Cutter wondered if young Felwyn would go barefoot on the open sands, should he find himself wandering them.

Satisfied, Cutter returned to collect the boy. The walk back to town was short and filled with silence. He desired another pipe, but his grumbling stomach suggested waiting until after a hearty meal.

"Have you eaten, boy?"

"Breakfast, sir. Bread and good cheese. If you're hungry…"

He smiled at the young man's generosity. It would not do to let him pass into the Prince's service. His stout heart and eager nature would be wasted on that petulant brat. Still, there were more options than pressganging him into service as a cook or luggage bearer.

"Do you know, Felwyn, I've never had a squire? Do you think you might be up to tending my horse, shining my boots, that sort of thing?"

"Oh yes, sir!"

"Very well. Here, hold on a moment." Cutter produced a ring from within his coats. It was gold with a green face, and when the hazy daylight caught it, it brightened. He squeezed it in his fist and passed it over to the young man. "Wear that and you may serve me. When you decide you're tired of my grumbling, simply return it and may we part as friends."

"Thank you, sir!" Felwyn dropped to one knee, bowing his head. Cutter realized he was expecting, what, to feel the flat of a blade against his head? Gods above and below.

"Get up, get up. We can't have anyone seeing you like that, take it from me. Bitter experience. I'll tell you about it someday." Cutter's finger found the length of his pipe within his pocket. That smoke might not wait until after lunch. "For your first task, go and secure us a table at the inn. Order well and expansively—you will be graded on your efforts. I'll be along once I've sorted out a small personal matter."

Cutter watched his new squire race off, unable to keep the smile from his face. The Prince would be furious, of course. He'd scream like a child and insist Cutter press the boy into his service. *Once the ring is given it cannot be taken back, only accepted when returned.* The Prince knew this, loath though he might be to admit it. It was possible he might attempt to lure the squire away from his master, if he got it into his head to try.

"Let the royal bastard try it," Cutter said, drawing out his pipe, *packing it, and striking a match on his thumbnail. Let the royal bastard try.*

The fresh mud sucked at their boot heels as they led the Prince to the intersect by the light of the falling moon.

"See?" Cutter said. "Bet you're glad for a good pair of boots now."

"Truly, sir." Felwyn hid his smile beneath a guise of concentration, taking his cue from the bodyguard's hushed tones.

"This mud alone is reason to turn back." Surprising absolutely no one, the Prince had been complaining in a steady stream since being roused from his bed just before midnight. "Really, you'd think there could be some consideration. Mud! This is worse than the horrid snow we rode through to get here. Where is the summery weather? Bad enough to travel at night, worse still to travel by intersect. Cutter, you *know* I hate using the intersects! Why didn't we account for this possibility as we traveled? Would it have been so hard to situate ourselves better than this?"

Cutter's face was a stoic mask as he turned. "My apologies, sire."

"Damn right *your apologies*. Next time we're in the King's lands, please remind me to bring up this whole 'three days' warning' nonsense. I don't know whose idea that was, but I'll have his head, mark my words. Three days? How is that even a reasonable timeframe? It's abuse is what it is, pure and simple. I wouldn't be one bit surprised to learn it's the Market-folk behind it. Waiting for us to be out in the hinterlands before raising the flag. 'Oh, it's time for the Market. Summon the Prince.' Who are they to summon me, I ask you? They'll hang for this, the lot of them. We'll find out who's responsible and stretch their necks like taffy-pudding."

They marched in single file. The trees seemed to have grown denser since their earlier visit, huddling together like old wives whispering gossip. The deeper into the woods they went, the more the Prince's servants needed to clear encroaching branches off the path, and it was not long before the party's pace had slowed to a crawl.

"Cutter, I need more light here," the Prince said. Cutter shone his lantern at the brat's feet, offering a hand to help him over a small obstruction in the road. The Prince swatted him away—then took his hand a moment later. "In the King's lands, intersects are better maintained than this. Guarded, protected, just on the outskirts of town. What woods there may be are fiercely tended, kept from growing into the path. These bumpkins, you'd hardly think they were aware of its presence."

"I expect they're not, highness. It's been some time since the widespread use of intersects was employed for Market travel. These days it's only folk such as ourselves—from the old lands I mean—with the knowing of these places."

The Prince sighed loudly. The sigh was meant to convey several emotions at once; his impatience with this never-ending march; his boredom with the mundane act of walking, especially when they'd left good, fresh horses back in town; his frustration at having to abandon his current plans and kowtow to the damnable Market-folk, who in their arrogance dared command him to do—well—anything; and worst, his sense of general superiority. It was beneath so august a presence as himself to travel at night, through thick, muddy woods, through an intercept which hadn't been used in who knows how long, to preside over a Market in a land which had twice in recent memory attempted to do away with him.

In addition, Cutter suspected the brat was hungover.

The woods grew thicker and thicker until Cutter lost all sense of direction. Only the tug of the intercept, a weight in his chest, kept them on course. He and Felwyn hacked their way through the branches as they strained, their trunks bent almost to breaking, to block the path.

"Sir, I do not understand," Felwyn said. "This path was wide enough to lead a horse through this morning."

"You don't understand. Stop thinking about it and listen. The answer will come on its own, I promise."

They fought their way through the tangle for several more minutes before Cutter heard his squire groan in frustration. "Sir?"

"Annoying, isn't it?"

"Does he know?"

"Oh yes, son. He knows. Sneak a glance when you feel confident he's not looking."

Felwyn ducked his chin and stole a look back as he navigated a particularly insistent branch. Cutter did not need to follow his eyes to see what the youth beheld: the Prince, in all his glory, walking the same path as they, unencumbered by branch or trunk or leaf. The trees withdrew at his approach as if afraid of being immolated by the lightest touch.

"Sir!"

"Now you're learning. Might be hope for you yet, boy."

It wasn't long, once Felwyn understood he only had to clear his own way and not the Prince's too, before they came again to the intersect. It remained unchanged. The two trees stood as before, branches crossing overhead, the air between them wavering like smoky water.

"Your highness," Cutter said, bowing low, indicating Felwyn should do the same.

"Ah, here at last, are we? And before daybreak—call it a miracle."

"Yes, sire."

"And the time?"

"Well past midnight, sire. You may proceed at your leisure."

"Very well." The Prince gathered his cloak behind him and stepped into the space between the trees. There was no flash of light, no thunderclap as the heavens protested the bending of time and space. He simply stepped up, then through, passing from this grove of trees to the faraway land of the humans.

Cutter and Felwyn guided the Prince's servants, those who'd caught up with them and those who'd been recently hired in town, through the intersect. When at last the two stood alone, Cutter stopped his squire with the palm of his hand.

"You can return the ring and turn back. No one would think the least ill of you."

"Sir?"

Cutter chuckled, striking a match and lighting his pipe. "Sorry, figured it was worth giving you a final chance. Some decisions, made in haste, should be allowed to be undone."

"I will stand with you, sir. You have my sword."

"Good to know, son. Let's hope I never need it."

They stepped through the intercept into the Market.

The doorway on the Market side of the intersect was not created by the joining of two trees. It was a great portal, twice as tall as Cutter himself, round in shape and decorated with intricate carvings whose meanings had long been lost to the tides of time. Those carvings had been the topic of much debate; some said they were runes, necessary to the operation of not only the intersect but the Market itself. Others insisted they were decorations. A history, perhaps, of the Market's original founders, a history of the Market itself.

Neither party, however, was willing to risk being wrong. The portal was guarded and maintained. None who passed this way were permitted to linger.

Cutter and Felwyn found only the guardian there to greet them. The Prince and his servants were already out on the street, attracting a crowd.

"Stay in one place long enough, I knew you'd turn up eventually."

"Invite me to visit and I'll turn up quicker," Cutter said. "How are you, Neesa?"

The guardian was several heads taller than Cutter, with skin the blue of a cloudless sky over a calm sea. She had four arms and six legs and carried enough weapons for three warriors. Cutter thought she was very likely the most dangerous thing young

Felwyn had seen in his entire life. Best to throw him right into the deep end, find out if the boy could swim straightaway.

Neesa skittered forward, the sight of her six legs working in tandem always a marvel to Cutter's eyes. He braced himself for an impact that never came as she threw all four arms around him in an exuberant hug.

"How long has it been, you dog?"

"Too long. We keep missing each other, don't we?" She noticed Felwyn standing, frozen, by the portal. "And who's this? One of his royal muckety-muck's toys?"

"My squire," Cutter said, bracing for this impact as well.

"A squire? You? By the Empress, I never thought I'd live to see the day." She disentangled herself from Cutter and offered one of her left hands to Felwyn, then realized her error and exchanged for the correct side. Cutter smiled, reminding himself that Neesa's people, the Shivari, had never quite gotten the hang of handshakes.

"Go on, son, she won't bite."

"No, I reserve biting for special friends only. How do you do?"

Felwyn took her hand. Cutter could see he was fighting to comport himself with dignity. "Ma'am. It is my pleasure."

Neesa howled with laughter. "Did you hear that, old dog? He called me 'ma'am.' It's been a lifetime, it has. Oooh, I like this one. Tell me, young sir, how has this scurrilous dog coerced you into his service? Return his ring and grace me with your presence a while."

Felwyn fumbled for an answer before Cutter stopped him. "She's only joking, son. Neesa is an old friend."

"The oldest," she said.

"She wouldn't dream of stealing you away from me."

"Absolutely not," she said. And then, leaning in close, "Unless you tire of his fastidious ways."

The portal flashed, signifying new arrivals. Cutter pulled Felwyn back and nodded at Neesa. "No glamour? Did you forget where we are?"

"I like to put it off as long as I can. Two legs? Whose bright idea was that?"

"Not mine," Cutter said.

"Your Prince lit out of here like his heels were on fire. Think I heard him on the street, announcing his arrival."

"Gods," Cutter said.

"Better get out there, and muzzle the fool before he attracts the wrong kind of attention."

"Such language from a lady of your breeding!"

She turned her head up. "He's no Prince of mine. My Empress would eat him whole, one gulp and gone. May her glory last a thousand lifetimes."

"A thousand lifetimes," Cutter said. He bowed, and was pleased to see the boy matching him.

The intersect flashed again and three travelers in cheap glamours stepped out onto the platform, looking confused and disoriented and in need of the Shivari's assistance.

"Let us leave you, milady, to your business."

"Sweet talker." She saw one of the newcomers extending a hand to touch the portal's carvings. "Hey, hands off the hardware!"

It was early yet. Only one sun had risen, and that only over the edge of the Market's horizon. Cutter paused to let the boy digest his surroundings.

They'd come out near the center of the Market. He recognized the intersection, though some things had changed since their last visit. The first change he noted was the most pronounced; two more Shivari stood guard outside the arrival center. Each was armed to the teeth and covered in gleaming jet-black armor. The armor was organic, grown rather than worn. A second, tougher skin. From what he knew of Neesa's people, Cutter judged these two were from the soldier caste, bred for ferocity in battle.

"Guards," he said. "Never needed guards before."

The Prince's inn was at the end of the street. Cutter recognized it as the same inn, but modernized somehow: a different cut to its once familiar lines, a different shape to its windows. Also, he realized, it was taller by three stories.

"That woman," Felwyn said, keeping his voice low. "She was blue."

"Aye."

"And her legs. It hurt my eyes watching her move about."

"You get used to it, I assure you. If we see her later, she'll be wearing a glamour to keep from scaring the visiting humans. You probably won't recognize her."

Felwyn nodded and did not comment.

They found the Prince out in front of the inn, holding court for all to see.

"You'd think he'd be more careful," Cutter said.

"Sir?"

"The last time we were here, the humans tried to kill him. He won't talk about it, but even odds say that's the real reason he was so resistant to coming. I suppose he expects it's safe being out like that as it's so early. Humans never get much of an early start, not if they can help it."

"I've heard they're savage creatures, sir. Never met one myself."

Cutter shook his head. "Mostly they're the same as you and I. Come for the pastries, the fancy clothes, the little clockwork wonders that sing your name when you come into the room. People just like anyone else you'll meet. Not bad, not good, just people. Come on, let's gather his highness and get him inside before he attracts too much attention."

The Prince complained when he learned the inn now went to eight stories instead of its previous five. He'd grown accustomed to having the sixth floor to himself and did not fancy tromping up eight flights of stairs to get to his suite of rooms.

When the innkeeper suggested a corner on the first floor as a likely alternative, the Prince sniffed and asked the man if he'd lost his mind. "The first floor? Only ruffians and paupers accept rooms on the first floor."

"Of course, your highness, of course. Forgive me for suggesting it."

"Certainly," the Prince said, the ice in his tone making clear that he had no intention of doing so.

It was Felwyn who stumbled upon the solution, suggesting they install the Prince's rooms above the eighth floor—for the view—but place the entrance in its usual spot on the fifth floor.

"That will be tolerable," the Prince said. He examined the boy as if seeing him for the first time. "Cutter, who is this young man? How long has he been traveling with us?"

"He is my squire, sire. He has only just recently joined our company."

"Your squire?" The Prince seemed disturbed by this development. What use could his bodyguard have for a squire? He'd never needed one before, had he? "Very well. Dreary work, I imagine. Please try to keep him occupied and out of the way."

The Prince installed his suite while Cutter directed the servants and settled their affairs with the innkeeper. There was the matter of payment, which the innkeeper tried to refuse, and which Cutter had to force on the man, insisting that royalty or no, it would not do for them to stay for free.

Cutter showed Felwyn to their rooms, installing the boy in a bedroom he was sure had not been there previously. Once unpacked, they waited for the Prince and then descended as a group to the common room for breakfast.

The Prince took his usual table at the center of the great room. Cutter directed Felwyn to the fireplace, which was stacked with cords of wood but not lit.

"I've always found this spot to have the best view in the house. See the entrance there and the kitchen there? Note the steps down to the cellar and the windows along the far wall. If you pay attention nothing can happen in this room that you will not see coming."

The squire nodded and practiced, under his master's direction, observing the ebb and flow of the room. Travelers entered through the front door, selecting tables and ordering breakfast. Cutter explained how far some of them had likely come. "The first day's crowd is always placid. Tired from long journeys. Still, no reason to let one's guard down."

"Yes, sir," Felwyn said. Cutter noted he'd fallen nicely into the habit of conversing without looking directly at him.

The common room filled up in short order. "I prefer not to dine when the Prince is at his business, as he is now. Food can be a terrible distraction, second only to women and perhaps cards."

"I never had the knack for cards, sir. Nor women, come to that."

"Small towns," Cutter said. "We'll soon cure you of that. But make sure you're the master of your habits and not the other way around."

"Yes sir."

The morning proved uneventful. The Prince remained at his table through the noon bell. The clientele changed to a mixture of travelers and visitors from the human lands. Cutter sized up each person as they entered, paying extra attention to the humans. More than once he directed Felwyn to watch as he cleared a disruptive sort away from the Prince's table. "Words will almost always serve better than force. The trick is to make your words forceful without being threatening. Give a man an excuse not to fight and he'll almost always thank you for it."

As the common room began emptying out, Cutter knew the Prince would soon be looking to venture out into the Market proper. "There are palms to press, cheeks to kiss. Some of it masks our true purpose in coming. Some of it is his duty to our King."

"True purpose, sir?"

"I didn't tell you, did I? Custom demands the Market have a representative of the royal family in attendance whenever it travels. You'll hear different theories as to why this is, but the one I prefer involves royal blood and the great power of the Market itself." He paused as two women, one with long blond hair falling like rain around her face, the other with strands of brown hair trailing in her eyes and a long braid down to the middle of her back, entered through the front door. He pointed them out to Felwyn. "Those two, what do you think?"

"I think my Captain has warned me against women and cards, in that order."

Cutter ignored the joke. "The taller one. She is familiar to me, but I cannot place her. Something about her face. Her eyes."

They watched in silence as the two women walked through the common room. Cutter waited for a sign that they'd come seeking the Prince, but neither of them spared him the slightest glance. They actually seemed to avoid looking in his direction, a feat which Cutter would have said was impossible given the racket the Prince's table was making.

"Wait," he said. A man entered the inn and stood in the doorway, looking over the assembled travelers, appraising the room. Cutter recognized him at once—and though it could not be possible, he knew who the tall woman was, as well.

"Quickly, with me."

He set off across the common room, horrified to watch the Prince spotting the two women and summoning them over. The blond one hung back, letting her friend slide into the suddenly empty chair beside the Prince. The smile on her face filled Cutter's heart with fear; there was not one atom of joy to be found there.

"Hurry. By the gods, hurry."

The Prince pulled the tall woman's chair so that it was touching his, and whispered in her ear. Cutter could only imagine what the daft fool was saying. He was too far away, too far away by half.

She laughed. The tall woman with the long braid laughed. She took the Prince's hand, looked into his eyes, and leaned forward as if to kiss him. Her friend drew back, the false smile vanishing from her face. Cutter was only steps away, but he would never make it in time.

"Sire!"

The Prince looked up as Ellie MacReady dropped a gold necklace over his head. As his eyes met Cutter's, there was a brilliant flash and a snap of collapsing air. The Prince's eyes burned red with hungry fire. His spun-gold hair turned to ash as his flawless skin became brown and scabrous. Only the top of his head could be seen as he sank beneath the edge of the table. And his voice, when he cried out for help, had lost its sonorous lilt and now resembled the wheezing of an ancient bellows over a blacksmith's flame.

"Cutter! Cutter, help me!"

Ellie dove away, scampering for cover before he could catch her. She vanished into the fleeing crowd along with her companion, their escape covered by the terror of people who remembered the last time the Market had come to the human lands.

Fools. What fools we were to come.

The Prince's chair was overturned, spilling him onto the floor. Cutter threw a table aside with no concern for where it might land. He had to find the Prince. His King demanded it. At all costs he must protect the Prince.

Felwyn found him cowering in the kitchen, crouching in the space beneath one of the sinks. The Prince had wrapped himself in a filthy chef's apron and refused to come out for fear of being seen.

"Your highness," Cutter said, kneeling to meet the burning embers of his eyes. "That time is past. Now our paramount concern is ensuring your safety."

"I will not go out. I will not be seen like this."

The inn rocked with a series of thunderclap explosions. Screams sounded from outside. What use was the Prince's vanity when people were dying nearby? His King reminded the bodyguard of his duty; to safeguard not only the boy's safety but the integrity of the throne itself.

"Give me your cloak."

Felwyn removed his cloak and handed it over at once. Together, they were able to fashion a makeshift sling and fasten it to Cutter's chest. In his true form, the Prince could hide within the folds of his bodyguard's cloak. They could make their escape without any more people seeing him this day.

"It will work, your highness, on my honor. But we dare not delay. Do you hear the fighting, the cries of the wounded? They are not so far away now. And this is the first place they will come looking for you."

How much of his charge's bravado was tied up in the glamour his father had cast? How much of his stubbornness was a result of the power he wielded but had never earned? Cutter resolved himself to clout the little pain and force him into the sling. He'd save the damned brat whether he wanted to be saved or not.

"I cannot," the Prince said. "They will see me."

Felwyn laid a hand on Cutter's shoulder. "I hear them coming, sir."

Cutter thought of his King and his course was clear. "Sire," he said, drawing his dagger and flipping it so the butt protruded from his hand. Small as the Prince was, it took the barest of love taps to chase his consciousness away.

"Help me secure him. Hurry."

The Prince weighed no more than a child. Hanging from the gold chain around his neck was a battered stone of purest black. Cutter attempted to remove the necklace, but try as he might, it would not budge. He gave up trying, pulling his own cloak closed over the unconscious Prince. If he was careful, and kept his cloak closed, no one would give them a second look. No one who wasn't already looking for them, that was.

The common room was a shambles. Most of the south wall had fallen in. Flames licked the rubble as if tasting it for flavor, deciding whether to take their supper here or search for better fare. Cutter saw three men moving among the broken tables and unconscious bodies. They were tall, much taller than the humans he'd seen before. They moved mechanically, more clumsily then humans. At first he thought they might be constructs, golems cast not of clay but of living iron. When they spoke, Cutter understood he was seeing men in armor.

But what armor!

Their arms and legs were jointed in the wrong places. Their heads did not match their bodies in proportion. When the light caught the armor's skin it glinted off, shimmering, reminding him of mirages he'd seen out on the open desert. Some kind of primitive glamour? He decided he'd save one of the men and ask him.

"Can you manage the third on your own?"

"Easily," Felwyn said with a confidence Cutter did not recognize. He sounded older somehow. The boy drew his sword and stood ready by his side.

"Very well. Wait until he is focused on me."

Cutter burst into the room at a sprint, head down, sword drawn. The men were moving in an alternating formation, but the one in the middle seemed to have less experience manipulating his armor. He stumbled as Cutter appeared, nearly losing his balance as he overcompensated, bracing himself for the attack.

Cutter swept past the lead man without touching him, confident of the confusion this would create. He took off the second man's leg at the knee with a swift, low arc of his sword, following it with three quick strikes of his dagger. The man was dead before he hit the ground, leaving Cutter to spin in place and attack the lead man even as Felwyn dragged the final attacker down.

"Ooh, look who's got a shiny swooord," the second man said. He was still standing, his leg intact; his armor had not a scratch on it. "Burt, did you bring your swooord?"

"Brought this," the first man said, his features visible through his armor's skin. Cutter froze, all his years of training and hard experience leaving him. How could he fight a foe he could not wound?

"Cutter, get down!"

Felwyn dove at Cutter, tackling his legs and dragging him to the ground an instant before their weapons fired. Cutter heard a faint whistle overhead, buzzing bees hurrying from flower to flower. Thin trails of golden smoke hung in the air, tracing the path of their projectiles. More lines of gold quickly followed, bearing down on him and the Prince where they lay, slicing through chunks of ceiling and furniture as if they were made of nothing more substantial than air. Cutter rolled in place, pushed up to his knees, and bolted for a gaping hole in the south wall. He couldn't see what waited beyond the dust and rubble, but it had to be safer than this.

Felwyn was at his back, shielding Cutter's escape with his own body. They tumbled together out onto the street, slamming into the far wall and rebounding without losing a step. A low buzzing sound drew Cutter's attention back the way they'd come. He saw the three men in their shimmering armor struggling to negotiate the fallen debris. Their difficulty did not prevent them from taking potshots at their fleeing prey.

What was the range of their weapons? What sort of projectiles were they firing? Cutter felt a burning pain in his shoulder, dodged around a corner, and paused to examine the wound. No barb, no arrow, nothing at all. It was only a tight, burning hole, smoldering like damp kindling.

"Sir?"

"Are you hit?"

"Twice, I think. What *is* this, sir? It burns!"

Cutter licked his fingers and dabbed at the wound. The pain flared for a second before beginning to ease. "It's iron, no mistaking it."

Felwyn hissed, his lips curling back in disgust.

The alley dead-ended, opening at its far end onto the high street. Cutter led them out, pausing just before the corner to gain the lay of the land.

The street was packed with combat. Shivari guards poured in from all other regions of the Market with their weapons high, battle cries on their dark lips. Some had taken the time to smear their bodies with rudimentary warpaint. Others had torn away their guards' uniforms and were fighting with bare chests and legs. They fell upon the human soldiers like berserker warriors of old, a raging storm pounding the shoreline, crushing all in its path.

"Out there. Go." Cutter pulled the boy out into the fray. The line of Shivari warriors surged forward and Cutter used them as cover, ducking and dodging to avoid being hit by the humans' weapons. It went against his nature, leaving others to fight while he fled, but it was his King's will. The Prince had to be protected. Above all other considerations, the Prince had to be protected.

The ground shook and Cutter beheld a sight from time out of memory. The giants, visitors to the Market in their man-size glamours, exploded onto the scene of the battle. He counted a dozen at least, towering creatures with craggy fists the size of houses. He yelled for Felwyn and dove out of the way, narrowly missing being squashed under the bare heel of a massive foot. He craned his neck and watched as the giant pulled its leg back and punted a handful of soldiers into the side of a building.

And the giants were only the beginning.

They came in groups and they came alone, all the creatures of the Market. Glamours cast aside, they sang the glorious song of battle. Red-skinned women hurled balls of roiling flame across the battlefield; a legion of fearsome dwarves, armored for battle, charged with their heads down and their axes high; a lithe black cat, big enough to ride, its eyes shot through with green and blue, tore at the humans' armor, its jaws stained with blood and flesh; and more, so much more. Things he had never imagined and things he'd seen so long ago he'd convinced himself they were not real, could not be real. Legends and dreams fighting the invading humans shoulder to shoulder and back to back.

Where the subtlety of the blade had failed him, the brute force of these assembled travelers was winning the day. The humans' armor could withstand his sword's edge, but had no defense against a giant's stomping foot or a bear's bashing paws. They began giving up ground, mere steps at first. Then he saw scattered groups of two and three human soldiers turning tail and running for their lives.

In short order, the street was theirs. The Market's creatures stood over many a corpse, the more bestial taking the time to pick meat and flesh from bones. Cutter was reminded of a bit of advice his father had given him the day he'd left to fight in the first royals' wars; *a fighting man eats when he can, battle or no.*

The giants roared in triumph, shaking their blood-stained fists in celebration. He watched one of them squat down to sit on the remains of a building. Its roof groaned and its remaining windows popped, but the building bore its weight well enough.

A general cheer went up as the last of the humans fled.

"That was too easy," Felwyn said.

"Entirely too easy. Come on, let's get out of here."

Cutter sheathed his sword, indicating for Felwyn to do the same. Their blades were of no use, but perhaps there were arms to be scavenged from the bodies of the fallen.

The boy hefted a great two-handed warhammer in his hands. It looked too large for him to hold, but as Cutter watched, he swung it in a great, controlled arc before him.

"When this is over, son, we're going to have a talk about who you are and where you're from. You're no duke's son."

"As you wish, sir."

Cutter's favored weapon had always been the quick, deadly blade, but the humans' armor resisted it. Blunt weapons—maces, morning stars, flails and the like—they lacked the clever grace of the blade. Still, as a carpenter uses the proper tools for the job, so too the warrior. He selected a spiked one-handed mace and a broad oval shield from the ground, tested their weight, and decided they would prove sufficient to the task at hand: the war which had come to the Market.

* * *

There were only two options: drive the humans out or escape with the Prince. The humans had been bested, but Cutter had no doubt they would return with a fresh bag of tricks. Humans were crafty, devious creatures, and if he'd learned one thing in all his dealings with them, it was that they relented only upon pain of death. There had been entirely too many of them still breathing when the battle ended. They would be back.

"We must make for the portal. It is our only escape."

"You wish to flee, sir?"

"I *must* flee. My King demands I protect his son."

Felwyn pointed with his new warhammer, showing Cutter the impromptu army which had grown around them. Even with the fighting stopped, more travelers had come, their glamours stripped away. "Your King would demand you fight for his Market. Save the Market and you save the Prince as well."

"No. My course is clear."

"Sir, begging your pardon, but your course is hardly clear. Look at this rabble. If the humans return, who will lead them? Who will command them? There is no one here to do it but you, and they would follow the legendary Captain Cutter into the jaws of hell itself."

"I've been twice already, son. I have no desire to return."

"If you do not, they will all be dead before nightfall."

Cutter felt the Prince shift against his chest. Vanity or no, in his current state, the whelp would not survive without his help. If the Prince went through the portal alone, he would likely be killed on sight. It had been too long since the royals had been seen in the many traveled lands. Few there were, if any, who would recognize the King's son in his true form.

"You do not understand. I have no choice. If you would follow me at all then you will follow me now. We must go."

The fight went from the boy's face. "I will follow, sir. But I wish you would reconsider. It is a foolish thing to flee a battle that can be won."

"No battle is ever won."

Cutter turned to leave, the portal building tantalizingly close. He was unsure of how to open the portal, but suspected the Prince might provide some instruction. Could they control where they arrived, drive straight for the shrouded lands and the King? It had been many years since Cutter had stood in his august presence. His heart swelled at the possibility.

A hand gripped his shoulder, halting him where he stood, snapping him back to himself.

"You are the Cutter, no?"

It was a Shivari warrior. Several more stood flanking him. And other creatures, besides.

"You are the Cutter," he said, repeating the words with slow precision. Cutter understood the Shivari was a new arrival, perhaps added only for this venture to the human lands. New travelers always spoke the same way as they became familiar with the Market's trick for melding strange tongues together.

"I don't know who you're talking about. Let us pass, please."

"He is the Cutter," the Shivari said, raising a hand to the assembled creatures, demanding, if not their stillness, then their attention. "You guard the Prince. Where has he gone? Why does he not protect his Market?"

Felwyn injected himself between Cutter and the Shivari. "He said he doesn't know."

Another voice broke the silence. "I know him! That is Cutter, the Prince's bodyguard!"

"You are the Cutter, then."

"If I am?"

"You guard the Prince. You know where he is."

"And if I'm not? If I don't?"

"You do. He must protect us. It is the compact."

Another voice spoke. "He knows where the Prince is! He must protect us from the humans!"

Cutter shot a brief look at Felwyn; *and this is the army you wanted me to lead?*

The boy jumped onto a chunk of stone and shouted for their attention. "People of the Market, travelers, we go in search of the Prince that he might save you this day. Please, let us pass!"

The crowd parted with some reluctance. The Shivari warrior who'd grabbed Cutter's shoulder refused to budge. His eyes burned with accusation, laying the blame for all the fallen at the Prince's feet, and by extension, Cutter's feet as well. "Stories I hear of the Cutter," he said. "All lies. The Cutter fights, not runs." He spat a great bloody gob onto the ground by Cutter's feet and turned away in disgust.

Felwyn hopped down from his stage and caught up with Cutter, who was already a dozen steps up the street and moving fast.

"Do you think that was wise?"

"Sir? It worked, didn't it?"

"And when we do not return? When the humans swarm over them to pick their bones clean, what then?"

249

The boy shrugged. "If that should happen, there will be no one to blame you, sir. And your Prince will be safe."

Cutter stopped. "I do not like lies."

"Then do not tell them, sir. Come, if you mean to flee, now is the time."

But Cutter did not move. Felwyn took several tentative steps, then turned. "Perhaps you are reconsidering?"

"No. My duty is clear."

"Why do you linger, then?"

He could not move. In his bones, Cutter felt the humans regrouping, massing their forces for the next attack. He knew it the way he knew the weight of a blade in his hand.

"They will all be killed. What if our staying could prevent that?"

"What of your duty?"

"My King speaks in my heart. He says son is above all others. He must be protected. That is my duty, but it has never felt so hollow."

"Then stay. Protect the Prince by driving out the humans."

"Is it so simple, then?"

"Of course. We are warriors. For a warrior, the choice is always simple."

Cutter couldn't help but laugh. "Oh, to be young again." He looked back at the travelers tending their wounded, mourning their fallen. Ahead, the white portal called, promising a swift end to this day's trials. Could the Prince guide them to the shrouded lands, to the safety of his King's throne?

"We will go, but we will make truth out of your lie. We will return with an army to split the heavens and let these foul humans weep at the power of my King. Let them know what it is to face his glory!"

He felt his King's approval, his gladness, fill his entire being. This was right. This was the way of things. They would enter the portal and—

"Sir?"

The ground shook. Dust and debris rained down from the ruined shells of buildings on either side of them. The street buckled and split, a jagged crack racing toward them with odd, predatory grace.

"Go! Go!"

The portal building was not far. If they could reach it in time, he could force the Prince out of his hiding and make him work the portal. Could he do it without his glamour? What cruel irony that, in returning to his true form, the Prince might have lost the ability to harness the power of his blood.

The tremors continued, growing in strength. They had only to run to the end of the street, not far at all. But the steady rocking caused them to stumble and fall, and the portal building pulled back, receding into the far distance, its wide doorway distorting into a fool's gaping mouth alight with vicious laughter. A moment later it was gone, along with the glow of the three suns hanging overhead.

Felwyn yanked on Cutter's cloak, pulling him out of the way an instant before an enormous metallic foot, too wide around to grasp, crashed down to flatten him. The peg-shaped foot drove into the street, extending spiny shafts that burrowed in all directions, anchoring itself anew with each step.

"Big," the boy said, staring up.

The beast crouched on all fours, its skin gleaming with the same shifting internal light as the humans' armor. Whatever hands had crafted those weapons were behind this monstrosity as well. Its shell was translucent, but they could see no moving parts inside, only swirling, living light and occasional flashes of a human form somewhere within.

"This is no beast," Cutter said. "It's just another type of armor."

"A bigger type of armor, sir."

"A bigger target. Come on, it's slow. We can get ahead of it."

They dashed out, Cutter in the lead, racing to where the Market's fighters gaped in awed horror. Murmurs of fear ran through the crowd. Cutter called out for attention, stamped his foot, bashed his mace against his shield. Nobody paid him any attention.

The mechanical beasts stopped. A low whine permeated the air as their feet drilled into the street, solidifying their position. Cutter counted a dozen of them surrounding the Market's defenders in a rough semicircle. At each beast's feet massed a horde of armored humans waiting for the order to strike.

Someone cried out that they should hide, run, flee for their lives. Cutter wanted to ask where they thought they could go. He wished he could apologize for his earlier cowardice.

A voice boomed through the air, soft in spite of its terrible volume. It spoke only a single word: "Fire."

As one, the dozen beasts directed cannons mounted on either side of their heads down at the travelers. They discharged their weapons in short, controlled bursts, aimed just shy of the travelers' position. A great amount of rubble and dust flew into the air, but so far as Cutter could tell, not a soul was so much as scratched.

"Cease fire. Hold positions. On my mark. Mark."

He tried to place the voice but could not. It nagged at him, dug into his mind the way these great mechanical beasts dug into the street.

"I will tell you," the voice said. "I do not mind harming you in the least. However, you have something I want. Your Prince and his guardian, my murderer. Give them to me at once and..." The voice's owner chuckled, leaving the connection open for all to hear. "Well, that would be a lie now, wouldn't it? A cliché older than me, really. Very well, give them to me at once and your pain will be *minimized*. Make no mistake, not a one of you is leaving this street alive."

More murmurs of dissent. Someone shouted, "Here he is! We've got him here—push him forward!"

Cutter felt a hand on his back. He braced himself to be shoved out into the ring of still-smoking craters but was instead pulled back. It was the Shivari warrior who'd spat at him. "You Cutter?"

"I am."

"You fight?"

"It's what I'm made for, big boy. You fight?"

"Oh yes." The Shivari clapped his upper right hand to his chest and smiled hungrily.

He turned to Felwyn, who'd overheard the exchange. "Well, he's in at least. What d'you think?"

"He wants us to fight, sir, no question. He doesn't think he can lose."

"We're going to prove him wrong. Here."

Cutter explained his plan. It was simple out of necessity. The Shivari, who did not share many of the Market visitors' aversion to iron, spread the word throughout their ranks. Felwyn made quick business of speaking with the ranged fighters and then collecting the fey among them who would be stuck fighting on the ground.

"I can count down from ten," the voice said, thundering overhead. "Doesn't that seem banal to you? Where are they, your Prince and my killer? Give them to me at once." He paused a moment, as if in thought, before adding, "Once more, for punctuation, fire."

The beasts had adjusted their aim; this time their cannons devoured the buildings behind Cutter's makeshift army. A fresh rain of broken glass, stone and wood showered down over the group.

"Aaaand hold fire. Any further thoughts? Anyone feeling like appealing to my better nature? I'll warn you, this is about the most fun I've had in a century. It would almost be a crime if you gave up without a fight." He sighed. The sound carried all through the Market. Cutter realized the mechanical beasts were acting as amplifiers for his voice. "Very well, take them."

The beasts opened fire as the armored soldiers surged forward. Cutter flew into the air as a giant scooped him up in its hand, away from the first of the humans' attacks. Atop its shoulders he found a dozen Shivari warriors. They'd retired their blades and axes in favor of smashing weapons.

"Hang on," one of the warriors said, a mad smile splitting his face.

The beasts aimed their cannons first at the fighters on the ground, however, it wasn't long before one of them realized what the giants intended to do and they redirected their fire. First they picked targets by proximity, each beast blasting away at the giant trundling directly at it. When that proved ineffective—Cutter realized with great pleasure that their weapons were ineffective against large targets—they concentrated all their fire on a single giant. It took ten or twelve seconds of sustained fire, long enough for the others to reach their targets, but when the smoke cleared nothing was recognizable except one of the giant's hands and a twitching foot.

"Go! Down!"

Cutter led his Shivari warriors off their giant's shoulders and down to the beast's back. The iron skin seared his feet, even through his good boots, but he ignored the pain, and focused all his energy on bashing through the armor to the beast's driver. He felt the Prince quaking against his chest and realized he'd forgotten the whelp was still there.

"You're mad," the Prince said, his voice small and inaudible to all but Cutter.

"Aye. No choice but to fight, sire. Keep your head down, will you?"

They smashed the beast's back again and again, digging a deep furrow into its skin. With every blow they came that much closer to the pilot within. The beast's cannons remained trained on the street. Whether that was by design or by choice, a weakness or a stratagem, Cutter didn't care to consider.

A sudden flare of agony erupted along his arm. Reflex alone made him crouch and raise his shield, ceasing the pain's march but not its smoldering remains. Where had the shots come from? Not the beast's cannons. He spun in time to see a fresh group of armored humans firing on them from the rear of the beast. Either they'd climbed up or they'd been hiding within its body the entire time.

A pair of Shivari shot off after the soldiers, their six legs enabling them to move much faster over the beast's skin than Cutter could. He told himself this was war and he needed to trust his soldiers, so he redirected his attention to widening the break they'd dug through the beast's thick armor. Another blow and the hole was large enough to wedge his mace into. He signaled his warriors to stop lest they strike him. In the moment's pause, the armor's skin glowed white and the wound sealed as if it had never been.

Cutter swore aloud, mind racing. The only hope was to bash and bash their way through the skin, never stopping, never letting up for an instant. He raised his mace and began assaulting it anew. His warriors wasted no time in following his example.

As Cutter fell into a steady rhythm, he spared a look back to see how his guard was doing. What he saw almost made him laugh aloud; the Shivari seemed to have tried fighting the human soldiers. Two lay dead on the beast's back as testimony to this effort. But one of the warriors must have struck upon an idea magnificent in its simplicity. Now, instead of fighting to the death, the Shivari simply used their greater reach and greater strength to push the humans off the beast's back. Cutter feared this might offer undue reinforcements to the fighters below, but he soon saw the soldiers climbing back up, ready for another go. It only took two of the Shivari to manage this cycle while allowing Cutter and his warriors time to dig. Looking out, he saw fighters astride the other beasts following suit.

"Here! We're through!"

They'd broken through the beast's armor to the womb supporting its driver. One of the Shivari, not waiting for his fellows, reached down to pull the human clear and silence the beast. In the time it took him to do this the armor healed itself again; it closed on the warrior's arm like teeth, slicing straight through the blue flesh. The warrior fell back, bleeding copiously. Of the lost arm Cutter could find no trace at all.

He stopped to survey the battlefield. Felwyn was directing the ranged fighters with unerring accuracy. The dwarven battalion held the human soldiers back, turning their axe-heads to the flat sides and bashing whatever fool ventured within their reach. The giants alternated between kicking at the humans on the ground and fighting the mechanical beasts.

His Shivari resumed their attack on the pilot. A flash from the corner of his eye made Cutter duck reflexively; armored soldiers were now scaling the front of the mechanical beast. One of them fired off a shot too early, giving away their attack.

"More from the front! You and you, get rid of them!" Cutter hooked the mace into his belt. "Keep at it," he said to the remaining warriors. "Don't stop, not for anything. I'll deal with the pilot."

He drew his sword and waited.

All around him the clatter of battle, his heart's song grown large. Shivari warriors fighting at the front and rear of the beast, knocking back the humans as quickly as they could climb. The rhythm of the digging warriors' weapons grew faster and faster as the beast's golden armor fought to compensate for their attack. He felt his breathing slow as the old, familiar calm washed over him, slowing time to a standstill.

A warhammer crashed down into the beast's skin, breaking off several shimmering fragments. They blinked away to nothingness once separated from the whole.

A mace smashed down, spiked and mean, missing its brother by a hair.

A morning star was next, its blades jagged like lightning bolts—and Cutter saw a break in the beast's skin, a sliver of a mouth, as if the thing were sneaking a quick breath.

He struck without hesitation or mercy, his blade slotting into the open mouth full to the hilt. A wail of dire agony shook the beast's frame, and with a pop of collapsing air, it was no more.

Cutter and his warriors hung absurdly in midair for a moment before falling. It was a long way to the ground, but they were lucky; a good many humans were waiting to cushion their landing.

His Shivari made short work of the soldiers before Cutter ordered them back onto the attack. "Join your brothers and sisters. Tell them how to bring these horrors down." It was not long before two more of the beasts were destroyed.

The war on the ground was not going as well. Felwyn directed the ranged fighters with unerring skill. Their arrows and hurled projectiles found the human soldiers with deadly accuracy, pushing them back, but only slowing them momentarily, as wounds closed faster than they could be inflicted. Up close, the stream of soldiers seemed inexhaustible, and their own fighters were growing tired. Even if they brought down the nine remaining beasts, they would soon be overwhelmed on the ground.

The giants were fighting away from the beasts' cannons, working to stem the tide of human reinforcements. It was a losing battle. No matter how many they crushed or swatted into the sides of buildings, more came. It was nothing but a numbers game. No matter how valiantly they fought, no matter the tricks they employed, given enough time the humans would flood the Market in soldiers, subsuming them all.

"We are doing well, sire, but we cannot win."

"Then we must flee." Cutter felt a rustling of motion and the Prince's head popped up out of the sling. "Can we make it to the portal?"

"Possibly. What if we organize a retreat, bring them with us?"

The Prince shook his head. "No. The humans will follow. We must spirit away while the battle rages."

"Sire, please do not ask me to. Perhaps we can still—"

"Still fail? Still die? If we cannot win, as you say, we will be taken. You may be lucky enough to die—that madman has a bone to pick with you—but what do you think he will do to me? No, Cutter, we must flee."

Cutter watched as a Shivari warrior fell beneath the combined assault of a dozen humans. Six of the mechanical beasts focused their fire on a giant, reducing it to man-size giblets, slathering the street and nearby buildings with gore. Felwyn directed bolts of lightning and balls of fire at the beasts, rocking them where they stood but doing no real damage. More and more of the armored humans poured onto the high street from every direction.

He could flee. His Prince had ordered it. His King would accept no other action. But a lifetime of battle and war had armored his heart against such an act of cowardice. Felwyn would see him, the Shivari and the dwarves and the others would see him. That they would soon be nothing but meat for the worms did not ease his mind. They would carry their dirge of Cutter's betrayal into the next world, and the winds would sing of his cowardice for eternity.

"No!"

A blaze of pain erupted from his hand. At first Cutter thought he'd been shot. The humans had finally recognized him as their prey and focused all their weapons on him. But his hand was not injured, no smoky trails of gold rose up from the site of his pain. Instead, a nimbus of purest white issued forth from the third finger of his right hand. From the ring he wore, placed there by the King himself, binding him to his service. Waves of destruction surrounded him, devouring a dozen of the armored humans as the pain grew greater and greater. Cutter screamed and fell to his knees, exhausted beyond belief.

The dusky gem shattered down the center.

It fell from his finger and was lost.

The Cutter who rose was not the same man who'd gone to his knees. His eyes were filled with fury and hunger for glorious battle. If this day brought his death, he would have it be such a death as the poets never ceased wagging their cursed tongues over.

"Flee! Flee!" His voice boomed out over the street. "I will not flee! Carry yourself away on your hands and knees if you will not fight, whelp!"

His words were nonsense to all except his squire, but there was no mistaking his actions. He flew into the heart of the battle with a furious snarl and set upon the foul humans, felling three and four of them with every blow of his mighty arm. He knocked aside their paltry attacks, and crushed them like pesky bugs. The Market's travelers swelled behind him as, impossibly, he began forcing the humans back off the high street almost singlehandedly.

The Market's fighters followed as Cutter pursued the fleeing humans. Three more of the mechanical beasts fell as he passed, as if his fury was enough to bring them low. He fought on and on, driving forward, sensing through his boundless rage that the architect of the day's misery could not be far.

He pushed on into the next courtyard, where more of the mechanical beasts waited. And astride the centermost beast, which was taller than the rest, Cutter saw people who could not be there. The Prince's bride, long since gone to die in the land of the humans, and the cook's boy, whom he'd bound to his service so many years ago.

Cutter snarled and fought onward, rallying the Market's forces behind him. Fire and lightning filled the sky, and two more of the beasts crumpled to the ground. Cutter found himself at the base of the large one and hauled himself up, ignoring the burning of iron on his hands and feet and face, ignoring the Prince's wails of protest as the iron burned him as well.

And finally it came to pass that Captain Cutter, hero of a thousand battles, found himself facing the humans' leader. Recognition pierced his mind, calming the fire within but not extinguishing it.

"You? I killed you!"

"Indeed you did," Commander Hart said, a mad smile on his face. "I'm here to return the favor."

Cutter charged at the madman, readying his mace for a killing blow—

—which never came. It flew from his hand with a mind of its own, clattering useless to the ground below.

Very well, the shield. Its edge would suffice, and the man had no armor. Cutter shifted his grip and swung at Hart's throat, intending to sever his head with a single blow. The shield crumpled to dust on his arm.

And the madman laughed to see his hated enemy brought low.

"Here, take a load off, will you, sir?"

Cutter's legs went out from under him. The sling bearing the Prince's weight fell loose as well. There was a burst of light and a wall grew between them, itself then sprouting additional walls until Cutter and the Prince found themselves caged.

"I'm a little disappointed, to be honest," Hart said. "It took you *ages* longer to get to us than I expected. And here I was thinking you were so fearsome, so ferocious. I really had you worked up to proper boogieman status. Shows what that'll get you, doesn't it?"

Cutter roared. The bars were cast from the same iron as the soldiers' armor, but that did not stop him slamming himself against them over and over again. Beside him, in his own cage, the Prince mewled and writhed in pain.

Hart observed the wriggling cloak. "What is this? A pet? I didn't take you for the sentimental sort."

Ellie stepped forward, dressed in black, a green cloak with gold edging hanging from her shoulders. When she touched the surface of the Prince's cage, sparks leapt off as if in a panic. "Allow me to introduce my husband, the Prince. Not much to look at without his glamour, is he?"

"This? This...thing?" Hart's eyes were wild. "I might question your taste in men, dear."

"I would be forced to agree." She knelt by the Prince's cage. His jewel was in her hand. "You! Hated beast! Long years have I served in your bondage. Set me free now or die!"

The Prince hid shaking beneath Felwyn's cloak. He coughed but did not speak.

"Set me free! Set me free!" She banged her bare hands on the Prince's cage again and again. "Damn you to a thousand hells, you will free me!"

Within his cage, the Prince shivered. The sound he made could have been laughter.

Ellie reached through the bars of the cage and seized him by the neck. Her eyes were filled with fire, her teeth bared in an animalistic snarl. "You will give me my freedom!"

The pitiful wretch opened his eyes, searching her face for nearly a minute before answering.

"I do not know you, girl."

She wailed as she dug her fingers into the Prince's shriveled throat, squeezing the life from him. The Prince's feet kicked, the cloak falling free, revealing him for all to see. His body was wasted, nothing but pockmarked skin and rickety bones. His head was too big for the rest of his body, lolling to one side as the strength went from him.

"Now now," Hart said. "More care, please, my dear."

Ellie ignored him. She passed her other hand between the bars, and now she was strangling him with both hands, wrenching him back and forth, the top of his head sizzling against the iron ceiling of his cage.

"Enough," Hart said. He touched Ellie's shoulder and a jolt of blue flame leapt from him to her. She flew back, colliding with the wall of their platform.

In his cage, the Prince wheezed, lungs rattling. Down on all fours, he coughed dryly, a thin bead of bloody saliva falling to fry on his shimmering floor.

Hart knelt down beside the Prince. "Can't blame her, really, *bucko*. Not after what you did. But I'm not through with you yet."

He rose and signaled for the cook's boy and a tall blond woman, standing nearby, to help Ellie up.

"Mind your manners, princess. This show's just getting started."

Ellie shrugged them off. Around her neck, the Prince's gem bubbled with power. "Don't you dare touch me, Commander. Do I need to remind you who you work for?"

"You don't, actually. But I've been thinking we're long past due for a contract negotiation. At the very least, I deserve a hell of a bonus." Hart waved his hand and Ellie was flung backward, over the edge of the platform. He rushed to the rail, perhaps hoping she'd splatter when she hit but he was buffeted back by the beating of tremendous wings as a tremendous, blue dragon swooped down to catch Ellie in the nick of time.

From his cage, Cutter called out to Hart. "You're in for it now, *bucko*."

Hart rolled his eyes and tapped a button on his throat. "Air support," he said, sounding bored. "Ten should do nicely—no, an even dozen."

Twelve of the armored soldiers gathered down on the street. One by one they raised their arms, and as Cutter watched, their armor grew and multiplied until each man was surrounded by the gleaming shape of an enormous, angular bird of prey. They beat their wings and leapt into the air after Ellie and the blue dragon.

The blue dragon held Ellie aloft, climbing high into the sky.

She screamed to be heard above the rushing wind. "You said you couldn't fly!"

"I was out of practice. Couldn't risk hurting you."

They rose higher and higher, into the clouds. At the apex of their flight, the dragon turned so its momentum would hold them in place, hovering with its wings spread. Bolts of golden fire exploded through the sky around them. The dragon turned and dropped, rolling to avoid being hit. It looked back, eyes wide at the flying attackers closing in on them.

"They can fly, too?"

"Some. Where are you taking me?"

"To safety, I hope."

"No! I have to get back to the Prince—he's the only one who can free me!"

Ellie was still trailing globes of white energy behind her. One of the fliers collided with the stream and disintegrated into a cloud of spreading dust.

"I've waited too long! It has to end today!"

The dragon dove, sweeping around a tower, letting the structure take the flier's bolts. It dug in with its claws, and let the fliers zip past them unaware, then brought Ellie up to its level so they could talk in a more civilized fashion.

"Revenge is never the answer, Ellie. Killing the Prince will get you nothing."

"It will free me. You don't know, you can't imagine what it's like."

"No? You freed yourself, didn't you? And what he did to you, it's what his kind does. You could no more blame the lion for stalking the gazelle."

"I'll blame the man who robbed me of my Joshua! Who turned me into a mindless slave for two centuries! Who cursed me to live like a rotted corpse!"

The dragon pulled back and examined her. "You don't look like a rotted corpse. How'd you manage this, by the way?"

"My friend, Bo. She's—well—she's amazing."

A shower of dust fell onto them as the fliers returned.

"They've got terrible aim," the blue dragon said.

It launched off the side of the tower, beating its wings, climbing over the surprised fliers. Before they could react, it tucked its wings in close and sank like a stone through the rushing air.

When it spread them again, arresting their momentum in a terrific *woosh* of air, they were skimming the very rooftops of the Market, passing over the high street and the scene of the battle.

"Take me back, take me back, take me back!"

"Not until you listen to reason. You *cannot* kill the Prince."

"I will force him to free me! I will have my revenge!"

"Ellie—"

The blue dragon's flight was interrupted as if it had slammed into an invisible wall. It flattened suddenly, dropping Ellie. She fell to the street and landed hard. The dragon's wings lost their air and it too fell, mashing a group of armored soldiers who'd been beating back a trio of heavily wounded Shivari warriors. The dragon raised its head, but before it could do more than look around, heavy chains of shimmering light formed on its neck, wings, legs and tail. A muzzle closed over its mouth. The chains pulled taut, pinning the dragon to the ground.

"Ellie," it said, muttering through its teeth. "Don't. Please don't."

She picked herself and dusted herself off. A long cut ran down the side of her head where she'd banged it falling to the ground. The gem at her neck had become a volcano of white lava, spewing forth destructive energy in every direction. It consumed humans and travelers without discrimination.

She stood on the street and screamed at the top of her lungs up to the platform.

"GIVE HIM TO ME!"

The light grew and grew. It reached out with unstoppable fingers, devouring one of Hart's mechanical beasts. Three of the fliers were unlucky enough to be caught in one of the tendrils of light and vanished without a trace. It reached up to the sky, dug down into the street. It swelled over the fleeing soldiers and travelers, feeding on her centuries of rage.

From above, Hart watched the growing destruction with an amused eye. Those around him—Bo, Clay, even Cutter and the Prince—could not tell if he'd gone mad or if he somehow did not comprehend that death was coming for him, coming for them all. He ambled over to the twin cages and lowered himself to where the Prince crouched, still struggling to breathe.

"You did this, you know? All of this."

The Prince frowned. "I do not know her."

"No? Funny, I'd say she knows you." He turned to Bo and Clay. "Refresh my memory, where did Ellie say this charmer picked her up?"

"Oberton," Clay said.

"Right. Ring any bells, your highness?"

The Prince peered through his bars at Cutter, pleading with him for help.

"The Scottish girl, you damned fool. You can't tell me you don't remember. You sent her away with the cook's boy"—he pointed up at Clay—"with him, actually, though I haven't figured that part out yet. Don't play dumb. Let her go or we're all dead. Even you."

"Do as he says, your highness. She's a mite angry, if you ask me."

The Prince closed his eyes, lowering his head in concentration.

"She liked to dance," Cutter said. "Remember?"

The Prince nodded. Of course, the girl who liked dancing. He said a word, a single word, too low for any present to hear.

Down on the street, the spreading flow of whiteness stopped.

Ellie sank to her knees. The fracture running through the center of the Prince's gem shrieked as if in pain. Several links on the heavy gold chain snapped and the gem fell from her neck. When it hit the ground, the gem shattered into dust, and was no more.

Hart grinned. He patted the Prince's cage. "Thanks, little guy. Knew you had it in you. Now..."

He threw himself over the side of the platform and landed deftly next to where Ellie knelt in the dust and debris. He brushed a bit of rubble off his sleeve and regarded her.

"Big lightshow," he said, walking around her in a wide circle.

The high street was deserted. All the fighters and soldiers had either fled or been reduced to dust and ash by Ellie's rage. "Tell you the truth, that's been my biggest fear, all these years. Couldn't die, couldn't kill you, couldn't risk getting the big bad on my case. 'Oh, yes mum' all over the place. What a thing it is, really. But I'll tell you something—you killed my friends."

He kicked her. Hart wore no armor, but his boot was heavy and the kick sent her sprawling across the rubble-strewn ground.

"Maybe you remember, maybe you don't. But you flashed your money and told us your fairy tale and you *knew* we didn't believe you. Knew we wouldn't learn the truth until it was too late."

He pulled her up by her long braid of hair. For a moment he paused, as if unsure of what to do first. There were so many options, so many ways to hurt a person. A flash of green light made up his mind in an instant.

"I suppose some of it's on our heads for taking the job in the first place. Fair enough. Still, there's a world of difference between taking a crazy old lady's money and tricking a guy into getting his friends killed. My friends, Ellie. *My friends!*"

By her hair, he dragged her past the blue dragon where it was bound to the street. Past the portal building, still untouched by battle, right up to the source of the green glow, the entrance to the tower that stretched up into the sky.

"You remember that day? Just another test for you, wasn't it? But not for me. Not for my brother. Your pal up there might have done the deed, but they were only there because of you. I've watched that replay a million times, watched him fight, watched him die. And I can't think of a thing in all the world better than watching you go out the same way."

He hefted her up, one hand still clutching her braid, the other up under her arm, snaking around from her back.

"Upsa daisy, dear."

Hart threw Ellie into the nexus, the heart of the Market. There was a sizzle of burning hair, a short scream that cut off almost before it began, and a distant boom of thunder.

And then nothing at all.

FIRST MARKET

SUMMER, 1726

Three suns overhead. Joshua's fine, strong hand around hers. A day, a magical day like no other. A promise and anticipation and then...what? A fair stranger with lies on his lips and white fire in his eyes. The world turning into a hazy, unreal thing.

Nothing but a dream.

Ellie opened her mouth, gasping for breath. Her ribs ached where Hart had kicked her. It hurt to inhale. It hurt to move. She did anyway, hauling herself up from the dewy grass. First to her hands and knees, then to an agonizing kneeling posture, and finally, after so very long, to her feet again.

"Where?"

She was in a wide meadow. The triple suns of the Market had not yet climbed high in the sky. The great wall of the Market loomed over her like a silent guardian. How many times had she seen it over the years, in how many different guises? In waking and in dreams, there had always been the wall. Surrounding her. Enclosing her. Even in her rage for revenge, it had been there.

Now she could see through it, past it, to the land of her birth. Earth. The human lands. She'd learned many names for it over the centuries, but it still held its oldest, truest identity for her: home.

"I'm home?"

She took a tentative step—and nearly fell. Pain shot through her left ankle as she put weight on it. Broken. Hart. It had happened so fast. The necklace had come off and she hadn't been able to think straight. He must have known, must have anticipated her confusion at being freed. His attacks had come with such swift ferocity, beating her back, never giving her a chance to collect herself and fight back. Smart. Just like a soldier. How long had he been planning this little coup?

A second step and a third. If it was just the ankle, just the ribs, she could have pressed on. Together, they hobbled her. Too much pain to walk, too much pain to draw a decent breath. It was all too much. She wanted to lie down and let it end. She was free. She had what she'd wanted. Whatever vengeance she needed against the Prince was nothing compared to Hart's. Her revenge would have been a mercy by comparison. Removing his glamour with Bo's little trick, exposing his true self for all to see. And she was free. It was over, finally over. She could let the pain take her and rest.

Except…she found she couldn't. Who was this Ellie who refused to fall, who kept walking beyond all reason? Was it the Prince's Ellie? Was it the Ellie who'd gone into exile with Rossi, mooning over the lover who'd cast her aside without a thought?

It wasn't the Ellie who'd built an army to hunt him across the ages; her heart was placid, the fires of her rage quenched at last.

She was free. He would suffer. Pursuing him further was only tying herself to him once again. A different kind of bondage. She would have no more of it.

Ellie stumbled. She nearly fell, catching the branch of a tree and holding herself upright through sheer force of will. The ankle. Something had to be done about it.

"Okay, Bo, let's see some magic."

She leaned back against the tree for support and dug into her pockets. Hart had wanted her, Bo, and Clay to wear combat gear like his soldiers. She'd refused, insisting on simple clothes to blend in with the other travelers. A dark skirt and a dark jacket. A green cloak trimmed with gold the hue of fresh grown wheat. And pockets. Secret pockets wherever she could stash them.

In one pocket she found a ring. It was twin to the ring she already wore, the one that had protected her and those around her from the Market Peace. A handy thing to have when you're marching to war.

Ellie removed the ring from her finger and swapped for one from her pocket. This carried the same protective glamour as the first, but it knew other tricks as well. Bo, sweet Bo, who'd grown her a new body and discovered working with glamours wasn't much different than tinkering with DNA. Once you had the code, well, there wasn't much you couldn't do.

She turned the ring once on her finger and quickly dug her hands into the tree. It occurred to her she might have sat down again, even laid down, but Ellie MacReady would have none of that. She would stand and take her medicine.

It wasn't that her ribs were healing, not exactly. It was that they were *wrong* and the glamour was correcting their wrongness. Bo'd tried to explain the science behind it, but in the end had fallen back on her stock explanation: "It works, trust me."

The pain in her ribs filled out like an inflating balloon. It wasn't pain, not anymore; it was air, the sweet, pure air of the Market flowing into her lungs. An ache in her back dwindled to nothing. The grinding agony in her ankle flashed warm, making her toes tingle. She fought to remain still, convinced moving would jinx the deal—even though Bo had told her it would not—and suddenly the pain had become so small it might never have existed at all.

"Okay, let's see." She stepped away from the tree, convinced she would stagger and fall. Two steps, three, four, ten—she was walking without the barest twinge of discomfort. If anything, she felt better than she had before Hart's attack. Sore feet from walking through the Market, a pinched nerve from tossing and turning all the previous night—they were gone as well.

"Good mojo, Doctor Beauregard. Have to thank you if I ever see you again."

She considered the healing glamour. Could it be harmful to continue wearing it once its work was done? She was embarrassed to admit she'd never thought to ask. *Better safe than sorry, isn't it?* Ellie removed the ring and slid the original onto her finger again.

Noise caught her ears, the sounds of the Market, rising up all around her. Had Hart injured her ears in some way? She realized she hadn't noticed much in the way of noise since opening her eyes to find that familiar trio of suns staring down at her.

Ellie walked in the direction the noise was coming from. It wasn't long before she came to a cobblestone street lined on either side with tinkers and cobblers and dressmakers and all manner of Market vendors. A hundred mouth-watering aromas filled the air. She bought two steaming hot rolls from a cart, scarfing them down not five paces from the vendor himself.

"Hungry?" the man said, grinning.

"Famished. I feel like I haven't eaten in centuries."

"More where that came from, missy, just you ask."

She thanked him and moved on to explore the Market. She realized that in all her visits, she'd never truly taken the time to just look around, apart from her short time with Joshua all those years ago. She wandered from stall to stall, trying on hats and jewelry, sampling piping hot muffins and cider which stung her nose. She played with mechanical animals and tried on a pair of sandals which allowed her to walk without touching the ground. She put on glasses which enabled her to see a great distance. She skimmed through a book which filled itself with words as she read, crafting the story according to her reactions.

More and more and more. She purchased a shoulder bag and began filing it with odds and ends. She was buying gifts, a bracelet for Bo, a jaunty cap for Clay. She saw a silver dagger that reminded her of Hart, which made her sad. She'd thought of him as a friend for so long, it was nigh impossible to see him now as an enemy. The vengeful part of her said to buy the dagger, hold on to it, hope for a chance to bury it in his traitor heart. She ignored that voice, told it to peddle its ill wares elsewhere. Ellie set the dagger back on the table and moved on to the next stall, where a doughy woman was selling scarves long enough to wrap herself in twice over. She moved to feel one knitted in warm, welcoming earth tones, but another woman was faster and got to it first.

"Oh, I'm sorry," the woman said, stepping back. Her voice familiar. "Did you want to look at—Ellie? Where did you go, dear? We thought we'd lost you."

She knew the woman but couldn't place her. Ellie studied her face, her eyes, the smirk at the corner of her mouth. So familiar. Almost like looking into a mirror...

"Mama?"

She spoke without thinking as a sea of distant memories flooded her mind. How could she have failed to recognize her own mama? Had she truly sunk so low, been gone so long that she could lose her mother's face? It was impossible.

"Mama?"

Ellie's mother smiled and wrapped the earth-tone scarf around her neck and shoulders. "What do you think, honey? It's nice, isn't it? And so warm! This will be perfect for winter, don't you think?"

Ellie stood rooted to the ground. Her ribs had healed, but there was no air in her lungs. She drank in the sight of her mother's face, the opal eyes which matched her own, the bun of hair which would fall to the center of her back when loosened, the crinkle which formed above her nose, telling Ellie she was concerned for her baby.

"Are you all right, dear? I've never seen you look at me so—"

The enormity of the moment overcame Ellie. The strength went out of her legs and she crumpled like a puppet with its strings cut. *That's what I am, after all. Nothing holding Ellie MacReady up anymore, is there?*

Strong arms stopped her before she could knock her head on the table's edge. "Joshua," she said, the word escaping her lips in a sigh. She looked up and found instead her father's face. It was more than she could take. Darkness came for Ellie. She went to it without fear.

Mama was stroking her hair. Papa cradled her head. Ellie was tempted, sorely tempted, to trick herself into believing this was life. All the rest, the Market, the Prince, Rossi, Bo and the rest ... it was nothing but a distant dream. Vivid and so cruel, but only a dream. Here she was, reunited with her family. Joshua would appear in a second and that would settle her. She could drift away, back to the life she'd lost. Another form of bondage? What did that matter, so long as it was a cage of her own choosing?

"No. No, I'm sorry, Papa. Let me up, please."

They were sharing a bench. Her head lay in his lap. She sat up, then stood. Her neck was stiff and there were tears drying on her cheeks.

"Ellie, what is it?"

"It's ... it's nothing, Papa." How could she explain? What could she say? *I'm still your little girl, but some things have changed. I'm over six hundred years old, for one thing. We went to the Market today and I was stolen away by a horrible monster. A beautiful prince. He mesmerized me and I left with him and I never thought I'd see you again. Only he got tired of me after a while and sent me away. To die, I think. But a wonderful friend looked out for me and cared for me and now here I am.*

She was imagining saying it all, but she was also saying it out loud. The concern she saw in their faces broke her heart.

"You gave him your name, didn't you?" Mama said.

Ellie was ashamed. "I didn't have a choice. He asked and I just…"

Papa leaned up to kiss her cheek, to kiss away the tears, the way he'd done when she was little. He could barely reach. "Ellie, are you taller?" He looked at her as if seeing her for the first time. "And your clothes… that's not what you were wearing this morning."

"No, Papa."

Mama's eyes grew wide. "It's true, isn't it? Everything?"

Ellie nodded. Her throat was too tight to speak.

"Where is he?" Papa said. "Where's your prince?"

And here was another Ellie to contend with. Seventeen-year-old Ellie, letting her papa negotiate for her dowry. Mama sending her to town on errands. *I've been everywhere*, she wanted to say. *Oh, the things I've seen!*

She stopped him with a hand. "No, Papa. You don't know what he's like. Especially now." Ellie remembered seeing him in his true form, withered and dark, like something sifted from the embers of a dying fire. "Now… now… wait." She froze, her mind racing. "Is today the first day of the Market?"

"Yes," Papa said.

"How long have you been here?"

"Not long. You and Joshua were over there not too long ago." Mama pointed over at a baker's stall Ellie remembered. It was where they'd conspired together before escaping into the Market. Realization knocked the wind from her. She was back, truly back. And she was also here. The earlier Ellie was here, in the Market, right now. She might be walking with Joshua, or picking a table to sit at while he ran his mysterious errand.

"Oh God—I have to go, right now. I'll...just stay here, okay? Don't try to follow me. I'm going to—that is, I'm going to try to ... well, I don't know if it'll work but I've got to—Joshua!"

Ellie broke away in a dead sprint, grateful for her modern boots, which adjusted themselves when they realized she was on the move. Her skirts billowed after her, but she paid them no mind. Let them fly off into the sky, if they must, if only she could get there before it was too late.

She wound her way through the Market with no clear plan in mind. Her only thought was to get there, to get to the little round table where her earlier self was waiting for Joshua. She could stop it all before it ever happened. Drag that other Ellie away, force her up, go after Joshua. If she wasn't sitting there, if the Prince didn't see her as he passed...

The Market is not a place for running. Travelers amble to and fro, sampling the wares of its many vendors, enjoying the feel of three suns' light on their skin. Children play, calling out to their parents to come and see, come and see, when they've found a toy they want or a snack too savory to resist. As she waded through the sea of people, Ellie became convinced she'd lingered too long with her parents.

"There! Oh, please..."

Ellie skidded to a stop in the center of the street. There was the eggplant building on one side. And the open seating area on the other. She picked Ellie and Joshua out of the crowd easily enough. He was saying something to her, smiling like a fool. He turned to leave on his errand.

"No! Stop!"

She ran up to them, waving her hands and calling out. They ignored her; Joshua continued over to the eggplant building as Ellie stood, mooning, watching him go.

"No no no no!"

She pulled on Joshua's sleeve but it might have been made of water. Or air. Her fingers passed through the cloth, unable to secure a grip. He walked farther and farther away, vanishing into the building with a final, eager step.

"You, then. I know I can stop you."

But she couldn't. Her younger self stood a moment in thought before making the fateful decision to find a seat while she waited. Ellie went with her, sliding into the empty chair, slapping her palms down on the table as hard as she could.

"Look at me! You don't know! He's going to be here any moment! You have to leave, run, go, just get away, just go, please go go go go go..."

The serving girl stopped to ask if the other Ellie wanted a drink.

"Ale?" the other Ellie said, a mischievous light in her eyes.

"Aye, and good too. Tempt you?"

She ordered two, and after the serving girl left, Ellie knew she was thinking about her conversation with Papa and how Joshua might have a question for her when he returned. She remembered walking with him the day before, how he'd lugged that ridiculous, heavy bag of flour more than half the distance to her parents' farm just to spend a few minutes with her. Joshua, whom she'd lost so many years ago and might yet be with again, if she could only make this foolish, stupid girl pay attention.

"Joshua," the other Ellie said, her tone reverent, almost a prayer.

Ellie kicked over a chair; it remained stolidly in place. She knocked over the glasses when they arrived, spilling their contents across the table and into the other Ellie's lap.

The drinks did not move. The other Ellie lifted her glass and sipped at its contents, crinkling her nose in delight. It was almost time. She had seconds left, no more than that. He would appear from out of the crowd, spot her sitting alone at her table for two and once the Prince had his hooks in, she'd never get them out.

A hand touched her shoulder. Ellie screamed and spun, expecting to find the Prince. He'd seen her and intended to trap her all over again. Two Ellies for the price of one. Well, this one wouldn't go without a fight.

"Papa?"

He was bent over, hands on his knees, panting for all he was worth. "Followed...too fast..."

She saw Mama coming up the street, holding up the front of her dress to keep it clean. She was too far away to help, too far away to do anything but bear witness to her daughter's fall.

"Papa, that girl over there. Don't ask me any questions—I know what it looks like—I need you to grab her and get her out of here. Quickly!"

She pushed him at the other Ellie. Surely the sight of her Papa come to collect her would shock the girl out of her reverie. All he had to do was turn her around and maybe the Prince would miss her and move on to someone else.

"Ellie?"

"Yes, Papa. I'll explain everything in a second. Please!"

He nodded, thumped his chest twice, and went to the other Ellie.

"Ellie, girl," he said. "Where'd you and your Joshua run off to? You know your Mama warned you to behave like a proper lady today!"

Impossibly, she ignored him. As Ellie watched, her other self sipped again from her glass and stared off into space, daydreaming. It didn't make a lick of sense. If the other Ellie couldn't see her, fine—Bo would have some math to explain how that worked—but she should be able to see her own Papa. He was here with her, part of the day. And he was her Papa, to boot. She should see him. She *had* to see him.

"Ellie!" Papa reached for the other girl's hand. He missed. She'd moved, that's all. Silently, Ellie urged him to try again. Papa walked his hand across the surface of the table and right through the other Ellie's hand.

This time when he spoke to her, he wasn't yelling; he was pleading.

"Ellie! Ellie, please! You've got to listen! Please!"

But it was too late. As her Papa begged her earlier self to see him, to come away with him, Ellie spotted the Prince coming through the crowd. He was perhaps as few as ten paces distant. He hadn't noticed her earlier self yet, but how much longer could it take?

She ran over, intending to tackle him, fishing in her skirts for another of Bo's rings. They'd only made the one disruptor, so she couldn't remove this Prince's glamour, but she still had some tricks. She could put up a fight.

The Prince stopped, and for a handful of drawn-out seconds, Ellie dared hope he'd seen her. Let him blast her to dust if only it kept him away from her younger self. If she could buy her freedom with her own life, rewrite the books so he never took her away with him, she'd pay the price gladly.

"Monster!"

Ellie swung at him with all her might. Half expecting her fist to pass through him, she couldn't have been more surprised when he neatly sidestepped her attack. Had he seen her? He gave no sign of it, apart from dodging her blow. He didn't summon Cutter or eradicate her with a single, searing glance. Just that quick, almost absent dodge and nothing more. Like swatting at a buzzing fly when you're involved in a heady conversation.

She tried again. She punched and kicked, and each time he slid to the left or right, pulled his head back or leaned forward to avoid being hit. He did this without giving the slightest sign of recognition or awareness. He might have been sleepwalking.

Until he spotted her. The younger her. His eyes lit up and a predatory smile crept across his face. "Oh, would you look at that. Her longing. Her expectation. Her *hope*. Cutter, she's perfect; I've found my anchor. Send someone to settle the arrangements. Make sure Madame Vlarta is waiting, would you?"

"Of course, your highness," Cutter said. Ellie watched him dispatch a man with a short wave. In spite of herself, she was fascinated.

The Prince patted the front of his jacket and indicated to Cutter that he and his men should stay clear. "Pardon me a moment, if you would. I need to get married."

Ellie couldn't watch.

She couldn't look away.

She was a statue in human form, unblinking eyes paying witness to her own history come to terrible life. The Prince had his bride, as he always had. The wheel of time continued turning, its momentum bigger and more fearsome than anything she could imagine. It felt to Ellie as if the Market itself was toying with her. Tossing her back to bear witness, taunting her with things she could never change.

"Fine," she said. "Fine, you win." And did he tilt his head just the tiniest bit, as if listening for a sound he wasn't sure was there? She leaned down and spoke right in his ear, catching him just as he stole her other self's glass for himself. "You win. But they're coming for you, you bastard. I'm coming for you. Your number's up and you don't even know it yet."

Ellie moved to leave. She didn't know where she was going but she couldn't bear staying here a moment longer. That was when she heard Joshua calling her name.

"Ellie!"

She thought he'd seen her, but he was shouting for her other self.

"Do something with the boy, would you?" the Prince said, dismissing Joshua with a wave of his hand. The crowd pulled him back, as mesmerized by the Prince as she had been all those years ago. They passed him from hand to hand, dragging him farther and farther away, wanting nothing in all the world but to spare their Prince of the shouting boy's offending presence.

Ellie moved without thinking, pushing through the mass of travelers and Market folk. She knocked one man aside and vaulted over a woman who'd stumbled in the confusion. It was slow going. Any space she cleared was filled almost instantly, the people flowing like water around her. She lost sight of Joshua a dozen times, but she wasn't going to let him get away. It was only as she reached the outer edge of the crowd, where three large, hairy men with teeth jutting up like tusks from their mouths were dragging Joshua away, that she realized she was no longer insubstantial.

She stopped short. Joshua's heels were digging deep furrows in the ground. Behind her, the Prince and her other self were even now making their slow march through the Market. Could she stop him now? Could she catch the Prince before he lifted the necklace over her head, binding her to him? She wished Bo were here to explain what was going on, why she could push these people but not stop herself from going with him. Was it something about him, the same aspect to his glamour which protected him from her? But that didn't make sense. When she'd tried talking to herself, the Prince hadn't arrived yet. The other Ellie didn't have a glamour to keep her away.

I can't affect myself. Maybe I can still help Joshua.

Mama and Papa caught up, breaking through the crowd. Papa caught Ellie's arm just as she was setting off after Joshua.

"Ellie!"

"Not now, Papa—they've got him!"

She took off after them like a shot, racing into a part of the Market she hadn't been to before. Ellie would have said that was impossible after all the time she'd spent here but there was no arguing with the evidence of her own eyes. Unfamiliar storefronts filled the streets on either side. And something else: houses. She saw a cottage with a green roof, smoke escaping through a capped chimney. Was this where the vendors traveling with the Market lived? If so, that explained why she'd never been here before. This was hardly the sort of place the Prince would have deigned to visit.

At the end of the street, the three hairy men had paused to argue about which way they should take their captive. She sped up to catch them, adjusting another of Bo's rings on her finger. It would increase her strength, giving her a chance against three foes who probably knew quite a bit more about fighting than she did. It would also, she reminded herself, protect them all from the Market Peace. These men were under the Prince's spell. She had no desire to see them dead, only to protect her Joshua.

As she reached them, Hart's voice piped up in her mind, urging her to attack swiftly and without mercy. They were the Prince's thralls, true, but no less dangerous for that. If she gave them a chance, they'd gut Joshua and then her for good measure. She gained nothing by giving them the opportunity to strike first.

Ellie slowed and approached, rubbing the phantom pain in her ribs as she went.

"Hold," she said, raising her hands to show they were empty. "That man is mine. I would have him back, if you please."

The two holding Joshua by his arms deferred to the third—their leader, she assumed—to answer.

"This *boy* displeases the Prince. He must be removed."

"Let me remove him. He will never trouble your Prince again."

"No! He honors us with this task. We will gain great prestige in his eyes by disposing of the boy."

"What honor can there be in harming one who is helpless? Give him to me and tell your Prince whatever tale you care to tell."

The third man, the leader, was bigger than the other two. His tusks gleamed with golden decorations etched right into their surface. No man at all, then. He waved his fists at Ellie as he talked, and she realized the glamour he and his men wore to attend the Market was bleeding off. Whether this was purposeful or a side effect of the Prince's influence, she couldn't have cared less.

"If this boy is such a treasure to you, perhaps we'll dispose of you both for the great Prince!"

The other two released their grip on Joshua's arms. The dull thud when he hit the ground was the same sound his sack of flour had made when he dropped it to hold her in his arms yesterday, all those years ago.

They advanced on her together, moving in a coordinated way she recognized at once from watching Hart drill his men. The two on the sides would angle to flank her, but their attack would come from the front.

"Very well," she said, lowering herself into a facsimile of the combat stance she'd seen her soldiers assume countless times. It was enough to give them pause as they seemed to confer, wordlessly, between themselves. *Does this girl perhaps know how to fight?*

Ellie held back a grim laugh. *No, she doesn't. And more's the folly.* How many opportunities had she had over the years to sit in with Hart as he drilled his men? How many chances since Bo had grown her this new body to do more than watch them train?

They continued advancing. She stepped back, letting them think they had her cowed. What she wanted was for them to continue spreading out as they came to her. She shifted to the left, making a small opening—the kind an amateur would make—on her right. She was inviting the leader in, hoping he'd attack before his men were in position.

He did, charging at Ellie with his fist cocked, ready to deliver a crushing blow. She sidestepped it neatly, bringing her right foot up in an almost lazy swipe at his leg as he passed. Augmented by Bo's ring and the glamour, it was enough to bring him to his knees.

"I'm sorry," Ellie said, snatching him by the hair with one hand and flicking his forehead, gentle as a feather, with the other. He flew back, skidding across the ground as if trampled by a raging bull.

She was quick, but not quick enough. The leader was down but the other two fell on her, pinning her to the ground and raining down blow after blow. Ribs that shouldn't have ached screamed in protest. One of them was biting into her shoulder, great tusks tearing through her tender, unprotected flesh.

"No!"

Panic overwhelmed Ellie and she flailed blindly. The biter went sailing through the air to flatten against the side of a nearby house. The one who'd been working on her ribs somehow managed to keep from being thrown clear. Ellie didn't like the way his arm hung dead at his side.

She huffed and puffed, pushing up from the ground. In a deep crouch she removed the glamour of strength, running through her pockets for the healing ring, rushing to find it before she bled out and lost consciousness. There were so many pockets to search through, so many places it could be. Which one was it in? Could she tell it by touch? Her fingers had become dumb, unable to do much more than jab senselessly at things. She felt the pull of the world on her, dragging her down. And blackness, sweet restful blackness. It would be good to rest.

"Ellie?"

Mama's voice brought her back—a short way—from the edge of the abyss. How was Mama here? Now? How could that be? It had been so many years, so many lifetimes since that morning she and Joshua had snuck away in the Market. But Mama had found her out, as she always did. Tricky lady, Ellie's Mama.

"Is this what you need, honey? Here."

Mama slipped the ring over her finger. Ellie was aware of this in the same way a person might be aware of a field mouse hiding, unseen, in the attic. Small footsteps and nothing more. Still, when the wound in her shoulder closed and the protestations of her ribs and back faded to faint, discontented murmurs, Ellie was able to open her eyes once more and see her Mama's face.

"Ellie?"

"Mama…"

"Your Papa and I—Ellie, what's going on?"

"Hold on." She was tired, so tired, but it wasn't safe yet. With Mama's help, Ellie was able to stand. She stretched, pressing at her ribs and the vanished wound on her neck.

"You were in a terrible way, honey. I don't understand—"

"Mama, I'm sorry," Ellie said, cutting her off. "Just give me a minute to clean things up and then I'll explain everything, okay? I promise I'll explain everything."

"Okay?" Mama said. A distant, curious part of Ellie tried to remember if that bit of colloquial slang had come into use yet. What if she'd just created it?

The first thing she did was go to Joshua. He was face down in the mud, but apart from a bruise on the side of his head, appeared unharmed. She slipped Bo's ring from her finger onto his. It was a space of seconds before he opened his eyes to see her leaning over him.

"Ellie?"

"My darling," she said.

"I don't—Ellie, who was that man?"

She frowned. "It's a long story. How do you feel? Can you stand?"

He could. They helped him up and she bade him stand and wait with her parents while she tended to the tusked gentlemen.

Their leader was the least injured but she went to him first. She didn't need Bo's ring to heal him, just a couple hard slaps in his face to bring him to.

"Miss?" he said, eyes glazed.

"Sir. Do you know me, sir?"

"You are... no. You are familiar, though."

"Aye. Can you stand and help me with your men?"

"I can, miss. Thank you."

She helped him up and made him stand by as she healed first the one nearby, whose arm had been nearly torn from his body, and then the other, who'd suffered multiple injuries from Ellie's wild punch and from his violent impact with the wall.

None of them, when back to their old selves, had any recollection either of the Prince or of fighting with Ellie.

"Thank you for your help, miss," the biter said, bowing low in gratitude.

She returned the gesture and warned them their glamours appeared to be slipping.

"Cheap charms is all," the leader said. "Gold don't buy what it used to, miss, an' that's the truth. Time was you could get a glamour to last 'tween Markets, but nowadays..."

Ellie left them to attend to Joshua and her parents, who had waited patiently by as she'd helped the three men back to health.

"Ellie," Mama said, putting a hand on her shoulder. "Please, can you tell us what's going on?"

"Of course, Mama. I think Joshua has something he wants to ask me, though. Don't you, darling?"

He nodded. "I do. Ellie, I... are you taller?"

SIXTH MARKET

SPRING, 2260

Watching was an unbearable torture.

Ellie and her parents hid in the shadows as Hart took the Market. It played out as she'd described, down to the last detail. Cutter's valiant charge, the fall of the giants, the destruction of the mechanical beasts; all of it, exactly as she remembered. When the smoke cleared and the travelers were either caged or killed, she knew the time for watching was almost at an end.

Papa crouched in the darkness. For perhaps the millionth time she corrected herself: *Reynold. Call him Reynold now. Or Rennie, if you can't manage the whole thing.*

"You going to be all right, hon?"

"I'll have to be. Don't worry about me. Just free Joshua and the others."

"All of them?"

"Yes, all of them. Yes, even the Prince—he's harmless now. But Hart, he's mine. My responsibility. My fault. Just clear them all away to safety."

Papa laid a hand on her shoulder but said nothing. Mama, who she was supposed to call *Tara* now, stood with tears in her eyes.

"You sure you're good?"

"Don't worry about me," Ellie said, her face dark.

"I'm not worried, it's just—I don't want you to do anything you'll regret."

"It's nothing to do with that anymore. I just want to set things right."

Mama hugged her, squeezing as hard as she could. "You make me proud, honey."

She vanished after Papa, leaving Ellie alone, curled up in the darkness. A pulsating flash of white light told her the time was almost here. The Prince's wedding gift was overflowing with power. She felt a morbid curiosity to witness her moment of freedom, but couldn't bring herself to look. What did it matter in the end? For her, the necklace was long gone, the Prince's hold forever broken.

She'd been dreading her beating at Hart's hands, but it was over with merciful speed. How many times had she relived that assault over the years? It was quicker and more brutal than she remembered. And in no time at all he was hoisting her into the air, lifting her like a paper doll, and flinging her into the nexus to be consumed.

A tingling sensation crawled over her skin.

At last.

Ellie closed her eyes and slipped the golden collar around her neck. For a moment, nothing happened. Then it seemed as if the entire world *bulged* around her. It was as if a larger Ellie was unfolding from within, the way a flower will open its petals to the sunlight.

She left the darkness, darting from shadow to shadow, rooftop to rooftop. For six hundred years she'd been curious to see what would happen next. Her best guess was he'd seek his revenge on Captain Cutter. Or would he go after the Prince first? She was embarrassed to discover she was excited to finally find out.

"Get him down here," Hart said, speaking to his men high up on the platform without raising his voice. There seemed to be a problem, some sort of malfunction. As Ellie peered out from her hiding spot, Hart's soldiers lifted Cutter's cage up several feet, only to drop it again just as quickly.

"Just kill it," Hart said. "Get him down here. The day's wasting."

Cutter's cage fell away like quickly melting ice. Ellie was a good way off, but she could still make him out quite well. His skin was singed in a hundred places, remnants of the iron nipping at him. His clothes were ragged, held together by threads. He had no weapons in his hands. His hair seemed lighter than she remembered, a little thinner than in her memories. She was on his left side and couldn't see his eyes, but it was safe money he didn't look happy.

"Send him down."

Cutter was beaten and weary, but corralling him was still a chore for the men on the platform. Eventually they managed to work him over the edge. He landed poorly, picking himself up without a moment's hesitation. A short sword was less than five steps away.

"Go on," Hart said, goading his prey. "I won't bite. Not yet. No fun in that."

Cutter dove for the short sword, rolling where he hit and coming up in a tight fighting stance, the sword drawn and ready to strike.

"Oh, bravo. Look at you. What a hero."

Hart wagged a finger at Cutter and the bodyguard's feet left the ground. He rose up several feet and dangled, unsupported, in the air.

Needing to be closer, Ellie made her way to the shade of a balcony directly above the two combatants. They might see her if they looked up, but for the moment each was focused entirely on the other.

Hart drew a long, curved blade from a scabbard on his belt. "Glamours. You people, you're so...uncreative. *Oh, I can make myself look human, how fun!* As if that's all they're good for." He gestured with his hand again, and Cutter shot straight up into the sky, a limp puppeteer's dummy being yanked away by his strings. He was a blur as he passed her hiding spot, but still Ellie suspected the canny old warrior had caught a glimpse. She withdrew from the daylight, cursing herself for a fool.

It was too early to be seen.

Hart toyed with Cutter a while, knocking him into the sides of buildings, jerking him this way and that. He called up after Cutter, "Having fun, Captain? I know I am. This is a long time coming."

Then, without warning, he cut the puppet's strings. Cutter plummeted to the ground, arms flailing for anything to grab hold of. He hit the remains of one roof, but slid off too quickly to snare a handhold, rebounding off a swinging wooden sign and slamming into the ground with a bone-cracking thud.

How Cutter pulled himself to his feet Ellie could not say. That he still held the short sword was nothing short of miraculous.

Unbothered by his foe's survival, Hart strode over, confidence hanging in the air around him like a stink.

"Such a gentleman, aren't you? Too polite to die before I've had my fun. People forget how important manners are these days, don't you agree?"

Hart rushed at him in a sudden, vicious frenzy of movement, his bare hands becoming a pair of gleaming golden blades. Cutter fell back, raising his borrowed weapon in a bid for defense against the deadly assault. He was quick enough—barely—but Hart was too strong. With every block, the bodyguard gave up more and more ground. It was plain to Ellie that fighting Hart this way was a short-term solution only.

Cutter stumbled, lowering his sword for a moment. Spotting his opening, Hart closed the distance, sweeping his blades down in a deadly arc. Ellie froze, sure the fight had just ended.

But Cutter was a canny foe. In stumbling, he'd widened the space between Hart and himself. When Hart moved to fill it, he overextended, leaving his midsection exposed.

"Ha!" Cutter drilled a deadly snap-kick into Hart's belly, knocking the wind from him. The soldier crumpled, giving Cutter the opportunity to follow up with another kick.

Doubling over, Hart groaned and clutched himself. The blades disappeared, leaving only a very ordinary-looking man curled in a ball on the street.

Cutter settled the point of his sword against Hart's throat. "Yield, villain, and I will show mercy."

Hart wheezed out a ragged cough which turned into a deep chuckle. When he looked up at Cutter, the three of them were so perfectly lined up that he might have been looking through the bodyguard and right at Ellie.

"Sure you will," he said. A lunatic grin broke across his face, and Cutter was flung back into a signpost. Hart unfolded himself and stood, unharmed.

"Nice shot there. Right in the breadbasket. You're some kind of tough guy, still going after the day you've had."

Hart waggled his fingers as if striking keys on an invisible keyboard. Panic rose in Ellie's belly as she realized what he was doing.

"Show you something neat, Cap'n. A little trick we cooked up just for you. Kind of a surprise but I think you'll get a kick out of it. You like surprises, don't you?"

A nimbus of shimmering yellow light surrounded Hart's body. As Ellie watched, the light solidified, building layer upon layer over itself, growing tall and broad, with the faintest splash of darkness at the center: Hart's body, driving the enormous suit of armor that had enveloped him.

He stood taller than any of the giants, towering over the Market street. His feet were those of the mechanical beasts, drilling into the ground with every step he took. When he stomped after Cutter, it seemed to Ellie as if the entire Market was trembling in fear.

Ellie leapt out from her cover, slicing through the air, and snatched Cutter out of harm's way a second before Hart could mash him to a bloody pulp. Hot chunks of street rained down on them as Ellie took several loping gallops to escape from the grinding maw at the bottom of each foot. Stabilizers. Sure.

"Hold on!"

She threw herself up at the rounded side of a rose-colored tower. Its face was smooth, but she had no trouble finding a grip.

Carrying Cutter, she could only climb with three legs. So long as Hart was confused, she could be fast enough, but she wanted to be in the air before he realized Cutter had gotten away.

The tower was only a few stories tall. Ellie reached the top with no sign of attack from the ground. She paused just long enough to flip Cutter from one claw to the other before exploding into the air, beating her membranous wings and climbing as quickly as she dared. There was still too much to fear on the ground; armed soldiers, the remaining beasts, and of course Hart himself. Given the choice, she was content to try her luck in the air.

Ellie had always been good at flying.

Hart's voice, amplified by his armor, followed her from below. "Another dragon?"

She caught an updraft, opening her wings to their full span, treasuring even in this chaotic moment the sublime pleasure of being one with the sky. Her scales were a deep ocher, her eyes the same glittering opal they had been when she was human. They never changed, the eyes, regardless of what form one assumed. It was a fact Joshua never let her forget.

"I can try and lose them," she said, shouting back to Cutter. "Buy us some time. I wasn't supposed to come out yet. It's still not safe."

A pair of fiery missiles from the approaching fliers punctuated her point. Hart had wasted no time in setting them upon her. She spared a look back and saw all six of them converging into a flying V formation. Why bother with fancy tactics when it was only one opponent you were chasing down?

She rolled onto her side, letting momentum carry her around another tower, placing it between herself and the fliers. Landing on an exposed terrace, Ellie was able to pause a second and catch her breath. She set Cutter down and flexed the claw that had been holding him.

"Papa said we should make me a harness in case I ended up with a rider. How does the man always know?"

Cutter had no response. He stared up at her in abject wonder.

"Hey, cut it out and focus. We need to buy a few more minutes."

"Your voice," he said. "I know it. How can that be?"

She tapped the golden collar around her neck. "Glamour. But it's a long story. As far as the voice, of course you recognize it. Honestly, I figured you'd know me no matter how I looked." She sat back on her haunches, tail curled around her forelegs like the train of a wedding gown. Her neck was long and graceful, but she looked down so he could see her eyes.

"Ellie?"

"Odd day, isn't it, sir?"

He shook his head. "I just saw you...the nexus, it isn't deadly, is it?"

"Depends on your definition. I suppose it would have been for most anyone else. But we've got more pressing worries. Any thoughts on how we stall these buggers for a few minutes?"

"What happens in a few minutes?"

"Big surprise. Tough to describe, but don't worry, you'll love it. Thoughts?"

"The outer districts? There's a broad meadow to the west which should negate their numerical advantage. If you're as fast as you seem, and if you can keep it up."

"Just you watch me. Um, should I leave you here or are you coming?"

He grinned. "Just you watch me. Lean down, let me see if I can free up your other claw."

Cutter removed his boots. Barefoot, he was able to curl his toes around the edges of Ellie's scales. That, and a length of thick rope, allowed him to create a makeshift harness, securing himself to her back.

"Comfortable?"

"Just go," he said, holding tight to the rope.

She dove off the balcony, tucking her wings in tight, letting gravity provide the acceleration. The wind roared in her ears, but she could still hear Cutter when he shouted from his new vantage point.

"Just in time! Look!"

She glanced back; the fliers had made short work first of the balcony and then the top section of the tower itself. So much wanton destruction.

"Ellie!"

Her wings burst open, arresting their descent, and they shot off to the west after Cutter's meadow. She wasn't sure how the open space would afford her an advantage over the fliers, but she was prepared to take him at his word.

She kept low to the ground, snaking through the Market's thin streets and dark alleyways. Much of what she saw was undamaged. The battle had been confined mainly to the center of the Market: the inn, the high street, and the surrounding shops. It was too narrow for her to fly properly, so Ellie alternated between dashing across low rooftops and touching briefly down on the street. As the shops became more scattered and the buildings lower, she was able to spread her wings and take to the air once more.

"There it is," he said.

Ellie did a wide, lazy pass over the meadow. It was dotted with lush trees and three gently flowing streams. Where the wall of the Market should have been was only a hazy border, like watching the air ripple over an open grill.

"It's there," he said. "Study the ground. Make a note. We're going to use the Market against them."

She nodded her approval, already visualizing aerial maneuvers she might employ to slam the fliers up against the stealthy barrier.

"Before you became the Prince's bodyguard, were you a soldier?"

"I was," he said.

When he didn't say *Why do you ask*, Ellie could only assume he understood the root of her curiosity. Cutter thought like a soldier. He looked at a barrier an opponent might not notice and saw it as a potential weapon. She'd seen plenty of that during her years with Hart, preparing for their final attack on the Prince. She sensed a difference between the two men, however. Hart had always been eager to go to war, almost hungry for it. When Cutter described the different ways he saw to bring the fliers down, all she felt from him was resignation. He would do this because it needed to be done.

"There!"

They appeared from within a copse of trees, a gleaming V of flawless construction, and moved as one, adjusting their flight path to intercept her and her passenger.

"This is my first dogfight," Cutter said. "Though I've been through plenty of sea battles. And I have fought a dragon or two in my day. When they get in range, they should scatter. They'll think it's going to confuse you."

"It's not?"

"No. Because when they scatter, you're going to pick one and fly right at him. You should be able to close the distance in only a few seconds, no?"

She knew the effective range of their weapons. She'd paid for them, after all. "That should work. I'll be exposed the whole time, though."

"Be quick about it, then."

Ellie continued her circuit of the Market, gradually increasing her altitude, noticing that the fliers were holding a steady course. Just before she was in range, they broke their formation, shooting off in every direction at once.

"Now!"

She picked the lowest one and bulleted right for him. The sky filled with gold smoke trails, but none of them came even close to touching her as she closed in on her chosen target. She spread her vast wings at the last moment, almost halting in midair. The flier dipped to avoid her and ended up presenting his belly to her claws. She slashed three times, tearing through the armor's layers. Quick as an eagle plucking a rabbit from the low grass, she tore the pilot right out of his harness.

The flier vanished in a brief flash of golden light.

"They did that before," Cutter said.

"Did what?"

"Vanished when we got to the human inside. I've never seen the like. And their touch burns."

Ellie crushed the pilot's control module and dropped him into the largest of the three streams below.

"It's more of our tech, I'm afraid. Ironlight. Solid light projections—like a very basic glamour—with a hint of iron added on the molecular level. Just enough to be truly unpleasant. In retrospect, not my best idea, but it seemed great when we dreamed it up."

"That explains why their projectiles burn."

"I'm afraid so, Captain."

He yanked his line to the left. Ellie went with it, narrowly avoiding a fresh barrage of golden smoke as it whistled past. She realized Cutter was doing what he could to steer her.

"My butt up here too," he said. Cutter's tone was light, half-joking. Cool as ice while riding a dragon through an aerial fire-fight. The result of too many years at war to count? Ellie felt her enormous dragon's heart thumping away inside her chest, racing to beat the devil, and decided she didn't ever want to feel as relaxed as Cutter clearly did during a life-or-death situation.

The other fliers reformed their V-formation, minus one member. Instead of scattering, now they bore down on her, guns blazing, dogging her at every turn.

Cutter dug his feet in to get her attention. "Head for the barrier. Turn to your right when you're close enough to touch it. Then skirt the edge as close as you can."

She nodded, thrashing her tail as she flew. The Market's outer edge, the hazy barrier, was not far away. She banked hard when she came upon it and held her wings out, letting herself glide right along the borderline. The fliers' shots followed closely behind, singeing her tail more than once.

"Keep going," he said. "You've got it. Just there…ha!"

A crackle of something like lightning shot across the barrier as one of the fliers edged too close, brushing up against it with a wing or one of his rear stabilizers. Ellie heard a surprised scream and then nothing else.

"Four to one. Odds are getting better. Okay, hold on, let's see—can you make for those trees?"

She nodded, changing course immediately. The trees Cutter wanted her to fly at were short, young things, hardly more than saplings. Much too small to provide her any cover. Much too frail for her to tear out of the ground and use as weapons. Still, she trusted his instincts and headed for them, only to be confused when Cutter shouted, "NOW!" a few seconds before they reached the trees. Ellie passed overhead unsure of what it was she was meant to have done.

"What was that?" he said, tugging on her line, guiding her away from a fresh volley of pursuing fire.

"What was what? You didn't tell me anything to do!"

"I thought it was obvious—you were supposed to breathe fire onto the trees. We could have used the smoke to hide. It would have played merry hob with their sensors and such."

"I can't breathe fire."

"You what?"

"I can't," she said.

"Have you tried? What kind of dragon are you?"

"A temporary one, I'm afraid."

Cutter swore. "So you *might* be able to breathe fire, then?"

"I don't know—I've never tried."

She felt him rise from his crouching position on her back. "Maybe this would be a good opportunity, no?"

Fire. How was she supposed to breathe fire? Flying she'd practiced, taking to the sky every chance she had. But fire was different. No one taught you how to do that trick, and it wasn't the sort of thing you worked on in the mirror. What if she succeeded and set the entire meadow ablaze? What if she burned down the entire Market?

Ellie circled around again, dodging and weaving to avoid all but the most glancing of blows. Her wings hissed smoke from the fliers' attacks, reminding her that in this form she was as vulnerable to iron as her passenger.

She picked a likely couple of trees and aimed herself on a course that would bring her directly overhead. She sucked in a great breath and, as she flew overhead, blew it all out in a great, heaving rush.

The trees did not catch fire. She was strong enough to create a good, strong wind, but nothing more.

"Don't talk nice to them—set them on fire! Think *fire! Fire! Fire!*"

Ellie inhaled again, but this time she held it. She picked a tree off in the distance and imagined it bursting into flames. There was a roaring furnace within her breast, and if she could just unleash it she could end this misguided war in a matter of minutes. She visualized fire exploding from her mouth, felt a rumbling in her belly. Zooming low, weaving back and forth to evade the fliers' shots, she dropped and, spreading her wings wide, came to a hovering stop just feet from the tree she'd selected.

"Atta girl," Cutter said, patting her shoulder.

Ellie spat at the tree; a great glob of dark saliva coated it from top to bottom. It curled the hairs inside her nostrils with its terrible, steaming reek. She hung there, beating her wings, hoping the tree might spontaneously combust, until a burning sensation peppered her back. The fliers. She'd remained stationary too long and they were opening up on her.

Their shots stung, but it was the iron insinuating itself into the skin beneath her scales that caused the real pain. Ellie folded her wings in, dropping to the ground as their shots whistled harmlessly overhead. She bounded off into another small grove of trees, crouching with her belly in the grass, hoping to buy a second to collect herself before taking to the air once more.

"Fire? Psh!"

Cutter sounded elated at her failure to breathe fire. She turned to face him.

He patted her shoulder again, digging his feet in. "Okay, I want you to fly straight up, fast as you can. Let them get as close as they can and then I want you to take 'em down, okay?"

"Take them down? How? You saw, didn't you? My 'fire' is just a great black glob of stink. Blech."

"Stink? Ellie, show me the tree."

She searched for it. There was no sign, only a dark, rancid puddle where it had been. It roiled and bubbled, eating away at the ground and surrounding grasses, but did not appear to be spreading beyond where she'd spat.

"Acid, Ellie. I've heard stories, but I've never seen a spitter before. Much worse than fire. Let's go."

She prowled through the trees, tracking the fliers overhead. Her natural coloration made her practically invisible beneath the shadow of the trees. A flier passed directly overhead, close enough that she was tempted to launch up and snatch him right out of the air. For a moment she saw his face through the layers of golden armor and recognized him from training.

It was so long ago, but still oddly prominent in her memories. Their years of preparation and research, plotting the best way to gain control of the Market, the most effective plan for taking the Prince out of action. How she had hungered for her revenge. It had consumed her every waking moment. By necessity, she'd told herself, but was she here today to make these fools pay for her weakness? She'd told herself she was returning to set things right. To save the Market, to even save the Prince. What was the point if she waded through the blood of these soldiers to get there?

"No. Already too many have fallen."

"What?"

"We just need to stall, Cutter. These men don't need to die. Not like that."

"Stall? Ellie, what are we stalling for?"

Before she could answer, blinding light pierced the darkness. One of the fliers had spotted them though the canopy. Ellie reacted without thinking, darting away a heartbeat before tracers of gold smoke tore through the trees that had protected them. She bounded through the shadows, picking up speed, and when she broke out once more into the daylight, her wings were already spread.

They surrounded her, cannons blazing, dogging her no matter which way she flew. Lashing out with her tail, Ellie bashed one of the attackers and knocked him clear out of the sky. Another was near enough for her claws so she raked at him, hoping to drag him from his craft. It would be worth the punishment she was taking if she could narrow the odds so there were only two of them left to fight.

"Ellie, fly!"

She glanced up and saw another dozen of the fliers bearing down on her position. From the east, another dozen, and still more from the north and south. Reinforcements. Hart had let the original six get her measure, and now he was moving in for the kill.

"Fly, dammit!"

She swept her wings in a great swath, clearing the space around her. The fliers were too near the ground for her to dip under them, so she climbed up, out of their killing box. They were converging at her from every direction. Only the space directly overhead was clear.

"Go go go!"

Up, into the sky, higher and higher. The triple suns blazed overhead, spectators in this oldest of games. How could she hope to survive with so many foes coming for her? It felt as if hours had passed since she'd wished her parents luck in their own endeavor, adrenaline drawing time long and thin like the blade of a knife. How long had it actually been? Could they have run into some difficulty of their own?

Cutter yanked hard on his line, dragging her away from a torrent of shots. The new fliers were everywhere, swarming around her in a cloud of golden light.

"You didn't tell me he had more than six of these buggers!"

"He has as many as he wants," Ellie said, ignoring the now-constant burn of their shots against her scales and wings. "It's the armor, it's—it's modular. I just didn't think…"

She couldn't talk any more. It was taking all her concentration to swoop and dive, to roll and twist out of the way of Hart's attackers. There seemed to be no reason or pattern to their tactics. It was a free-for-all. Ellie remembered there had only been a handful of soldiers capable of piloting the fliers with any competence. Those must have been the original six who'd opened the pursuit. He was throwing these new ones at her in a mass, hoping their sheer numbers would bring her down.

Ellie tore off toward the Market wall, changing course at the last second. The barrier erupted with crooked bursts of light as the inexperienced pilots careened into it head-on. If the originals had forgotten to tell the newbies about the Market's barrier, they were doing it now. She would not get away with that trick a third time today.

No matter how she flew, high or low, weaving about or straight as an arrow, they were on her. There were simply too many to evade. She stole a glance back toward the Market proper, but there was a wall of them hovering in place. At least fifty more fliers hanging back, blocking her retreat.

"Any thoughts?"

Cutter grunted in pain. "Just keep doing what you're doing. We'll hold out as long as we can. Stalling, right?"

She collided with a flier, found herself face-to-face with him for a prolonged beat as the two of them turned midair. The soldier inside couldn't have been more than twenty years old. He looked terrified. She seized his wings, swinging him around as they fell, her claws burning. Another flier dipped in too close and she bashed one with the other.

"I can't keep this up forever!"

"Hang in there, you're doing great, Ellie. Just hang in there."

She was too low. The fliers came in close, driving her with their endless stream of golden fire. She dodged as well as she could, but one group forced her into the sightline of another. Her entire body burned as they forced her slowly but surely to the ground.

"Ellie! Ellie! It's Tara, come in!"

"Mama?" she said, still unable to use her mother's first name.

"We're here, honey. It'll be online in another ten seconds or so. What's going on? We saw you run out and grab the captain. Are you hiding somewhere safe?"

She shook her head, fighting through the pain. Ten seconds. What could she do with ten seconds? How high could she fly?

"Hold on," Ellie said, hoping Cutter could hear her over the din of battle. She might have tried to leave him on the ground—what she was about to do would be very unpleasant for her rider—but the fliers would have shredded him in seconds.

"Hold on?"

"Yeah. This is... this is really gonna suck."

She thrust forward, snatching two fliers out of the air and flinging them, end over end back at their compatriots. It was too tight for evasive maneuvers, and they had the equivalent of a twelve-car pileup before her eyes.

A moment later there was a hole where they'd collided. She dove into it, passing through the opening before they could close up around her. The damaged fliers all recovered and followed as she fled up, up into the sky. Their blasters nibbled at her scales, burning through her natural armor, singeing the soft skin beneath. She ignored them, casting away everything but the need to climb, the need to go as high as possible. Cutter guided her by urging her this way or that. She didn't want to think about the shape she'd be in without him watching her pursuers.

She considered pausing a moment to hawk another lungful of acid down at the fliers. How high had they flown together? Would any of them survive if their wings suddenly melted away? With each passing second, flying higher and higher, it seemed less likely to Ellie that she'd be able to hold out long enough for Mama and Papa to save her.

"Bringing you up now, honey. Good luck."

Mama's voice, speaking through the implant at the base of her skull. It wasn't supposed to work with anything so mundane as radio transmissions but they'd found a good frequency. Only for "necessary communications," or so the story went. Hart shouldn't have been able to listen in, time being what it was. And now? Now, Ellie hoped it didn't matter. She hoped beyond anything she had a right to hope for that it didn't matter if he heard them or not.

"I love you guys. Thank you. Ellie out."

Higher and higher. She had them all coming up under her now. A few overzealous fliers were climbing nearly alongside her now. She could see them struggling to keep up, jerking their wings, hoping to get a shot off.

It wasn't going to be easy getting them all to the ground in one piece.

"Captain, I'm sorry," she said, putting on a final burst of speed. "Don't let go."

She closed her eyes and left her body behind. It was the space between moments and she knew she was falling out of the sky; knew it intellectually but not through any physical means. If only she was high enough to get back before they hit.

Command subroutines...power systems flow...okay, let's see here...

Her initial idea, when discussing this plan, had been to kill the power to the soldiers' armor and let the Market travelers rout them. Papa had pointed out that wasn't likely to work, especially if there were as many as she'd described. At least some would likely find handheld weapons from the street, and there were enough of them to overwhelm any small force, dragons or otherwise.

"What then, Papa?"

"You'll never be able to call me 'Rennie,' will you?" He'd sighed. "Can you control them, do you think? Order their armor to just march them out the way they came?"

She hit the fliers first, ordering them to fill into a formation and fly right for the Market gate. External sensors and eye-cams confirmed that her orders were being followed; they'd stopped shooting at her and were flying away.

The ground soldiers were next. She disabled their weapons systems and ordered them to start marching. They'd double-time it right out of the Market.

And finally, the mechanical beasts. She minimized them down to a more manageable size, and had them fall in at the rear of their marching comrades.

Computer time is different from real time. Ellie's perceptions were used to real time, however, and it was dangerous for her and for Cutter, who must be scared witless right now, to remain here any longer than necessary. Still, she spared a processor cycle to scan the system and confirm that every instance of armor running at that moment was pointed toward the Market gate. Then she pulled herself together and logged out, mentally crossing her fingers that there would be a body for her to return to.

Cutter was screaming and pounding the scales on her back with his right hand, holding on for dear life with his left. Confined back in her body, it took Ellie a couple of seconds to remember where everything was. Claws, tail, head, legs. And wings. Oh yes, can't forget about the wings.

She spread them wide, letting them fill with air perhaps as little as fifteen feet from the ground. A gust of wind nudged her with its breath. She let it take her and savored the momentary pleasure of gliding along without a care in the world.

"Ellie! Ellie!"

"It's okay, Captain, I'm here." She banked softly, hoping for a view of the fliers as they vacated the meadow. It was a glorious sight to behold; there must have been a hundred of them flying in four orderly lines. From above they looked like worker ants returning to the anthill.

Cutter collapsed against her back. She selected a likely spot and let herself drift to a gentle, lazy landing.

"Can you get down on your own?"

"Kicking me off?"

She nodded at the fliers. "Fight's over. We won. Thought you might like to stand on your own two feet, stretch your legs."

He removed his feet from between her scales one at a time. Then he leapt down, making a show of kneeling and kissing the ground. He brushed off, retrieving his boots from where he'd tied them to his back. They were scorched in a hundred places but otherwise quite wearable.

"Want to tell me what just happened?"

Ellie examined herself as she explained. "The ironlight tech is powered remotely. The system lets you do some interesting things if you're the system admin."

"And you are?"

She raised the dragon equivalent of an eyebrow. "I wouldn't

have guessed you'd know much about modern human technology."

"I don't. But I've been around enough different kinds of magic that I can fake my way through just about anything. I assume a 'system admin' is the person running the show, no?"

"Sort of. There actually isn't an admin, not in Hart's system. But he's using my old system, where I used to live back when . . . well, before I solved certain problems with my situation. He had it closed off against outside intruders, so we had to connect a hard-line before I could take it over."

"I see." He jerked a thumb in the direction the fliers had gone. "And where are they going?"

"Out. They'll circle until we catch up. I told you, they're soldiers just following orders. *My* orders mainly."

"And the rest?"

"Going with them only on foot. They won't be any trouble." She saw disbelief on his face. "Trust me, Captain. It's all over. They can't lift a finger without my say-so, and the only thing I'm going to let them do is leave. The Market's been through enough today, don't you think?"

"What about their leader?"

"Hart?" She frowned. "I shut down everything there was to shut down. He should be walking home with the rest of them. Hold on, I'll check." She activated her mic and asked Mama what was going on back at the center of the Market.

"We're working with your friends to free everyone from these cages," Mama said, sounding frustrated.

"How's Joshua?"

"Uncomfortable. He says he's ticked at you."

"Any sign of Hart?"

"The commander? No, he left with the rest of the soldiers. Why? Is everything all right?"

"Just Cutter being paranoid. We'll be back soon, Mama."

"Tara."

"Right, sure. See you in a few." She met Cutter's attentive gaze. "She says we're all clear. They're just wrestling with the cages. We should get back. They could probably use my help."

They returned to the center of the Market in relative silence. Cutter had questions, but Ellie was in such tremendous pain, her scales leaking golden smoke in at least a dozen places, that she didn't have the strength for more than terse, single-word responses.

"Please," she said at last. "Let's get back and make sure everyone's safe. I'll answer all your questions then."

She could have removed the glamour, and with it a dragon's natural vulnerability to iron. Her wounds might not have vanished, but at least they wouldn't burn any longer. What a relief that would be.

But flying was quicker, even with the pain. So long as her wings could catch air, she decided to let it do the lion's share of the work. Walking from the distant meadow would have taken forever, and bad as the pain in her back was, she suspected her legs bore more than their fair share of damage from the battle. Best to get the unpleasantness over with as quickly as possible.

There was still so much to do. Freeing the travelers was the first order of business. Moreso than anyone, they were the innocent victims in this whole mess. What was their crime, apart from trying to defend their home from the invading humans? She owed each of them the deepest of apologies. That she'd ultimately saved them did not excuse her having put them in harm's way in the first place.

And then there was Hart and his soldiers, marching for home. She'd ordered them away from the Market, but beyond the gate she'd need to deal with seeing them all safely home. Dismantling their armor once they were away from the Market required but the press of a button. Sending them back to the lives they'd left behind to fight her personal war, that was an entirely different matter.

Most daunting of all, she found, was the prospect of her own freedom. The Prince's necklace had been shattered long ago, but it was only now, as she was able to step back into her life, that she felt its weight had truly been lifted. How many times since passing through the nexus had she found herself unable to act, unable to be seen or heard? Bo could explain the peculiarities of time travel to her, but there was one thing Ellie felt in her heart to be true: she was, at long, long last, her own woman.

She leaned back to speak to Cutter. "Do you have a home, Captain?"

"A home? Once, long ago. Why do you ask?"

"I saw you during the battle. You are no longer bound into the Prince's service."

Cutter sneered. "I never served that brat. It was the King into whose service I entered."

"Oh," she said, abashed. "I had no idea."

"How could you?" He dug into a pocket and removed the ring the King had presented to him, long ago. Its body was shot through with cracks. Of the gem once mounted on its face, there was no sign apart from four scorch marks where it had been held in place.

"Did you enter into his service willingly?"

"He was my King. I thought that meant I owed my life and service to him. Part of me, as I imagine you might understand, still does." When she did not answer, he continued. "I bent my knee to him in the name of war. My bodyguarding duties came later. In retrospect, I suspect it was a way for him to extend my service without facing undue criticism."

"Critics of the King? I think I would like to meet them."

Cutter laughed. It was a sad sound, filled with regret. "They would bore you, I believe. But who could argue with the King tasking his most decorated captain with the care and protection of the Wayward Prince?"

She cocked an ear at the word. "Wayward?"

"It's a long story, and much meaning would be lost without a proper telling, but suffice it to say your...the Prince has not been welcome home for quite some time. Honestly, I'm not sure what's to be done with him after the removal of his glamour. That is what your trick did, no? It's gone for good, isn't it?"

"It is."

"Ah, pity. He'll have to be returned home to obtain a new one. That won't please his brothers one whit, I can tell you."

In spite of herself, she said, "Brothers?"

The surprise on Cutter's face was genuine. "No? He never said?"

"He never said much at all, and don't pretend you don't know that. Your brat was never so interested in anything as much as the sound of his own voice. For all that, of course, the majority of his blather was self-serving garbage. Did he ever mention brothers? Cutter, he never mentioned anything to me apart from how handsome he looked and how pleased I must be to be seen with him. The kid's a real charmer."

She beat her wings several times, increasing their altitude, banking wide around a tower they had no chance at all of hitting. Was she angry with Cutter? How many times had he been accomplice to the Prince as he seduced and stole innocent girls as his brides? How deep had his loyalty to his King gone? How much responsibility for what had happened to her could she lay at his feet?

"A person could go crazy," she said at last. "Portioning out blame. The Prince seduces me and you stand by while he does it. Rossi too—funny how I never think of the time he spent in the Prince's service, only about when he looked after me. If Hart did all this damage today, am I not to blame? I brought him into this mess all those years ago. And when he died, did I let him rest or did I keep bringing him back and bringing him back? He was the assassin all those years ago, so in a way, he's the one who started all this. Would the Prince have sent me away to dispose of his weapons and armor, or would he have held on to me for another century or two? Where does the guilt start and where does it end? Cutter, it's just too much. I can't blame everyone."

They were turning broad, lazy circles over the center of the Market. How long ago had they arrived?

"Ellie?"

"I know, I know. I'll sleep it off and I'll feel—"

"No! Ellie, turn! Turn!"

The blast caught her completely by surprise. She was hit dead center in her underbelly, where her scales were thinnest. It was unlike anything she'd felt before either as human or dragon. There was iron in the blast, but it was more than that. So much worse than mere iron. Past the heat was a cold so severe it seemed she must have been frozen solid. She would topple out of the sky and shatter when she hit the ground. Her remains would be nothing but shards of ice scattered across the streets and rooftops of the Market.

"Ellie!"

Cutter rolled from her back. The loss of him snapped her back to herself. Could she still move? Yes. Then she had to try and save him. Whatever had hit her, she would deal with it once he was safely on the ground.

"Captain!"

Another blast, but this one she saw coming. It moved slowly, like a tight wave rolling up onto a narrow shore. She had plenty of time to swing around it, to dive and catch up with Cutter. Only her wings protested. Her tail was caught by the blast and reduced to dead weight. The loss of her tail affected her maneuverability in a terrible way. Even if she managed to catch him, she'd never be able to pull out of her dive in time.

It didn't matter. She'd find a way to save him if only she could catch up. She drew herself long and thin, a javelin hurtling through the air. Her wings tucked themselves in at her sides, peeking up only the slightest bit, using the rushing air to propel her faster, faster.

He was right below her, close enough to grab, but she forced herself to wait until she drew alongside. Then she snatched him out of the sky and cradled him to her chest. If she couldn't pull up, at least she could protect him from the impact.

"Ellie, no!"

She popped her wings and braced herself. Whether they hit or not, it was going to be a violent stop. Her limp, heavy tail was an anchor dragging her down. She ignored it, focusing on holding her screaming wings out. It wasn't enough. They were going too fast. There was nothing she could do to—

Ellie gasped aloud as she felt a familiar pair of arms wrapping around her body. Great, wide wings added their power to her own, slowing her descent, guiding her into a controlled spiral that ended with them tumbling free onto the rubble-strewn street.

"Ellie!"

She'd known him from the first touch. Even like this, there was no mistaking him for anyone else in creation.

"Joshua!"

The great blue dragon, who'd be making fun of her forever for not recognizing him in New York, knelt over her amid turned-up chunks of street, shattered glass, and the bodies of the fallen.

"Are you all right? I was watching you circling but then—"

"I'm fine. I'm fine *now*. Nice catch, hon. That was one in a million."

She pushed up to her feet, shaking off the dust and debris.

"Did anyone see who was shooting at us?"

"I was too busy catching you before you splatted on the street."

"I only saw the blast coming for us," Cutter said.

Ellie swore. "It has to be Hart. There's no one else. Some weapon he had saved up that I missed. Dammit!"

Cutter seized her claw. "We'll worry about him in a minute. Let's get under cover before he gets a bead on us, shall we?"

"No." She rose to her full height. If she was in pain, if she'd been injured, it was impossible to see it in that moment. "It's enough already. No more blood on my hands. Joshua?"

"Right behind you, love."

"Cutter?"

He was bent over. "Let me just get my boots off."

Ellie couldn't help smiling at the puzzled expression on Joshua's face. He was bigger than her, his scales gleaming under the Market's three suns. When Cutter climbed up onto her back, slinging his line around her neck, the understanding that dawned on Joshua was beyond priceless.

"He's been riding you?"

"Jealous? I'd have died more than once without his help."

"Then I am jealous. Captain, any suggestions?"

"Yes," Cutter said, a devilish grin on his face. "Learn to breathe fire. Quickly."

When Ellie was a girl, years before the Market came to her village of Oberton, her Papa brought her along to the city to make a delivery of goods. She rode next to him on their cart, pestering him the entire way to let her hold the reins and drive. As their horse was well-trained and the road well-maintained, he acquiesced to her wishes—probably more than her Mama would have liked.

It was only two days' journey from their farm, but to Ellie it seemed an unfathomable distance. Would they stay overnight in the city? Where would they stay? What would they eat? Could she bring home a present for Mama, perhaps a new dress or a hat to replace the one she'd lost the past winter during a wild snowstorm?

No matter what she asked, Papa's answer was always the same: "We'll see when we get there, Ellie-dear." And by the close of their second day, as the city grew closer and closer, she had so many things she was looking forward to that the girl who'd one day grow up to marry a prince couldn't decide what she was most excited about. The city was all her dreams come true, everything she'd ever wanted plus a host of things she'd never dreamed might exist—but which she was confident she'd want as well.

And when they rolled through the city gates and Ellie saw the reality of it? That the buildings were taller than those of Oberton but still made from stone and wood? That the bread smelled like bread, and tasted like bread, no matter where it had been baked? That the bed she slept in that night was hard and lumpy and no match for her own back home? Was she disappointed?

Not in the least. Because the city she found was so much more than the city she'd imagined. It was filled with energy and a life that took her breath away. If they'd stayed a month she wouldn't have felt she'd seen everything. A year might not have been enough, and when they rode for home the next morning, Papa's business done, she spent the entire ride carrying on about what she'd seen. When could they go back again? Would the city change much between now and then? Could Mama come next time?

It was late on the second day, still a ways to go before they arrived, when Papa asked Ellie to hold her tongue a moment.

"Let me tell you," he said, his voice serious but filled with an unfamiliar wonder. "Let me tell you, Ellie-dear, about the Market which comes once in a century and then only for three days…"

She was hearing Papa's words again as they made their slow way through the wreckage of the high street. Joshua by her side, Cutter astride her back—somehow it felt like coming full circle. Papa had promised her a place of wonders, but she'd turned it into a battleground.

"Anthony! Anthony, come out! It's all over!"

"You really think he'll, what, surrender?" Cutter said into her ear.

She shook her head. "No, but I have to give him the chance, don't I?"

The street was still rotten with debris, but Ellie was pleased to see the golden cages had all been dismissed. Where had the travelers gone? Were they hiding from the fearsome dragons? No, she decided. There was something worse here than dragons to hide from.

"Anthony! Please come out!"

Next to her, Joshua cleared his throat and snarfed a fist-size ball of fire from one of his nostrils.

"Better, boy," Cutter said.

"Id burnth," Joshua said, hacking dark smoke onto the street.

"Not as much as on the receiving end. Keep working on it."

The silence was becoming oppressively loud. The street was so wide that she and Joshua could have spread their wings side by side with room to spare. It should have been teeming with people. She felt her blood run cold, thumping in her veins. If Hart was going to attack, it would happen at any moment.

"Be ready to fly," she said, nudging Joshua. He nodded, eyes comically large as he strained to turn his inner heat into real flame.

Cutter patted her shoulder. *Patience*, the touch said. *Let it happen when it will.*

The street rumbled beneath their feet. Ellie heard a sound like the sky itself splitting open and a stone as big as her head crashed to the ground, shattering into a thousand pieces.

"Fly! Fly!"

She leapt into the sky, a split-second behind Joshua, as a four-story building to their left collapsed onto the spot they'd been standing in. It toppled not as a solid building but as a shower of stone and wood, brick and glass. An eruption of dust followed the collapse, and Ellie fought to stay ahead of it as it grew and spread, covering all the high street in a shapeless gray cloud.

"Damn, almost got you!" Hart's voice reverberated through the sky. It was impossible to tell where he was speaking from. "The old-fashioned way, then."

A blast of energy shot from within the cloud, closing in on Ellie with a lazy sort of certainty. She dodged it, flying directly into a pair of smaller, faster moving blasts. One hit her leg and it exploded in a burst of pain. The second caught her right wing, tearing a tight hole in the membrane. She cried out in pain, struggling not to fall out of the sky.

Joshua flew up in front of her, placing himself in Hart's line of fire. "He's shooting from within the cloud!"

"Genius your man is," Cutter said, growling, leaning up as far as he dared to peer over Ellie's shoulder. "Wait…okay…there!"

She felt him tugging on her line, pulling her off to the left. She followed his direction, hoping Joshua would follow their lead as another slow blast came at them from within the dust cloud. Again, several smaller shots followed in quick succession; she had no problem evading these blasts with Cutter's help.

"Do you see?" he said.

"I think so. What're you thinking?"

"Let's draw him out."

"No."

"No?"

"No—I'm going in. Coming?"

She couldn't see it, but Ellie had no trouble imagining the hungry smile on Cutter's face.

"Hell, yes," he said. "It's about time we went on the offensive."

Ellie beat her wings to increase her altitude. She called over to Joshua. "Wait here. We'll flush him out."

Then she lowered her head and dove straight into the dust cloud after Hart. She expected to find herself fighting through the shroud of darkness cast by the cloud, but her dragon's eyes were well-suited to the poor visibility. She couldn't see fine details—if she had to read a road-sign to find him she would have been out of luck—but shapes stood out clearly through the dusky haze.

She glided down through the dust, past a pair of good-size buildings. Ellie opened her wings, slowing her descent, trying to place her location within the Market from memory. She knew the landscape well enough but one of the buildings didn't seem to belong. It was tall and broad, but otherwise had no distinguishing characteristics.

The building moved.

She rolled away just in time to evade Hart's blast. It was one of the big ones and would have grounded her with even a glancing blow. He followed it with a fresh volley from his smaller cannons, crisscrossing the air right in front of her nose with a steady stream of projectiles.

"Cutter! He's right here!"

"Hit him, then!"

She slashed out with her claws, raking the face of the building. The searing pain that found her a moment later was exquisite in its depth. It felt to Ellie as if the ends were melting off from her claws. She recoiled, narrowly avoiding another barrage of shots from Hart's smaller cannons.

"His armor! I can't touch him!"

"Then don't!"

Realization was swift, action swifter. She let herself drop to avoid the next, inevitable discharge from his cannons. A sweep of her wings and a flick of her tail brought her up and around, circling past where Hart stood in his tremendous suit of armor. It had been anthropomorphic earlier, with a head, arms, legs, and a torso. She didn't know if that was still the case or if he was as she saw him: a building-size block piled high with cannons and blasters. Either way, she reasoned if Hart was in there some-where, he'd be roughly at the armor's center of mass.

She reached to the burning at her core and hawked a giant lungful of acid down onto Hart's armor.

The dark, stinking smoke instantly began cutting through the cloud of dust. Ellie pulled back, confident it would be several seconds at least before Hart fired again. An idea struck her and she acted without consulting Cutter, beating her wings as fast and hard as she could while holding her position steady.

The dust cloud began dispersing.

"Again! Hit him again!"

She wasn't able to muster as much acid this time but what she brought up proved more than sufficient. Hart wailed and for a moment Ellie thought her acid had gotten to him, boiling him in-side his own armor. She paused and peered into the haze for some sign of him. If it wasn't too late to help, she was ready to go in.

A giant, spiked fist swung out at her from within the dark-ness. She avoided the bulk of it but caught a glancing blow as she dodged out of the way, afraid he would follow up with another of his great, paralyzing blasts.

She lost control. Her wings went limp and she began falling, twisting as she fell, struggling to catch some air. She ended up knocking into the side of a building and rolling several times when she hit the ground.

"Was that a fist?" Cutter said.

"I think we've got his attention, at any rate. Ready for more?"

He dug his feet in, bettering his position. She could feel him strengthening his grip on the line around her neck. "Let's take him apart."

She ran a few steps and launched back into the air, separating the dust cloud before her. Hart's armor was almost in full view now. It had the same basic shape of the thing she'd swooped in and saved Cutter from but it was bigger now. In a funny way it resembled a Shivari warrior with its long body, multiple legs, and the innumerable cannons mounted on its shoulders, torso, and limbs.

"Time to go."

She climbed away, thinking she could put some distance between herself and Hart and avoid his ranged weapons. The air filled with buzzing golden projectiles. She wove and ducked away from the worst of it, suffering several hits on her back, chest, and tail.

Joshua was hanging above her position, hovering in place. As they passed him, Ellie heard Cutter shouting, "Let's see some fire, kid!"

As she turned, unable to look away, Joshua roared a holocaust of flame down onto Hart in his monstrous armor. It absorbed the damage, but dragon's fire would continue burning a long time on the iron-imbued light.

Cutter slapped Ellie's back in celebration. "Did you see that? Your fella's a natural!"

She didn't respond. Instead, Ellie dipped low and spat a fresh gout of acid across Hart's chest. His armor sizzled and cracked in a dozen places. The acid, coupled with Joshua's fire, had to be making life quite uncomfortable for Commander Hart.

Unless it wasn't, of course. She'd boned up to refresh her memory, but most of the tech was beyond her understanding. Ellie was a natural with computers. Remembering how the air-conditioning system inside a soldier's armor worked, especially when the soldier swapped out his armor for a better kit, was a different matter entirely.

She hovered in place, watching Hart stumble as his armor melted around him. "I see him! Look, there!"

At the center of the golden machine was a dark blur that had to be Hart. She swooped in low, too close for any of his cannons but not for his arms, and tore at the armor's skin right where the dark spot was. It was agony, but it was working…until the wounds she'd inflicted sealed up again while she paused to adjust her position.

"I can't do enough damage!"

"I've got an idea," Cutter said. She dropped low to avoid another blow from Hart as Cutter described what he had in mind.

"Oh, I love it. Hold on."

She waved for Joshua, who had continued his fiery assault while she and Cutter went in close. Ellie realized she didn't feel the heat from his flames and hoped the same would hold true for her acid's effect on him.

"Come down!"

Joshua caught her eye and nodded to show he'd heard her. Ellie dodged another swing of Hart's arm, and then bolted under it and around his back. She fastened herself to his armor's skin, digging in with her claws as hard and fast as she could.

She ignored the pain, ignored everything but her claws and the work she'd put them to. She could see Hart in there, a dark blur against the translucent golden metal. How far did she have to go? How far could she go before it healed up around her?

"Give it a shot," Cutter said, peering over her shoulder.

Without stopping her claws' furious digging, Ellie unleashed a wide spray of acid into the trench she'd created in the skin of Hart's armor. It flashed white, and then copious amounts of dark gray smoke began pouring off the wound.

"Let's see," Cutter said, pulling back on his line.

Ellie separated herself from Hart, beating her wings, waiting for the dark smoke to clear. She felt Joshua by her side but could not drag her eyes away from the smoldering hole.

"A little fire if you will, son."

Joshua paused to inhale, then arced a narrow line of fire directly into the source of the smoke. It broke through the darkness, revealing what Ellie hadn't dared allow herself to hope for.

The wound was not closing. The acid was holding back the repairs and now, she saw, Joshua's flame seemed to have cauterized it.

"Incredible," she said. "Captain, I could kiss you."

He patted her back. "Okay, you two kids, get to it."

Joshua pushed past Ellie and took a stab at widening the hole she'd made in Hart's armor. He was larger than her and had not suffered her injuries, but he was also unprepared for the blinding pain of the iron's touch on his dragon's flesh. He raked Hart's skin once and then fell back, yelping in pain.

"How can you stand it?" he said.

"I have to. Here, let me."

Joshua's mouth narrowed to a thin, determined line. "No, I can do it."

He returned to Hart's armor with renewed vigor, digging deep furrows with blinding speed. Ellie hung back, watchful for fresh tricks from the old soldier. When she sensed Joshua's attack losing steam, she dipped in and fired another spray of acid all over his handiwork.

"Holy—Ellie, you almost got me!"

"I don't think it can hurt us, love. I'll be more careful."

He pushed off and covered the expanded hole with a fresh blast of fire. Through the smoke and the edges of the hole, she thought she could make out some of Hart's features.

"My turn now," she said, flying in close.

But before she could lay one claw on his skin, Hart's armor began shifting and changing shape. The wound did not close but two pairs of massive hands sprang like fast-growing trees from either side of the scar. They grabbed Ellie before she could react, crushing her wings to her side, mashing Cutter against the thick scales at her back.

Its head spun around and she saw, not in the center of the chest but behind the face, peering out at her from behind cold golden eyes, Hart's blazing hatred.

"There you are," he said, sounding immeasurably pleased with himself. "Aren't you a pesky thing?"

Hart swatted Joshua clean out of the sky, batting him away with a casual flick of one massive hand. Ellie watched as he became a streaking blue comet crumpling against a distant wall.

"No!"

"No? I say yes! That is you in there, isn't it, Ellie? Another one of Bo's tricks, isn't it? Such creativity! I might have to take that one for a spin myself."

She ignored him, knowing she only had a precious few seconds to free herself and Cutter. Even crazed as he was, Hart wasn't one for long, drawn-out speeches. He'd take his moment, call her a rude name, and flatten the two of them against the ground with his palm.

"Cutter…"

"'m here," he said, his voice weak. For the first time it occurred to her how much worse the burning touch of Hart's iron must be against his skin. She had to get him out of here before he was overwhelmed.

"Hold on," she said. Hart heard her talking and squeezed the air right out of her lungs. Air? Fine, let him have it. She had worse things in her, after all.

Ellie turned to find the mechanical hand's wrist joint. With her last gasp of breath she covered it with a fresh spray of acid. It began sizzling immediately. From somewhere far, far away she was aware of Hart yelling at her to stop. What did she think she was doing? Another hand blotted out the sky, closing itself around her.

But it was too late. She and Cutter dropped out of Hart's grip. She reached for the captain but was too slow. As she fell, it was all she could do to shift her weight and take the impact on her thicker back scales.

"Oh no, you don't," Hart said. He bent to retrieve her, but Ellie scampered away, using reserves of strength she didn't know she had. Loping through his massive fingers, one leg dragging limply behind her, she found a shred of cover and had a second to catch her breath.

"There you are!" He flung the rubble away, blasting at her with every weapon he had. Ellie darted behind new cover, tucking her wounded leg in tight to avoid catching it on anything. She needed her wings. If she could leave the ground, she might have a chance.

He caught her with a barrage of perhaps half a dozen shots, all in her back. The pain rushed through her like adrenaline, urging her forward, drawing her up, up into the sky that might prove her last refuge against him.

Ellie stumbled and fell, rolling through the dust and the dirt. She felt her wings open, but could sense no life in them. How much had they suffered this day? Would they be able to hold air? She imagined leaping up at the Market's suns, a moment of weightless joy and then plummeting face-first into the rubble-strewn ground. How could Hart possibly miss her in that condition? At least it would be over quickly.

He was everywhere, all at once. He sprouted new arms and legs, filling the high street with his body, knocking down walls and flinging aside roofs to get at her. She kept running, kept fleeing, racing blindly at any shadow she could find, moving again when he tore it away a moment later. There was no escaping him, nowhere she could go to get away.

"Mama...Papa...Joshua..."

Ellie ducked around the remains of a building and found herself facing a dead end; a wall which had survived undamaged. She swore and flattened herself against it, hoping she might buy a few precious seconds to rest and hide.

"Oh no, you don't." He wagged a finger at her. "Naughty, naughty!"

Hart uprooted the wall intact, tossing it aside as if it were made of paper. Ellie dove clear and found herself teetering on the edge of a deep hole that had not been there a moment earlier, the collapsed basement and foundation of the building that had stood on this spot for so many years before their arrival today. She caught her balance and stood staring down into the blackness when inspiration struck. In the end what it came down to was a simple decision: if this last, desperate gambit didn't work, at least she could deny Hart the satisfaction of killing her himself.

She leapt into the darkness, spreading her wings, telling herself it was possible the damage wasn't as bad as it felt. She fell and fell, down into the black, begging her borrowed wings to serve her just one final time.

The air was still. She heard the trickle of running water nearby. Distantly, she could sense the outline of the cavern's bottom, craggy and threatening, not far below.

Falling was almost like flying, and Ellie allowed herself to enjoy what might be her final moments. She closed her eyes and imagined the open sky, the clouds and the suns overhead. If she carried them with her, was it so bad being down here in the dark?

No. But there were others, above in the light, who would suffer without her.

How long would it take for Hart to find Mama and Papa? What would he do with Joshua once he learned his true identity? She thought of Cutter and Bo and Clay, all up there in the light. She told herself they would manage without her, that they would find a way to beat Hart, to escape his rage. It was one lie she could not make herself believe, no matter how she tried.

Her wings were torn and battered, but the rushing air caressed their delicate skin. She felt a measure of control returning and tested it out, beating her wings once and adjusting her course down through the void. She whipped her tail to the side and turned with no small measure of difficulty. Again she flexed her wings, and now she was rising from the darkness. She was weak beyond belief, aching in a hundred places. Did she have enough strength left for one final attack?

"Yes. I have to."

She rose to the light, to her friends and family, to face the monster she'd created.

He was waiting when she emerged, but here Ellie's exhaustion worked to her favor. Hart snatched at her, filling the sky with blazing projectiles. She had none of the speed she'd previously exhibited. His attempts to catch her failed as his blasts overshot, vanishing into the distance.

She ignored him, fighting for all the altitude she could get. Higher and higher she flew, telling herself he would wait for her on the ground. His strength was there, his armor designed to be an unstoppable, moving fortress. He would not follow her. He would wait for her to come to him.

She would only get one chance.

Soon she'd flown high enough that only the meanest evidences of the day's damage were visible. The high street was ruined but the majority of the Market was intact. It was lovely, her Papa's fairy tale made real. She wished she could go back and find the girl she'd been and bring her to this moment. Ignore the fighting, ignore the danger, and behold the wonder that was the Market.

Hart fired up after her. She thought she heard him screaming for her to return and fight honorably. Easy for him in his unstoppable weapon. Easy for him with no injuries and no loved ones in harm's way.

There was only one building this tall in all the Market. Ellie flew to it, and not trusting herself to rest even for a moment, hovered in place as she struck at it with what remained of her claws. She raked at the very tip, cutting into the stonework until she'd broken through. With quickness that belied her weariness, she swept around and caught the tip of the tower before it could topple over on its own.

"There," she said, wishing Cutter was here to offer his opinion on this latest bit of foolishness.

It was no trick finding Hart at this distance. His armor had become greater than any of the Market's buildings. The triple suns reflected off his golden skin, their faces becoming distorted as it shifted and continued growing.

Ellie made a wish for Joshua and, gripping the point of the tower, turned to point herself at Hart.

She made no attempt to control her descent apart from focusing on her target. Faster and faster she fell, wings tight to her sides, tail straight back, forelegs clutching at the point of the tower. It was difficult balancing, so Ellie braced the flat, wide end against her chest, using her whole body to aim this crudest of missiles.

"Joshua…"

Hart began firing on her as soon as she was in range but Ellie was falling too rapidly for him to more than graze her. One claw slipped from the point of the tower. She sunk her talons deep into its skin and held on by sheer force of will. This was it. Win or lose, this was all she had left.

She pushed it away at the last second, spreading her wings in what she knew was a futile gesture. The point of the tower hit Hart's armor on what Ellie thought was a shoulder, splitting it from top to bottom, sending a long, running crack through its entire body.

"Joshua!"

She tore the collar from her neck and where Ellie the dragon had been now there was only Ellie the girl, falling uncontrollably at her foe. She slipped into the chasm in Hart's armor with her eyes closed, a mumbled word in the old language on her lips. Mama would have recognized it, even all these years later.

Protection.

The armor closed around her, healing itself as swiftly as it had been damaged. It caught Ellie, absorbing some of the force of her impact, cushioning her body as it closed in around her. It was enough to keep her from liquefying on contact, but not enough to keep her bones from splintering, her organs from exploding. Ellie held what breath she had and prayed she would have enough time to get her work done.

Behind her closed eyes, a heads-up display appeared as the old, familiar user interface flooded into her mind. She was aware of shouted words and a desperate frenzy of movement, but he couldn't get to her in time. He was up in the armor's head and she was wedged somewhere in the shoulder.

Enough, Anthony. Enough.

His control unit was set only to broadcast. That was how he'd avoided her shutdown order, why he hadn't appeared in her system when she scanned for him. Hardwired as she was now, however, there was nothing he could do to stop her. It was still, after all, her tech. Her system.

She killed the power and they fell together to the street. She braced herself for the impact, a part of her savoring one more time the feeling of flight.

Hart picked himself up before Ellie. He beat at the control unit on his hip, screaming at it to turn itself back on. She ignored him, concentrating instead on trying to lift herself up. Where was her dragon's collar? Where was her healing ring? It was no use; she was a rag doll, broken, battered, and unable to move.

"You! Always you!"

She tried to say, "Hello, Anthony." Her muscles weren't working. Her jaw felt a thousand miles away.

"Kill you! Revenge!"

He threw himself at her, clutching for her neck. Tall as she'd become, he was still taller, and outweighed her by a significant amount. Even uninjured, she couldn't have fought him off. He pinned her to the street with his knee, crushing it into her battered ribs. His hands around her neck were impossibly strong. She struggled to breathe and the coarse, rattling sound made her head swim. This was it. No more glamours, no more tech. Just a man she'd once considered a friend squeezing the life out of her with his bare hands.

Beneath her, the ground rumbled. Shifted.

Anthony. No.

His eyes were blind, his lips foaming with fury. "Revenge! Revenge! Kill you!"

Twinkling stars filled the edges of Ellie's vision as she began to lose consciousness. She found she didn't mind, not really, dying after all this time. How many years had she had, after all? Hadn't she found Joshua again, and her parents as well? Hadn't she soared through the sky? Hadn't she lived? All the years the Prince had stolen from her, she'd won them back in the end.

Darkness swept over her and it was a familiar sight. She felt the ground shift again, wriggling like a bed made of snakes. It reminded her of something she'd learned long ago, something she couldn't quite recall in this, the moment of her death. Bright light suffused her entire being, and suddenly the pressure was gone from her chest. The pain was gone from around her throat. Ellie stood in her body, whole and undamaged. She stretched her fingers and touched her neck, expecting soreness and finding none.

She'd been pulled into the system. Yanked out of her body a heartbeat ahead of death.

She saw her own face, dirty and bruised, hair singed, eyes open in a blank stare of shock. Hands were clenched around her neck, straining as if holding on for dear life. Ellie peered into the window and the world rushed forward so now she was looking down at herself, down at her lifeless body.

Looking out through Hart's eyes.

The ground rose up around her, thin tendrils of dark, broken street wrapping themselves around the clutching hands, obscuring her view, pulling her away from her own body, drawing her back, consuming her, dragging her down, away, into the ground. She screamed with Hart's voice, and Ellie's heart broke as with no glamour and no armor to protect him, the Market finally claimed Commander Anthony Hart.

"I'm sorry," Bo said, speaking from behind her.

Ellie turned. "Bo?"

"It was all I could think to do. You saw him, Ellie. There was no stopping him."

"You let the Market take him? The Market Peace?"

Bo shook her head, frowning. "There was no way to stop that. But you're safe, at least. It was all I could think of."

"What about my body?"

Bo brought up a screen. Ellie realized the UI had changed so they were sitting in her old house in Maine. It was the house she'd shared with Rossi, the house she'd returned to after the disaster in New York all those years ago.

"Broken bones, a bunch of organs to replace. Your left hand's in fine shape, interestingly enough. Not sure how you managed to pull that one off. Anyway, nothing we can't fix, so long as you're safe in here. Brings you back, doesn't it?"

"My parents? Joshua? Cutter?"

"Everyone's fine. Your mom's sweet."

Ellie felt the weight of years drop from her shoulders. She fell back into the cushions of her favorite chair and wept with relief.

"I didn't want to come back," she said after composing herself. "I was free—finally free. No more Prince, no more Market. No more fighting." One of the dogs piled into her lap. She rubbed the skin behind its ears, savoring the wintry smell of its bristly coat. "But I couldn't stay away. It was all my fault, Bo. All of it."

"Ellie, you didn't—"

"Didn't what?" she said, cutting Bo off. "Didn't sacrifice the lives of good men over my pathetic little war? Didn't march an army into the Market without a single thought for the innocent people I'd hurt? Sure I did."

Bo stood and came over to join Ellie on the couch. "You came back, didn't you? Give yourself credit for that much, at least. You tried to make it right."

"Putting out the fire I started is hardly heroic."

"It's more than most would do," Bo said.

"Too little, too late."

Bo punched her shoulder. Ellie felt it throughout her entire body, as if her injuries in the real world were somehow agitated by her doctor's virtual punch. "Ow!"

"Serves you right."

Ellie could have booted her out then; she probably would have once upon a time. Instead she rubbed her sore shoulder and thought about banishing the comfortable sitting room. A moment's thought and Bo would find herself outside in the cold, knee-deep in fresh snow. In her underwear. But she left the sitting room where it was. The fire kicked and writhed, the program perhaps affected by her state of mind.

"I came back," she said. "But I didn't want to."

"It's enough, Ellie. It's enough if you let it be."

"I'm not so sure."

"I'll tell you what," Bo said. "Promise you won't start any more wars and we'll call it even, okay?"

Ellie thought for a long while before answering. "I think I can live with that," she said. And was pleased to find it was the truth.

THE END

Ellie MacReady will return in

THE KING'S GLAMOUR

David Hoffman is the author of *The Seven Markets* and the forthcoming *Beautiful Handcrafted Animals*. He and his wife live in Westchester, New York. He is currently working on two books, and really ought to sleep more.

The Seven Markets is his first book.